"Engage," ordered
Captain Benjamin Sisko . . .

Dax frowned despite herself. She was hardly unaware of the risk the captain was taking, if it turned out they were wrong, and there was no attack, no need for them to have turned around to check on the station . . . well, everyone aboard *Deep Space Nine* might as well kiss their careers goodbye.

The *Defiant* surged forward, but almost instantly it wrenched back to impulse power; and, simultaneously, every warning horn, tocsin, and claxon on the bridge began to shriek.

"Report!" Sisko shouted over the din.

"Benjamin," Dax said. "You know that feeling you've been getting about us not being alone out here?" She did not wait for his reply. "You were right. . . ."

Star Trek: Deep Space Nine®

The Search • Diane Carey
Warped • K. W. Jeter
The Way of the Warrior • Diane Carey
Star Trek: Klingon • Dean W. Smith & Kristine K. Rusch
Trials and Tribble-ations • Diane Carey

#1 *Emissary* • J. M. Dillard
#2 *The Siege* • Peter David
#3 *Bloodletter* • K. W. Jeter
#4 *The Big Game* • Sandy Schofield
#5 *Fallen Heroes* • Dafydd ab Hugh
#6 *Betrayal* • Lois Tilton
#7 *Warchild* • Esther Friesner
#8 *Antimatter* • John Vornholt
#9 *Proud Helios* • Melissa Scott
#10 *Valhalla* • Nathan Archer
#11 *Devil in the Sky* • Greg Cox & John Greggory Betancourt
#12 *The Laertian Gamble* • Robert Sheckley
#13 *Station Rage* • Diane Carey
#14 *The Long Night* • Dean W. Smith & Kristine K. Rusch
#15 *Objective: Bajor* • John Peel
#16 *Invasion #3: Time's Enemy* • L. A. Graf
#17 *The Heart of the Warrior* • John Greggory Betancourt
#18 *Saratoga* • Michael Jan Friedman
#19 *The Tempest* • Susan Wright
#20 *Wrath of the Prophets* • P. David, M. J. Friedman,
   R. Greenberger
#21 *Trial by Error* • Mark Garland

Star Trek®: Voyager™

Flashback • Diane Carey
Mosaic • Jeri Taylor

#1 *Caretaker* • L. A. Graf
#2 *The Escape* • Dean W. Smith & Kristine K. Rusch
#3 *Ragnarok* • Nathan Archer
#4 *Violations* • Susan Wright
#5 *Incident at Arbuk* • John Greggory Betancourt
#6 *The Murdered Sun* • Christie Golden
#7 *Ghost of a Chance* • Mark A. Garland & Charles G. McGraw
#8 *Cybersong* • S. N. Lewitt
#9 *Invasion #4: The Final Fury* • Dafydd ab Hugh
#10 *Bless the Beasts* • Karen Haber
#11 *The Garden* • Melissa Scott
#12 *Chrysalis* • David Niall Wilson
#13 *The Black Shore* • Greg Cox
#14 *Marooned* • Christie Golden
#15 *Echoes* • Dean Wesley Smith & Kristin Kathryn Rusch

Star Trek®: New Frontier

#1 *House of Cards* • Peter David
#2 *Into the Void* • Peter David
#3 *The Two-Front War* • Peter David
#4 *End Game* • Peter David

Star Trek®: Day of Honor

Book One: Ancient Blood • Diane Carey
Book Two: Armageddon Sky • L. A. Graf
Book Three: Her Klingon Soul • Michael Jan Friedman
Book Four: Treaty's Law • Dean W. Smith & Kristin K. Rusch

Star Trek: The Next Generation®

Look for STAR TREK Fiction from Pocket Books

Star Trek®: The Original Series

Star Trek: The Motion Picture • Gene Roddenberry
Star Trek II: The Wrath of Khan • Vonda N. McIntyre
Star Trek III: The Search for Spock • Vonda N. McIntyre
Star Trek IV: The Voyage Home • Vonda N. McIntyre
Star Trek V: The Final Frontier • J. M. Dillard
Star Trek VI: The Undiscovered Country • J. M. Dillard
Star Trek VII: Generations • J. M. Dillard
Enterprise: The First Adventure • Vonda N. McIntyre
Final Frontier • Diane Carey
Strangers from the Sky • Margaret Wander Bonanno
Spock's World • Diane Duane
The Lost Years • J. M. Dillard
Probe • Margaret Wander Bonanno
Prime Directive • Judith and Garfield Reeves-Stevens
Best Destiny • Diane Carey
Shadows on the Sun • Michael Jan Friedman
Sarek • A. C. Crispin
Federation • Judith and Garfield Reeves-Stevens
The Ashes of Eden • William Shatner & Judith and Garfield
    Reeves-Stevens
The Return • William Shatner & Judith and Garfield Reeves-
    Stevens
Star Trek: Starfleet Academy • Diane Carey

#1 *Star Trek: The Motion Picture* • Gene Roddenberry
#2 *The Entropy Effect* • Vonda N. McIntyre
#3 *The Klingon Gambit* • Robert E. Vardeman
#4 *The Covenant of the Crown* • Howard Weinstein
#5 *The Prometheus Design* • Sondra Marshak & Myrna
    Culbreath
#6 *The Abode of Life* • Lee Correy
#7 *Star Trek II: The Wrath of Khan* • Vonda N. McIntyre
#8 *Black Fire* • Sonni Cooper
#9 *Triangle* • Sondra Marshak & Myrna Culbreath
#10 *Web of the Romulans* • M. S. Murdock
#11 *Yesterday's Son* • A. C. Crispin
#12 *Mutiny on the Enterprise* • Robert E. Vardeman
#13 *The Wounded Sky* • Diane Duane

And the weapon slid right to Spock. He snatched it up, heart racing faster than a proper Vulcan should permit, and pointed it at Sered.

"Can you kill a brother Vulcan?" Sered hissed, unafraid, from where he lay. "Can you?"

Could he? For an endless moment, Spock froze, seeing Sered's fearless stare, feeling the weapon in his hand. Dimly he was aware of the struggle all around him as the invaders grabbed hostages, but all he could think was that all he need do was one tiny move, only the smallest tightening of a finger—

Can you kill a brother Vulcan?

He'd hesitated too long. What felt like half of Mount Seleya fell on him. Spock thought he heard his father saying, *Exaggeration. Remember your control.*

Then the fierce dawn went black.

were kindred, of Vulcan stock; surely they could be reasoned with—

As Sered could not. Spock faltered at the sight of the drawn features, the too-bright eyes staring beyond this chaos to a vision only Sered could see. Few Vulcans ever went insane, but here was true madness. Surely his followers, though, clearly Vulcan's long-lost cousins, would not ally themselves with such insanity!

Desperately calm, Spock raised his hand in formal greeting. Surak had been slain trying to bring peace: if Spock fell thus, at least his father would have final proof that he was worthy to be the ambassador's son.

They suddenly seemed to be in a tense little circle of calm. One of the "cousins" pointed at him, while a second nodded, then gestured out into the chaos around them. The language had greatly changed in the sundered years, but Spock understood:

"This one."

"Him."

It may work. They may listen to me. They—

"Get back, son!" a Starfleet officer shouted, racing forward, phaser in outstretched hand, straight at Sered. "Drop that weapon!"

Sered threw back his head. He actually laughed. Then, firing at point-blank range, reflexes swifter than human, he shot the man. The human flared up into flame so fierce that the heat scorched Spock's face and the veils slipped across his eyes, blurring his sight. He blinked, blinked again to clear it, and saw the conflagration that had been a man flash out of existence.

Dead. He's dead. A moment ago alive, and now— Spock stared at Sered across the small space that had held a man, his mind refusing to process what he'd just seen. "Halfblood," muttered Sered. "Weakling shoot of Surak's house. But you will serve—"

"Got him!" came a shout. David Rabin hurled himself into Sered, bringing them both down. The weapon flew from Sered's hand, and Captain Rabin and Sered both scrambled for it. The woman touched it, Sered knocked her hand aside—

He tore off his austere robe. Gasps of astonishment and hisses of outrage sounded as he stood forth in the garb of a Captain of the Hosts from the ancient days. Sunlight picked out the metal of his harness in violent red and exploded into rainbow fire where it touched the gem forming the grip of the ancient energy weapon Sered held—a weapon he had brought, against all law, into Mount Seleya's amphitheater.

"Welcome our lost kindred!" he commanded, and gestured as if leading a charge.

A rainbow shimmer rose about the stage. *Transporter effect,* Spock thought even as it died, leaving behind six tall figures in black and silver. At first glance they were as much like Sered as brothers in their mother's womb. But where Sered wore his rage like a cloak of ceremony, these seemed accustomed to emotion and casual violence.

For an instant no one moved, the Vulcans too stunned by this garish breach of custom, the Federation guests not sure what they were permitted to do. Then, as the intruders raised their weapons, the amphitheater erupted into shouts and motion. From all sides, the guards advanced, holding their *lirpas* at a deadly angle. But *lirpas* were futile against laser rifles.

As the ceremonial guard was cut down, Sarek whispered quick, urgent words to other Vulcans. They nodded. Spock sensed power summoned and joined:

"Now!" whispered the ambassador.

In a phalanx, the Vulcans rushed the dais. They swept across it, bearing T'Pau and T'Lar with them. They, at least, were safe. Only one remained behind. Green blood puddled from his ruined skull, seeping into the dark stone where no blood had flowed for countless generations.

"You dare rise up against me?" Sered shrilled. "One sacrifice is not enough to show the lesser worlds!" He waved his weapon at the boys, at the gorgeously dressed Federation guests. "Take them! We shall make these folk of lesser spirit *crawl.*"

Spock darted forward, not sure what he could do, knowing only that it was not logical to wait meekly for death. And these intruders were not mindless *le-matyas!* They

"You honor me," replied T'Lar.

"I live to serve," said T'Pau, an observation that would have left Spock gasping had he not been getting sufficient oxygen.

Both women bowed, this time to the youths who stood waiting their presentation.

Again, the adept struck the gong.

T'Lar raised both arms, the white and silver of her sleeves falling like great wings. *"As it was in the beginning, so shall it always be. These sons of our House have shown their worthiness . . ."*

"I protest!" came a shout from the amphitheater.

"I protest," Sered declared, "the profanation of these rites. I protest the way they have been stripped of their meaning, contaminated as one might pollute a well in the desert. I protest the way our deepest mysteries have been revealed to *outsiders."*

T'Pau's eyebrows rose at that last word, which was in the seldom-used invective mode.

"Has thee finished?" asked T'Lar. Adept of *Kolinahr,* she would remain serene if Mount Seleya split along its many fissures and this entire amphitheater crumbled into the pit below.

"No!" Sered cried, his voice sharp as the cry of a *shavokh.* "Above all, I protest the inclusion of an outsider in our rites—yes, as leader of the men to be honored today—when other and worthier men, our exiled cousins, go unhonored and unrecognized."

Sarek drew deep, measured breaths. *He prepares for combat,* Spock realized, and was astonished to feel his own body tensing, alert, aware as he had only been during his *kahs-wan,* when he had faced a full-grown *le-matya* in the deep desert and knew, logically, he could not survive such an encounter. *Fight or flight,* his mother had once called it. That too was a constant across species. *But not here. There must not be combat here.*

"Thee speaks of those who exiled themselves, Sered." Not the slightest trace of emotion tinged T'Pau's voice. "Return lies in their power, not in ours."

"So it does!" Sered shouted. "And so they do!"

nia back—and up to the entrance of the amphitheater. Two masked guards bearing ceremonial *lirpas* presented arms before his father, then saluted Spock for the first time as an adult. For all his attempts at total control, he felt a little shiver race through him as he returned the salutes as an adult for the first time. The clublike weights that formed the *lirpa* bases shone, a luster of dark metal. The dawn light flashed red on the blades that the guards carried over their shoulders. At the guards' hips, they wore stone-hilted daggers, but no energy weapons—*phasers*—such as a Starfleet officer might wear on duty. Of course, no such weapons might be brought here.

Lady Amanda removed her fingers from her husband's and smiled faintly. "I shall join the other ladies of our House now, my husband, while you bring our son before the Elders. Spock, I shall be watching for you. And I am indeed *very* proud."

As, her gaze told him, *is your father.*

She glided away, a grace note among the taller Vulcans.

Spock fell into step with his father, head high, as if his blood bore no human admixture. *As it was in the beginning* . . . Silently, he reviewed the beginning of the Chant of Generations as he glided down the stairs.

Everyone in the amphitheater rose. T'Lar, adept and First Student, walked onto the platform. Then, two guards, their *lirpa* set aside for the purpose, entered with a curtained carrying chair. From it, robed in black, but with all the crimsons of the dawn in her brocaded overrobe, stepped T'Pau. She leaned on an intricately carved stick.

Spock's father stepped forward as if to help her.

"Thee is kind, Sarek," said the Elder of their House, "but thee is premature. When I can no longer preside unassisted over this rite, it will be time to release my *katra.*"

Sarek bowed. "I ask pardon for my presumption."

"Courtesy"—T'Pau held up a thin, imperious hand—"is never presumptuous." Her long eyes moved over the people in the amphitheater as if delivering some lesson of her own—but to whom? Carefully, she approached the altar and bowed to T'Lar. "Eldest of All, I beg leave to assist thee."

Instead, he concentrated on his parents' progress. Sustained only by the light touch of Sarek's fingers upon hers, veiled against the coming sunrise, Amanda crossed the narrow span as if she had not conquered her fear of the unrailed bridge only after long meditation.

Few of the many participants from the outworld scientific, diplomatic, and military enclaves on Vulcan could equal her grace. Some had actually arranged to be flown to the amphitheater just to allow them to bypass the bridge that had served as a final defense for the warband that had ruled here in ancient days. Others of the guests crossed unsteadily or too quickly for dignity.

Vertigo might be a reasonable assumption, Spock thought, for beings acclimating themselves to Vulcan's thin air or the altitude of the bridge.

"The air is the air," one of his agemates remarked in the tone of one quoting his elders. "I have heard these *humans* take drugs to help them breathe."

All of the boys eyed the representatives from the Federation as if they were xenobiological specimens in a laboratory. Especially, they surveyed the officials' sons and daughters, who might, one day, be people with whom they would study and work.

"They look sickly," the same boy spoke. His name, Spock recalled, was Stonn. Not only was he a distant kinsman to Sered, he was one of the youths who also eyed Spock as if he expected Spock's human blood to make him fall wheezing to his knees, preferably just when he was supposed to lead his agemates up to the platform where T'Lar and T'Pau would present them with the hereditary—and now symbolic—weapons of their Great Houses. By slipping out early into the desert to undergo his *kahs-wan* ordeal before the others, Spock had made himself forever Eldest among the boys of his year. It was not logical that some, like Stonn, would not forgive him for his presumption, or his survival; but it was so.

A deferential three paces behind his parents and two to the side of Sarek, Spock strode past a series of deeply incised pits—the result of laser cannon fire two millen-

Vulcan, Mount Seleya
Day 6, Seventh Week of Tasmeen,
Year 2247

Dawn hovered over Mount Seleya. A huge *shavokh* glided down on a thermal from the peak, balanced on a wingtip, then soared out toward the desert. Spock heard its hunting call.

Where it stoops, one may find ground water or a soak not too deeply buried, Spock recalled from his survival training. He had no need of such information now. Nevertheless, his gaze followed the creature's effortless flight.

The stairs that swept upward to the narrow bridge still lay in shadow. Faint mist rose about the mountain, perhaps from the snow that capped it, alone of Vulcan's peaks, or perhaps from the lava that bubbled sullenly a thousand meters below. Soon, 40 Eridani A would rise, and the ritual honoring Spock and his agemates would begin.

It was illogical, Spock told himself, for him to assume that all eyes were upon him as he followed his parents.

VENGEANCE

Dafydd ab Hugh

POCKET BOOKS

New York London Toronto Sydney Tokyo Singapore

An *Original* Publication of POCKET BOOKS

POCKET BOOKS, a division of Simon & Schuster Inc.
1230 Avenue of the Americas, New York, NY 10020

STAR TREK is a Registered Trademark of Paramount Pictures.

A VIACOM COMPANY

This book is published by Pocket Books, a division of Simon & Schuster Inc., under exclusive license from Paramount Pictures.

ISBN: 0-671-00468-9

First Pocket Books printing February 1998

10 9 8 7 6 5 4 3 2 1

POCKET and colophon are registered trademarks of Simon & Schuster Inc.

Printed in the U.S.A.

VENGEANCE

CHAPTER
1

QUARK—TEMPORARILY BARLESS, unbusy, at loose ends—walked a frenzied pattern around and around the deserted Promenade, trying not to notice the empty kiosks, locked doors, and dimmed or missing welcome signs. He felt his face flush; he knew he was a bright, pinkish orange color that would doubtless elicit a double-sneer and cutting remark from Liquidator Brunt, if they were on speaking terms. Never before had the Ferengi bartender debased himself so thoroughly . . . parading around the Promenade wearing a sandwich-board advertisement! *I might as well be as naked as a female under here,* he thought with some bitterness, though he wore his best suit in a futile effort to recapture a shred of dignity. But of course, no one could see it past the flashing lights and animated holocharacters cavorting across his chest and back. No, they were all too busy drinking up and having a smoking time at the holomated Quark's Place.

Grim-faced, the Ferengi quick-walked around and around, hoping to drum up the merest smidgen of business. *One customer! Is that too much to ask? One, stupid freighter captain, a passing smuggler, even a human!* He was aware that the cheery image of unclothed, prancing nymphs and satyrs having a grand old time at the bacchanalia on his sandwich board contrasted sharply with the bitter, warning snarl on his face; Quark's lip curled back from a set of teeth razor-sharpened that morning in a frenzy of ablution. But he couldn't stop himself from baring his naked fury. With the general evacuation, Quark had not had one, single customer in three days—well, just one: Morn, of course.

Already hurting more than he would admit from being cast off the loving accounts of the Ferengi Business Alliance, now he had to admit that he was failing at the one piece of identity he had left: Quark was a failure as a businessman.

By the Profits! Why not just apprentice myself to Rom and make the humiliation complete? Or show up on Nog's doorstep at the hu-man Academy and say "Good morning, Nephew—I'd like to enlist!"

Instead Quark walked, not quite staring at the empty shops, abandoned enterprise zones, lonely benches, and somnambulant security guards. Constable Odo stood near one of the benches, a spot from which he could see a quarter of the Promenade, from Garak's clothier's—not even Quark had patronized the Cardassian's shop lately; he had no money even for a new suit!—all the way around to Quark's Place, at whose flashing lights and enticing holomation the Ferengi stubbornly refused to look.

"Still carrying around that ridiculous, obscene billboard?" growled the constable.

"No, I died about three hours ago, Odo; this is my ghost you're talking to."

"I thought Ferengi went to the Divine Treasury when they died. Weren't you greedy enough?"

Quark stiffened and stopped, glaring at the tall, austere, and now thoroughly solid constable—a fancy term for cop. "Greed is never enough, Odo. A true Ferengi combines greed with pure corruption and a passion for staying *out* of other people's business unless there's a profit to be made. I'm pleased to note that you fail all three tests of Ferengi character."

Odo snorted, his *"hnh!"* indicating he had been bested by the Ferengi, as usual. "Take off that ridiculous sign!" he commanded, to no purpose, as usual.

"Why should I? Is there a *law* against advertising a perfectly legal, perfectly above-the-table business?"

"You look utterly absurd. Who are you advertising *to?* And you're contributing to the net ugliness of this station—"

"That's like contributing to the bad temper of a Klingon. And *who* is being disturbed?"

"I'm tired of that thing flashing in my eyes. Take it off! Consider that an order."

"You have no authority to give such an order!"

"Then consider it a . . . a *favor.*" The constable rolled the word around his mouth as though it had a disagreeable flavor.

"A favor?" demanded Quark, incredulous. "You want the sign gone? Fine. How much is it worth to you?"

"What?"

"Everyone has his price . . . even dear, old Constable Odo. How much is your sanity worth to you?"

"I would think you could remove it out of simple courtesy!"

"Well, that's not the Ferengi way, is it? How do you expect me to get to the Divine Treasury if I go around doing favors for every Tom, Dick, and Odo?"

"Quark, someday, I hope to see you thrown out an airlock, drifting away like yesterday's garbage. You'll beg me to rescue you, and you know what will happen?"

"The alarm clock will go off, and you'll wake up."

"Hnh!" Odo stalked away, hands clasped behind his

back. Quark smiled grimly; *he's as bored to death as I am!*

Ferengi and constable had a symbiosis that very nearly allowed each to read the other's mind. Odo fretted, Quark knew, because the dangers that menaced *Deep Space Nine* were wholly beyond the constable's ability to affect them. Odo understood all manner of internal disruptions, from simple drunkenness and assault to full-scale riots, from burglary to sex crimes—some races that visited the Federation had not even the *concept* of self-control—to homicide to religious discrimination; Odo had gotten much experience dealing with that particular crime now that Bajor was such a powerful force on the station. Odo understood financial misman- agement of all sorts, from thievery to fraud to high-end smuggling operations, much to Quark's chagrin.

But the constable knew nothing, absolutely nothing, about war and invasion. He was as useless in defending the station against an attack by his own people, the Founders, as a hu-man would be to judge a Ferengi civil- court action.

Now that Odo was gone, Quark peeled the sandwich board off and threw it to the ground, as he had been dying to do until Odo started barking orders. Massaging his aching shoulders, he gave the board a savage kick, shorting out one quadrant of the holomation: now the nymphs coupled with satyrs, headed toward Quark's, and vanished into a mysterious, enticing black square. That might even have been more effective at drawing a crowd to Quark's Place . . . were there any crowd to draw, that is.

The billboard had been a last-ditch attempt by the Ferengi to maintain his sanity. He had let go all his employees. Why pay Dabo girls to spin the wheel for an empty bar? Why pay busboys to clean tables that had not been dirtied for days? Now Quark faced the prospect of living on his replicator rations, of all things! Like a hu- man!

And all it had taken to empty *Deep Space Nine* was a single, nasty encounter with the Jem'Hadar on a planet altogether too near the wormhole for the comfort of the cowardly, sheeplike civilians living on the station. One battle, and it wasn't even conclusive!

But the mob, the "mobile class," had lived up to its name by quickly booking passage on any and every ship leaving the station for points closer to the central maw of the mass of tentacles that was the Federation ... as though that would save them if the Founders really did come through the wormhole again.

"Miserable consumers!" shouted the Ferengi, sitting on one of the many, many unoccupied benches, though there was nobody in earshot. "How *dare* they just leave? If they have no concern for their own career options, can't they at least have some consideration for me, their hardworking, profiteering bartender?" No one answered.

Quark stared at the flashing sign at his feet, felt the eerie silence, even the pulse of the station reactors, many levels down, generally not noticeable above the roar of the mob. Maybe Rom was right. Maybe, in this miserable, altruistic, hu-man Federation it made sense to have a *trade* to fall back on, something other than business. Quark's own, personal modification of the Sixth Rule of Acquisition read "Never allow the hatred of family to stand in the way of opportunity." After all, Quark didn't live on Ferenginar anymore, did he?

And never would again, echoed an unwanted voice in his head, the voice of Brunt.

Quark shook his head. *It takes more than a little adversity to hurl* this *Ferengi out of orbit.* Still, Quark's brother was pretty busy, even now: Master Chief Miles Edward O'Brien had Rom hopping all over the station, repairing every electronic combat device and sharpening the station's teeth.

Quark snorted, then jumped as he realized he sounded

just like Odo. *Two coins in a purse,* he thought bitterly. *I wonder what my brother—*

". . . what my brother is doing now?" asked Rom. Chief O'Brien stared incredulously back at his Ferengi crewman; the chief was, more than usual, exasperated and frustrated at the inept, clunky Cardassian circuit design.

"I should think you'd have more important things to do than wonder about your crooked brother," he said.

"Quark is not crooked! Well, uh, okay, maybe a little, but his heart's in the right place." Rom couldn't quite meet O'Brien's eye, the chief noted.

"Your brother's heart is in his cash register, along with his conscience and his loyalty. He couldn't care less what happened to any of us unless it affected his bottom line!"

Rom nodded curtly. "Apology accepted," he said. O'Brien rolled his eyes and returned to the photon torpedo circuitry, which was failing left and right on every test run. With war and the rumors of war coming at *Deep Space Nine* from all sides, Captain Bejamin Sisko had ordered a complete overhaul of every combat system on the station, which meant everything else on DS9 was going to hell in a handbasket, along with the special retrofit on the *Defiant's* cloaking device that Chief O'Brien had worked out in theory.

Suddenly, O'Brien's comm badge beeped, echoing like a screaming baby in the tight confines of the upper firing chamber of pylon II. The chief jumped and dropped his plasma infuser, and cursed like an Irish sailor.

"Chief," said the voice of Major Kira Nerys, department head of Weapons and Defenses, "something urgent has come up. Drop everything and—"

"I just *did* drop everything, Major!" barked O'Brien. "Now I have to pick it up. Can't you wait until I finish adjusting the—"

"Now, O'Brien! This is an all-senior-hands briefing by the captain. I think you'll want to hear this, anyway."

"Hear what?"

"This isn't a secured channel, Chief. Come on up to Ops."

O'Brien paused. A *secured channel?* Whatever had just happened, it was so secret, O'Brien realized, that Major Kira wouldn't even say it over the comm link for fear Garak or some other spy might be eavesdropping. "On my way, Major," he said, softly; he tapped his comm badge to sever the connection. "Rom, how would you like to finish realigning the firing chamber wave guides?"

"Would I!" breathed the Ferengi, overjoyed at the prospect.

"Well, don't have too much fun; this is supposed to be work, you know." With a last, nervous glance at the delicate guides, Chief O'Brien began the painful and delicate operation of extracting himself from the chamber, climbing over the Ferengi—whose small size probably gave him a job advantage over the bulky chief anyway—and sliding down the pylon without slipping and killing himself.

Twelve minutes later, the turbolift popped up into Ops, disgorging Chief O'Brien. A teenaged ensign (well, he looked like a teenager to the chief!) said, "In the captain's office, Master Chief," pointing in case O'Brien forgot the way up the ladderway.

"Aye, sir," said O'Brien; then he saluted, just in case the kid didn't catch the sarcasm the first time. The ensign returned the salute without glancing away from his scanner panel.

Hustling up the ladderway, O'Brien entered through the nasty, dilating, Cardassian security door to find the entire senior staff, including Odo, staring at him, impatient to start the meeting. "Um, sorry," mumbled O'Brien, slithering into his seat. "I got—hung up."

"Now that all of us have arrived," said Captain Benjamin Sisko, "I will explain what prompted so much drama." Sisko smiled, his cold, glittery smile that always made O'Brien swallow. It was the *we who are about to die* smile that they doubtless taught at the Academy: *use this expression, cadets, when you tell your troops you're about to lead them on a suicide mission!*

Captain Sisko stood, his back to the tableful of officers (and one chief), staring at the main viewer. The Starfleet planet-logo popped up, followed by a series of security tags, including Eyes Only. The hairy face of some admiral O'Brien faintly remembered meeting once superimposed itself over the logo, which faded behind him.

"Captain," said the recorded voice, "one of our deep-cover humints relayed a very disturbing piece of intel to FleetIntCom."

"If I may interrupt," said Dr. Julian Bashir smoothly; the image froze. "What race are the Humints? I've never heard of them before."

"Human-intelligence units," said the captain. "It's an ancient term for actual spies planted inside the enemy camp. Inside the Dominion, in this case. They probably aren't actually human, but Admiral Montgommery is of the old school."

Chief O'Brien squirmed uncomfortably; a top-secret message from the vice admiral in charge of Fleet Intelligence about the Dominion could mean only one thing: *so it's finally happening,* thought the chief, wondering where he could send Keiko and Molly, his wife and daughter—if they would even agree to leave Bajor!

Bashir slumped in his chair, probably chagrined at not knowing an old Earth term for a spy. "Continue playback," said Sisko.

"You have already seen the reports of the minor clash near Charlie-Lima-202 and Delta-Lima-201, 'Carlos' and 'Diana,' we're calling them, in the Gamma Quadrant. Well, the clash wasn't as minor or as random as we initially believed. In addition to the two Starfleet ships destroyed, the *Parallax* and the *Delphine,* there were seven ships that joined the battle in progress . . . possibly rebels from the Dominion sphere of influence. And on at least one other ship, the *T'Pau,* there was an infiltration. The Founder was detected when she bolted before a routine blood-screening; unfortunately, she escaped on a shuttle before the ships returned through the wormhole."

The department heads nodded; evidently, rumors had already gotten out, though O'Brien hadn't heard them. He had heard about the battle, of course; everyone had. It had emptied the station! But O'Brien had not heard about the infiltration of the Vulcan ship. That was a bad blow, considering the security measures already in place. *Great, now we'll need to get even tighter!* Lieutenant Commander Jadzia Dax smiled cheerfully . . . another sign of bad things to come.

The admiral continued: "We now believe, Benjamin, that the attack was not a random contact between flanks, but an attempt to keep the fleet away from a particular sector of the Gamma Quadrant. Captain," Admiral Mongommery leaned close to the screen, his face looking tired and mechanical, "FleetIntCom is convinced that a massive assault is imminent and focused in some fashion on a sector near where the Carlos–Diana battle occurred. We don't know why that sector is important or what's going on there. We're worried it might be a new Founder weapon, or perhaps an alliance or conference to bring more parties into the war. But all border units are hereby ordered to full combat alert status . . . and more than likely, at some point not far in the future, Fleet Intelligence is going to draft you and the *Defiant* as intel operatives."

Lieutenant Commander Worf did not react, but O'Brien knew his friend well: the Klingon was exulting on the inside with the joy of pending battle, especially a dangerous mission behind enemy lines as a spy. Dax was

Dax, of course; she would go wherever there was action. But Major Kira seemed curiously reluctant, less blood-thirsty than even just a year before. *I wonder if impending motherhood—even impending surrogate mother-hood—is permanently changing her personality?*

Julian looked pensive, arms folded across his slender chest. Odo showed no change in his expression, of course; it would have required more effort than he cared to expend on such trivialities.

The message continued, giving more specifics of other tiny bits of "intel" Starfleet had managed to pick up, most of it sounding ambiguous and useless to the chief. But the admiral seemed convinced, and Captain Sisko held his own grim, gray grin throughout. The recorded, scrambled transmission ended with the usual formalities, and the screen went blank.

"Chief O'Brien," said the captain, "have you finished modifying the cloaking systems on the *Defiant?*"

O'Brien cleared his throat, slightly embarrassed. "No sir; the system is still based on the Romulan model, and there's no logic to it. It's a dog's breakfast of and-or's and Y-branches; there's no elegance or—"

"How long?" snapped Worf.

"Another week at best," admitted O'Brien. "Assuming something else doesn't blow up in my face. I'd have been done a week ago if the photons hadn't crashed. Captain, should I switch back to the ship?"

Sisko mulled over the question, then answered with one of his own. "Is Rom up to the job on the photon torpedoes? I won't leave the station defenseless, no matter what the orders from FleetIntCom."

"Well . . ." O'Brien looked to Dax for help; she was training the Ferengi in the scientific and engineering theory involved. O'Brien had a hard enough time keeping his temper while teaching Rom standard Starfleet maintenance procedures! The Ferengi had spent too much time around his brother. He always looked for the quick and dirty shortcut, not thinking about the problems it might cause down the road.

"He can do it, Benjamin," said Commander Dax. "It'll take longer than if the chief does it, of course. And there's no way he can do the cloaking retrofit," she added.

"Fine, Old Man," said Sisko, "it's against my better judgment, but I suppose our best allocation of resources is to move O'Brien back to the *Defiant* and let Rom finish the photon-torpedo alignment. Worf . . ."

"Aye, sir."

"Put together a skeleton crew for the *Defiant,* in the event we get the mission: volunteers only, with excellent hand-to-hand, in case we run into Jem'Hadar."

"Aye, sir!" The Klingon could not keep a snarl of battlefield pleasure out of his voice.

"People," concluded the captain, "we've known this was coming for a long time, ever since we first ran into the Founders. They will not be satisfied until the entire Alpha Quadrant is under the control of the Dominion, and we're all as dependent upon them as are the Jem'Hadar.

"I don't know whether we can survive. With the Klingons and the Cardassians, together, we might have had an excellent chance, but under the present circumstances?" Sisko shook his head, smiling again. *I* hate *that smile!* thought Chief O'Brien.

Sisko continued. "But this is *not* what we are going to tell the troops. For their ears, the war is winnable. We beat the Klingons; we beat the Borg. We can beat the Founders. That's what we'll tell them, and that's what we'll believe. And *that* is an *order!"* His smile changed to one of genuine mirth, and the senior crew chuckled, even O'Brien.

"Now unless anyone has anything to add, this briefing is—"

Dax's viewer beeped, and she held up her hand; Sisko

paused, waiting to see what was so important that the duty ensign would interrupt a high-level staff meeting to signal the science officer.

"Ship coming through the wormhole, Benjamin," she said, "and it's broadcasting a Federation priority-one distress call!" She stared at the screen for a second. "Captain, there are two ships following the first, firing on it—and they're Klingon!" She looked up at Sisko. "Benjamin, if we don't get out there in the next five minutes, they're going to destroy that ship!"

"Worf, Dax, O'Brien, you're with me on the *Defiant;* you too, doctor—we may need to rescue survivors. Kira, red alert. You have the conn . . . and remember, phasers only! We don't want to fry poor Rom."

Worf slapped his comm badge; "Emergency crew recall!" he commanded, summoning the *Defiant* on-duty team from wherever they were and whatever they were doing.

Why would the Klingons try something here? thought O'Brien. *Well, they're in for quite a donnybrook if they pick a fight in front of* this *station!*

CHAPTER
2

JADZIA DAX WAS momentarily confused with both the captain of *Deep Space Nine* and the captain of the *Defiant* on the bridge at the same time. Benjamin had immediately turned over responsibility for the ship's launch to Worf while he demanded a detailed briefing from Dax on recent Klingon activity around the wormhole. At the same time, Worf was barking orders at her in her capacity as helmsman and weapons officer!

Meanwhile, the two Klingon ships fired three more disruptor blasts. Two deflected off the shields of the target ship, the last partially penetrated and drew blood from the starboard engine pod.

"Aye, Commander—I'm sorry, Captain?—engine spin-up, seven-six-five-four. Yes, sir, five ships in the last two weeks; can't say for sure they were Klingon, but they were cloaked and they were in and out of the wormhole. Release docking clamps, chief. Aye, Commander, reverse one quarter . . .

Captain Sisko stood and walked away from Dax,

reluctant to interrupt her while she performed the whip-turn and got the *Defiant* cruising to attack speed headed toward the wormhole, where the battle raged. Now one of the birds-of-prey fired a torpedo of some sort, briefly illuminating the smaller ship's shield structure to the naked eye.

A fourth blip appeared for a moment in the glare, but Dax quickly classified it as most likely a sensor echo. Something seemed strange, however. Could it be another cloaked ship? *Well, we'll soon see,* she thought; *it has to decloak to shoot anything.*

"On screen," said Worf; he didn't say, but Dax knew he meant the combat. They watched as two Klingon birds-of-prey harried a smaller vessel of unknown design, a ship that scarcely would have attracted the station's attention except for two points of interest: it was squawking a Federation distress call, and it was being cut to ribbons in their own backyard.

Worf inhaled, but before he could ask, Dax responded, "Four minutes, Commander." Another disruptor blast rocked the presumed Federation ship, skewing it from its path and sending it careening into the teeth of the second bird-of-prey. "Captain," said Dax, "their shields are holding remarkably well. We should be there in plenty of time."

"Let's hope so, Old Man."

The lieutenant commander watched her oldest human friend pace back and forth. His face was impassive, but the Trill could read it like a tricorder, so long had she known him. There were rumors of high-level, political contact between Gowron and the Federation Council, but nobody had given the word to the high muckety-mucks of Starfleet, let alone a mere captain commanding a space station in the quadrant boondocks. The Klingon-Federation alliance was off; no, it was on again; no, definitely off—absolutely, definitely, positively—well, maybe not, but they weren't exactly sure.

The captain, Dax understood, fretted that yet another incident between the *Defiant* and Klingon warships might have diplomatic repercussions far beyond the problems of a Federation pleasure yacht or ore-hauler that had stupidly poked a stick into a Klingon anthill. But how could Benjamin Sisko possibly stand still for a Federation ship being mauled within eyeball range of a heavily armed Federation fortress?

O'Brien spoke up. "No response to the hail from the Klingons, Captain. I mean, Commander." Dax smiled.

"They heard us?" asked Worf, touching all bases.

"Yes, sir. They're just giving us the cold shoulder."

Now Worf rose from his command chair. "Captain, I insist you either give me full command of this mission and let me lock phasers or take command yourself."

"I'll take the conn, Mr. Worf," said Benjamin decisively. He strode to the command chair as the Klingon vacated to the XO's position. "Full power to the phaser array, Old Man. Lock on both targets simultaneously but don't fire yet. Mr. O'Brien, try one more time . . . tell them to stop immediately or we'll blow them out of the sky."

"Can I quote you on that, sir?" asked O'Brien, but he was already sending the message.

"Two more shots, Benjamin," said Dax. "Their shields are still at sixty-five percent."

Sisko stood, staring at the forward viewer. "That should hold until we can hose them down and separate them."

Suddenly, Dax saw an energy surge; her suspicions were confirmed. "Captain, there's a third Klingon ship!" The new ship, a small, lightly armed patrol vessel, decloaked practically at the side of the Federation vessel. "Their shields are powering up, but they don't have any disruptors."

"I've had as much of this as I'm going to take. Fire on the birds-of-prey. Let's bloody their noses and see if *that* catches their attention!"

Abruptly, Worf leaped from his chair and raced to Dax's console. "Commander, did you say the small ship has *no disruptors?*"

"Yes, sir. Firing now, Captain." She tapped the touch-plate, still incongruously called a "trigger" even centuries after the last mechanical lever dropped a hammer on a firing pin. The twin bolts appeared instantaneously—actually at just a hair under lightspeed, but close enough to infinity across such a short distance—cutting through the weaker side-shielding of both birds, crippling the disruptor alignment module of one ship and slightly damaging the aft environmental controls of the other. Call it one hit and one near miss.

"Readying photon torpedoes," announced Chief O'Brien, in case the captain decided to finish them off.

"Just shields?" demanded the Klingon in Dax's ear, urgently.

"Huh? Oh, yes Worf, just shields. Why, is there something I should—"

"They're modulating their shields!" shouted Worf. "Captain, we must reverse course and put as much distance as possible between us and the Federation ship!"

"Why must we do that, Mr. Worf? That ship needs our help."

"That ship is already dead, sir!"

Hesitating only the briefest of moments, Sisko made an instant decision to listen to his second in command. "Full stop, reverse full impulse. Get us out of here, Old Man." His voice seemed a bit sulky to Dax; Benjamin was not happy about withdrawing when he seemed to have the upper hand.

The small, unarmed Klingon ship began to modulate its shields, extending them. Suddenly, every sensor on

Dax's console shot off the scale, and she actually *felt* a hard, electrical shock pass through her body.

Both ships now drifted naked, the two shield systems gone. "Hold tight," said Commander Worf.

"Benjamin, the Klingons are beaming something—"

She never finished the sentence. The forward viewer flared white, giving the *Defiant* crew an instant of spectacular rainbows as the viewscreen filters tried to damp the electromagnetic energy by separating it into component bandwidths. The computer finally gave it up as a lost cause, and immediately substituted an instrument readout in place of the visual.

A moment later, Dax restored visual contact. The Federation ship was a dark, twisted hulk of metal, shredded beyond recognition as a starship except for the telltale warp signature residue and other forms of radiation associated with hyperluminous travel. The smaller Klingon patrol boat was nowhere to be seen, not even with a sensor sweep.

"Faith," whispered O'Brien, eyes as wide as Dax's must have been.

"Dax," shouted an unexpected voice from the turbolift, "scan for life signs!"

When did Bashir come up to the bridge? she wondered.

"The two birds-of-prey—where are they?" said Sisko. The words broke the spell that had held the others motionless.

Dax quickly remodulated the scanners, swept the entire system. She had totally lost track of them when all the instruments maxed out. "Captain, they're heading back toward the wormhole at full impulse. We can't catch them before they're in the Gamma Quadrant."

Sisko stared, silent a long moment. "Better let them go, Dax. We have no idea what reception committee might be waiting for us on the other side, and I think we'd better discuss this one with the flags before going anywhere."

He sat at his command chair, looking heavy and tired. *He hates this part,* thought his friend. "Take us to the— the remains of the ship, Dax. We'd better make an inspection, file a complete report. Bashir, Dax, pull some EVA suits and meet me in Transporter One. Doctor, bring your forensics case. Let's at least try to figure out who they *were.*"

Lieutenant Commander Jadzia Dax laid in the rendezvous course and engaged, then she rose from her console and shuffled toward the turbolift, feeling quite heavy herself.

Doctor Julian Bashir sealed up his pressure suit, feeling the perfect fool, and stepped forward onto the transporter pad. Listening to his own breath rasping in and out his helmet stimulated his adrenal gland; his heart raced, and his breathing grew ragged. By the time PO1 Swenson pulled the transporter slides forward, energizing the away team, Bashir's hands were shaking and his knees felt weak, as if he couldn't support himself.

He didn't need to. There was, of course, no gravity on the exploded wreck of a hull: no lights, no air, no gravity—no life that Bashir could see. Materializing, he could not stop his feet from twitching as his stomach lurched, and he launched himself gracelessly across the belly of what once had been the main deck. The others, even the captain, had similar problems.

The comm channel squawked loudly in Bashir's ear. "Good idea to tether us together, Benjamin," said lovely Jadzia Dax. The doctor quite agreed and said so.

The away team comprised Captain Sisko, Lieutenant Commanders Worf and Dax, and Lieutenant Bashir, but it looked like a single, four-bodied, sixteen-limbed organism connected by thin, vascular cables. "Everyone *freeze,*" ordered Sisko, straining against the pull of three other bodies with their own momentum, their own velocity.

Singly, the captain reeled them in slowly; one tug was all that was necessary, Bashir noted—he'd "known" it, of course, but studying zero-G in books at the Academy was different from actually experiencing it in a ghoulish hulk of a once-was starship! Even the two training exercises he'd received were inadequate.

As the captain pulled Bashir closer in turn, the doctor tried to shake off the fantasy that he was a fly in a web being drawn in by a hungry spider. "Everybody loosen your tether reel," said Sisko. "Just move slowly and don't exit the ship without my authorization."

Suddenly, Bashir blinked. He'd just seen movement, something about the walls. Staring at a particular bulkhead, Bashir suddenly realized what he had seen: "Captain, the hull is contracting!"

Sisko winced inside his nearly transparent helmet. "Good eye, doctor. O'Brien, is this ship stable?"

"Um . . ." The chief activated his tricorder, which flashed silently in the vacuum, and he spun slowly in place. "No sir; it's not stable. It could go at any second. Maybe we'd better get out of here."

"Set up a forceshield to reinforce the hull," ordered the captain."

"That'll give us a whole half an hour," muttered O'Brien.

"Then monitor it carefully, Chief. I don't like surprises."

While O'Brien set up the minishields, Bashir bounced gently to the center of the black cavern, trailing his gossamer tether; looking out—there was no up or down—he saw stars through gaping holes in the skin of the ship, holes with jagged edges pushed outward presumably by a terrible explosion. Ground-zero was not yet determined; that was Worf's job. Bashir unslung his medical tricorder, set the scan depth, and kicked the deckplates to begin a slow pirouette, searching for lifesigns the ship's scanners might have missed—

though how anyone could still be alive on this frozen, airless hulk is beyond me, he mentally added. As expected, the only lifesigns he detected were those of the away team.

Bashir began to grow dizzy; he was still breathing too rapidly, hyperventilating, and the short, shallow breaths were scrubbing his blood of carbon dioxide. Starting to panic, he tried to stop his rotation, but he had drifted out of contact with the deck. He closed his eyes, but that was worse. Forcing himself to inhale slowly, taking long, deep breaths and holding them, the doctor finally calmed himself. His stomach continued to roll and lurch, however . . . he *really* didn't like zero-G!

"We're alone!" he reported.

"Ouch! Doctor, there is no reason to shout. I can hear you perfectly well over the comm link."

"Sorry, sir," said Bashir, chagrined. "No further life signs."

Dax spoke up; Bashir heard tension in her voice, too, and this made him feel better, though he didn't know why. "Julian, try scanning for organic molecules."

"Right, Jadzia." The task required recalibrating the tricorder to a more sensitive scale, which of course required closer proximity to what he was scanning. "Captain," he said, cutting off his words too crisply, "request permission to—to untether. I cannot conduct a full DNA scan while tied up like a dog on a leash."

Sisko was a long moment answering. "If you think it's necessary, Doctor. I don't like it. Report every few minutes, so I know you haven't drifted through a hole and into empty space."

Julian reached down, hesitating a moment; he gently rubbed his fingertips together, then quickly disconnected before he could change his mind. Holding on to the base of a chair, bolted to a bulkhead (or had it once been a deck?), he stared around at a dozen rips and gaps easily large enough to "fall" through. *Even if I did, the*

Defiant *would still catch me,* he told himself; his stomach and knees refused to believe him.

The hull lurched again. "Sorry, Captain," grumbled Chief O'Brien. "This jury-rigged fairy box isn't going to hold much longer."

Pushing away the fear with thoughts of duty, Bashir began a laborious scan across each flat surface for organic molecules. He struck rich ore right away: nearly every deck, overhead, and bulkhead was coated with a fine spray of DNA, the gigantic, easily detected coding molecule found in varying forms in every species of animal or plant in the quadrant. "Good Lord," he whispered, forgetting he was hot-miked.

"Find something?" asked Sisko.

"There was somebody—there were several some-bodies here all right, um, I count six; but they were . . . *vaporized* is the only way I can put it. They were blown apart by a bomb, I would guess, so powerful that all organic entities aboard this ship were taken apart, mole-cule by molecule, and dis—" Bashir swallowed, feeling nauseated at the thought, "and distributed in a fairly even coating approximately a hundred and fifty ang-stroms thick throughout the ship."

The guttural voice of Commander Worf cut through the soft conversation like the blare of a trumpet in the middle of a string quartet. "Captain, I was afraid of this. The Klingons have perfected a weapon they were only testing when I was last on the homeworld."

"A new weapon, Mr. Worf?"

"To be more accurate, sir, a new weapon-delivery system. I do not know how familiar you are with Klingon battle tactics."

"I'm reasonably familiar, Worf; I had a good instruc-tor." Bashir could hear the smile in Sisko's voice; he recalled that Curzon Dax, Jadzia's former host and a mentor to the young Benjamin Sisko, had befriended many old Klingon warriors.

"Then you know about the legendary battle of Fom Kerdeth."

"I think I recall," said the captain. "Perhaps you should enlighten us anyway."

"At Fom Kerdeth, Bardak Linron the traitor fought the forces of Kahless to a standstill. Many dead were recorded during those six days, and many songs have been sung. But Kahless finally lost the battle when Bardak sent his best general, Renarg, to negotiate terms for separating the combatants. Renarg entered the tent of Kahless's high command with an arrogant list of demands, but his terms were a ruse, for he had strapped high explosives all around his body, concealed beneath his armor and clothing. He detonated the munitions, sacrificing himself to kill Kahless's entire general staff. It is only by a miracle that the Emperor himself survived; he had stepped out to . . . to relieve himself from the night's drinking."

Bashir waited; evidently Worf wanted some prodding, which Dax supplied. "A charming story. How does it relate, Worf?"

"We have long theorized that any ship, of any size, can be destroyed by transporting a bomb directly to the engineering deck next to the antimatter containment field, or to the bridge if you want to preserve the ship as a trophy. The idea is to detonate a bomb aboard your own ship, transporting it just as the explosion initiates, so there is no time for the target to transport it into space or back aboard your own ship."

"You can't transport a bomb or anything else through shields, Worf," said Sisko.

"That has always been the difficult point," agreed the Klingon. "The High Council spent years secretly funding Project Renarg, trying to develop a method for momentarily interrupting a target ship's shield. Two years ago, I took the initiative to quickly read through a classified abstract of the current theory: the researchers believe that if you pilot a ship without a shield up to the target, then activate the shield set to a frequency whose wave crests and troughs are the exact mirror image of the target's shield, it will cancel out both shields."

"Only for a moment!" exclaimed Dax. "Only until the target realizes what has happened and remodulates its shields. A second or two, no more."

"A second or two is all you would need, Commander." No one spoke for a moment, then Worf continued. "I have found the center of the explosion, and it is not at a location where it could have occurred by accident or in the heat of battle. There is no evidence of concealment; the explosive device seems to have materialized exactly where it exploded."

"Project Renarg," mused Bashir.

"Yes, doctor. I believe the project has been successful. The Klingons now have the capacity to destroy any ship in the Federation fleet."

CHAPTER
3

"CHARMING," SAID DAX. *The Old Man doesn't sound particularly charmed,* thought Captain Sisko.

"Mr. Worf, this raises an interesting question," he said; "assuming your analysis is correct, why would the Klingons tip their hand by using their secret weapon right here, within smelling distance of a Starfleet starbase?"

Worf sounded almost apologetic—an odd tone of voice for a Klingon warrior! "That is the part I cannot fathom, Captain. I can think of no strategic advantage to letting us know of their new capacity."

Sisko smiled, noting the faint emphasis Worf placed on the words "us" and "their"; *making sure I know which side he's on,* thought the captain. Worf made a point of doing it every few days, as if concerned that fellow members of Starfleet might start to grow suspicious of the only Klingon member of the service, given the circumstances.

"They would 'let us know' by blowing up a Galaxy-class starship with a patrol boat," Dax chimed in.

"Unless . . ." came a hesitant voice.

"Yes, doctor?" encouraged Sisko.

"Unless whatever they had to destroy was more dangerous than allowing knowledge of their success to leak out."

Sisko grunted assent. It was the only likely explanation. "So what could have been so valuable aboard this small, private yacht? What did they want so badly to destroy? Spread out, everybody. Untether and search this entire ship—carefully. I want to know what skeletons are buried here."

Heeding his own advice, the captain released the trigger on his cable reel, and the cable silently rolled tight through the airless ship onto Dax's reel. Turning, Captain Sisko played his helmet lamp around the ruined chamber. There was virtually nothing recognizable left. "I suggest we move to the farthest ends of the ship, as far away from ground-zero as we can. We won't find anything intact anywhere else. And people: if O'Brien shouts, be prepared for an emergency beam-out. As he said, those forceshields will not last forever."

Sisko himself moved aft—*at least, I think it's aft,* he corrected—until he began to see the skeletons of corridors and shards of doors; then he searched room to room, looking for clues amid the destruction.

Movement, flicker; Sisko's heart lurched, and his hand jumped of its own accord to curl greedily around the phaser. He froze, drifting slowly in the zero-G corridor, time frozen. After a moment, he took his hand away from the weapon, feeling a thin layer of ice crack around his elbow joints, condensation perhaps from a gruesome "humidity" of fine blood droplets not yet condensed against the metal surfaces. He reached to a bulkhead and tugged himself along the corridor again.

The movement was his own shadow, thrown into

relief by the floodlights of the *Defiant* reaching through the torn skin of the wayfaring corpse. Sisko's shadow danced on every surface, surprisingly three-dimensional, as he moved past more holes blown through the hull.

Whenever the captain came across a shadowy or buried corner, he pulled away whatever debris concealed the space, looking and hoping. A thick table or titanium hatch might have shielded a body or log-clip from the blast—*something* to prise the secret from the silent ship's skeleton! His breathing became more ragged as he exerted himself, sweating like a horse. More times than he could count, the captain reached up and tried to wipe his face, only to bump his hand into the unfamiliar helmet.

Farther along the corridor, the force of the internal explosion *(like swallowing a phaser-grenade)* had twisted the ship's orientation; Sisko "swam" through a vaguely helical corridor, as if he were an RNA messenger molecule surfing the monstrous DNA helix for the protein code that would whisper what happened.

At last, nearly as far aft as he could get before the ribbons of ship became so disjointed he could no longer unambiguously call it inside or out, Benjamin Sisko found a cabin space. It was still just barely recognizable for what it once had been: the infirmary. Here, so far from the focus, the force of explosion had not obliterated all traces from the room. Instead, the room was *compressed* fore to aft, contracted into a space many times smaller than it once occupied, but still recognizable. And, amid the rubble, the shatter of glassware, the ubiquitous spray of bio-residue, to be polite about it, were the remains of some model of personal log and recording device.

The box was nearly crushed beyond recognition by the compressive force, but still visible was a company logo glued to the side of the machine: *Levanian Biomedical Survey Pangalactic Consortium,* it read in Levanese, as near as Sisko could tell; he was not an expert in the

Levanian language. But there was one other symbol on the box that caught Sisko's eye: the stylized red cross that still, after hundreds of years, signified something medical on most planets in the Federation.

Sisko stared for a moment, breathing twice with a catch in his throat; then he touched the helmet transmit switch with his chin and spoke into the microphone inside his light, clear helmet. "Bashir, come aft, home on my signal. I've found . . . something."

"On my way, sir!" The relief in the doctor's voice was palpable. Julian Bashir was unsettled by a dead ship that would not yield its dead.

Within ten minutes, the captain was joined not by Bashir alone, but the entire away team except for O'Brien, who still tended the force shield. None had found anything worthwhile, so they all responded to the promise of something, anything. "Doctor," asked the captain, taking Bashir's arm and launching him toward the find, "what *is* that piece of equipment?"

With difficulty, Bashir maneuvered himself upside-down with respect to the captain's orientation, not that it made any difference in zero-G. The doctor pulled his face close to the remains of the electronic device, studying it carefully for several minutes before responding. "Sir," he said at last, "as near as I can make out, I should think it's a—it once was a medical log. Of course, I'm not as familiar with this model as with the modern Starfleet version."

Sisko couldn't help licking his lips. "That is what I thought, Doctor. Julian, if Chief O'Brien can salvage that medical log, would you be able to deduce where the ship was and what it was doing to incur such wrath among the Klingons?"

Bashir rotated, then seemed disconcerted when he realized he and Captain Sisko were inverted with respect to each other. "I . . . well, that is, I really cannot say, Captain. The medical officer *should* input the stardate before every entry, and we should be able to extract the approximate location. But sir, this isn't a Starfleet ship, and I cannot guarantee his accuracy or diligence. Or her diligence, whatever he or she was."

"Do *you* generally describe the station's current mission in your own logs, Doctor?"

Bashir managed to blush and preen simultaneously; *quite a feat while floating on his head!* thought Sisko. "Well, of course, my own log entries are hardly typical. I'm a very thorough doctor. I don't know about these . . . whatever they are."

"Levanians," supplied Sisko. "Dax, see if we can rescue the remains without losing any circuitry or breaking it any further than it already is."

It took the station's science officer more than ten minutes to gently detach the box from the bulkhead into which it had been thrown. The rest of the team tethered around the room in various orientations and fidgeted, forcibly prevented from "helping" the Trill by stern command of the commanding officer. Such ham-fisted help from, say, Worf was more likely to pulverize the fragile, remaining bits of electronics than actually to *assist* Jadzia Dax.

Worf remained at alert, outside the corpse of the starship, with the away team inside. Julian Bashir gave advice to Dax, as if his specialized knowledge of medicine automatically extended to all electronic devices ever used by doctors. The captain hovered, literally, nearby, trying to keep the doctor occupied so he wouldn't bother the Old Man—young woman.

Finally, Dax loosened the last contact point that had fused metal-to-metal. She gently teased away the entire unit with a single, sharp tug, then pulled her hands away. The data-pack of the medical log "rose" from the mess of machinery and drifted in zero-G across the room. It barely rotated on its axis . . . Jadzia Dax had quite a delicate touch, far more so than Curzon had!

She captured it in a shield-containment module, what used to be called a magnetic bottle in the more colorful jargon of bygone centuries, recalled the captain with a flicker of a smile.

"Activating a zero-G containment field," Dax said, touching the appropriate buttons. "This thing is about ready to fall apart, and the *Defiant*'s gravity field might just do it."

At that moment, the urgent voice of the engineering chief cut through the chatter in Sisko's command comm circuit. "We're losing it—get us out of here, Captain!"

Sisko chinned his comm switch: "Away team to *Defiant*: emergency beam-out! Four to beam back, plus a memory-pack in a containment field that should be beamed directly to engineering."

As he materialized, Captain Sisko saw the hull collapse under the tidal stresses of the distant Bajoran sun and the ship's own mass. As they materialized on the transporter pad, O'Brien was looking at his timer: "thirty-eight minutes, twenty seconds. I'd say we got our money's worth, Captain."

Chief Miles O'Brien took custody of the medical log, but one look persuaded him to leave it alone until he had it all the way back on the station. As well-equipped as the *Defiant* was, the job was too delicate to be conducted remotely.

The chief would have preferred to work alone; failing that, he would have rather worked with *anybody* than Doctor Bashir. Although O'Brien had become fairly chummy with the doctor lately—playing darts, kayaking—Bashir still tended to ask a fairy-mound of annoying questions, which O'Brien was obliged to answer politely, since Doctor Julian Bashir was a commissioned Starfleet officer while O'Brien was only an engineering master chief.

Bashir leaned forward, peering over the chief's shoulder; O'Brien felt the doctor's breath on his ear and almost cringed away before catching himself. "Julian, if you *don't mind?*"

"Eh? Oh, terribly sorry, Chief. I was just trying to see what you're doing."

"What I'm doing is scanning the edge of the spool-pack to find sections with the property parity; that's the only spot we're likely to decipher."

"Ah. Yes. Of course." Bashir nodded vigorously.

"You don't have a clue what I just said, do you?"

"Certainly I do. Well, no I don't; not really."

Gently pushing the doctor back into his chair, O'Brien explained the engineering theory behind the recording and how it might have survived the Klingon bomb. The biggest danger was not the actual force of the explosion, since the log was shielded by a metal desk. Most of the damage would have been done by the intense pulse of electromagnetic energy that would accompany any detonation of that size: it was worse than running through a data-clip library with a huge electromagnet tucked under one arm!

On the first run-through, O'Brien found nothing but snow on the visual channel and white noise on the audio, with just a few fluctuations here and there: but those fluctuations actually contained more information than the human ear could detect. In the second play-through, after digital enhancement, O'Brien turned the volume all the way up. He and the good doctor listened in mounting nervous fascination to a loud hiss masking the eerie echoes of a distant warning: the words recorded by the female doctor of the Levanian Consortium sounded urgent. The tension in the woman's voice was evident, even though the words were so far unintelligible.

A ghost from beyond the grave, thought O'Brien, shivering, thinking of the Banshee of the Scots; *she's come to warn us,* if *we can heed her words.* But first they had to *understand* her words . . . and that required more delicate digital construction than the computer could do by itself. It required the full attention of Miles Edward O'Brien.

The chief caught himself working feverishly, as if everyone's life depended on hearing the Levanian doctor's last warning. Well, maybe it did; until they knew what the warning was, they had to treat it as extremely serious, after all, the Klingons had been willing to kill, even to reveal the existence of their newest weapon, in order to silence her. It was up to O'Brien to give her a voice again.

He clipped individual word fragments, compared them to intact words elsewhere, and made shrewd guesses where insufficient information stumped the computer. The trouble with computers was that they were so literal. It still took a human to make the intellectual leaps of faith necessary to reconstruct words obliterated by an electromagnetic pulse, to drag the warning back from the Other Side.

Finally, after nearly nine straight hours of "reconstructive surgery,"—during which Doctor Bashir remained every bit as alert and concentrated as did the chief, impressing O'Brien more than he would admit—they were ready for another playback. Gingerly, the chief said "computer, play tracks four through six." No stardate was intelligible from the tapes. They were identified only by the physical track on the bubble-recording medium.

There were seven sentence fragments, all that remained of the life and death of the Levanian doctor, all that remained of her urgent warning. The annoying hiss remained. O'Brien was reluctant to eliminate it, since it might contain information that so far had eluded him. But he had the computer mostly suppress it for the playback. Each batch of now-intelligible words was separated from the others by many minutes of visual snow and audio steam. Still, O'Brien and Bashir listened intently, even during the long gaps:

SURVEY NEARLY CONCLUDED . . .

APPROACHING GAMMA GAMMA KILO NINER SEVEN FOUR
TO CONDUCT . . .

FOUND THEM, NEVER KNEW THE JEM . . .

—DISRUPTED! THE JEM'HADAR HAVE FLANKED . . .

BESIDE THE KLINGONS; WE DON'T KNOW WHAT THE HELL
THEY'RE . . .

—WORKING TOGETHER! THIS INTELLIGENCE IS SO CRITI-
CAL, WE *MUST* BREAK AWAY IMMEDIATELY TO REPORT IT
TO . . .

—'HADAR *TRAINING WITH THE KLINGONS* ON GAMMA!

O'Brien swallowed hard; he was a man who remembered his history. The Federation had had many con-
flicts with the Klingon Empire, each time Starfleet
barely winning against their more aggressive and vicious opponents for one major reason: the Klingons
were impetuous and tended to attack before they
were fully ready. They didn't wait for a workable
strategy; they never quite had the technology to match
Starfleet.

But things were different this time, weren't they? In
the past, Starfleet always held the technological and
strategic edge. But the war between the Federation and
the Founders—fought mainly by the latter's slave-
warriors, the Jem'Hadar—was just the reverse: it was
the *Jem'Hadar* who enjoyed a decisive technological and
strategic advantage, in addition to the Founders' ability
to shapeshift. In fact, the Dominion was so far held in
check *only* by the Founders' evident reluctance to attack
outside the Gamma Quadrant.

"All they've ever done is infiltrate, manipulate," said
O'Brien aloud. He didn't need to clarify whom he was
talking about. Dr. Bashir understood.

"The Gowron incident," said Julian. "They've never attacked us directly. Maybe their power is stronger inside the Gamma Quadrant than outside?"

"Not anymore," said the chief, feeling his stomach start to hurt. "Not if they've allied with the Klingons. With Jem'Hadar technology and the Klingon presence throughout the Alpha Quadrant, the Founders can project their force anywhere in the bloody galaxy!"

Chief O'Brien and Doctor Bashir looked at each other with the same understanding: the few scraps of data left in the Levanian medical log indicated the ship had stumbled onto a secret training base at Gamma GK-974, an unnamed planetary system deep and cold in the cold heart of the Gamma Quadrant, a base where *Klingons and Jem'Hadar trained together.*

O'Brien swallowed; a stone weight fell from his throat into his stomach. "Doctor, are you thinking the same thing I'm thinking?"

"I think so," said Bashir, nervously glancing back over his shoulder to make sure no Klingons or Jem'Hadar were sneaking up on them; it was a nervous gesture, and O'Brien understood it completely. "Can we make it any clearer, Chief?"

O'Brien shook his head. "See these batch of electromagnetic spikes? This first one is where the pulse itself washed across the log. These fainter lines in both directions are the electromagnetic echoes off the metal bulkheads and equipment in the infirmary. There's a total of eleven refraction echos, plus the original: we're damned lucky to have recovered *any* of the log at all."

"Yes, I thought as much," said Bashir, sighing. "I was just clutching at straws. Do we have enough to take to the captain?"

O'Brien turned back to the log, again replaying the fugitive scraps of intelligence: *the Jem'Hadar—beside the Klingons—working together.* "We have enough that we don't dare *not* take it to the captain. There's something else here, something I'm not one hundred percent sure about: I'd swear that this log was erased *before* the Klingons blew up the ship."

"Before? What are you saying?"

"I'm saying, Julian, that somebody aboard the Levanian ship deliberately erased the medical log, or tried to; looks like he ran a powerful electromagnetic field over it, but he missed a few spots. That's why there's so little left. Believe it or not, the bomb itself would have left more fragments, and each fragment would be longer."

Julian Bashir had nothing to say; it was a puzzling and sobering development. Twelve minutes later, O'Brien made his presentation to all assembled: the captain, Major Kira, Lieutenant Commander Dax—and of course Worf, the fugitive Klingon, and Constable Odo, the renegade, now-"solid" Founder. Worf and Odo both stiffened visibly; they didn't quite move away from each other, but O'Brien was sure it took inhuman control for them to stand their ground. Worf flushed darker than his usual Klingon complexion, and Odo squeezed his fists so tightly, his knuckles actually cracked—a feat that would have been impossible back when he was still a shapeshifter.

Major Kira was first to speak. The Bajoran ex-resistance fighter (and very pregnant birth-mother of O'Brien's second child) sounded an aggressive note to open the grim meeting. "I'm inclined to believe this log, Captain," she said, studiously avoiding Worf's frosty glare. "It definitely smells like a Klingon tactic. Uh, no offense, Worf."

"I choose not to take offense," rumbled the Klingon, in a tone of voice that meant he took very great offense indeed. Lieutenant Commander Dax shivered when she heard it. "But I do *not* believe the report of Klingon–Jem'Hadar alliance. That would be dishonorable," concluded Worf.

You're dancing on very thin ice, Major, thought O'Brien. Of course, he didn't say such a thing out loud.

"If you want my opinion," argued Kira, not backing down, "attacking *Deep Space Nine* was pretty dishonorable, too."

Worf had no response, but Dax took up the cause. "The Klingons I've fought with were all honorable warriors," she said, folding her arms and crossing her legs. "Well, at least since the Cult of Kahless arose a few decades ago. I can't believe that even Gowron would ally with the Founders. That's too much to swallow, especially after what they almost did to him!"

A pensive Captain Sisko frowned. "I don't like the fact that someone aboard the ship tried to erase the log. Were they trying to cover up what they saw? Did they hope the Klingons would allow them to live if they removed all evidence of the alliance—assuming for the moment that there really was an alliance?"

O'Brien shrugged. The other possibility was that one of the Levanians was a traitor to the Federation, or perhaps they were carrying a non-Federation passenger? It was another disturbing aspect of the medical log, but not their primary problem.

Odo shook his head sadly. *Have we been looking at him differently since we found the Founders?* wondered the chief. O'Brien felt his face heat slightly. Even he had been a little more *guarded* around Odo since the troubles started; he'd looked at the constable differently, held back a little more information than he should have. *It's hard, staring at that face, knowing it's one of their faces.*

"There is only one minor point I should make about that tape," said Constable Odo. "Whatever the Klingons may think, my people do not even have the concept of alliances and treaties: they recognize only masters and slaves. If you're not the master, you're the slave." He paused, but no one spoke, especially not Worf. "When I was briefly in the memory pool on my homeworld," continued Odo, "I received many impressions. One that came through very clear was the Founders' fascination with the Klingon Empire: they see the Klingons as the

Alpha Quadrant version of the Jem'Hadar, the best material to be . . . converted into servants of the Dominion. I'm sorry, Commander," he added with unexpected tenderness to Worf.

"You're saying the Founders will betray the Klingons?" asked Major Kira.

"Let's not be too hasty," said Sisko, relaxing the tension. "We *don't* even know there is an alliance yet."

"I mean, Major, that the Founders see the Klingons only as the means to an end," continued Odo. "Like every other race in all four quadrants, to the Founders the Klingons are tools, used until they're dull, then cast aside."

"I still don't buy it," griped Lieutenant Commander Dax.

"Commander," said Chief O'Brien, the first words he had spoken since presenting the medical log data, "might you be, ah, overly influenced by the memories of Curzon? It's—it's a different era now. If those days of Klingon glory and honor were still here, then Worf would be honored by his people, not discommodated." The chief had been trying to cheer up Worf, but it seemed to have the opposite effect; the Klingon glowered at the deck, and O'Brien kicked himself for not phrasing it better.

Captain Sisko said nothing, but O'Brien saw his jaw muscles bulge as he clenched his teeth. *Maybe he's still brooding about the log being erased,* the chief thought. Then Sisko seemed to push his personal misgivings aside: an immediate decision was required. "Old Man," he said at last, "any chance Gamma GK-974 is the base for the assault that FleetIntCom was looking for?"

Dax stood and studied the map of the relevant sectors of the Gamma Quadrant displayed on the viewscreen. "If it's true—and that's a big if—then it would be pretty well suited for a staging area to order the invasion. Gamma-Kilo isn't all that close to either Carlos or Diana sectors, but it's only a couple of days at warp nine. Other than that, it looks . . ." She trailed off, but everyone knew what she meant, including O'Brien.

"It looks pretty deadly," concluded the captain, not pleased with the confirmation. "Mr. Worf, you haven't said much. What do you think about the possibility of alliance between Gowron and the Founders?"

If O'Brien's old Klingon friend had looked stiff before, he positively fossilized now. "Sir, I cannot imagine that any *honorable* Klingon would sign a secret treaty with the Dominion." Worf paused; no one interrupted the silence . . . the Klingon had not finished. "But Gowron has acted without honor before. He betrayed the Cardassians. And as Major Kira reminds me," now it was Kira's turn to stare down at her feet, O'Brien noticed, "he treacherously attacked *Deep Space Nine,* his Federation allies, without warning."

Worf stared at the map, at the transcript of the log, anywhere but at Captain Sisko. "Sir, I cannot entirely rule out the possibility," he grudgingly allowed.

The captain pressed. "So this message could be accurate: there could be an alliance between the Klingons and the Founders."

"It could be accurate."

"And there might actually be a secret base at GK-974 where Klingon warriors are training side by side with Jem'Hadar shock troops."

"It could be so."

The chief swallowed; he knew what would have to be done. Silence fell across Ops like a heavy, woolen shroud over a corpse. Captain Sisko turned to O'Brien: "Prepare a summary message to Fleet Intelligence, Chief. Worf, begin working up the *Defiant* crew for a dangerous run. I suspect we are about to be drafted."

"Aye, sir," said the engineer and the security officer simultaneously.

"Sir," said Odo swiftly, "I would like to accompany—"

"Of course you will," said Sisko without hesitation.

CHAPTER
4

LIEUTENANT COMMANDER DAX was unsurprised when the order came back from Starfleet Intelligence less than three hours after the chief sent the priority message, even though it was probably a fleet record for making a decision of this magnitude. But she was nonplussed when Benjamin called her into his office and said, "Old Man, I'm going to have to leave Commander Worf behind."

"You're joking."

"I need an experienced battlefield commander in charge of the station. There are still Klingons about, and the Founders might still come through the wormhole."

"But what about Major—"

Benjamin leaned close and whispered, as if the major might hear them even through the Cardassian-steel bulkhead: "Major Kira, in case you haven't noticed, is nearly ready to have a *baby*. I cannot exactly see her squeezing through the corridors with a phaser in each hand."

"Can you see her manning the phasers on the *Defiant?*"

"I sincerely hope it will not come to that, Old Man," Sisko winked. "This is an intelligence-gathering mission, not special-ops. We'll stay cloaked, keep our mouths shut, and our eyes open."

Dax nodded. "Yes, I can see where that would be hard enough on Kira."

"I need Worf here, not because he can fight, but because if he's here, he probably won't *have* to fight. Not many commanders would attack an angry Klingon with several thousand photon torpedoes in his pocket, at least not without a brigade. Worf stays."

Dax swallowed. Sisko had a point, but Worf wasn't going to like it. She was just as glad she wouldn't be present when her old friend issued this particular order.

Worf's reaction was more sedate than Jadzia Dax expected, possibly due to the growing closeness between them. "No! This is *not acceptable!*" he growled.

"Worf, those are the captain's direct orders!"

"I will *not* be left behind like a—like a *Ferengi!* They are my people, my problem, my mission!" The Klingon clenched his teeth and began to look around, presumably for something to throw. So much for his taking it well.

Dax's first impulse was to bolt, get away from the raging bull, but she had long since learned that Worf's Klingon rages burned themselves out quickly . . . even when he had as much cause as for this one.

"Commander Worf, *yItamchoH!*" The Klingon blinked in surprise, freezing in mid-rant. "Do you still have any honor left . . . or are you a *verengan Ha'DIbaH?*"

Worf said nothing. He stared at Dax. She swallowed, facing him down. By Klingon law, Jadzia Dax had just challenged Worf to combat . . . potentially to the death.

Am I his comrade in arms now? she wondered, *or just his woman?* If the latter, she might be dead before his Starfleet training could reassert itself: Klingon women did not lightly insult the honor of their men.

Worf took a deep breath, then another, and Dax knew she was safe. "I apologize for my outburst, Jadzia; I have felt the rage since I first heard about the alliance."

"Possible alliance," she corrected. "That's what we're going to find out, Worf." She half closed her eyes, feeling her own sense of shame at the honor of her old friends impugned. "My gut still tells me it's not true, but we have no choice: if the Klingons really are training at a Jem'Hadar camp, it changes everything. It would mean—"

"It would mean having to rewrite the entire order of battle," said Odo, having joined them so quietly that Dax jumped at the sound.

"Worf," she added, "Benjamin needs you here. Who's going to defend the station if Gowron attacks again . . . Kira? Before or after she gives birth? Julian? Quark?"

Worf sucked in a third deep breath and let it out in a snort, curling his lip in disgust. "You are right. It is the proper course of action for the captain to take. I will change the voice-codes and command authority at once." He stomped off toward the turbolift, pylon IV, the *Defiant.*

Constable Odo stared at the wreckage of the bench. "I suppose the maintenance crew isn't terribly busy these days anyway," he sighed.

Not four hours later, Dax expertly tapped the impulse thrusters to nudge the *Defiant* away from the pylon, while her captain brooded over the transcript of the recovered medical log.

"Three contacts in this sector," said Kira, staring at her sensor readout. "Standard lights, no hostile indicators, no fire-control sensors . . . looks like a Lonatian freighter and two Federation science surveys where they're supposed to be, according to SigInt."

Sisko didn't respond, but he didn't need to; the major was merely stating for the log that there was no hostile activity in the vicinity of the wormhole.

"That freighter is a smuggler who sometimes works with Quark, our resident one-Ferengi crime wave," muttered Odo, not so much because it was important, Dax realized, but merely to have something to say. Not even Odo was immune from nervousness—though Benjamin still sat silent as a statue.

The *Defiant* seemed eerily empty with only the four of them and two ensigns aboard, Janine Wheeler and Tarvak Amar. Dax missed seeing Chief O'Brien scurrying about, adjusting controls that were already reading perfectly, and she even missed feeling the longing gaze of Julian on her neck speckles whenever he thought her back was turned. Most of all, she missed the comforting bulk of Commander Worf, his confident snarl, the savage way he barked orders at the cringing junior officers. But Worf was needed on the station, and there was no reason to risk the lives of the engineering senior-chief and the station doctor: as Benjamin said, this was an intelligence-gathering mission . . . four days of tedium at peak sustainable warp, cloaked; a few days of observation at Gamma GK-974 to quash the ugly rumor—or confirm the even more ugly truth—and then another four-day high-speed run back through the wormhole and into *DS9* again to transmit the intel, for good or ill.

Well, here goes nothing . . . I hope! On her own initiative, the Trill turned the ship and headed toward the electromagnetic and gravitational singularity that was normally invisible to the naked eye—except when a ship passed through—but was lit up like a supernova in the high-end of the spectrum from ultraviolet to X-ray. "Shifting to warp two," she said. "Entering the wormhole now."

The multicolored "tunnel-wall" effect encased the ship like a cocoon, and Dax clenched her teeth: they were flying invisible, thus unshielded, into the belly of the beast . . . and Jadzia Dax feared what she might find inside.

Master Chief Petty Officer Miles Edward O'Brien prowled around inside his "pit," the engineering well from which he could, in a pinch, control virtually every aspect of the station from weapons to environment to rotation to communications—even, though few were aware of it, to station *movement,* as if *Deep Space Nine* were a gigantic, albeit slow, starship. Worf eschewed the captain's office, preferring to command from Kira's weapon station, for typically Klingon reasons, O'Brien supposed.

"Chief O'Brien," snarled Worf, becoming formal in his agony, "will you please cease whistling? It is bad enough I was left behind two days ago. I do not wish to endure audio torture as well."

The chief stopped, embarrassed; he hadn't realized he was whistling so loudly. With a guilty start, O'Brien realized he was actually *happy* that he wasn't on the mission—but he was terrified for Kira, and for his and Keiko's second child, artificially implanted in Major Kira after Keiko was injured. Happy, frightened, and guilty, his only outlet had been to sing, and the only song he could think of would have been more appropriate in Quark's, or in a Dublin pub, than in Ops.

Again, O'Brien felt disturbingly as if someone were staring at the back of his head. He couldn't resist the temptation to turn around and look behind him; of course, he saw only the wall of the well, and further back, the doorless turbolift leading down into the rest of the station. "Worf, don't you find this rather creepy?" He gestured around. "This, I mean—the whole station is empty, and now even Ops is deserted."

"In fact," rumbled the Klingon, "I find the solitude refreshing. I just wish the station were also empty of a certain pair of Ferengi. I am uncomfortable having to take Odo's place in watching them."

"Oh, come on, Rom's not bad," said O'Brien, defending his budding protégé.

"Rom is the brother of his brother! He is still under the thumb of Quark."

"He only goes there to eat; I haven't seen him palling around with Quark since . . . since I don't know when."

"I will reserve judgment," conceded Worf. *That's probably the closest he'll ever come to admitting he's wrong about Rom,* mused the chief.

O'Brien glanced at the readouts on the power grid; he had noticed some odd fluctuations in the past three days. Whenever an intense electromagnetic field, such as a starship, interacted with the EM field of the power conduits, an interference pattern developed that the chief could detect on some of his sensors. But there had been no ship activity around the station since the *Defiant* left two days earlier, and the fluctuations and interference patterns persisted.

"Probably one of the grids is flickering," muttered O'Brien.

"Please say that again. I did not hear you."

"Talking to myself, Worf. That's what happens when you're the last living being in a dead station." The Klingon's only response was half grunt, half snarl.

Spinning on his stool, Miles O'Brien touched three screens in rapid succession, bumping up the scale of the displayed interference pattern. He stared, puzzled. No matter how he sliced the data, more than anything else, they resembled starship fields interacting with the power grid. But there was only one problem: there *were no* ships. Sensors confirmed the only unnatural objects nearby were small runabouts and one-man skiffs. Suddenly the floor lurched under them.

"What the *hell?*" O'Brien exclaimed, gripping his console as he stared at a sudden, inexplicable surge in the pattern degradation of the power grids.

"Chief, I have just lost all communications carrier waves, and my sensors have darkened."

"Commander, we were just hit by a huge electromagnetic pulse!"

"Is this an attack?" demanded the Klingon, his hands already flickering across his battle stations; O'Brien's view in the well was good enough to see Worf power up all the station's weapons.

"I don't *think* so, sir; I don't see . . ." The scanners flickered in and out of operation; during the moments when they worked, the chief scanned all headings, all bearings, but saw nothing. "I don't see any ships. All I see is—good God!"

"What? What do you see? My instruments are blind here."

O'Brien stared in disbelief. A partially functional video sensor showed a scene so bizarre, the chief could barely believe it was real: the entire subspace emitter superstructure had been *sheared off!* "It looks like . . . no, can't be."

"Chief O'Brien! I must have complete information if I am to command this station!" Worf seemed more snappish than normal, certainly more than the situation warranted.

"Sir, it looks like the damage that would be caused by a ship colliding with the subspace emitter, but there are no ships out there. Wait a moment," O'Brien scanned for warp trails. "No sir, there's been no warp activity since the *Defiant* departed two days ago. We must have . . . maybe a meteorite?"

"Or a cloaked vessel," growled Worf, curling his lip and baring his sharp teeth.

The chief stared at his friend. "Worf, you're saying a ship—a *cloaked* ship—sheared a piece of the station away?" Again, he stared at his readouts. "I said there's no indication of any warp signature since the *Defiant* left; before, even . . . not for two days!"

"Then the ship has remained stationary for two days." Abruptly, the Klingon stared around Ops, as if looking for lurkers in the dark. "There is a spy out there. Has anyone beamed onto the station recently?"

O'Brien checked. "No, not according to the records. Of course, if someone beamed into, say, the habitat ring and— Worf, a ship just decloaked by the sliced emitter!"

"Shields up!" shouted Worf, but three events occurred simultaneously: Miles O'Brien positively identified the ship as a Klingon destroyer. A spherical object materialized in the middle of Ops—the *very* middle, hovering three meters above the deck, and a terrific flash bathed the entire room in a hellish, blue-white light.

O'Brien never had time to raise the shields. He had grabbed the lip of the well while he leaned down to the defensive-systems console. As the invading sphere flashed, his right hand and arm jerked convulsively. He grabbed them, and they throbbed angrily, the digits tingling.

"Worf! Worf, are you all right?" he cried, but then, the tingling in his arm expanded until it enveloped his chest and finally his brain; logy from the disruptor blast, O'Brien discovered that he could not focus his eyes, and he felt flushed and nauseated: *symptoms of disruptor stun!* his confused mind finally concluded.

The well had shielded O'Brien from the full force of the bomb, else he would be down and out for the count. Worf did not answer, and neither did the only other person in Ops, a green ensign (literally green; she was a Lysenian, tinted a charming teal) named . . . named . . .

The chief could barely remember his own name. He dimly recollected something about shields, but he couldn't for the life of him remember what they were or how one went about activating them. As O'Brien staggered to his feet in the well, he realized he could hear nothing and could barely see; every eyeblink dragged back the afterimage of the disruptor bomb that had just exploded.

Out—get out! It was the only thought that screamed clearly enough to be heard in the tumult of his disordered brain. He tried to grab the lip of the well to vault out, but his right arm still would not move. He stepped on a console and managed to slither up the side like a worm, wallowing onto the deckplates and tearing his uniform and the skin on his knee.

"Get . . . out." The task sounded reasonable enough, just two words. But he couldn't make his body work! O'Brien humped along on his belly, elbows digging into the wire-mesh above the deckplates themselves, crawling toward the turbolift. *They're coming—they're here!*

He reached the turbolift and rolled into it just as the first, characteristic vertical patterns of a Klingon transporter appeared in Ops: a dozen Klingons beamed aboard *Deep Space Nine,* standing amid the bodies of Worf and the young ensign.

One of the Klingons looked vaguely familiar, but O'Brien had no time to chat him up. They stared around Ops, pointing disruptors in every direction. *Strange,* thought a confused Miles O'Brien, *why not bat'telhs?* That was a more usual weapon for a Klingon to carry for hand-to-hand combat.

The Klingons spotted the bodies immediately. One invader, the obvious leader, crouched low over Worf and examined him closely, then he snorted and rose, speaking rapid-fire orders: "Secure the rest of the station. Use the turbolift."

That's my cue, thought the dazed engineering chief. "Computer," he gasped, praying that the disruptor blast hadn't burned out voice-recognition circuits, "engineering—stat!"

The Klingons turned as a man to stare. "It is talking!" shouted the slightly familiar one.

"No! *Really,* son of Noggra?" The sarcasm of the strike-force commander's response drew a round of snickering among the other troopers.

Just then, the turbolift started to descend, taking O'Brien to his command destination. *"The prisoner is escaping!"* shouted the increasingly observant "son of Noggra."

"Shoot the control mechanism!" shouted the leader, but those were the last words O'Brien heard as he dropped below the Ops level. All that he heard after that was the shrill whine of a Klingon disruptor, and then the turbolift ground silently to a halt, the safeties tripping until the computer could diagnose whether the lift was in danger of falling—and leaving Chief O'Brien lying half-stunned on a platform, ten meters above the next deck down. *Level one and a half,* thought O'Brien bitterly.

There was only one way down to the Promenade. In a couple of seconds, he was going to be looking up into a dozen angry Klingon faces. If he wanted to get down to the next deck, he was going to have to jump—and pray for a soft landing.

Miles O'Brien was not an agile man, but his hands were quick and his fingers had never failed him, not while rotating a Bradford spar into place or curling the most delicate fiberoptic cable into its connection. In the dim light from Ops, he could *see* the power conduit just a meter and a half below the lift platform . . . close enough that with luck and a strong grip, he wouldn't drop down the shaft to his death. But one hand still tingled madly and barely worked.

Brilliant, he thought, *after twenty years, I've finally become a maintenance monkey!* He lay on his belly and reached his good arm as far down and forward as he could. The conduit was still well out of reach. He would have to drop and make a grab as he fell past.

"There—stop him!" shouted a voice in Klingon above him. O'Brien didn't waste time looking up. He knew who was doing the shouting. He muttered a quick wish for the dexterity of the wee folk and lowered himself headfirst over the side of the turbolift.

Dropping upside-down through the air, it was all he could do not to close his eyes—it would have been fatal. He made a wild, one-handed grab at the power conduit and connected! For a second, he balanced on one arm, feet still up on the turbolift platform.

But the chief discovered, too late, that a fine mist of lubricant from the stone-age Cardassian turbolift tracks had coated the conduit pipe . . . his hand slid right off the side of the cylinder, letting him drop straight down-ward.

His shoulder and face thunked into the same conduit he had just slipped from. This time, he wrapped his good arm around it in a death grip, then his legs as soon as they fell onto the steel bar.

O'Brien swung around until he dangled freely from the pipe, staring straight up into the nasty end of a Klingon disruptor seven meters above. The Klingon snarled something unintelligible that O'Brien assumed was Klingon for "eat flaming red death!" and thumbed the contact.

The chief squeezed his eyes shut and gritted his teeth; his last thought was of Keiko, his beloved, and of his darling little girl, Molly.

O'Brien's next thought was to wonder how the Klingon could possibly have missed such a thick target as himself at such close range. Cursing, the attacker fired again, and this time O'Brien saw the trouble: the electro-magnetic power grid surrounding the turbolift interacted with the essentially electrical discharge from the disrup-tor, and the beam actually bent outward to pour harm-lessly into the power mesh.

The chief wasted no time contemplating his brush with the final reward. He reached down with one foot and managed to kick open the maintenance access ladder for servicing the conduit. Hooking his knees on the rungs, he swung himself onto the inspection catwalk. *Must remember to thank the gentry,* he swore, *lest they take offense and tie Molly's hair in knots.*

The Klingon commander shouted something, and O'Brien caught the word for "follow"; the chief grinned. Let them try! *I'd match myself against anyone, even Rom, for crawling the hidden paths through the station!*

CHAPTER
5

WORF, SON OF MOGH, commander in Starfleet and captain of the *Defiant* (when Captain Sisko was not taking the ship out for spy missions), loyal and honorable subject of the Klingon Empire of a most ancient and honorable house (a house that was experiencing a few technical difficulties at the moment), awoke to a throbbing pain in his head. He sat up, wincing, trying to reconstruct what had happened.

As soon as he realized he was locked into one of Constable Odo's own cells, and that a Klingon wearing the uniform of a colonel general was staring at him through the forceshield, Worf was able to make a shrewd guess.

The general's face was shadowed, deliberately, Worf presumed. The Starfleet commander angrily opened his mouth; but before he could speak, the captain said "Oh yes, I will."

"What?" thundered Worf. *The voice . . . it is so familiar, so—*

"You were about to say, 'You will never get away with it!' Were you not?"

"You cannot succeed."

"Oh yes, I can." The general grinned; "and you are going to help me, Worf, son of Mogh."

Worf controlled himself outwardly, but his stomach lurched, not just at the insulting implication of faithlessness, but at the increasing sense of familiarity about the general. He was a Klingon from Worf's past, a face and name he could not quite pull into the light, but one with whom his destiny was intertwined, even before the colonel general captured *Deep Space Nine*.

Years earlier, back on the *Enterprise*, or even a year ago on *Deep Space Nine*, Worf would have spit some angry insult at his captor in response to the prediction that Worf would sanction the loss of his own command. But he was older; he *felt* older. And today, he did not react as impulsively as the green lieutenant he once had been. He said nothing, only rose slowly to his feet and stared at the general from a distance of five meters—by Klingon custom, far enough not to imply an immediate challenge, close enough not to appear cowed.

The general stepped into the light, and Worf sucked in a breath of sudden recognition.

"I am Malach of the noble and honorable house of Razg." Behind Malach was a phalanx of a dozen Klingon warriors. Something was peculiar about them, but for the moment, Worf's concentration was fixed upon Colonel General Malach.

"Did you think I would forget you, Malach?" For a moment, Worf could think of nothing else to say, though myriad thoughts exploded through his brain. *Malach! Malach . . . my blood brother.*

"A house of honor," continued the Starfleet Klingon, "would not launch a sneak attack without much to gain. And you have nothing to gain by attacking this station, Malach, Son of Razg."

Malach stared Worf full in his eyes, silently demanding Worf remember the oath he had sworn as a boy to the boy Malach. The general threw his head back and smiled at the ceiling, eyes closed. "Oh, but we have so much to lose, son of Mogh. We both have so much to lose." After a moment, he snapped his head down and stared at Worf. "You know the fear."

Well, if he is not going to mention it, I will not be the first. "If the Founders come through the wormhole," insisted Worf, "we *will* stop them here."

"I am sure you will fight well, son of Mogh, my brother. And you will earn an honorable peace in Sto-Vo-Kor," Malach curled his lip, "but that will not help the Empire much. Or the Federation . . . I do not know where your loyalty lies most, my brother; but either way, if the Founders are not stopped here, they will overwhelm both Federation *and* Empire. I launched this—"

"Criminal assault."

"This military engagement not only for Klingons, but for humans and their lackeys in the Federation."

"So it is necessary to kill them in order to save them! Is this what the honor of my blood-brother has fled in favor of, a criminal act of cowardice?" It was a calculated thrust. Worf had not seen Malach for many years, more than two decades, since they both were young boys at the military academy in Emperor Kahless Military City, in the year before the House of Mogh removed to Khitomer. It was while Worf and Malach were at the academy that they swore the blood oath. Worf was six and Malach was eight, but the oath was official and witnessed.

Malach did not even blink at the deadly insult, which in any other Klingon would have provoked a challenge to fight to the death. In fact, he smiled. "You cannot anger me, my brother; do not even try. We have killed no one, and we *will* kill no one. I have issued strict orders: for a Klingon in my command to kill, or attempt to kill, or even to act in wanton disregard for Federation life on this mission, is to earn the dishonorable death of a traitor."

Worf stared, astonished at sheer audacity of the general's lie. "But I felt the blast! I—" He froze as one by one, the strands of observation pulled together at the center.

The honor guard behind Malach carried disruptors, but *no bat'telhs.* Disruptors could be set to stun. The *bat'telh* could not. And in the beserk fury of battle, what Klingon could resist taking an arm, a leg, or a head, if he held the bladed crescent in his hands?

And clearly, the bomb that exploded in Ops *had been set to stun,* not kill, or Lieutenant Commander Worf would not still be sucking air.

Finally, the astonishing control that Malach exerted when Worf—his own blood brother!—called him a coward and impugned his honor, and that of the House of Razg—not once, but twice!—began to percolate through the commander's skull like the morning's first raktajino.

Worf was still at a loss for words; everything he had seen or heard indicated that Malach was telling the truth: that this was an invasion without casualties. Having nothing to say that could advance his cause—and Worf was very clear where his loyalty lay—he stood mute, waiting for his blood brother and captor to continue. It was clear Malach thought he could persuade Worf to cooperate. The burden was on the general to push the conversation.

"My brother," said the general, "you must work with me. I swore to Gowron that you would cooperate."

"You should not have sworn for another. I will not help you take control of this station."

"Worf, I already have control of this station! These troops," Malach indicated the warriors behind him—they glared at Worf with nothing but contempt, knowing who he was and seeing the uniform he wore—"are not as circumspect as you and I." Malach grinned and shrugged, acting more like a Cardassian plotter than a Klingon, Worf thought. "I can give orders, but warriors can also disobey. Your friends could die if I do not maintain control, if I must pick another hero to do your job."

Worf hesitated, and knew he had nothing to gain by open defiance—*open* defiance. Not yet. "What would be my job?" he asked darkly.

Again Malach shrugged. "The obvious. Herd the defeated into the portable cells, contact Starfleet, demand ships to transport the hostages back to Federation territory in exchange for recognition that this station is now *Klingon* territory." Malach raised a finger, curling his lip. "And one more thing, brother: one of the senior crew, the enlisted man, escaped. He will raise a force among the remnants of the crew and lead a rebellion, and people will die on both sides. Worf, your first duty will be to track down the maintenance chief petty officer who was on the bridge with you."

The bridge? It took Worf a moment to realize Malach meant Ops. "Where is he now?"

"He has not left the station. Other than that, I know nothing."

Feeling a bitter taste in his mouth, Worf nodded. "I will find O'Brien. You will give me your word as a Klingon warrior *and as my blood brother* that no defender will be hurt."

Malach nodded faintly; it was enough. *May the Emperor Kahless ensure it is enough,* prayed Commander Worf.

"He could be anywhere," he growled. "O'Brien knows this station better than any person alive, except perhaps for Gul Dukat."

A trace of a smile flickered across Malach's face. "For reasons that should be obvious, the *gul* is not presently available for service." Worf glared at the general, never having liked his absurdist humor even when they both were children.

Malach nodded to one of his men, and the forceshield sealing Worf's cell from the rest of the brig vanished. Stepping forward, Worf stood nose to nose with the Klingon he once would have defended with his life. "You will clearly instruct the Starfleet ships when they capture you that I betrayed my oath only to save the hostages."

"Nobody will capture me, Worf, so the situation will not arise."

"It is inevitable."

"On the contrary, it is utterly evitable. My men control Ops, so there will be no communications until I choose to initiate them through my ship. We destroyed your subspace emitter, so even if one of your Federation friends broke free—O'Brien, perhaps—and tried to call for help, he would not be heard. The station is nearly deserted, and your captain and his ship are in the Gamma Quadrant. They will return too late to do anything but marvel at the glory of the Empire!"

Worf searched his memory. *Was my brother always such an egomaniac?* he asked himself. Taking a deep breath, Worf agreed to the terms: "If leading this search is the only way to protect the lives of my command, then I will agree to lead the search."

Malach grinned, in pleasure, not in challenge. "Welcome home, son of Mogh," he declared, not noticing that Worf had, in fact, not exactly *sworn* to anything; the statement was conditional.

So it has come to this, thought the commander; *I pass from warrior to space-lawyer!* His cheeks stinging from the humiliation, Worf pushed roughly past his blood brother toward the door. But as he passed one of Malach's honor guard, Worf glanced at the warrior and froze, staring.

"You . . . know this man?" asked Malach curiously.

"I have seen him before," said Worf in a strangled voice, struggling to find his center of balance.

"He is Rodek, son of Noggra. A fine family. He was

wounded in the Cardassian war and has lost the memory of his former life, but he is a brave and honorable warrior with an astonishing natural grasp of strategy. I think he could perhaps command his own ship or cohort someday." Rodek, son of Noggra, stood tall, his suspicious gaze never wavering from Worf's face.

Never wavering, never recognizing. He did not recognize the Klingon who was his brother in another life, his *real* brother. Rodek, son of Noggra, was what he called himself now, not knowing any better.

But a year earlier, he had been Kurn, son of Mogh; a year before, Kurn was Worf's brother, a general who commanded his own *fleet*. "Perhaps I do not know him after all," said Worf quietly, suppressing the emotion that could—at the hands of his *blood*-brother—threaten his brother's life.

A year before, Kurn was unable to live with the shame of his brother Worf dishonored, their house discommodated. Kurn had demanded to die at his brother's hands during the rite of *Maukto'Vor,* but Captain Sisko would not permit it aboard *Deep Space Nine.*

Instead, Kurn's brain had been whitewashed, his entire identity obliterated, and the name Rodek, son of Noggra, painted across the now-blank canvas. *So really, there is no more Kurn, and I have told no lie.*

Turning his face from Rodek, son of Noggra, Commander Worf pushed through the honor guard and exited into the outer office of Constable Odo. He clenched his teeth and forced his hands to his sides, lest he grab a weapon from the desk—phaser, baton, anything!—and begin killing everyone around him.

Seeing Kurn—Rodek—shook Worf more than he allowed himself to admit. It was not just the sight of a familiar, unfamiliar face; it was the knowledge of what drove him to the horror of identity obliteration—the *pride* of a Klingon, the *face* that must at any cost be saved!

The memory tasted like ashes, and Worf turned away

from Rodek, from the memory, from confronting the damage wrought by the core of Worf's soul, the core of any Klingon: *honor*. If honor led to this, the blank face of what used to be Kurn, then what was honor but a bitter joke played upon Worf by the cruel, jesting gods of Klingon folklore?

Worf did not look back. He was afraid the punchline might be gaining on him.

Jake Sisko, raconteur and troubadour, was engaging in the time-honored tradition of mopery with intent to gawk. He was stationed at his normal spot, on the second level of the Promenade, at the railing high above the people below, the place where he and his erstwhile constant companion Nog used to hang to observe the teeming ants on the Promenade. But with Nog off at Starfleet Academy—where Jake always presumed he would be forced to go one day, and which fate he had escaped only by discovering a talent for writing—and with the anthill mostly empty with the rumors of war, Jake was more than usually bored.

He amused himself by inventing fanciful stories for each of the few people still puttering around the wide, circular Promenade: this one was an unlucky gambler hiding out from his loan sharks; another was a Cardassian spy, surgically altered to look like a chubby maintenance worker; a third was a rich merchant getting ready to purchase the entire planet of Bajor for her own private estate.

Suddenly, a swarm of Klingons burst onto the scene. For a moment, Jake was surprised at the vividness of his own imagination; he often visualized invasions or romantic interludes, but never this distinctly!

Then he gasped and leaned farther over the rail, abruptly realizing that this was no dreamy hallucination: this really was a sudden invasion of Klingon warriors!

He stared, transfixed, as the tiny figures drew their disruptors and swept the small, scattered crowd. The victims collapsed into heaps where they stood, offering no resistance. *They don't even know what's happening!* he thought.

He was about to bolt to the turbolift but stopped himself, his heart pounding. What the hell was he going to do, fight the Klingons bare-handed?

It took only a few seconds for these thoughts to race through his mind, then he saw a phalanx of Odo's security force attempt to charge out of the security office, only to be mowed down mercilessly by the Klingons. The shrill whine of disruptors and the piercing throb of phasers drifted up to where he stood, and in half a minute, Jake began to smell the metallic tang of ozone produced by the electrical discharges around both weapons.

He stood frozen at the handrail, staring down at the tableau, unsure whether there was simply nothing he could do and nobody to tell, or whether it was just another manifestation of his own cowardice. The same feeling of senseless, unreasoning panic gripped his gut as he'd felt during the seige on Ajilon Prime, when he'd deserted Dr. Bashir and fled randomly across the countryside.

But even when he forced his panic down and desperately tried to think of something to *do,* he still found nothing! The security forces obviously knew as much as Jake did and couldn't even get out of the squadroom that had become their trap, and Jake's father, Captain Sisko, was far, far away, on the other side of the galaxy, as a matter of fact, in the Gamma Quadrant.

"Where the hell *is* everybody?" he demanded of himself. All right, Odo and Kira were on the mission with his father, but where was Chief O'Brien? And *where was Worf?* Odo might have had primary responsibility for crime on *Deep Space Nine,* but surely defending the station against an armed Klingon assault was Worf's job!

Unless . . . Angrily, Jake dismissed the thought. He

had no doubt about the Klingon's loyalty to the Federation, after all, hadn't Jake's father personally picked Worf for the station security slot? *He can't be involved— he can't! Dad's the best judge of character in all Starfleet!*

And then, staring down at the carnage—just beginning to feel the horrific sense of unreality of a witness to massacre—Jake saw him. It was Worf, no question. He still wore his red Starfleet command uniform.

And he was leading the Klingon forces as they circled the Promenade, hunting down survivors and shooting them.

"No!" shouted Jake impulsively. He dropped to his belly, somehow feeling closer to the scene than when he was standing over it. *"No, you dirty . . . !"* For several minutes, Jake watched Worf clearly lead the Klingon expeditionary force in a search-and-destroy pattern around the lower level of the Promenade. Then the Klingon traitor left a holding force on the bottom level and led the rest up to the second floor, just below Jake. It wouldn't be long before they searched the top floor too, and Jake Sisko would be a cardinal anomaly in a sea of casualty statistics, dead as a Ferengi's charity.

For a moment, Jake broke through his own terror and helpless rage to thank fate and the circumstances of coincidence that his dad was *not* on the station. *At least one of us will live to see tomorrow,* thought the young man bitterly.

At the thought, the rage boiled over into berserk fury. Jake jumped up, leaned over the railing, and screamed a stream of obscenities down at the traitor, Worf. *What the hell, I'm going to die anyway!* He climbed onto the railing itself, balancing precariously and hanging on to the overhead catwalk. For the first time in his life, Jake felt the fear of death drop away like a torn cloak, and he felt himself filled with the recklessness of desperation that produces heroes and martyrs. But in the tumult of battle, the warrior didn't even hear the poet.

But other ears did hear. As Jake balanced on the handrail, one of the Klingons looked up and saw the young man, the boy, furiously waving his fist. The Klingon raised his disruptor and fired. The first shot hit the railing beneath Jake's feet, causing his legs to spasm with the electrical jolt. He lost his footing, barely grabbing the catwalk with his other hand to dangle twenty meters above the floor that was littered with the bodies of victims.

The Klingon raised his sights for the second shot, striking the catwalk itself. Another jolt of current flashed through Jake Sisko. It was all he could do to cling grimly to the bars, his face paling and his stomach convulsing with the impact. He swallowed bile, knowing the next shot would either kill him outright, or cause him to lose his handgrip and plummet to his death below.

But the most extraordinary thing happened. Staring down at the man who would kill him, Jake saw another Klingon, one wearing a much-decorated uniform of high rank, reach out and grab the assassin's throat in a headlock. The second Klingon yanked and twisted his arms savagely, and the sniper fell to the floor, his legs and arms jerking randomly! Even from Jake's height, he could see that the Klingon's neck was broken: *his own comrade in arms had killed him.*

But there simply was no time to worry about the vagaries of Klingon table manners, even without another helpful blast from a disruptor, Jake was in imminent danger of losing his grip and his young life.

Terrified—especially so, now that he thought he had a plan for escaping, but still might not make it—he began to swing back and forth, desperately struggling not to look down or think about the huge, empty space below his feet. With every swing, he got closer to the opposite platform, until at last he hooked one bootheel over the lip. He shimmied and squirmed until he managed to haul himself up and onto the maintenance walk that ran all the way around the Promenade, close to the ceiling. He collapsed onto his stomach, utterly spent.

Shaking, he peeked over the edge. His Klingon guardian angel watched him narrowly, but made no move to shoot. In fact, as soon as the officer saw that Jake had made it, he turned back to the invasion, directing troops to remove the body of the dead Klingon.

Jake lay on the steel grid, panting and exhausted from the *one* pull-up he had done! Absurdly, the thought that echoed round his skull was of his father urging him to spend more time on physical training two years before. His face flushed as he remembered his snotty response: "How many pull-ups do I have to do to pass the writers' test, Dad?"

Jake Sisko staggered to his knees, then his feet, and jogged lead-footed along the platform, looking for a maintenance hatch leading up out of the Promenade. If he could get into the access tunnels and conduits, he had a chance, assuming he didn't get lost and starve to death! But beyond the immediate, he had no plan and no strategy, except one: get as far away from the mob of bloodthirsty Klingons, led by Worf the Betrayer, as he possibly could.

If I can just hold on, avoid capture until Dad gets back, he'll know what to do! And if he didn't? Jake refused to consider the possibility.

CHAPTER
6

MILES O'BRIEN WATCHED the carnage on the Promenade from the grating of an air vent high above the main floor, fuming with frustration—and feeling the most horrific sense of *déjà-vu. I've seen this before,* he raged, but there was nothing he could do. The air vent grill was bolted tight, and even if he could remove it, all he could do was drop ten meters to the deck, break his ankle, and then be mowed down by the Klingon invaders.

But what hurt most, tearing at his innards like a Klingon *bat'telh,* was how quickly Worf had reverted to his own kind. O'Brien ground his teeth as Worf led the assault, rounding up the Starfleet and Bajoran personnel who still remained on the station—then watching, doing nothing, as the forces under his command poured disruptor fire upon them. The bodies fell to the deck, twitching for a moment, then lying still. Odo's security force put up a valiant fight, but without the changeling—*ex-changeling,* O'Brien reminded himself—leading the point-defense, and without benefit of Kira, Sisko, Dax, and, of course, the traitor Worf, the good guys were overwhelmed by the Klingons.

The chief couldn't watch anymore; he was sick to his stomach. Turning his back on what used to be his station—his own friends, allies, comrades—Miles O'Brien crawled through the air vent, thanking his lucky stars that Keiko and Molly were safe on Bajor, attending a conference on "vertical gardening" and playing among the springferns, respectively, and that his nascent son was still growing in the womb of Major Kira, the child's surrogate mother, where he was reasonably safe in the Gamma Quadrant.

The thought struck O'Brien so hard, his head rang. Bajor! He had to get a message out to the Bajorans. They could send warships and contact Starfleet. O'Brien slapped his comm badge, but all he heard was a persistent, annoying buzz. "So, jamming the signal, are you?" he muttered. "Well, anything you can fuzz, I can stabilize."

O'Brien began the long, slow descent to the engineering levels, where hc could control every aspect of station operations, including the entire communications system. Obviously, the Klingons must have left *some* channels open, even if encrypted, after all, they had to communicate with one another. It was just a matter of finding the open channel and exploiting it.

But he had one stop to make. He couldn't make the trip alone, and he would also need an extra pair of hands when he got there. *God, I wish I knew where Rom was,* he thought. Alas, the Ferengi had been off-duty, and could be anywhere from Quark's Place, just outside the air vent grill, to his quarters on the habitat ring, to the cargo hold.

But there was one obvious second choice, the only other person aboard that O'Brien could trust. "Next stop, Saint Julian's Infirmary," he said.

* * *

With no patients to care for and nothing much else to do, Dr. Bashir was running diagnostics on the medical equipment in the infirmary, some brand-new Starfleet-issue, others left over from the Cardassian era. Not that the station residents were unusually unhealthy of late, but they were unusually absent . . . with the threat of war with the Dominion, recent clashes and dire warnings, it seemed to Julian that the entire station had abruptly migrated to Bajor or even deeper into the interior of the Federation.

At first, he didn't even hear the screams, so deeply was he concentrating on aligning the cortical stimulators just so. Then he looked up, his mouth open in astonishment: through the clear windows of his operating room, over the desk of the head MedTech, and out the open door of the infirmary itself, Julian saw people running in absolute panic, closely followed by . . . "By *Klingons?*" he demanded incredulously.

The doctor bolted toward the open door, getting halfway across his medical lab before the folly of running *into* a panic slammed home. He staggered to a halt, then spun to take a quick head-count. He slapped his comm badge and shouted, "Computer, emergency medical beam-out of four personnel *from* the infirmary *to* the . . ."

Julian paused. He slapped his comm badge again. It did not even make the normal chirping sound, which meant the computer was either completely offline or else it couldn't "hear" the high-frequency, subspace throat-clearing by which a comm badge got the computer's attention. "Uh-oh," he said.

"Doctor, what is it?" demanded the senior staffer present, MedTech-2 Janaholt Jaas, still wearing his greens from the one operating procedure earlier that day. Fortunately, the patient had already left to recuperate in her living space in the habitat ring.

Julian stared out the door. Now it was mostly Klingons running past, firing their disruptors as they ran. It was only a matter of seconds before one of them looked inside, saw the medical crew and took them out with a few, well-placed blasts.

He looked around the room for a hypo to fill with a sleeping aid, a breakfast tray, *anything* to use as a weapon. Alas, Julian's technicians were too well-trained—they put everything away when the doctor was finished using it!

By the time the first Klingon hesitantly poked his snout into the infirmary, the three MedTechs had already caught up with Julian in figuring out what was going on, and how little they could do about it. As the attacker raised his disruptor and pointed it at the gaggle of men and women, Julian caught himself thinking, *You know, it never would have occurred to me in a million years to stock the infirmary with phaser rifles.*

The Klingon fired. Julian braced for the impact of death, the physical blow he expected would end his short life—worse, his Starfleet career!—in a flash of glory. But the blow never came.

Bashir opened his eyes. Evidently, Jaas had panicked at the last moment in the face of certain death—*I can hardly blame the man!*—and had bolted sideways to escape the shot, but instead of dodging the disruptor blast, the poor chap had wandered directly into the brunt of the blast radius, and in the process, had completely shielded Dr. Bashir.

The realization flashed through Julian's mind in a microsecond, so quickly that the other three were still just beginning their long, slow fall to the deck. *Strange,* thought the doctor in his accelerated mental state, *why didn't they simply phase out of existence?*

But as Jaas was thrown forward by the convulsions of his own muscles, Julian had a flash of absolute, utter clarity, as if his spirit had just jumped out of his body, out of time, and could spend hours or days figuring out exactly what to do next.

As the MedTechs fell, mown down by the disruptor shot, Julian Bashir jerked convulsively in exactly the same way, falling to the floor almost in unison with his department petty officer. It was so perfectly executed that one of the other enlisted technicians, MedTech-4 Yvette Tang, actually fell on *top* of him!

This is crazy! This is useless . . . Surely, as soon as the Klingons examined the good doctor and discovered he hadn't attained room temperature, they would simply slit his throat with a *bat'telh* or cave in his skull with a well-aimed bootheel. Bashir stayed very still. His position was very awkward, which was good, they were less likely to examine him closely. But it was also very uncomfortable, and Julian had to struggle against himself not to shift ever so slightly to a different position.

Two Klingons stomped around the med-lab, nudging their victims with toes and prodding them with meaty forefingers. When one of the pair—the foulest smelling Klingon Bashir had ever run across—leaned close over the doctor and stared at his face, Julian didn't even breath for nearly a minute.

The attackers did not bother feeling for a pulse. *They're so damned cocky,* thought Bashir. A bitter rage tore at his insides as he thought about his dead comrades lying around and on top of him. Outwardly, he was as close to a corpse as you can be with a functioning circulatory system and cerebral cortex. But inside, he felt such desperate horror at such death and destruction . . . and for what? What did the Klingons hope to gain from slaughtering the inhabitants of *Deep Space Nine? What the hell did they want with us?* he raved, all without so much as twitching a single muscle in his face or body. *Why, why, why?*

But his friends were unable to respond, and for obvious reasons, the Klingons chose not to enlighten him. So still in ignorance, Julian Bashir suffered being dragged from the scene of the crime, out onto the Promenade, and deposited among a large heap of bodies a few meters distant.

Bashir waited in mounting impatience for the Klingons to go away. Instead, another batch came and dragged all the bodies, the doctor included, to a new spot that seemed no different or better than the old spot. Then a Klingon non-com popped round and screamed at the troops to haul them all *back* again.

Lying against the bodies and trying not to move, breathe, or otherwise reveal his continued presence among the living, Julian suddenly made the astonishing discovery that *other bodies* were also still living. He didn't dare talk to them or try to find out if they, like he, were simply faking death, but as soon as he noticed the incongruity, Bashir began edging his hands out ever so slightly to gently touch a carotid artery here, a wrist pulse there. He shifted his eyes and observed long enough to see that chests were rising and falling all around him.

In fact, to Julian Bashir's confusion, he could not find even one, single dead body! Everyone he was thrown against, everyone crowded into his particular heap of bodies, was alive.

Still, nobody else was raising his head to peek around, so the doctor had to mimic them and not attract Klingon attention. Every medical impulse in his brain screamed that he should jump up and see who needed emergency help, but if he were killed or incapacitated, that would leave everyone without medical care now and into the future.

At last, his most burning question—did the Klingons *know* that their victims were still alive?—was answered in the affirmative: one of the "bodies" began to groan audibly, and the sharp-eared Klingon non-com heard her. He told his subordinates to "take her to the portable cell right away, the damn disruptor is wearing off."

The discovery simultaneously relieved and astonished Bashir: the Klingons were deliberately avoiding killing their victims! The thought was so boggling that he almost stood up and demanded to know why.

Then his question was answered. Someone who sounded exactly like Lieutenant Commander Worf stomped into view, bellowing at the Klingons: "Stop prodding him with your foot, you miserable worm! I will tear your cowardly eyes from your head!" The Klingon grumbled and shuffled off, but Bashir was stunned into paralysis. Worf! *My God, Worf was commanding the attack!*

Unable to resist, Bashir raised his head slightly, peeking over a stunned, barely clothed Dabo girl, he saw Worf himself. Worf, the *Deep Space Nine* security officer; the Klingon who had turned his back on the Empire for the Federation; the man for whom honor and loyalty defined his life. The traitor leading the assault upon his friends!

Suddenly, Worf turned, seeming to feel Bashir's eyes on the back of his neck. The doctor froze, not wanting even to lower his head for fear of attracting even more attention by the sudden movement. Worf scanned the bodies for the source of the offending feeling, *and he saw Bashir,* looked him right in the eyes.

They stared thus at each other for a beat. Worf's face was flooded with a sadness and desperation wholly inappropriate and unexpected in the face of a Klingon. Then he shook his head, so imperceptibly that Bashir was hardly certain he had really seen it. Commander Worf turned away and began barking orders in the typical Klingon style, accompanied by threats and snarling denunciations of his troops' honor and courage, and marched away to see to the comfort of other victims. He did not look at Bashir again and did nothing to help him, but neither did he make a move to order him restunned or shifted to the "portable cell" where they'd taken the previous, still-conscious prisoner.

Julian lowered his head excruciatingly slowly. No one else had noticed him. But he couldn't get past the strange interlude or decide what it meant. He knew only one thing for sure: something horrible and strange was happening to the station's resident Klingon, and Worf felt compelled to cooperate with the unexpected, inexplicable invasion. But whether the compulsion was something the rest of them would understand, especially Captain Sisko, Bashir could not possibly guess.

The Klingons had stacked Dr. Bashir's heap of bodies in a small room off the Promenade that once was, he recalled, a bistro serving bad Klingon food. *How gruesomely appropriate,* he thought bitterly. The Klingon cook—whom Worf never patronized, saying he preferred replicated human food to badly prepared Klingon food—had left with the first wave of emigrants, probably because he could only survive as a restauranteur with a population density high enough that some were *forced* to patronize his eatery by necessity. But the place still smelled like rotting flesh.

The other victims didn't object, and Bashir concluded, without even examining them, that they must therefore be stunned into unconsciousness. At the maximal stun setting, a Klingon disruptor, he remembered, would put a human or Bajoran out for a least three hours. So, probably, no one would be back for a long time—unless they decided to move the bodies again.

Before he could decide whether to risk standing up and getting out, Bashir began to hear a strange metal-on-metal scrape from above. He stayed still, desperately wishing he could look up and see what was making the sound.

A moment later, he heard the wrench of some large piece of metal, followed an instant later by a hushed curse, then a loud clatter as an access hatch or panel or something crashed to the ground a couple of meters away.

Julian felt a wild surge of relief: the curse had carried the distinct accent of an Irishman and could belong only to one person. After two minutes of total silence, during which O'Brien was surely waiting and listening to see if any Klingons would come running at the noise, Bashir heard a loud thump, followed by another round of whispered cursing and moans of pain, and "damn this ankle! Why don't I just cut the bloody thing off and be done with it?"

On impulse, Bashir remained motionless. He wasn't sure why. "Oh no," said O'Brien aloud. "It really *is* you. Julian, why'd you have to be standing in the way when the bastards started shooting?"

The shock of the engineering chief was genuine, and Bashir realized that O'Brien didn't know that the bodies were still alive! For Julian, it was the first thing he'd noticed, shoved up against them. Once again, he was amazed at the quickness with which lay people assumed a still, unmoving body must be dead.

He almost rose and reassured O'Brien that he was still using up the station's oxygen, but a morbid impulse stopped him, made him lie still and listen to what O'Brien might say over his "corpse." *Probably the closest I'll ever come to hearing my own eulogy,* he rationalized.

Miles O'Brien was silent a long moment, long enough that Bashir risked peeking through slitted eyelids. The chief looked less like a mourner than a student faced with an unexpected question, trying to drag the right answer from a dimly remembered study session. His brow furrowed as he bit his lower lip, staring up at the ceiling he had dropped from. "I guess you weren't a bad sort," he said at last. Bashir almost leapt up in outrage at the faint obituary. "Though you did get on my nerves once in a while. Well, quite a few times, actually. To be fair about it, it was pretty constant; you always . . . But enough of that. I really will miss you, Julian. You were a good friend, and that makes up for a lot.

"I'm sorry this isn't more flowery, but I was never good at that sort of thing, you know. Maybe your friend Garak could've put something together that was a bit more, well, like you'd probably have done yourself. But what the hell. It's the thought that counts, isn't it?"

During the final sentence, a thoroughly offended Julian Bashir was creeping his unseen hand closer and closer to O'Brien. With the last question, he grabbed the chief firmly by the ankle, sat up suddenly with a wild look, and snarled, *"No it bloody well isn't the thought that counts, you ungrateful rat!"*

Chief O'Brien gasped like a dying man and turned white as an albino Denebian bloodworm. He stared at Bashir as if the doctor were a zombie come back from the dead to vent his wrath upon the living. He skittered back, face now turning the pinkish-orange color of Quark, mouth working soundlessly.

"You . . . you . . . *you!* You son of a—" For the next several seconds, O'Brien let loose a string of cussing that would have put a drunken Klingon to shame and make him take the pledge, resolving to devote the remainder of his life to good works among the unfortunate. Alas, Bashir missed the performance by talking over it, a terrible breach of swearing etiquette.

"You heartless bolt-tightener! Is *that* the best you can do? I wasn't a *bad sort?* I *got on your nerves?* And what, *exactly,* did you mean by saying my friendship *made up* for a lot of things? What things?"

The two stared at each other for a long minute, while O'Brien's color and respiration slowly returned to normal and Bashir's ire subsided into inarticulate grumbling. They both looked away, glancing at each other sidelong.

"That was a pretty dirty trick," accused the chief.

"Well *that* was a pretty pathetic eulogy!"

Another long, uncomfortable silence. "Friends again?" offered the doctor at last, feeling more guilty than he would ever acknowledge about having played dead and then scared the bejesus out of Chief O'Brien.

"I guess so," agreed the chief, picking at his boots. "I guess I could've been a bit more, you know, deep about it. But I couldn't think what to say. I'm not really a talker, you know."

"I know. And I'm sorry, Chief." Bashir shrugged. "Usually, the person delivering the eulogy has a prepared text, anyway. I'm sure you could have done better if you'd had some preparation time."

"Now why didn't I think—I mean, yeah, that's probably true. Friends again, I guess." He suddenly jabbed a thick, pink finger at Julian. "But *don't* you go tellin' anyone about this, right?"

Julian half-cringed back, smiling and putting his hands up. "Oh, I wouldn't breathe a word of it! I promise." He smiled and winked, and O'Brien scowled. "And now, the burning question: What in heaven's name are the Klingons *doing* here? And why is Worf helping them?"

"I think we'd better wait on those burning questions, if you don't mind, Julian. We've got a more important problem: How do we transport two wanted escapees off the Promenade, and where do we find reinforcements?"

"Ah," said Julian, annoyed that he had missed the more urgently practical point. "I think I know someone who might be able to help us."

"Who?"

"Why, you should know, Chief. You were the one who suggested him."

Shaking his head, O'Brien hoisted Julian up until the doctor could grasp the lip of the air vent. After pulling himself into the shaft, the doctor returned the favor, reaching down to haul the chief up beside him. They left the cover on the floor. The Klingons weren't likely to notice it, and there was no way to replace it in any event.

CHAPTER
7

CAPTAIN BENJAMIN SISKO sat cross-legged in his command chair, tugging absently at his beard, frowning, scowling, grunting, and, in general, annoying the living daylights out of Jadzia Dax. "Benjamin," she said sweetly, "will you *please stop fidgeting?*"

"I'm troubled, Old Man. Something just isn't right here."

"What?"

"That's why I'm troubled: I don't know what."

"Ah, my favorite kind of complaint." Dax pushed a few buttons uselessly. They were still en-route to Gamma GK-974, a solid day into the four-day journey, and there was nothing to look at: no anomalous stars, no peculiar gas clouds, no inexplicable energy sources, no chronotron particles or emergency beacons or planet-devouring alien machines. They had crossed paths with three Dominion ships along the way, but, cloaked, the *Defiant* had slipped right past without so much as a ripple in the ether, not even a warning call via subspace.

And Jadzia Dax was, quite frankly, bored to tears. Dax had never been a patient Trill, not in any of his, her, and its bodies. Jadzia was not as impatient as Curzon, but in times of tedium, the spirit of Curzon tended to loom forth and make his complaints very public.

She swiveled around to observe her oldest non-Trill friend, now her commanding officer. But Sisko said nothing more.

"You know," said Kira to Dax's right, "I'm feeling something too."

"Something?"

Kira made a face, looking down at her bulging abdomen. "I think the littlest O'Brien is going to be a dancer," she added. "But that's not what I meant. I keep looking over my shoulder, like something's coming up from behind."

Dax swiveled back to the sensors, grateful for something to do at last. "Well, nothing that I can find, Nerys."

"I know. I already . . . already . . ." Then Kira was off on another sneezing spell, spoiling yet another handkerchief. *Take it easy,* Dax counseled herself. *Bajorans can't help it.*

Yes she could! rejoined the wicked side of her brain, the Curzon-devil. *She could have refused to take the baby. She did it just to annoy us!*

Constable Odo still paced back and forth in the rear of the bridge, hands clasped behind his back. He was nervous, Dax could tell; he was not happy. In fact, even through the plasticity of Odo's face, Dax could tell that the erstwhile changeling was actually frightened. "I think we're all just jumpy being out here," he said in his sexy, gravely voice. "This sector is empty enough that there's no reason anyone would be looking here. And nobody knew we were coming . . . it's not as if there were any ships around the station when we left."

"Yes," said Sisko, "I noticed."

Odo nodded, mistaking the captain's disappointment

for the constable's own relief. "Yes, that's at least one good thing to come from this war: at last the station's population is down to a manageable size."

Sisko glanced at Odo and couldn't help grinning. He winked at Dax. "So, Constable, how do you suppose things are getting on back at the station?"

"Oh, I'm sure my deputies have things well in—"

"With an unsupervised Quark on the loose back there?" added the captain, as if innocently completing his thought.

Irritated, Odo opened his mouth to reply before realizing someone was tugging at his fetlock. He contented himself with a loud "Hnh!" and turned to face the forward viewscreen, ceasing his pacing at last.

But Sisko was not done worrying about his feeling, Dax noticed. "Benjamin, what's really bothering you the most?"

"I just don't like coincidences, Old Man."

He paused, and she raised her eyebrows.

"Well, for example, it was quite a coincidence that the Klingons didn't manage to destroy the ship until *after* it passed through the wormhole."

"True. But the Levanians could have made a monumental effort to break through the wormhole, thinking the Klingons wouldn't dare follow and kill them right out in the open."

"Then there's the matter of the log we found. Think of the astonishing coincidences connected with that log! First, the Klingons blow up the entire Levanian ship, just to stop us from discovering intelligence about this Klingon–Jem'Hadar training camp, but they *don't* destroy the very log that will tell us!

"Third, somebody tries to erase the log with a magnetic sweep. But who? And why? Was there a traitor aboard the Levanian ship? If so, why destroy the ship and attract our attention? Or was it the doctor himself, afraid that someone *would* find the log?"

"Well, those are good questions, Benjamin." Dax pursed her lips, trying to visualize a set of circumstances that would lead the Klingons to pursue and destroy the ship, but not to destroy the most important piece of evidence aboard the ship. After blowing it up with Project Renarg, why not pump a few more torpedoes into the shredded hulk before the *Defiant* arrived?

"And then," continued Sisko, "there's the most curious coincidence of all: the entire medical log is erased, hundreds of hours of routine medical reports . . . *except* for just a few words that just happen to be the very clues we'd most be interested in!"

Dax exhaled noisily, resting her chin on her hands. "That is pretty coincidental," she admitted. "You've got a point there."

"If you ask me, it is entirely *too* much coincidence all around."

Throughout the exchange, Kira had been turning her head back and forth like a spectator at a tennis match. "Oh, come on!" she exclaimed at last, "are you actually working yourselves into believing this whole thing is an elaborate conspiracy? But *why?* If someone wanted to lure us off to destroy us, why hasn't he struck already, like right here?" She gestured around them, meaning the sector they traversed, Dax presumed.

"You've got a point too," she pronounced. "The problem here, from a scientific standpoint, is that we're speculating way, way, *way* beyond the data. All we know is that a ship was destroyed, the medical log gave us a clue to a possible secret Klingon base in the Dominion, and that Starfleet has directly ordered us to check it out."

She looked to Odo for another opinion. The ex-changeling shrugged. "In light of the orders, I don't see that we have any choice, Captain."

There was a long pause, during which Benjamin continued tweaking his beard and squirming. *He's really bothered by this mission,* she realized, and the thought worried her: almost invariably, Benjamin Sisko's intuition was far smarter than it had any right to be. "For the moment," he said at last, "Constable Odo has the winning argument. Until we have a lot more substantial evidence than my fretting and a few strange coincidences, we must proceed on course to examine this . . . Gamma Gamma Kilo niner seven four."

His face lightened, and Dax knew he had thought of something for her to do. "In the meantime, Old Man, I want you to go back and examine the record of the automatic sensor logs taken while we passed through the wormhole. If there were a warp-speed chase going on that ended there, we might have picked up evidence of the ion trails left behind the ships."

"I'm on it, Benjamin," she said, already calling up the raw data.

The *Defiant,* like other Starfleet ships, automatically scanned 360 degrees heading and bearing around itself, unless the science officer specifically turned off the autoscan, for "silent running," for example. But Captain Sisko had thought it more important to have advance warning of anyone approaching, and Dax had continued the scans.

Normally, the autoscan logs were kept only twelve hours before being erased and recorded over. But Jadzia Dax had discovered ages ago that sensor logs were inadvertently shadowed whenever the ship overwrote them, and the "echo" could still be retrieved as long as four days later, if one had a well-trained retrieval demon, which, of course, Dax developed for every new ship or command she served on, including the *Defiant.* Thus, even though the book declared it impossible, she was able triumphantly to announce her success three minutes later, preceded by a computer-generated fanfare sound.

"Got it! I have the logs."

"Miraculous, Old Man."

"Was there ever any doubt?" Dax reviewed them carefully for ion trails. The critical period was just before they entered the wormhole and just after they exited into the Gamma Quadrant. The sensor autoscan did not work properly inside the wormhole itself.

"This is . . . peculiar, Benjamin," she said after a few moments.

"Peculiar?" said Odo, looking as puzzled as one can look without actually changing expression. "Peculiar in what way?"

"Everything on our side of the wormhole looks perfectly normal. But on the Gamma Quadrant side, all the ion trails come from different directions."

"So?" Odo still didn't understand the significance, but Dax noticed that Benjamin was starting to smile grimly.

"Odo," she said, "do you think everyone involved, Klingons and Levanians, *met for the first time* right at the wormhole and started the chase there? What did they do—flip a coin to see who would be the chaser and the chasee?"

Kira leapt in immediately, protecting her friend Odo from Dax's sarcasm. "Well, maybe somebody else was chasing the Levanian, and . . . and the Klingons tried to head him off at the pass. But he snuck through first."

"It's a possibility, Kira, but it's starting to smell suspicious," Dax replied.

If Odo noticed her sarcasm, he didn't react to it. "Are you saying that the chase might have been *planned?* That they gathered, then created the illusion of a chase to catch our attention?"

"That's . . . a chilling thought, Constable. Is that the kind of thing criminals might do?" That was, of course, exactly what Dax already suspected, but now they had entered Odo's realm: the criminal mind.

"Commander, criminals can and *do* contrive anything they can to hide the truth. It's the sort of thing a Ferengi

78

would do by second nature, and I daresay even a Klingon could think of it if he turned his mind to being devious. Ferengis have no corner on duplicity." Odo folded his arms across his chest, pleased to be able to contribute at last to the mission. "If my guess is correct, and they did stage this so-called chase for our benefit, then that calls into question all the evidence about a Klingon–Jem'Hadar training facility."

"And raises a most disturbing question," interjected Captain Sisko. He sat cross-legged in his command chair, steepling his fingers and resting his lower lip against them, deep in thought.

"You mean *why,* Benjamin. Why would the Klingons want us to think they were in league with the enemy?"

"Well," said Kira, struggling for an explanation, as they all were, "Cardassians do that sort of thing all the time: keep everyone guessing whom they're allied with today and who's about to receive an unexpected visit from a Cardassian battle fleet."

"But Klingons aren't Cardassians," griped Dax. *Damn it, can't anyone in the Federation understand the Klingon concept of honor?* It was a neverending source of frustration for the Trill. In her many lifetimes, she had more than once fought alongside Klingon blood-brothers and sisters, developing a tremendous respect for that culture. Neither she nor any Trill could ever understand the shortsighted view of the Federation and the Empire toward each other. When both sides allowed it, they worked so perfectly together!

"Tell me about the ship, or what was left of it," said Odo, who had not, Dax remembered, ever seen it.

Dax waited, but the captain said nothing. So she began to talk. "The ship was wonderfully eerie . . . a dead hulk, no gravity, no air, and not even a ghost aboard."

"Doctor Bashir—" Odo said the name as if he suspected the good doctor was not the quadrant's most reliable witness to anything—"Doctor *Bashir* reported finding Levanian remains aboard."

"Well, in a manner of speaking, I suppose," said Dax.

Odo scowled, shifting his hands to the behind-the-back hold. He had yet to master the lifelike hand movements of a "solid." "What does *that* mean, Commander? Either you found Levanian remains, or you didn't."

"What she means, Constable, is that we found a fine mist of vaporized cells that contained Levanian DNA."

"Exactly," said the constable, who clearly had read the report closely and was leading them along a train of criminological deductions. "You found, in fact, *no* bodies! Despite Doctor Bashir's extravagent claims to the contrary."

Kira was staring back at her chum. "What do you mean? They found what was left of the bodies after the Klingon bomb."

"Really?" Odo leaned forward inquisitorally. For a moment, Dax realized what it must feel like when the man actually suspected a person of a crime, and she felt a pang of pity for Quark, which she quickly suppressed.

Odo asked the next question in his cross-examination. "Was the bomb blast evenly felt throughout the ship?"

"No," she answered. "The aft end suffered much less damage. That's where we found the medical log, still more or less intact. Apart from the erasing, I mean."

"And also where you would have expected to find the bodies of Levanian crew members, also 'more or less intact.' Wouldn't you?"

Dax looked at Kira, who stared back, hand on her belly again, waiting for another kick. "He does have a point," the Bajoran admitted.

Lieutenant Commander Dax turned back to Odo. "Are you saying there never were any bodies? That the Levanian body cells were just . . . sprayed in beforehand?"

"I'm saying," clarified the constable, "that we don't *know* that there ever were any living Levanians aboard that ship, and now we can't even establish that there was an actual chase before they arrived at the wormhole. Isn't that interesting?"

"Old Man," said Sisko, "I am starting to get a *very* bad feeling." The captain leaned forward, raising one finger as if pointing to the overhead. "Let's pretend, just for a moment, that there never really was any pursuit, no Levanians, and no Klingon–Jem'Hadar training facility. We're right back against my original question: *Why* should the Klingons want us to think they're allied with the enemy?"

"Uh oh," said Kira, staring down at her console.

"What?" asked Dax, hurriedly scanning for close encounters of the Dominion kind: nothing.

"I think I just figured out a reason they might, I say might, want to trick us."

"Which is?" asked Benjamin Sisko.

"Which is—exactly what we're doing. Going out chasing a green puffin."

"A green *puffin?*" demanded Dax.

"A snipe, a red herring, whatever."

"That," said Sisko, "is exactly what I was afraid of."

"You mean they wanted to *lure* us out here? Or just away from the station?" Dax was already starting to get angry: she still could not accept the idea that Klingons would actually ally with the Jem'Hadar, but she could buy more easily the notion that they could trick Starfleet into *worrying* that they were allying with the Jem'Hadar, enough that they would order the *Defiant* through the wormhole to check on the rumor—and away from the station, leaving it defenseless against . . .

"An attack?" she suggested.

"That's a terrible thing to say, Old Man, and I'm afraid you may very well be right."

"Again?" Dax felt the Curzon memories start to rise in fury at having been tricked once again by the Klingons. *Maybe,* corrected Jadzia Dax to herself. "On the other hand, Benjamin, this is all still speculation."

"Yes," added Kira. "What if the original information

is true after all? If we turn around because we suddenly get paranoid about the Klingons, we'll be disobeying a direct order from Starfleet, *and* we'll never know whether there really is a joint training camp."

Odo now turned 180 degrees and began to argue the other side. Dax was annoyed, but she understood he was only doing his job: examining every aspect of the evidence, just as he would for a particularly puzzling crime. "Captain, it's important we never lose sight of the duplicitousness of my people. They are perfectly capable of either allying with the Klingons, or else tricking them into thinking they're allied. Or even of taking the form of Klingons to trick *us* into thinking they're allied."

Sisko turned to look back at Odo. "You sound like you're saying that no matter what we do, we may be wrong."

"I'm afraid so."

"That there is no right choice."

"Well, I didn't say that, exactly."

Sisko rose from his command chair. Everyone else fell silent and waited for the captain's decision. "Kira's point is well-taken. We have direct orders from Starfleet to proceed to Gamma GK-974 and investigate the possibility. But my primary duty is to defend my command, which is the station."

"Captain," interrupted Major Kira softly, "are you sure you're not being, um, unduly influenced by the fact that Jake is still back there?"

Benjamin Sisko paused a long moment. "Of course I am," he admitted, "and why shouldn't I be? Jake is my son, but there are still other civilians aboard, including children. Not everyone has left. It is my duty to defend them."

"So you're just going to throw out all the evidence aboard the Levanian ship?" Kira seemed amazed that the captain would make such a decision. *She spent too many years in the Bajoran underground,* thought Dax, *saw too many kids die.*

"No, Major. I have weighed that alleged evidence against the points that Odo brought up, and I find the thesis lacking credibility." Sisko turned to Dax. "In the end, Old Man, I trust your judgment about Klingons more than I trust an unknown medical log on a destroyed ship. Ensign Wheeler, plot a course back to the wormhole at maximum warp and let me know when it's ready."

"It's ready now, sir," said Janine Wheeler, as quiet as Kira had been. Neither she nor Tarvak had participated in the conversation on the bridge. They had almost faded into invisibility, trying to stay out of the way of the senior officers.

"Engage," said Sisko with finality. Kira shrugged, and Odo frowned.

Dax wasn't sure what she felt. she was hardly unaware of the huge gamble the captain was taking: if it turned out they were wrong, and there was no attack, the station was fine, and then the Klingons and Jem'Hadar staged a joint attack on the Federation . . . well, everyone aboard *Deep Space Nine* might as well bend over and kiss their careers goodbye, that is, assuming they and Starfleet Command managed to survive long enough to come to a parting of the ways.

Wheeler turned the ship expertly, of course. She was only an ensign, but she had spent eleven years in Starfleet before attending the academy, rising to the rank of senior chief petty officer. The ensign engaged maximum warp.

The ship surged forward, but, almost instantly, it wrenched back to impulse power and, simultaneously, every warning horn, tocsin, and klaxon on the bridge began to shriek: *crash warning!*

Dax instantly transferred control to her own console and veered hard to starboard, praying that whoever or whatever was heading directly toward them had the same emergency procedure. When seconds passed and they hadn't turned into a huge fireball of matter-antimatter reactant, she breathed a sigh of relief.

"What the hell was that?" demanded Sisko.

Dax tapped furiously at her console, backing the *Defiant* away carefully. "Um, Benjamin, you know that feeling you've been getting about us not being alone out here? Well, you win the blue ribbon for intuition."

CHAPTER
8

Now THE CAPTAIN was pacing furiously on the bridge, and Kira was desperately trying to reconfigure her sensors to target on a cloaked . . . what? "Captain," she said, "any idea what kind of ship we're facing? Cardassian, Romulan, Dominion?"

"Try Klingon!" snapped Sisko.

"They're not supposed to use cloaking technology," said Dax.

In a pulak's eye! thought the major. "Maybe this one has a problem with authority figures," she said politely. The Trill could be so touchy about her Klingons, especially now that she was romantically involved with one. "Or maybe he's not even a member of the official Klingon fleet. Dax, after this long, don't you think everyone in the galaxy, public and private, has managed to beg, borrow, or expropriate cloaking technology from *somewhere?*"

Dax said nothing, but she snarled, which Kira took as grudging agreement.

"I don't know that this has ever happened before," said the captain, landing at last in his command chair. "Two cloaked ships, no shields, facing each other blindly with phasers and torpedoes." He smiled, but without mirth. In fact, he looked a little like Shakar, leader of Kira's resistance cell, and now boyfriend, sort of, sometimes. "I can't say I like being the test case," Sisko added.

"On the other hand," mused the science officer, "there was a subspace surge just as we missed that did look a little like the warp signature of a Klingon bird-of-prey. Khitomer class, ironically enough."

Kira stared longingly at the shields console. "Sir, maybe we should just drop the cloak and raise shields?"

"Mm-mm," said Dax, emphatically shaking her head, "can't power up the shields until we complete dropping the cloak, but the bad guy can fire a torpedo as soon as he *starts* powering down his own cloak. And that would give our friend almost five seconds to torpedo us into constituent atoms."

"Perhaps if we simply made a speed-run back toward the wormhole?" Odo suggested.

"No chance," said Sisko. "Major Kira, what would the Klingon do?"

"He'd follow along behind, guessing where we were headed or following the ion trail, shooting randomly. Eventually, one of his torpedoes or disruptor blasts would slide right up our warp engines, and we'd light up the sector." *At least that's what I'd do,* she added to herself.

"I don't understand how the ship followed us in the first place," continued the constable. "Isn't the cloak working?"

"Evidently," said Kira, "otherwise we'd have been destroyed by now." She found her hands actually shaking. *I'm no coward! What's happening to me?* Then at once the explanation sprang into her forebrain: *it's the baby, stupid!* She forced her hands to remain on the weapons console, though she had a nearly irresistable impulse to touch her belly, feeling for her baby's kick.

No! Keiko's baby, Keiko and O'Brien's . . . not mine! Not for the first time, she wondered whether she would really be able to give the child up, having borne it for so many months.

But now was not the time to worry about it; trembling or not, she had to force her hands to dance across the console, teasing out whatever slight sensor readings she could, waiting for a partial lock or even a manual target. Something to shoot at. Now was the time for Kira the major, not Kira the mother.

So began the slow, deadly dance, each ship maneuvering blind and invisible, reaching out with gentle fingers on the triggers of terrible weapons. *First to stumble loses!* thought the young major from Bajor.

"What?" demanded Miles O'Brien, jerking upward and banging his head against the ceiling of the ventilation shaft. "You're not planning to invite that doddering, old fraud, are you?"

"Old? He's no older than you!" retorted the doctor.

"Well, he *acts* like a grandfather."

"And you know as well as I that *you're* the fraud. Mr. Garak is the real article."

"Oh, and I suppose you're in Garak's league? Bashir . . . Julian Bashir. Secret agent!" O'Brien sounded distinctly nasty. "All right. Then I don't want to involve us with that middle-aged, competent, but *totally untrustworthy* Cardassian spy!"

"And why not?" responded Dr. Bashir, irritated that his friend still, after all these years together, didn't seem to trust the judgment of Bashir, Julian Bashir. There was something about the hard-headed master chief, something annoying. "Garak may sometimes look like a traitor or act like a traitor—"

"And flap like a duck and quack like a duck. Julian, he's a duck! He may not be a spy anymore, but head games are his blood, Julian. We're much better off trying to get to the subspace emitter and repair it, so we can call for some help, than wandering around the station looking for the last surviving member of the Obsidian Order!"

"Have you got an envirosuit in your pocket? Do you think the Klingons will leave the airlocks unguarded? I really hate to do this, *Chief* O'Brien, but I'm afraid I'm going to have to make it an order."

O'Brien stared incredulously. "Julian, you're ordering me to help you find that Cardassian threadneedle?"

Bashir took a deep breath. He so rarely pulled rank, it felt like pulling on an old overcoat that had shrunk over the years. "I'm afraid so, Chief."

Miles glared at him for a moment. "Aye-aye, sir," he said tonelessly, and Julian felt the sting. *Friendship is only possible between equals,* he remembered. Until the crisis was settled, Julian and Miles would have to be *Lieutenant* Bashir and *Chief* O'Brien.

The chief set out along the shaft, scuttling so very like a spider that Bashir could barely keep up. O'Brien was at home in the nooks and byways of the station, but the doctor had never climbed up a turbolift shaft in his life and had only rarely crawled along a ventilation shaft. The experience took him back to his carefree days in the Academy, where only a ventilation shaft connected the male and female cadet quarters.

It was hot and very dry work. The air in the shaft was thoroughly scrubbed of water vapor, to reduce the possibility of molds and airborne bacteria spreading through the station, and within a few minutes, the skin on Bashir's face began to crack, and his eyes, leached of moisture, felt achey and heavy. He tore his uniform at the elbows and knees, then started working on the skin, but he had to press on. And of course, Miles—Chief

O'Brien, that was—didn't complain, so neither could the officer.

So creeping, scuttling like rats, they closed on the barricaded tailor's shop, desperately hoping the once and future Cardassian spy had managed to hold off the Klingon invaders. Bashir knew that O'Brien's heroic plan to warn Starfleet was something between desperation and despair. If they were to have any hope of remaining free and retaking the station, they would need allies, as many as they could get. Bashir was already thinking ahead, beyond Garak, about whom they could trust in a pinch.

Quark was "tending bar" when his brother, the white sheep of the family, burst in screaming incoherently about some silly disturbance or other. Quark put the phrase tending bar in quotation marks in his mind because the reality of tending bar included, he was pretty sure, having actual *paying customers*, which were in such short supply lately that he was seriously thinking of packing up and moving to someplace more rollicking, like Vulcan, perhaps.

Nevertheless, there were two remaining customers: an ancient, retired Bajoran judge and, of course, the perennial Morn, forlornly drinking Rigelian bloodwine and spinning the Dabo wheel, though there were no gorgeous Dabo girls to take bets. While there was even a single slip of latinum in Morn's pocket, it was Quark's Ferengi duty to relieve him of it.

Quark was scurrying from behind the bar with a trayful of drinks, one for Morn and four for the judge, when Rom charged into the room, grabbed his elder brother by the elbow, and caused Quark to spill the entire tray over Morn's table, lap, and head.

"You blithering idiot!" screamed Quark at his hyperkinetic sibling. "You . . . you altruistic nonprofit volunteer! Look what you've done! Well, that's going to come

out of your—" Quark paused, groping for words, he had been about to say "wages," but of course, Rom no longer worked for his brother. Instead, the little Ferengi had taken the most un-Ferengi-like tack of becoming one of Chief O'Brien's *engineers!* Worse, he had allowed his own son, Nog, to run away and become a decidedly unprofitable cadet at Starfleet Academy, an embarass-ment surely caused by Rom allowing Nog to fraternize with the hu-man boy Jake Sisko.

Quark still worked his mouth, though now no words came out. But Rom didn't even notice. He was still shouting something about barbarians or invaders or tax collectors—the Ferengi word he used could have meant any of the three.

"We've been invaded by *tax collectors?*" shouted Quark, suddenly realizing what his brother was saying.

"Worse!" responded Rom.

Quark was puzzled. "What could be worse than tax collectors?"

"Klingons! We've been invaded by Klingons!"

Quark stared at his obviously demented brother. "Rom, ring up the sum! Klingons can't collect taxes here, it's not their financial jurisdiction!"

Suddenly, Rom seemed to go crazy. He grabbed Quark by his lapels—"my best suit!"—and shook him vigor-ously enough that when he let go, Quark's ears rang and his sense of balance was halfway back to Ferenginar.

"Open up your ears, brother!" bellowed Rom, eyes almost as big as his lobes. *"The station has been invaded!"* For-real invaded, by Klingons, not tax collectors, and they're killing people in the Promenade, just outside the bar!"

Dizzy, Quark grabbed hold of the nearest stationary object, Morn's head, to steady himself. "What are you babbling about? There are no Klingons!"

Just then, the loud and unmistakable noise of a disruptor sounded just outside the open doors of

Quark's Place, followed by a series of screams and the battle-shouts of Klingons in full cry. Quark vaulted over a chair and dashed to the door. After a second, he turned back. "We've been invaded by Klingons, you idiot!" he snapped.

"That's what I've been trying to tell you! And they've taken over Ops, and the comm grid is down, and we're alone and cut off and I want . . . I want . . ."

With two long strides, Quark bellied up to Rom and shook his fist under the younger Ferengi's nose. "I'll *earbind* you if you say one word about wanting your Moogie!"

Rom sniffed but didn't say the hated phrase. "I was fixing a weird comm grid problem that was piping all the Ops communications down to a public restroom on the Promenade when I heard Worf say something about the subspace emitter being sheared off, and then there was an explosion, and then I heard the voices of Klingons, and—"

"Rom, will you shut up! I need to think. We have to do *something*, but should we bolt with the loot or stay and defend the place?" Quark heard another volley of disruptor blasts, followed by a pathetic, few phasers in return fire. "Well first, we'd better at least shut the door!"

The two Ferengi ran in opposite directions, Quark to the door and Rom to the two customers, pushing and shoving them out the rear exit. Quark poked his head out for a moment. The battle seemed to have passed right by Quark's Place. Presumably, the Klingons wanted to secure the entire Promenade before they started assaulting the shops, one by one. But Quark had no illusions that that wouldn't be the next phase of invasion: plunder! *Why else would anyone attack anything?* he thought. *War is just organized robbery anyway!*

Then he pulled the heavy doors closed and threw the brand-new deadbolt. The old Starfleet-supplied lock would probably have lasted about five seconds, he figured, or just long enough for the first Klingon to set his disruptor on the highest setting and vaporize the locking mechanism. The new duridium bolt should be much better . . . *twenty* seconds of disruptor fire, if they were lucky!

Then he ran back to Rom, who was already cleaning out the latinum safe into a tablecloth. "Rom, we're not leaving! We're going to stand and—hey, how did you get my *safe* open, you little sneak-thief?"

"I pick your lock every couple of days," answered the young Ferengi without a trace of embarassment, "just in case of an emergency!"

"You do?" Quark stared at his brother with new respect. *Maybe there's hope for him yet,* he thought. "We're not going to be driven away by a pack of wild Klingons, Rom! This bar is mine, and I'm going to fight for it!"

"Good for you, brother!"

"Help me move the cash register. I've got a little Klingon surprise hidden under the deckplates!"

Quark stooped and began tugging at a barely visible tab that poked from the deckplates no more than two centimeters—any larger, and he figured that formerly shapeshifting goon Odo would have found it. But it was devilishly hard to get a grip on such a small bit of metal! Sudden shouts, followed by the pounding of a steel-shod bootheel against the door lent urgency to his tuggings.

At last, the trap flew open with a groan, just as one of the Klingons outside shouted to use a disruptor, as Quark had predicted. "Hah!" snarled Quark, poking an arm into the black dark hole and retrieving first one, then another, phaser rifle. The heavy shoulder-weapons were a little too big for Ferengi hands, but Quark supposed they would manage.

"Where did you get those, brother?" asked Rom, staring incredulously.

Quark looked up, annoyed at the query when he

should have heard congratulations at his cleverness. "From Mrs. O'Brien's magnificent phaser collection in the schoolroom!"

"Uh, that doesn't look like something Mrs. O'Brien would—"

"Oh for acquisition's sake, Rom! What difference does it make where I stole—I mean bought—I mean *found* them. Take one and shoot anything big and warlike coming through that door!"

"Yes, brother!" Rom fumbled the rifle when Quark tossed it to him. As it twisted and spun, finally falling to the deck, Quark squawked and dove for the ground, cringing; the gun didn't fire, fortunately.

"Rom, you idiot! It's not enough you ruin the family's reputation by becoming a hu-man engineer . . . now you want to *fry* me?"

"Uh, I'm sorry, brother." Sheepishly, Rom picked up the rifle and hefted it. "Does this feel a little light to you, Quark?"

"Light? *Light?*" Quark bared his sharp, crooked teeth at his brother. "Well, why don't you just hang the first Klingon corpse from the barrel to make it heavier?"

"Oh, here's why it's so light." Rom stared into a slot he had just opened. "Uh-oh."

A slow, red, creepy feeling spread through Quark's innards. "Uh-oh? What do you mean, *uh-oh?*" Gingerly, he turned his own rifle upside-down and popped the hatch.

It used to hold a battery, the battery that supplied the phase-energy that supplied the phaser shots. "It's empty," announced Rom, master of the blindingly obvious.

Quark suddenly felt nauseated. He quietly buried his face in his hands as Rom ticked off a list of possible suspects.

". . . and he could have traded the batteries for a can of Hyperian beetle snuff," the engineer finished triumphantly.

A defeated Quark shook his head. "It doesn't matter who took it, you imbecile. The point is, my entire family is now as good as dead."

"Don't be silly, brother—the whole family isn't going to die!"

"Oh! Really? How is that possible?" the bartender drawled skeptically.

"Well . . . Moogie isn't even here."

Quark stared at his brother for a second. "Rom, *get your lobes into the bolthole!*"

CHAPTER
9

THE KLINGONS WERE still pounding on the doorlock, which was a brand new, duridium deadbolt Quark had just bought from a Lonatian trader. He hated bargaining with them so much—they spoke only in rhyme, and one had to conduct negotiations in iambic hexameter to get anywhere—that he had allowed the trader to get the better of him.

Well, at least we'll get to see whether he actually cheated me or merely overcharged. Quark dashed for the Ferengi bolt-hole on the heels of Rom, who was still Ferengi enough to grab the bag of latinum *en passant,* the pitiful fruits of all the years of Quark's labor in the bar. The Ferengi were practical businessmen, and they always believed that no matter how good things were going, at any moment, the marks might figure out the actual rules of the game, at which point, they would storm the Ferengi shops with torches and pitchforks.

Thus, it was standard Ferengi business practice,

though never formalized into a Rule of Acquisition, always to build a last-ditch escape tunnel, or bolt-hole, into every Ferengi establishment. In fact, "block his bolt-hole" was a common Ferengi expression meaning "don't give him any options or room to negotiate."

Rom dove over the bar and hit the deck rolling, just as a final kick from the lead Klingon snapped the duridium dead-bolt like a wooden spoon. *Hah, you lantern-headed Faav lizard!* thought Quark, already imagining what he would do to the Lonatian if he ever caught up with him again; *he's not a trader . . . he's a traitor!*

Rom grappled with the ventilation grating in the bulkhead; Quark elbowed him aside and grabbed for it himself. They wasted precious moments in a wrestling match for who would get to open the bolt-hole and escape first, but a blast from a Klingon disruptor that split the difference between the two Ferengi settled the matter: Rom had his hands on the grill for the moment, and Quark leapt back screaming threats and imprecations at the attackers, allowing his brother to wrench free the metal grating.

The Ferengi bolted into the hole in reverse chronological order, the younger brother going first. Just as Rom cleared the lip, the first enraged Klingon leaned over the bar, saw the escaping proprietor, and bellowed an order to halt immediately. "Yes sir, right away sir!" screamed Quark to confuse the behemoth. While the Klingon vaulted the countertop, Quark dove through the hole after his brother.

The Klingon made a blinding lunge and barely managed to catch one of the Ferengi's boots, but Quark had just had one of the Dabo girls, Deppi An, polish the footwear before she emigrated—and the Klingon's grip slid right off!

Quark scuttled backward like a spidercrab. The Klingon's shoulders were much too broad to fit into the bolt-hole, but, of course, he could stick his gun-hand inside. And he did.

But a Ferengi bolt-hole would be suicide without a back door to slam in the face of the pursuing enemy! As the Klingon shoved his arm and one shoulder into the hole, bending to bring one angry eyeball into view and his disruptor to bear, Quark lashed out with his foot and kicked the "panic panel."

With a bang like a huge, Cardassian firecracker, explosive bolts blew three rods made of DS9 hull material across the tunnel, blocking the entrance, and incidentally impaling the Klingon's arm in the process. He screamed in agony as one of the rods passed right *through* his forearm. Then his Klingon machismo took control, and he clenched his razor-sharp teeth and fought back another scream. But for all intents and purposes, the bolt-hole was permanently blockaded.

"Let that be a lesson to you, Rom," said Quark, gingerly retrieving the pinioned Klingon's disruptor, which had fallen inside the tunnel; "always trust traditional Ferengi values, like the bolt-hole, ahead of newfangled, duridium technology."

They scurried through the "tunnel"—actually the gap between the shops of the Promenade and the station core, too small even for Ferengi to crawl through comfortably—as it made several right-angle turns. They dropped through a hole in the floor, then wriggled up a ladderway. When Quark and Rom stopped at last to catch their breath, there was no line of sight between them and the Klingons, not even a good three-cushion shot for a projectile weapon. "Ah, I have a question, brother," said Rom. Quark said nothing, he was too busy staring back the way they had come and thinking about the wreckage of his business, his standing in the Ferengi community, and his life. "Where are we going?"

"Straight to the Land of Perpetual Poverty," muttered Quark, "not the Divine Treasury, not the Lake of Latinum."

"Actually, I meant where are we going right now?"

Quark shrugged. What was the difference? With the bar gone, occupied, in enemy hands, one hiding place was as dead and worthless as another.

"Well, if you don't have anywhere in mind," said Rom, "I suggest we find Chief O'Brien. He probably wants us to, uh, defend the station or something."

"Perfect! Why not?" Quark turned to glare at his brother. "It's not as if I had *anything to live for* anymore! Might as well go out in a blaze of bankruptcy."

Rom still sat in the tunnel unmoving. "Well?" demanded Quark, "take me to your boss."

"I don't know where he is!" wailed Rom.

Any minute now, he's going to start blubbering for Moogie, predicted Quark. "Look, Rom, there's nothing more to do here. We're going to have to abandon the bar and the station and get help from somewhere. We'll head for the cargo bays and try to steal a runabout. Then, when the hu-mans and the Klingons finish fighting it out, we'll return in triumphant glory to reopen the bar." Suddenly, he saw a faint metaphoric glimmer at the end of the proverbial bolt-hole. "Say . . . maybe the Federation will pay us a reward!"

"We can't abandon the station, brother. The chief would never forgive me!"

Quark rolled his eyes. "Well, aren't we just as likely to find *O'Brien* in one of the cargo bays as well? Getting off the station and getting help is probably the top priority on his mind, too." Quark didn't mention his own idea what was the most probable "top priority" thought in O'Brien's mind at that moment: justifying himself before the Divine Treasury, or wherever it was hu-mans went when they were fried into a cloud of submicronic dust by a disruptor blast.

"Well, you may be right," conceded Rom.

"Am I ever wrong?" added Quark, his bad mood returning as the Federation reward receded farther and farther in his mind, hidden behind a mountain of dirty, dangerous work.

Rom looked dubious, but he seemed to have no better plan. The two Ferengi set out through the bolt-hole, trying to find the main ventilation shaft that they would take toward the cargo bays.

Chief O'Brien kept a pretty face, but inside he was groaning and complaining like a bent, old woman struggling up Tara hill. The extended crawl through the shafts and vents was killing him. He didn't want to admit he was getting to be an old man, and he surely wouldn't let Bashir see him crippled and limping—the kid was thinner than O'Brien had ever been, and wiry enough to slither like a snake through the narrow holes of the ventilation system, and Miles O'Brien would be damned before he'd let on how much he was hurting!

It would be different if he were alone, better, but with another person bumping up against his feet every few seconds, the chief's chest tightened and he felt more than a dollop of frustration, exacerbated by Bashir's incessant chattering.

"How far do you think we've crawled, Chief? I'll bet it's at least a couple of kilometers. I never realized how extensive was the ventilation system in this station! I guess that makes sense, though . . . I mean, it has to supply air to thousands of people and filter the atmosphere of every room on *Deep Space Nine*. Have you ever thought of installing lights along here, Chief? No, I suppose there's no need . . . I wish you'd let us use hand-torches, instead of these glowtubes, but I agree there's too much danger of the Klingons tracking the electro-magnetic fields produced by the current-flow in flash-lights."

O'Brien stopped so suddenly, Bashir ran right into him, yelping in surprise. The chief turned his head; his body was too tightly wedged to move. When he spoke, his voice was more than subtly tinged with irritation: "Will you please kindly *shut the* hell *up?* Sir?"

A few moments before, he wouldn't have thought it possible, but O'Brien found the ensuing silence even more troubling. He felt guilty. Bashir wasn't a bad sort, really, just a bit of a blatherer.

"Garak's shop is just ahead, Julian, if you're still interested in that wash-up," O'Brien continued in a gentler tone. "I think he sleeps there too."

"Oh, he won't be there," predicted the doctor. "Klingons and Cardassians mix like acid and base."

O'Brien stopped again, but this time Bashir was farther back and avoided bruising his cheek against the chief's boot again. "If you'll pardon my asking, then why the hell did we just crawl all the way around the damned Promenade?"

"I expect him to have left, but I hope he left behind a clue to his whereabouts." Bashir's voice floated from the darkness beyond the red light of the glowtube. It was strange to talk to a person whose face was shadowed. O'Brien never realized how much of communication depended on visual cueing; he felt he was talking to Bashir over a comm link.

"Why would he leave a clue?"

"So I would know where to find him, of course."

O'Brien rolled his eyes, but Bashir probably couldn't see it in the dark. "He left it for *you* to follow?"

"Of course; he knows I would try to find him, were I able to do so. Who else could serve as the nucleus of the resistance force against the Klingon occupation?"

"But he wouldn't know the station was being invaded until the Klingons burst into his shop. There'd be no time for a note to you! And the Klingons would find it and use it to hunt him down anyway."

"I'm sure he had advance warning, Chief. He probably heard you and Worf talking about it up in Ops."

O'Brien began crawling again; the annoyance provoked by the conversation was getting him agitated again. "Julian, you think the station *tailor* has planted a bug in Ops?"

"Why not? He's also the only resident member of the Obsidian Order."

"Ex-member."

"Chief, there is no such thing as an *ex*-member of the Obsidian Order of Cardassia. No matter what Garak may say. 'Death will not release you,' as they say."

O'Brien merely grunted in response. He was too busy trying to fit through a particularly close section of the tube.

If the shaft narrowed any further, though, O'Brien would stick; he was already cursing himself for not following Keiko's advice and losing a couple of inches around the waist. *I'm sure that skinny bastard Bashir is having a grand, old time.* But he crept forward.

They came to a sharp bend that intersected the main shaft. The course they followed was a long, circular route—"a commodius vicus of recirculation," thought the chief—circumnavigating the Promenade, and the right-hand bend led inward, toward the core, right about the point that Garak's shop should be. "I think we're here, Julian. I think this turning is the air-supply to Garak's place."

"What turning? I can't see a thing over your enormous—ah, boots."

"It's up here. You'd better go first, sir; if it's a wrong turning, I might not be able to back out again."

O'Brien crawled forward past the T-intersection, allowing Bashir to squirm into the very narrow gap and hump forward on elbows and belly.

The chief's glowtube was fading. *Time to crack the last one,* he thought. But before he did, he poked his head into the black-dark and thought he saw a faint glow of light in the distance, diffuse, as if it were reflected off a dull material with a low albedo.

After a couple of minutes, Bashir's voice came from far down the darkness. "I see light, Chief! I can see into a room, and it's *definitely* Garak's shop . . . I think."

"Wait, you *think* it's *definite?*"

"Nearly so, I'm pretty sure."

"You can't tell?"

"I mean," said the doctor, "that I think it used to be Garak's shop, but it's been turned."

"Searched?"

"By somebody with a wrecking crew, it looks like."

"Can you break open the grill and make your way out? Julian? *Julian?*" Now where had he gone?

O'Brien turned and crawled along the inward shaft as fast as he could. As the glow of light became strong enough not to deny anymore, he found another baffle, an S-turn; negotiating that took time and ingenuity—he imagined Bashir had just bent around it casually without giving a second thought to his thicker partner.

Around the baffle, O'Brien saw what Bashir had seen, and the stylus-thin doctor was right: it *had been* Garak's shop! The grill was missing. Since the chief hadn't heard it wrench out, he presumed the Klingons had already pulled it off when they searched the room, but the baffle was clearly too narrow for any Cardassian (especially Garak) to squirm around, or a Klingon, for that matter, preventing a search of the shafts by the invaders.

Chief O'Brien crawled to the lip of the shaft and lunged out, head-first; there was no way to turn around in any event. He fell onto his hands, and his right wrist spasmed in pain, provoking a yelp from the chief, hastily cut off in case they were not alone.

The doctor came running. "Chief! Good heavens, I entirely forgot to tell you it was all right! Please forgive me." Bashir instantly noticed the way O'Brien was flexing his hand and wincing. "Let me fix that for you," said the doctor, fishing out the medical kit he could now reach.

Bashir played the cylinder, whatever it was, up and down O'Brien's wrist, and the pain ebbed quickly. The chief took the opportunity to look around the tailor's shop, trying to make sense of the chaos the Klingons left. Racks were broken apart and the pieces flung into corners, walls were torn out, the desk was smashed, and Garak's computer screen was kicked in. And everywhere were clothes, or their remains: shreds of teal and emerald, happy pink and crimson, somber mauve, brooding cobalt, maroon, and midnight, epic argent and auric for trim . . . what once was the wardrobe for every nefarious character who slunk the Promenade or stalked the corridors of *Deep Space Nine,* from Klingon to Ferengi to Bajoran to Starfleet captain.

Now, the ruler of Garak's shop would be nothing but a king of shreds and patches; he could adorn himself as the world's most colorful beggar, or be misapprehended as a wandering Ferengi rag merchant.

Bashir began to tour the shop, muttering inanities to himself *"All right, my clever, Cardassian friend, what devilishly brilliant hiding hole could you have—"* But O'Brien rushed first to the door to check whether they were likely to be dodging Klingon disruptor blasts in the next few minutes. He listened carefully. Hearing nothing, the chief crept close enough to the door to activate the auto-open.

The door remained shut, and O'Brien bumped his nose against the door hard enough to break the proboscis. "Damn it!" he yelped, pulling away a hand dripping blood. Then the nose began to throb, then itch, and he felt a terrible need to sneeze, which would have been terribly painful, he knew.

Gritting his teeth, he stomped back to the doctor. "Loog, Duliab," he said, wincing from the pain, "I habboo bobber ooh, bu' cabboo . . . ?" He pointed at his nose, as if Bashir wouldn't notice without a visual aid.

"Chief, Chief, how *do* you get into so much trouble in such a little bit of time?" Shaking his head, the doctor once again broke out his medical tricorder and repaired the damage.

O'Brien sniffed a couple of times, satisfying himself that the nose really was straight once more. "Thanks, I particularly appreciate the bedside manner." He turned his back and returned to the curiously inactive door. "They must've cut power to the automatic servos," he announced, "probably to deactivate any automatic security systems. The Cardassians left a few surprises on the station, if you remember."

"Oh, how could I forget? Just the picture in my mind of the entire Ops crew crouching behind control panels while Gul Dukat's alarm system fired . . ."

The chief tuned Bashir out, concentrating on forcing open the doors despite the inactive servos and the high-friction sliding tracks. When they were wide enough for O'Brien to exit, he poked his head onto the Promenade.

"My God," he breathed; "it's completely deserted!"

"No bodies?" asked Bashir, his head appearing directly below O'Brien's, giving the chief a start.

"Looks like your hypothesis was correct, Julian. I don't think they're killing anyone. There's no blood, either. So where would they take everyone?"

"They talked about a portable cell, whatever that is. Probably some sort of forcefield gadget they've rigged."

"Clever," said O'Brien. "It means they don't have to waste manpower actually guarding the prisoners." He stepped back into Garak's tailor shop. "So what do we do now? You took charge, remember?"

Bashir shrugged. "The only thing we can do, we find whatever message Garak left us."

"And if he didn't leave a message?"

"Or we can't find it? Then . . . then I guess we crawl back into the ventilation system and try to find somebody else. Or we find suits and try to make it to the subspace emitter. Don't ask me—I'm a doctor, not an insurgent!" With the final admonition, Bashir resumed his hunt for a mythical message from an Obsidian tailor.

VENGEANCE

CHAPTER
10

THE SEARCH WAS ON, and O'Brien found himself drawn, unwillingly, into his friend's fantasy. *So maybe Garak left a message . . . so what! You can't trust him farther than a pregnant Irish bull!*

But Bashir was obsessed, and Chief O'Brien really had no better plan. So they searched every corner of the shop, looking for an invisible message.

And they found it. Actually, horrifically enough, it was O'Brien who spotted the ink scrawl on the wall, near the smashed remains of computer, below the trim, above the deck-mounted mike pickup for the main ship's computer, ahead of the holo-projected fitting dummy (now MIA with the death of the servos), and behind the intact latinum safe. "What the hell is that?" demanded O'Brien, squatting to stare at the strange symbols. "Looks like chemistry," he said. It was his least favorite subject at school.

"That's exactly what it is," said Bashir excitedly, on his hands and knees to stare at the scrawl. "It's

Cardassian biochemistry, actually . . . a Cardassian amino acid, you might say. It's part of their DNA; it can substitute for cytosine when a human mates with a Cardassian. Um . . . corrigor? Corregidor? No—corigan something." He leaned close, counting something.

"What is that supposed to mean? A Cardassian amino acid—is he hiding somewhere where there's a lot of acid?"

"Corigan Nine-Five, a rare, amino-acid disorder of Cardassian children that causes them to be born with no cerebral cortex, kind of like anencephaly in a human."

"Well, that certainly fits," said O'Brien, but again, the sarcasm was lost on Julian, who seemed never to notice it.

Bashir struck a pose, resting his chin upon his palm, the elbow resting upon his other arm, which folded across his pencil-thin chest. "But what could Garak possibly mean by drawing a picture of Corigan 9-5?"

"That he felt his brain leaking out his ears?"

"If you wanted to conceal information from a Klingon, what would you do?"

"Tie it to a carrier-tribble?"

"I'm serious, Chief!"

"All right, I'm sorry, Julian." O'Brien paced; his brain seemed to work better on the go. He kept his eyes on the deck, so as not to stumble across the strewn debris and detritus. Something tugged at the tip of his forebrain, a thought—where could a Klingon never look? What would they never think of? *What does Worf lack, for example?* he asked himself.

Suddenly the chief snapped his fingers. "Julian, I've got it! What does every Cardassian have, but few Klingons possess?"

"I shudder to ask," quipped the doctor.

"That's it exactly! A *sense of humor.* Cardassians love to pull intricate, complex gags on their friends and enemies. They mock, they gloat, they laugh at everyone else. They pull pranks, like that alarm set-up you mentioned: Gul Dukat wasn't content to set it and leave; he wanted to watch us sweat, so he could laugh at us."

"You're saying if a Cardassian wanted to conceal information where a Klingon would never find it, he would—"

"He'd hide it in a joke, Julian. A play on words, a pun."

"Corigan. Corridor?"

"Too obvious. Besides, the corridors were crawling with Klingons just a bit ago."

Now the doctor paced as well. They nearly bumped into each other, and O'Brien altered his flight plan so they could orbit without intersecting.

Bashir suddenly stopped. "Word play, you said?"

"Would a Klingon ever notice it?"

"How about an anagram?"

"An anagram? You mean rearranging letters of one word to form another?"

Bashir smiled. "Corigan can be anagrammed into the phrase 'in cargo.'"

O'Brien froze as well. They stared at each other. "That's perfect!" said the chief. "There are a lot of cargo bays on this station, and each has hundreds of individual cargo pods! And all the private cargo is shielded against sensors unless you get right up on top of it, so a Cardassian stowaway could escape detection for a long, long time." O'Brien paused, pensive. He called up the mental image of the cargo holds on the station . . . it was a very big picture. "The only trouble is—which one?" He looked at Julian, who was staring upward so intently, O'Brien's own gaze was drawn to the ceiling.

But Bashir was just thinking hard. Abruptly he relaxed, rolling his eyes and shaking his head. "Of course, what an idiot! It's staring us in the face. That wasn't just the amino acid Corigan he drew; it was a specific *damaged* version, with a unique name: Corigan Nine-Five."

"Yeah, so?"

"Nine dash five? How about nine *minus* five?"

"Corigan four . . . 'in cargo' bay *four!*"

"That has to be it, Chief. How fast can we be there?"

O'Brien looked back at the ventilation shaft they had tumbled out of, and he shuddered. "Faster than a speeding snail, Julian."

Captain Benjamin Sisko strained forward in his command chair, staring at the viewscreen, as if that would enable him to see his invisible enemy better. *This is bad morale,* he lectured himself. *I cannot allow the crew to see me so agitated!*

The *Defiant* was edging sideways, so gently—impulse engines at 0.001 percent—that he hoped the Klingon would miss the faint radiation surge against the cosmic background radiation of three Kelvins.

"Benjamin, surge at forty-three mark minus nineteen!"

"All stop," commanded Sisko. Ensign Amar reacted instantly, killing the impulse engines quickly; Wheeler sat back, her hands in the air to signal that she was not touching a thing on the Nav console. "Old Man, are we flanking them?"

Though the engines were silent, the *Defiant* would continue to drift in space relative to her previous position, of course. Two centuries of subspace science had not managed to overrule Newtonian physics when it came to macroscopic objects traveling at nonrelativistic speeds: objects in motion remained in straight-line motion unless acted upon by an outside force, such as an impulse engine.

If they were lucky, if the *Defiant* were moving relative to the Klingon ship (assuming it was a Klingon ship), then after a few minutes, they should clear the obstacle. *And* then *what?* he asked himself, again. So what if they managed to clear the Klingon ship? They couldn't jump to warp speed; the ion flux and warp signature would give them away, even if the Klingons couldn't *see* them because of the cloak. *They sure as hell would know where we were headed!* All they would have to do is fire a few torpedo volleys in the direction of the wormhole. If the *Defiant* was unlucky enough to catch one up her exhaust vent, that would end the story: they could not raise shields while maintaining their cloak. It was one or the other.

But suppose we didn't follow a direct line to the wormhole? Suppose we tacked back and forth? That would minimize the chance of a torpedo strike, but . . .

Sisko sat back in his chair, making an elaborate pretense of cool serenity, probably the hardest but most important job of a senior officer. *No, that wouldn't work. The Klingons would figure out that that was our likliest evasive pattern; they would follow their own torpedoes at maximum warp straight to the wormhole—and arrive first, because we'd be monkeying around.* The thought of a blind fight at the mouth of the wormhole did not appeal to the captain.

"Benjamin," said Dax quietly, "the energy pickup over the passive radioastronomy antennas isn't diminishing." She looked up at him and explained before he could ask what that meant. "I can't pinpoint them because of their cloak, but I can tell when they're close. And they haven't gotten any farther in the last four minutes since our burn."

Sisko frowned, rubbing the close-trimmed beard he had adopted for greater military bearing. "They must have detected the increased radiation to one side and correctly deduced what we were doing."

"They matched us, Benjamin, speed for speed. They're still too close to risk heading toward the wormhole . . . even if we could figure a way around the torpedo question."

It was unusual to have Odo aboard, and the captain

decided to take advantage of the occasion by picking the constable's brains. "Odo, you understand the situation we're in?"

The constable stood with his hands crossed rigidly behind his back, staring at the viewscreen. "It's rather like a security officer and a Ferengi loose in an enormous, pitch-black cargo bay. Neither can see the other, but they can hear each other breathing, so they know they're close. They each have a hand-torch, but whoever turns on his torch first signals his whereabouts to the other, and he'll be incapacitated before he can swing the beam around and find his foe."

Sisko nodded, impressed. "You have it exactly, Constable. It is essentially a game of cops and robbers . . . now how do we find the bad guy before he finds us?"

Odo turned up the corners of his mouth in an expression that almost looked like a smile. He had been practicing it ever since he became a solid. "I suppose it's out of the question to shapeshift into a creature that sees in the dark?"

"Perhaps the next model of the *Defiant*."

"Then I would program my torch to light automatically in ten seconds, put it down, and walk away from it."

Sisko pondered a long time. There was something there, something he could use; he was sure of it. But he couldn't quite pull it out. "Dax . . . what do you think of Odo's idea?"

Actually, the logical person to ask would have been Kira. There were several alliances and cliques developing on *Deep Space Nine*, which didn't bother Captain Sisko a bit; they made for competing theories, which usually arrived at a workable answer faster than a single, top-down heirarchy: Dax and Worf were now an "item," which was hardly unusual, given Curzon Dax's friendship with Klingons over the decades coupled with Jadzia Dax's fascination with the physical side of things; this gave her great insight into the Klingon mind.

Kira and Odo had been friends for several years, originally owing to the fact that both were egregiously maltreated by the Cardassians: Kira tended to back Odo and vice versa, sometimes without really thinking it through.

Then there was the puzzling and absurd coalition between Dr. Bashir and Garak, former member of the Cardassian Obsidian Order. Alas, both were back at the station, where Sisko hoped they were enjoying a lunch, during which Garak would hint at the various intrigues of espionage he was engaged in, while the young doctor tried desperately to sort fact from fancy.

"I don't see how that helps us," groused Dax, responding to Odo's suggestion. "There's nothing we can set and walk away without it instantly becoming visible to the Klingon." Odo was a technical naif compared to Dax, and she was impatient at a suggestion that sounded nonsensical.

"Wait a minute, Jadzia," objected Kira, as the captain had known she would. "Don't just dismiss it out of hand! This is a police situation." Now that the Bajoran major had opened her mouth, she had to struggle not to put her foot in it. She would think through Odo's suggestion more furiously, Sisko predicted, than if he had simply asked her directly in the first place, then she would have said "yeah, sounds great," which wouldn't bring them any closer to a plan than before.

"The walking away wouldn't matter if . . . if it were a light point-source, rather than a beam. The whole room would get bright, and you'd see him the same time he saw you," Kira said.

"So we'd each shoot each other! Benjamin, what's Odo getting at?" Dax asked.

Sisko hadn't a clue, so he merely sat silently in his command chair with a faint smile, as if he were the Sphynx demanding an answer to his riddle. But he knew, he just *knew* they were on the verge of something.

"No," said Kira, "you don't get it! Sure, he'd see us the same time we saw him . . . but *we'd be expecting it!* He wouldn't—I figure I can get one clean shot while the Klingons are saying 'What the hell was that!'"

And suddenly, no one was talking about cops and robbers. Now it was a concrete plan for the *Defiant* against the presumed Klingon bird-of-prey that stalked them invisibly.

Now Dax was getting excited, seeing the possibility for some flashy pyrotechnics. "Benjamin, if we could create some sort of bright pulse, something heavy, but with a wavelength less than four or five times the length of his hull, we might be able to see it bend around his ship like ripples around a leaf floating in a pond."

Benjamin Sisko raised his hand in benediction. "So mote it be," he intoned.

"Kira, what about a hyperphasic pulse?"

"Yes!" shouted the former terrorist. "The soliton pulse through subspace would have to deflect slightly around the cloaking field itself. It's kind of like how we used to detect Cardassian transports coming in to land."

What an amusing irony, thought Sisko, *to detect a ship* because *of its cloak.* It would only work because of the incredible proximity: if the ships were more than five hundred or so kilometers apart, the effect would be too minuscule to detect.

The women dove for the warp drive circuits, ripping away the cover panel without getting into each other's way, astonishingly enough. Sisko turned to his constable. "A brilliant idea, Odo."

Odo nodded gracefully. "Thank you, sir."

"I think you may have solved our problem."

"Perhaps. It's a good start, at least."

Captain Sisko turned to watch his science and weapons officers attacking the ship's controls. Quietly, he added, "You haven't a clue what Dax and Kira are doing, do you?"

"Not the vaguest idea, sir."

Sisko smiled broadly.

"Ensign Wheeler," he said, loud enough to attract her attention, "at random intervals every few seconds, fire up the impulse engines to point zero zero one, random heading. Just to keep them on their toes."

Fifteen minutes passed, during which the captain strained his eyes so hard, staring at the starscape through the forward viewer, that his vision went out of focus and he had to blink for half a minute to restore it. Dax called out, "Got it, Benjamin! We're set up for the hyperphasic pulse whenever you pull the lanyard."

Eyes closed, Sisko asked, "Can we raise shields while we pulse?"

There was a pause. In between blinks, he saw Dax and Kira looking at each other and communicating silently via nods and shrugs, as two conspirators often did. "Sorry, sir," said Major Kira. "It's too much drain on the ship's systems. In fact, we won't be able to do *anything* that requires a power-drain for almost ten seconds after the pulse."

"Can you lock on phasers and torpedoes?"

"Sure, but we can't fire until the storage cells recharge . . . nine point nine seconds."

"That will be fine. If we're lucky, the Klingons will still be blinking from the flash."

"Captain," said Odo, "perhaps I'm not following the technical side of this conversation, but wouldn't it take even more power to raise shields than it will to fire the phasers?"

Kira agreed. "Can't even start for nine point nine seconds; then it'll take three and a half seconds for forward shields, if that's where they are."

"But what if the Klingons don't happen to be directly forward?"

The major shrugged. "Well, after we identify their bearing, it's nine point nine seconds to full power, then three point seven seconds to start raising the appropriate shields, and a final four seconds before full shields can be raised. Almost eighteen seconds for full shields, assuming nobody trips over their own fingers."

"So what you're saying," Odo persisted, "is that if we don't destroy the ship or at least disable their weapons systems, then after we get one free shot, *they'll* get one free shot. And neither of us will be shielded."

"That," said the captain, "is the chance we will have to take." He stood, folding his arms across his chest. "Secure all emergency hatches, all hands to crash positions. Dax, activate the pulse on my command: four, three, two, one, now."

At the final word, Sisko sat quickly and thumbed the crash-restraints on his command chair. Dax touched her console.

The hyperphasic pulse was so powerful, the captain actually felt it himself, right through his body: it was like a sudden glass of particularly rough, moonshine whiskey, the kind he used to drink with his father in the bayous of Louisiana when he was Jake's age, but instead of starting in the throat and spreading down to the stomach, thence to the rest of his body, the hyperphasic pulse erupted from his brain and spinal column and spread along his nervous system to the extremities, hands and feet, fingers and toes.

Sisko jerked and grunted, blacking out for a microsecond. He shook himself and pulled his shaky hands over his own command console, ready to take control from Kira if she were still unconscious from the pulse. She was awake, but the ship's systems were dead!

Just as the fact registered in Sisko's mind, along with the mild regret one feels when "the best laid plans of mice and men aft gang agley," the bioelectronics burped and abruptly came online again.

"Searching," shouted Kira, unnecessarily, since nobody's hearing was affected by the pulse. "Where *are* you? Where the hell *are* you?"

"Yes!" shouted Jadzia Dax, touching a single button that shot the coordinates directly to Kira's console.

"Got it," said the major. "Thanks . . . come on, little ones; come back to me—come on back to me!" Evidently, the phaser cells had ears; they responded almost instantly to Kira's summons. She did not wait for orders. She fired a full spread of phasers and photon torpedoes. "Blessed be the Prophets," she mumbled, almost as an afterthought.

"Incoming!" shouted Dax. Before she could finish the word, the entire ship shuddered, as if it had been smashed by a giant sledge hammer. With a second blow, the starfield began to race past the viewer. It took Sisko almost a second to realize the ship was spinning rapidly from the force of a blow.

"Inertial dampers?" he inquired.

"Normal parameters, Captain," said Ensign Amar. he looked a little green nonetheless.

"Correcting for the drift and spin," said Wheeler, her hands jerking across her navigation controls.

"Unfortunately," said Dax, "the Prophets giveth and they taketh away. The Klingons got their shields up before the torpedoes arrived, but we did wing 'em with the phasers."

"How bad is our damage from the return shot?"

Dax held her hands up, staring at her diagnostic screen. "Looks *good,* Benjamin! We got the jump, and our shields came up just before their disruptor blast. That was the first jolt. It was their torpedoes that started us spinning, but there's no serious damage. The shields were nearly full-power."

"And the Klingon?"

"One of Kira's phaser shots popped him right in the weapons pod. He won't be shooting again for a couple of days, I think. Got a partial on the warp engines. Benjamin, I can't tell for sure with his shields up, but I think he's crippled!"

"That was an extra-base hit, Major," grinned Sisko. "Now set a course back to the wormhole, maximum sustainable, Ensign Wheeler, and get us the hell away from here."

"He'll follow," said Kira, as the ensign lay in the course and engaged the warp drive.

"But he has a weak arm," said the captain, still in a mood for baseball metaphors. "And I'll bet the *Defiant* can beat the throw to the plate anyday."

CHAPTER
11

MAJOR KIRA TOOK control of the *Defiant* away from the irritated Ensign Wheeler, who rose from the nav-chair when requested and fairly stomped to the "woodshed," the fold-down jump seat used for visitors on the bridge, where supernumeraries and cadets sat to observe the bridge. Janine Wheeler had done nothing wrong, but it was only her third navigation-propulsion watch on the *Defiant,* and the captain wanted a more senior hand at the helm.

Kira verified the course every half hour; "landmarks" were distant enough in the Gamma Quadrant, which was so sparsely scattered with stars, that there was insufficient parallax for the computer to reliably navigate: the stars were so far away that they didn't change much as position changed, and it was easy to drift from the course. But on many long trips in the quadrant since the discovery of the wormhole, Major Kira had developed various seat-of-the-pants navigation techniques, such as a "sideways glance" at a particular planetary system they skimmed, judging by the relative position of the well-mapped planets whether they were on course, or how much of a correction was needed.

"Wheeler, stop pouting and watch what I'm doing," snapped the major. "I know what they taught you in your Academy, but that's theory. The reality is that there is *no such thing* as 'coordinates' in real space."

"I don't understand," said the ensign, still fuming.

"Coordinates are measurements from a zero-point. . . . Earth, in the case of Federation coordinates. But Earth doesn't sit still; it revolves around its sun, Sol; and Sol revolves around the center of the galaxy and is tugged by other star systems."

"We account for all that!"

"But you *can't* account for the fact that the relative length of whatever unit you use for measurement changes, depending on what direction you're approaching the coordinates from, and how fast you're moving relative to Earth when you drop out of warp into sublight velocity."

"Huh?" The ensign looked blank, and Kira silently cursed the allegedly "practical" approach to astronavigation that taught Starfleet officers only what they *needed* to know about special relativity and quantum mechanics.

"I mean," explained the Bajoran, with rather more patience than she actually felt, "a ship approaching the so-called coordinates from one star system going ninety-nine percent lightspeed actually measures a *different-sized* meter or kilometer than a ship coming from somewhere else going ninety-nine point ninety-nine percent lightspeed."

"Wait," said Wheeler "you're saying they two ships might come to two different spots, and each one would think it was at the right coordinates?"

"Exactly!"

"But, which is right?"

Kira couldn't help groaning aloud. "Janine, *neither* is right. Or they both are, however you want to look at it.

There *is no* exact correlation between coordinates and some fixed position in space. All you can do is note landmarks and correct when you get there." Kira read the numbers the computer just finished crunching from the sighting she just made. "That's what I'm doing here, see? I know certain landmarks—every pilot has her own set—and I take a peek, calculate the deviance, and correct."

Wheeler stared for a long time, trying to absorb the lesson. When she spoke, her voice was softer, meeker than when she was banished. "It sounds like you're saying the whole science of navigation is . . . fuzzy."

"It's not a science, it's an art. It's like . . ." Kira groped for an analogy, looking back at Captain Sisko.

The captain had been following the conversation more closely than even Kira realized. "It's like throwing a ball to a friend," he explained. "There's no precise answer to when to let go of the ball, because you never swing your arm exactly the same way twice."

"Only in this case," Kira added, "you're on one runabout, and your friend's on another going a different direction."

Dax chimed in. "Actually, our friend is going the same direction . . . and he just increased his speed. He's gaining on us, Kira!"

The ensign instantly forgotten, Kira stared at the rear-mounted sensors on her threat board. Indeed, the image of the Klingon in the sensor array was "blueshifting," the term used by analogy with light, indicating he was moving closer to them. The Klingon was catching up. "How the hell is he *doing* that?" demanded Kira, almost rhetorically.

Dax took it as a real question. "He's overcranking his engines, Nerys. Got hot spots all over the pods. It's a miracle that thing hasn't blown a gasket by now."

"Blood of the Prophets," swore Kira. "I don't believe it."

"Believe what?" asked Captain Sisko. "Major, if you know something we don't, please tell us."

"He has no weapons," she said.

"Yes, I told you that!" griped Dax.

"And his engines are damaged. He might not be able to make it all the way back to the wormhole . . . it's two days travel." Kira Nerys paused, but nobody spoke. The silence was eerie, and she quickly filled it. "So that leaves only one choice for our Klingon friend: he has to close the gap and *ram us.*"

Sisko pursed his lips and touched his beard. He looked pensive. "I cannot think of an alternative," he said at last. "Circumstances dictate tactics." He paused for a moment, then turned to Dax. "Old Man, we have to match velocities. We can't let him catch up. Can you modify the engines to get higher than maximal warp out of them?"

"Benjamin," she said cautiously, "we could burn out *our* engines. And if we did, then we'd be stuck here, a sitting duck, long enough for the Klingons to finish repairing their weaponry. I can pretty much guarantee we wouldn't make it back in time to stop—"

"Stop whatever surprise party the Klingons planned for Mr. Worf and Chief O'Brien," finished Sisko. "Nevertheless, we have little choice either, just like the Klingons: *their* tactics dictate ours. We must go faster. But Dax—"

"Yes?"

"Don't overrev it all the way to maximum, and don't burn out the warp drive; that's just what the Klingons want. As long as they're gaining more slowly than they are now, we should be all right."

"Aye-aye, Cap'n."

Dax dove into the wiring again, obviously unhappy. But looking down at her screen, Kira saw that the bird-of-prey had closed the gap by 8 percent of the separation in only a few minutes. *At this rate,* she calculated, *they'll be close enough to smell the raktigino in ninety minutes!*

"Hm, one question, Benjamin," mused Dax from under the propulsion console, her voice muted by the mass of fiberoptic bioelectrical wiring, "the only two places I can divert power from for extra speed are the shields or the phaser banks. Which would you rather lose?"

"Kira?" asked the captain.

The major opened her mouth to choose the former, then closed it to think a second time. "If we drain the shields, and it turns out the Klingons fix their disruptors faster than we expected, we're dead meat. I can live without the phasers. We still have plenty of torpedoes."

"Phaser array it is," muttered the barely audible Dax. Kira sat back and stared as the Klingons crept closer and closer; she had to force herself to divert some attention to course corrections, so concerned was she about the pursuing ship.

A few minutes later, Dax managed to goose the warp drives, and the *Defiant* began to shudder. Kira gripped the edge of her console and tried to read the blue-shifting, difficult with the buffet from engines operating at 105 percent or 110 percent normal capacity. "He's . . . not gaining quite so fast," she announced. The good news sounded tepid. She should have hollered "he's falling back!" but the sensors showed otherwise.

Sometime in between glances, while Kira was poking at the nav stream, nudging the ship on a better course for the wormhole, the blueshift changed to redshift. "Oh!" she declared, and almost forgot what she had been dying to say. "He's not—the Klingons are—Captain, I think the bird-of-prey slowed down. We're pulling away from him, now."

"Excellent!" declared Sisko. But the triumph was short-lived, within two hours, the color had changed once again, and the Klingons were once again trying to overtake the *Defiant.*

For more than eight hours, the tug-of-war continued: both ships nursed their engines, prayed hard, and goosed the nacelles just a little faster, then backed off the heavy-warp when warning lights exploded like a string of supernovas across the engineering consoles. Sometimes the *Defiant* gained; more often, the game went to the Klingons. By the time another bridge-watch had passed, and Ensign Janine Wheeler had been replaced in the woodshed by Ensign Tarvak Amar, Kira, who still sat in the driver's seat, felt a terrible, shooting pain in her eyes. She couldn't keep them moist enough, and she had to take a thirty-second break every bell to drip saline onto her corneas.

The Klingon bird-of-prey had closed the gap to just one quarter of where it had started out, after the *Defiant* got the first, big jump at the very beginning. Their lead had eroded to virtually nothing, and still the Klingons came!

"This is ridiculous!" complained Dax. "Their engines are hotter than a stellar core—and I mean that literally—their ship is shaking apart, the dorsal and ventral stabilizers are stuck open, so the damned thing is rocking like an elephant in full gallup. Why hasn't their ship exploded or shot off in a random direction by now?"

"Jadzia," said Kira, "we're not much better off. Except for not taking a hit to the warp pods—and it doesn't seem to have affected them much—we're in as bad a shape as they are."

"Speaking of which—damn it, not again!" Dax swore fluently under her breath. Once again, she killed the extra-power feed from the phaser array into the engines that had been salting the matter-antimatter reaction for just a jot more power.

"Kira," said Sisko, "are they in torpedo range?" She jumped. It was the first question he had asked in hours.

"No, sir. Can't lock onto the target from here."

"Major Kira," he continued smoothly, "have you ever heard of a minefield?"

Of course she had. The Cardassians had regularly buried the deadly, indiscriminate explosive devices along routes followed by Resistance columns, either troops or supply trains—or civilian traffic, as the routes were generally public. "You mean—just drop photon torpedoes behind us and hope the Klingons run into one?"

"Do you have a better idea?" asked the captain. Since the answer was no, of course, Kira began the process of "mining" the path behind them. Every five minutes, she allowed two or three torpedoes just to "roll" out of their magazines, set to proximity fusing. The first time caught the Klingons by surprise, and they drove directly into a torpedo. The blast diminished their shields by 11 percent, but from then on, the Klingons were watching for Kira's little surprise packages and were able to dodge them. Still, the evasive maneuvers slowed the pursuers down and prevented them from applying full warp power toward catching up.

With every mine Kira dropped—she preferred to think of them as depth charges; she had seen the results of Cardassian mines on Bajoran children—the Klingons fell back to drive around it, then overcranked their warp nacelles to play catch-up.

"Kira, what are you doing?" asked Dax. "Their engines look like they're ready to burst!"

"It's not the torpedoes, it's the speeding up and slowing down," said the major, not taking her eyes off her threat-board. Again she dropped a depth charge, then again, then once more. "Um, Dax, how close do you think they are? We're starting to run low here. If we run out, we're defenseless: no phasers, no photons."

The Trill hummed skeptically. "How many do we have left?"

"Four. That leaves us bone dry."

"Well, four more spurts of power *ought to* blow their

engines, but I've been thinking they're going to blow for some time now, and—"

"And they're still turning over," Kira completed. *Damn! What are they running on?*

The captain spoke from behind Kira. "It's your call, Kira."

Kira discovered herself silently praying to the Prophets . . . something she had been doing more and more recently, since getting pregnant with another couple's baby. She rested her hand on her swollen belly, something else she had started doing all the time. Ordinarily, Kira would suggest standing and fighting, but not every person aboard the *Defiant* had chosen the danger: there was one aboard who had never chosen anything, not yet.

Why did I go on this mission? she berated herself, but it was too late now for recriminations. The mission was supposed to be a routine trek through the Gamma Quadrant: *get close to the planet, do a passive scan for Klingon and Jem'Hadar lifesigns, get out quickly before anyone even knows we're there.* Instead, they were racing across the galaxy with a bird-of-prey literally in hot pursuit, desperately trying to make it back to the wormhole—and having no idea what they would find on the other side. *If the station fell under attack, are the O'Briens still alive?*

Kira remembered that Keiko was down on Bajor, and she breathed a sigh of relief: at least one O'Brien was all right, no matter what may have happened to the station when the Klingons drew the *Defiant* away on a wild Jem'Hadar chase. But of course, that also meant at least one O'Brien stood to suffer the most horrible blow a parent can suffer: the death of a child, should Kira make the wrong choice now. Worse, Kira couldn't remember whether Molly was aboard with Miles or on Bajor with Keiko!

"Dax," she asked, her throat was too dry to speak, and

she had to clear it. "Dax, what's the pattern on their warp-engine overload?"

"You mean each time? Um, it rises steadily as they accelerate to about twelve percent past redline, then they scale back."

"Which do they use as the mark: the speed, or the engine temperature?"

"Oh! I hadn't thought of that." Dax typed at her console, then reported back. "You're right, Kira—they're cutting off their engines when they reach closing speed, regardless of the engine temperature!"

Got 'em! "All right, people, here we go: let's see how slow they have to go for *four* depth charges."

With a final *amen,* Kira dropped the last four torpedoes out the aft end of the *Defiant.* hoping the ship's name would live up to expectations. She watched helplessly; with no more ammunition, there was nothing Kira could do. Dax could reroute power back to the phaser array, slowing the ship, but the bird-of-prey would run right up the *Defiant's* aft end, possibly destroying both ships in the ensuing collision. The final depth charges had to work! The alternative was not to be considered.

Because they were just dropping the torpedoes out the back of the ship, not firing them, it was impossible to predict the pattern they would take. Kira held her breath, praying they wouldn't all line up on one side.

They didn't. In fact, the torpedoes spread nicely, forming an impassable "picket fence" directly in front of the Klingon ship. The pursuers did the only thing they could: they slowed dramatically and altered course to avoid the explosive barrier.

But when ships are moving at what Bajoran scientists called *hyperluminous velocity*—that is, faster than lightspeed—slowing "dramatically," even by a few tenths of a warp number, meant that, all of a sudden, the *Defiant* was *way* ahead of the Klingon ship: in the ten or so seconds during which the Klingons had to drop from warp 9.72 to warp 9.20, the Starfleet ship pulled ahead by some three and a half *million* kilometers . . . that was more than eleven light-seconds.

The determined Klingons commenced their overheated burn to catch up to the *Defiant,* and Kira gritted her teeth: here was the last chance they had to shake the pursuit! The Klingons had not been this far behind since they began to overburn their engines, and they threw caution to the solar winds, revving their warp engines up to 110 percent rated capacity. Within seconds, inside the nacelle containment field, the matter-antimatter reaction superheated to the core temperature of a mid-sized nova. Closer and hotter, the measurements stood in indirect proportion to one another. By the time the Klingons had almost caught up, the subspace tachyon and chronotron output from their blighted ship was probably lighting up sensor arrays across the entire sector, as dozens of spacefaring races were staring at their own threat boards and saying "What the *hell* is that?"

A Klingon bird-of-prey is a sturdy ship with plenty of built-in safety margins. But no safety margin ever made could contain a point-source as hot as those engines. There was a flash that burned out several of the *Defiant's* sensor contacts and probably fried all the unshielded electronics throughout the ship. Kira's screen went dead for several seconds, during which she sweated and cursed silently. Then the array flickered back into existence, the computer having switched to backups.

She searched behind them for two solid minutes, but all she found was microscopic debris that *might* have been the remains of the bird-of-prey, but they would never know for sure. The ship did, however, vanish from the sensors: whether it had blown up or burned out and put up its cloak, she couldn't tell.

"That did it, Captain," she said, licking her lips like a Prophet-Bobber lizard. "I don't know where they are, but I know where they *aren't.* We're clear from here to the wormhole . . . unless he had a friend who's still running silent."

"That is a chance we shall have to take," said Sisko. He tried to appear calm, but Kira saw his pale knuckles and the imprint his gripping fingers made on the upholstery of his command chair, and she was not fooled, not for a minute.

CHAPTER
12

JAKE SISKO WAS surprised to find himself less terrified than he had been earlier, much less than he had been under the bombardment on Ajilon Prime. *It wasn't just the fear of death,* he realized, *it was the helplessness!* Struck by his revelation, he crept along the corridor, back against the bulkhead, trying to look forward with one eye and back with the other . . . an untenable position. But he hadn't seen a Klingon in several hours.

For the first four hours after fleeing the Promenade, Jake "ran into" the invaders left and right. The enemy were making no attempt to be silent—hardly unusual for Klingons—and fleet-footed Jake, silent as a ghost, was always able to evade the troops. He knew the station well enough to avoid dead ends, and he was lithe and wiry enough to duck into the most astonishingly narrow spaces, where wide-bodied Klingons wouldn't even think to look.

But there were some hairy near-misses, such as the time he hung by hands and feet from a fire-suppression sprinkler pipe not three meters above the heads of a Klingon patrol, who had previously spotted him and were looking. They looked everywhere but up.

Now Jake stalked empty halls and silent passageways, and he wasn't afraid—not *that* afraid—but he wandered aimlessly, from nothing to nowhere. Until he found himself turning a corner, shading into a shadow when a pack of braying Klingons scuffled past, looking for stragglers. Jake had seen none for more than an hour, the station was secure. But when the Klingons passed, and Jake continued on his ostensibly aimless route, he found himself standing at the entrance to Cargo Bay 4, and at once the plan that had eluded his stunned brain became clear: if he could steal a runabout and escape the station to Bajor, he could warn his father and Starfleet!

Jake stared at the locked door, his palms itching and sweat beading on his forehead. A moment before, he was calm, accepting the situation as immutable. But now that he abruptly had *something to do,* all his old fears and insecurities flooded back. He was grateful for the fear; it meant he was still alive. For many leaden minutes at the beginning of the crisis, Jake Sisko had wondered whether he, too, had been gunned down, and his consciousness was nothing but a ghost walking the site of his physical death.

At first, his brain froze; then he remembered the standard access code for station personnel, which he wasn't technically allowed to know, but his father was captain and had given him access. *So file a complaint,* he once told Odo when the constable raised the issue, back in the days when Jake and Nog made mischief and menaced quietude on the station. Jake typed the code . . . and nothing happened.

Of course, the Klingons encrypted all the access pass-

words. Well, what did he expect, incompetence? From a Klingon operation?

Jake smiled. The Nog era was about to pay off yet again. To prove he would never be bested by a mere human, Nog had demonstrated his own methods of breaking into allegedly secured facilities and quarters, methods that didn't require a father who ran the station to give his little precious a security-access code. Jake, roundly impressed, had learned the techniques, the easy ones at least.

He scavenged the deck until he came to a cooling duct, as usual wrapped with tight coils of insulating material. When uncoiled, the material was stiff but bendable, and could be flattened into a shiny strip a meter and a half long and four centimeters wide.

Stretching as high as he could—Nog always needed a leg-up—Jake flattened his thumb against the insulation at the top of the jamb. Pressing up hard, he created a gap just thick enough to slide through the strip of unrolled insulator. He inserted it as far as he could, retaining just two fist-widths, then he bent the stiff material downward and inserted it a little farther, until the bend was right at the top of the door.

Jake gently pumped the insulator up and down, and the shiny, reflective surface caught the motion-sensors on the other side of the door. With a faint hiss, the door slid open, the door-eye thinking someone approached from the inside to exit. Exiting was allowed from the cargo bay by default, unless the function was specifically turned off, and disabling the mechanism had simply not occurred to the Klingons. Besides, presumably they were moving in and out themselves, and it was convenient not to have to type an encrypted access code with an armful of weapons.

Jake slid into the darkness of the bay, crouching low to make a small silhouette against the bright corridor. He froze, his pulse pounding in his ears. His chest ached, and he realized he was so tense, he probably wouldn't be able to move even if a raging Klingon burst through the boxes directly ahead of him, sweeping his *bat'telh* like a scythe.

Jake forced himself to relax, slowing his aching heart, taking long breaths silently through his mouth. As his pulse quieted, he could hear the noises of the cargo bay, normal noises, but faintly behind them the insistent buzz of low, guttural conversation.

Creeping closer, shackled by a strange chill, the young Master Sisko caught a word here and there, deep and harsh, an ugly sound to the speech. But somehow, it didn't sound quite Klingon enough. He mentally cursed his universal translator: he knew what Klingon speech sounded like, if only the damned technology would get out of his way and stop translating everything into his own tongue! What finally tipped him that he was not dealing with a Klingon enemy was the *height* of the noise, which he finally localized by twisting his head every direction until he pulled a muscle. Unless the Klingon were squatting on the ground or were a dwarf, it was doubtless a Ferengi—a *pair* of Ferengi, now that he listened closer. One pair of Ferengi: hardly enough even to open the bidding!

Jake closed the distance, treading quietly enough to avoid alarming the two little men, but not so quietly as to sneak up on them. His efforts were for naught.

Rom was so startled he could barely open and close his mouth, but Quark let out a satisfying yelp. Then the Ferengi bartender grabbed his brother and shoved him forward. *"It was Rom!* It was all Rom's idea—take him, not me!"

Brother Rom found his voice. "This is Quark, the infamous smuggler! I'll be happy to inform on him . . . I've often heard him talk about how dishonorable and cowardly the Klingons are!"

Jake stepped out quickly, before the Ferengi caused

irreparable damage to their sibling relationship. Quark and Rom stared, mouths open. The elder Ferengi was furious, which didn't bother Jake in the slightest, but he did feel a twinge of conscience at Rom's reproachful look. "Um . . . sorry, I didn't mean to scare you."

Quark straightened his coat of many colors. His ears had turned pink, almost glowing in the darkness of the cargo bay. Starlight from the open bay door, covered only by a forcefield, illuminated Quark's lobes from behind and picked out the blood vessels.

"We've been running from the Klingons for hours," Rom said almost apologetically.

"Well me too!" said Jake defensively. Then his shoulders slumped. "Oh, never mind. Guys, what are we going to do? Is there a runabout here?"

Quark snorted, sounding remarkably like Constable Odo. "If there were, do you think *we'd* still be here?"

"I, uh, think the Klingons took them," Rom said. "All. Some time ago. This is the third cargo-launch bay we've, ah, investigated."

Great. Another brilliant Jake-Sisko idea shot to hell! He sat on a box, tucking his long, thin legs beneath him and resting his chin on his knees.

Suddenly, Quark jumped to his feet. In the dim light of distant suns, Jake saw the Ferengi's eyes go wide, staring over Jake's shoulder, as if he was looking at a ghost.

A Klingon ghost? "Oh, cut it out, Quark!" said Jake.

A monstrous paw suddenly grabbed Jake's shoulder. The boy blanched, his breath stopping in his throat, as the insistent power of the huge, bearlike hand gripping his flesh rotated him all the way about to stare at a lightless figure that loomed between Jake and his escape.

"It was all *Rom's* idea—"

"I'll be happy to inform—"

Jake didn't waste his breath shouting. He lashed out with all the pent-up fury produced by hours of terror, helplessness, and the destruction of everything he had called home since he was a young boy. His fist struck the assailant full in the face, numbing Jake's arm and nearly splitting his knuckles wide open.

The figure stepped back, blinking, otherwise unaffected. "What a peculiar greeting you humans have for fellow freedom-fighters," said Garak, contemplatively.

"You're not a Klingon," announced Jake.

"I would have expected a bit of leaping about, clapping on the back, cheers and such. Or perhaps a reserved, Cardassian smile and bow."

Jake squirmed. "Garak, could you let me go, please?"

"Ah, I might have known the Ferengi would manage to evade capture. They've always been so . . . practical." Garak let go of Jake's shoulder, allowing the boy to slump backward and almost stumble over a launching stanchion. The Cardassian was dressed in a thoroughly practical Cardassian military jumpsuit, but without the battle armor that, for example, Gul Dukat would wear over it. Garak smiled, and Jake immediately felt an urge to step back uneasily; he suppressed it.

"Garak, I'm really, really glad you're here," gushed Jake hesitantly. He thought for a moment and added what the Cardassian probably wanted to hear, "Good thing we have someone experienced in, ah, resistance fighting now."

Quark was in a sneery mood. "Oh yes, we're just brimming with military effectiveness now . . . a poet, a tailor, an innkeeper, and a nitwit! We'll send those Klingons packing in two hours."

They sat in the dark talking in hushed tones, while Jake stared out the bay door at the stars slowly rotating past his view. He said little, grunting agreement now and then or adding an observation, while Quark, Rom, and Garak filled in what had happened so far in the invasion. They diagrammed *Deep Space Nine* on the floor using the tailor's chalk Garak carried, and Rom and the

Cardassian sketched where the forces had moved: the Klingons were following a quick but pedestrian invasion route, starting at the hub, the Promenade and Ops, and working outward and down toward the habitat ring at one extreme and the lower engineering levels down to the reactor room at the other.

Jake said nothing about his most important and controversial observation, but he knew he would have to spill it eventually. Still, he cringed like a Ferengi when Rom raised the very point that Jake was hoping to avoid: "Uh, I know Odo's off the station—"

"*Everyone* knows Odo is off the station," interrupted Quark, rolling his eyes.

"But . . ."

"But *what*, Brother?"

"But where's, you know, Commander Worf. I mean, if Klingons are invading the station, shouldn't Worf be fighting?"

Jake winced. "Well, he is fighting, sort of."

"Where is he fighting? I haven't seen him."

Garak smiled mysteriously. "Would you like to tell them, Jake, or shall I? Nothing to say? Well, Rom, Worf *is* fighting—at the head of the Klingon invasion!" Six eyes snapped to the Cardassian.

Quark broke the tension. "Worf is fighting *with* the Klingons?"

"He is."

Rom sought clarification. "You mean he's fighting, uh, leading the Klingons? Against the station?"

"I know this is an unpleasant fact, gentlemen, but we must face unpleasant facts. They don't go away by ignoring them. Isn't that right, Jake?"

The young man jumped. "Oh. Yeah."

Garak of the cursedly sharp eye continued, "But you don't seem very surprised, Master Sisko. In fact, if I weren't sure you would *never* hold back such a vital piece of information, I would almost say you already knew that Worf was leading the Klingons before I mentioned it."

The Ferengi brothers turned accusing eyes toward Jake, who pressed his lips together and exercised his right to remain silent. As was usual, exercising the right appeared to implicate him more thoroughly than a denial would have—rightly so. "All right!" he confessed. "I saw Worf on the Promenade, and it looked, I mean *sort of* looked, like he was leading the troops."

"I never did trust that blasted Klingon!" shouted Quark, turning to kick a huge box labeled "Spare Replicators." It was a mistake for which he paid, dancing and swearing for several seconds.

"Fortunately," announced Garak, "we have our own weapon to use against them." He reached into his coat pocket and extracted what looked to Jake like a small comm badge, or comm earpiece, actually, connected to a phaser-sized piece of electronics. "I managed to liberate this from one of our friends out there on the Promenade."

"What is it?" demanded a peevish Quark, who had removed his boot to massage his injured toes.

"Uh, looks like a communications device," said Rom. "Does it work?"

"Well, in a sense." The Cardassian pressed a button, and a pair of lights began blinking. All Jake could hear was faint static, though he thought he picked up a pattern within the static.

"Encrypted," muttered Rom. He reached for the communicator, and after a short but gingerly struggle, got it from Garak. "I, uh, think it's supposed to be run through, ah, through a passkey system the Klingons wear in their battle helmets. I think we're picking up the transmissions but—"

"What you're saying, brother, is that Garak's piece of junk is totally useless."

"Well, unless we can decrypt it somehow, yeah. Can't use it."

Garak was frowning. "After all the trouble I went through to win it! Such gratitude."

"Oh, you probably picked it up off the floor," accused Jake, still smarting from having been exposed by Garak.

"Off the floor!" The Cardassian drew himself back, pressing his hand against his exquisitely tailored coat and raising his eyebrows at Jake's effrontery. "Let me tell you what I had to go through, the pain, the suffering—"

"The bolts of fabric," sneered Quark.

"Please don't, Garak," said Jake, but it was no use. The Cardassian tailor, whom Dr. Bashir always insisted was a former member of the infamous Obsidian Order, had already begun his epic narrative.

The Tailor's Tale

For some time, I have been receiving communications from sources of mine that the Klingons were preparing for an assault upon the station. I know that Dr. Bashir believes I was once a member of the patriotic, visionary order you've all heard about, but I assure you that even the lowliest tailor has access to more intelligence information than you might imagine. After all, people buying suits tend to talk; you know how it is, Quark, in your position as bartender! You hear things, and you cannot always decide just how much credibility to assign to the drunken ramblings of Morn, or the tall tales of a merchant-fleet captain you've never seen before in your life.

But when you hear the same stories over and over, after a while, you begin to lend them some credence in your head. So it was that my sources informed me for several days now that this attack was imminent, and I was prepared, of course, with several contingency plans: just as would any good . . . tailor.

When the attack itself came, I must confess to being in a rather awkward, that is not to say undignified situation, however; as one of your human books says, no man shall know the hour or the day, and there are certain duties to which we each must attend once or twice a day, if you know what I mean. Yes, Rom, I am aware that you were attempting to fix the problem. It must be embarrassing for Ops communications to accidentally be rerouted to a public washroom—however did you manage that? As I said, I was in a rather awkward position when I realized the invasion had begun, but I extracted myself as quickly as I could and rushed back to my shop, where I had prepared my plans for response to the impending assault.

Well, as your human poet Burns wrote, the best-laid plans of mice and men oft go awry. I hadn't quite made it back when . . . Oh, all right, Jake, gang agley, whatever that means. No, I'm sure your father has the quotation correct. I had not quite made it back to my shop when the first wave of Klingons materialized on the Promenade and began to lay down cover fire.

I saw right away they were not aiming, merely shooting to force everyone down to the deck, helpless, where the Klingons could dispose of them at their leisure. Taking advantage of their own tactic, I kept my feet and charged across the deck directly at one of the attackers!

Oh, it was a glorious fight, reminiscent of the grand days of the Empire. In fact, I daresay I felt a small surge of the patriotism that members of—of that order must feel as they ferreted out disloyalty, corruption, and treason among the more libertine civilians of our populace, or that a soldier in the front lines must have felt when confronting the barbarians ship to ship, Cardassian wits against Klingon *bat'telhs!* The Klingon saw me coming, but too late! He raised his disruptor and fired, just as I dove through the air and rolled across the deck. I felt a tingling in my back as his bolt o'ershot me.

Coming out of my roll, I rose before him and, remembering my training, I struck with—I mean, my training in school, of course, Jake; I know what Dr. Bashir thinks, but he is rather a romantic soul—I was too close for fists or feet, but remembering my *schoolboy* training in the manly arts, I struck at the Klingon warrior with my elbows and knees, knocking the wind out of him right through his battle armor. And let me tell you, were I some fragile species like human or Ferengi, instead of a proud Cardassian, I'm certain I would have done myself an injury!

As it happened, though, I dropped him to the deck and snatched up what I *thought* was his disruptor. At that moment, the other Klingons belatedly realized their danger, and they concentrated their fire upon me.

Dodging disruptor blasts is quite an invigorating exercise. I highly recommend it for, ahem, sedentary bartenders, Mr. Quark. But I realized that I was somewhat outnumbered—though they were only Klingons, hence a little, shall we say, thick—and decided discretion was the better part of valor, an expression we civilized Cardassians try to live by. I exited and circled the Promenade to my little tailor shop. It was only then that I realized that my talented fingers, quite on their own initiative, had liberated this particular piece of technology from my assailant as I pulled him to the deck. Quite an accomplishment! I only wish the good doctor had been there to witness it. It amuses me to feed his charming fantasy about the Obsidian Order.

I left a short hint to the doctor that I was headed here. Now don't fret, Jake. I assure you, the Klingons will never understand the message, if they even find it. It will just be so much gibberish to them. I only hope Doctor Bashir is as subtle as he wishes and more subtle than he appears!

And that is my tale. And if Quark does not *immediately* cease rolling his eyes so rudely, I shall surely do him an injury!

CHAPTER
13

EN ROUTE TO Cargo Bay 4, Miles O'Brien hesitated before entering the long, dark crossover bridge connecting the hub of *Deep Space Nine* with the habitat ring. "I don't like the look of this," he said. "Why are the lights out?"

"Maybe the Klingons like the dark?"

"Very funny, Julian. It looks like the perfect place for an ambush." Glaring at the doctor, who retained his semipermanent smirk, O'Brien led the way into the tube, walking along the catwalk that fronted the turbolift shaft. The chief tried to watch ahead and behind simultaneously, which resulted in a headache. Human eyes couldn't point like that.

"Um, chief?"

"Yes, Julian?"

"What happens if a turbolift uses this particular tube while we're in it?"

O'Brien hesitated a long moment. He had hoped the doctor wouldn't think of that particular eventuality.

"You'd better hold on really tight, sir. At that range, the damned turbos will probably shake your eye-teeth loose."

Bashir stared at the chief. O'Brien could barely see the discomfort in the doctor's face in the waning light from the tunnel mouth. "Oh don't worry, Julian. What are the odds that it'll happen in the exact half hour or so we'll be in there?"

Truer words were spoken every day and twice on Federation holidays. No sooner did the reassurance leave O'Brien's lips than he knew he had just sealed their fate: what god of mischance would pass up such an opportunity as the chief had just handed him?

By an incredible stroke of inevitability, they were a third of the way along the shaft when Chief O'Brien began to feel a rumble in his feet. He crouched, putting his hand against the Cardassian steel-mesh to feel the vibration. "Wonderful," he announced, "absolutely perfect timing!"

Bashir stared wildly around. "Chief, there's no place to hide! There's nothing to hold onto!"

"Damn, there's a spar a hundred meters up, but we'll never make it."

"They'll see us!" shouted the doctor.

O'Brien blinked in the darkness—that was a side-effect he had not even considered. If the Klingons saw them in the shaft, they could stop the lift using the emergency socket-kill, assuming they could figure out how to use the Cardassian circuits, then step out and blast doctor and maintenance chief into oblivion.

"Quick, lie flat, Julian. Unless they're sharper than they have any right to be, they won't even notice."

Bashir and O'Brien threw themselves down to the mesh and tried to flatten against it, the vibration became unbearable, then finally turned into sound, a low-frequency roar that reminded O'Brien of the fusion reactors in the bottom level of the station.

Momentarily, a bright halogen beam cut the blackness, seeking them out in their hide-in-plain-view position. The single, unwinking eye of the turbolift washed the walls of the crossover bridge white, so bright it painted over the colors that lesser illumination picked out: the beam was bright enough to reflect off every water droplet, every smooth segment of wall, dazzling the chief.

He averted his eyes from the direct glare. The reflection from below the catwalk silhouetted him like a scarecrow against the rising sun, and he lay perfectly still, hoping Bashir didn't succumb to the temptation to raise his head and stare: the Klingons would see, and the doctor wouldn't . . . not for hours while his eyes recovered!

Then the vibration turned to a shake, and O'Brien gripped the railing to hold himself from being shaken off the walkway. The turbolift galloped past, a herd of a thousand horses with bright flame snorting from nostrils and lightning flashing in their hooves. He gritted his teeth to hold back the scream as the lift, which ordinarily would be rerouted if a crewman were known to be doing maintenance in the crossover bridge, scraped past not a meter distant at a horrific velocity.

At that speed, it was past them in a fraction of a second, and O'Brien cautiously raised his head. He froze: the instant he moved, he realized it was a stupid reaction of premature relief—the blood-red tail lamp of the turbolift caught him in perfect relief, and Miles O'Brien stared into the startled eyes of the tail-gunner Klingon looking aft through the cracked doors of the Promenade-to-habitat express.

The Klingon recovered quickly, raising his disruptor for a shot at the chief. He missed, of course. It would have been the bull's-eye of bull's-eyes if he had hit them on the draw from the rocketing platform. But it made little difference. Klingons would be in the habitat ring in seconds, and they would call in reinforcement and sweep the crossover bridge on foot. "They can't miss us," O'Brien bitterly concluded after explaining the situation to Doctor Bashir.

For a long moment, the pair stared at the receding dot until it stopped. They could not see Klingons getting off, but they knew they were. They couldn't hear them call for backup, but it was moments away. *Think, think, think!* thought O'Brien, but the only plan that suggested itself was a pell-mell dash back the way they had come . . . and surely the Klingons would swarm the crossover bridge from both ends, anticipating just such a retreat. "Damn it, there's got to be somewhere to go!" he said, half aloud.

Bashir had a peculiar, faraway look on his face. "What?" demanded the chief, grabbing the doctor's arm to bring him back to the here-and-now.

"Chief, how tight is the forceshield around this station?"

"What?" O'Brien scowled. "Julian, what are you on about now?"

"Does . . . does the forceshield that surrounds *Deep Space Nine* fit *exactly* against the outer hull? Or is there a gap?"

Chief O'Brien's frown deepened. How did Bashir always manage to find a safe spot? "Normally there wouldn't be any gaps, but this station is a crazy-quilt of Cardassian technology with—"

"So there are gaps," Bashir interrupted.

O'Brien's eyes narrowed, then suddenly widened. "Oh, you're not thinking about . . . You're crazy!"

Bashir raised both eyebrows. "Wouldn't it work? Couldn't it?"

O'Brien ran through the technical specs in his head. There were a few places where he'd been keeping the fields extended. Bloody hull always needed some repair or other. The chief understood what Bashir was suggesting. It was just crazy, though!

Yeah, crazy like a fox. "Come on, Julian, we don't have all day!"

Miles O'Brien led the doctor along the tube toward the

habitat ring. Spaced evenly along its length were various access ports for maintenance, and the nearest was twenty meters outward. O'Brien took the top and Bashir the bottom as they untogged the pins, then the chief rotated the wheellock at the center of the hatch. He rolled the door back toward them, then pulled it open.

They stared out at the stars whirling past as *Deep Space Nine* rotated majestically on its axis. "Uh, after you, sir."

"Well, it's your station, Chief."

"Excuse me, but it's your idea, Julian." O'Brien insistently gestured with his hand. The doctor gritted his teeth, grimacing, and edged through the hatch to the outside of the station.

Chief O'Brien followed. As soon as he cleared the hatch, he was jerked around and found himself hanging from the lip of the access port, for "down" was now directly outward toward the habitat ring. They were outside the jurisdiction of the artificial gravity generators, propelled now by the momentum of the station's rotation.

The chief stared outward at the spinning stars, down at his feet and the habitat ring, up toward the core of *Deep Space Nine*. A terrible, reasonless panic gripped him: *Outside without your pressure suit, bucko!* It was every spacer's worst nightmare. But there was a thin envelope of air surrounding the skin of the station, trapped by the forceshield and simply part of the station environment, as far as the environmental controls were concerned. But the thin hull that separated O'Brien and Bashir from the crossover tube may as well have been an iron curtain between living and dying in the chief's bruised psyche.

Cautiously, holding tight with both hands and wedging one foot in a handrung, O'Brien extended his left foot in front of him, like a Ferengi Lobette. When he saw the shimmering ripples surround his foot, he yanked his leg back. They had about half a meter, no more, between the hull and a messy death: blood boiling, lung alveoli bursting, skin and eyeballs freezing solid.

His boot wasn't cold—it had only been in the vacuum of space for a second and hadn't had time to lose heat. Paradoxically, the sweat on his trousers had boiled away: in vacuum, any temperature above freezing is automatically boiling, because there's no air pressure pushing down on the water to keep it liquid. "Freeze-dried laundry," he mumbled. Bashir didn't answer.

Doctor Bashir clung to the handholds, looking frightened and more than a little sorry he had ever thought of the idea. Straining himself, O'Brien did a pull-up, reached in, and pulled the hatch door to. Just in time. Looking through the tiny, pinprick porthole, the chief saw a light bounce past, swing high to illuminate what once was the ceiling, then sweep side to side: Klingons, bearing flashlights.

"All right, here they come," said the chief. His voice sounded a little distant, as the air pressure was lower in the "bubble" than inside the station, but it was perfectly discernible.

"Can—can they see us?" stammered the doctor; he looked pale. *I probably look even paler,* thought O'Brien.

"I don't know, Julian. It's kind of bright out here, what with the floods and all."

"Can we kill the lights?"

"Oh, *that* wouldn't attract any attention, no sir!"

The doctor remained silent. O'Brien kept his own mouth shut, grateful for the chance to worry uninterrupted. He stared through the porthole as the Klingon search party got closer, their dozen torches casting bright beams in every direction, swirling spotlights looking for the *little men who were not there.*

> *I saw a man upon the stair;*
> *A little man who was not there;*
> *He wasn't there again today;*
> *Gee, I wish he'd go away!*

Then he heard the faint tramp of boots, ironshod boots of warriors unafraid to be seen and heard. The sounds were faint through hull and in the thin air of the pocket, but they approached, and O'Brien ducked his head until just one eye cleared the porthole. A mob of Klingon warriors rolled past, looking in every direction, including under the catwalk and "overhead," which was actually sideways from O'Brien's viewpoint.

Then the chief saw a sight that caught his breath: in the midst of the enemy invaders was one very familiar Klingon face. Lieutenant Commander Worf's grim visage appeared among the mob, floating "above" the others (Worf was the second tallest Klingon O'Brien had ever personally seen). Worse, it was evident from the body language, though there was such a confused babble of sound that the chief couldn't distinguish words, that Worf was *leading the assault* on *Deep Space Nine.*

Worf a traitor? O'Brien forgot himself and his predicament and actually rose to stare full-faced through the porthole, fury overwhelming good sense. *You* bastard! *You treasonous snake!* "So it's war you want, is it, lad?" he said aloud, "have the decency, at least, to take off your Starfleet uniform before you dishonor it!" But it was absurd, and O'Brien abruptly felt the uneasy indecency. Worf could never betray them. Something— *something*—must have happened to the Klingon . . . something horrible.

Worf looked up toward the porthole. For an instant, it almost seemed as if their eyes met. In Worf's face, O'Brien saw only a cold, emotionless determination, an inhuman but thoroughly Klingon savagery that spoke of imperial fantasies and glorious dreams— *Worf the Magnificent! Worf the Terrible!* Worf the traitor was making his name in the Empire by sacking his own former post! The pain struck O'Brien like the sharp point of a *bat'telh* beneath his ribs, and he realized he was clenching his teeth so hard his jaw throbbed. *No, it's stupid. Worf* couldn't *be a traitor—it's not possible for his Klingon brain.*

But Worf gave no sign of recognition. He did not smile and wink, or call the troopers' attention and bang outside to fire on the two men. Instead, his eyes passed along without a moment's pause, without even a flicker of surprise . . . either Worf had never seen O'Brien, or else he had a promising career as an actor.

Lieutenant Commander, now Brevet Colonel, Worf scanned the crossover corridor, hoping *not* to find who he was looking for. From the description given by the corporal of the guard, there was no question the corridor had moments before contained Miles O'Brien and some other person, probably a female, judging from the physique.

O'Brien! Worf silently cursed his luck that he, Worf, wasn't safely aboard the *Defiant* when the attack had come. It wasn't cowardice or lack of confidence that he would somehow be able to thwart the invasion, it was the certainty of what his "treason" was doing to his honor. *Comrades in arms at each other's throat,* he thought bitterly, *with my blood-brother pulling the strings. I should enjoy it . . . it is a Klingon opera!*

As the soldiers made happy, grunting noises rooting around for the Federation escapees, Worf tracked his eyes up and down the corridor, wondering where they had managed to hide. Perhaps he could contrive to miss the spot in his search? Then he turned to glance at the porthole, and the sight he saw nearly stopped his heart: O'Brien was *outside looking in*—without a pressure suit!

It was absolute, utter madness. *I have gone insane, and now I see ghosts and hallucinations!* It took every erg of willpower the Klingon possessed not to make a sign, gesture, or even just stare. He managed, barely, not to give any outward indication of what he had seen.

"There is nothing here," snarled Worf, shoving the nearest man into a group of soldiers bending over. Two of them toppled, but they forbore to challenge his authority. "Go away! Kleeg and Drach saw shadows of their own bloodlust—there are no Starfleets here!"

* * *

After conferring, Worf moved the soldiers further down the corridor, leaving Bashir and O'Brien hanging tight. "They're gone," said the chief, trying to force his shoulders to untense. It was impossible, and they began to spasm.

"Now what?" asked Bashir. He seemed in better spirits now that the Klingons had passed and the pair were still free and alive.

O'Brien took a deep breath, feeling explosive pressure behind his eyeballs. It wasn't decompression. The force came from his sinuses, and behind them, his brain, what he had just seen. Reluctantly, he told Bashir what he had seen: Worf, leading the expedition! Worf, hunting for them at the head of a pack of Klingons!

"That's ridiculous!"

"You think I'm *lying*, Julian?"

"Of course not!"

"But I saw him—Worf is leading the invasion."

"Of course not! Chief, there has to be another explanation. Did he have a disruptor to his back?"

"No."

"A frightened expression on his face?"

"Not in the least!"

"Well, how about a dour and angry expression?"

"Of course; he always has that."

"Well, there's your answer! They threatened him with something."

"Julian, he looked . . . determined. I saw him when he looked right at me: he wasn't scared; he was *efficient.*"

"He looked right at you?"

"Through the porthole. I guess he couldn't see me through the glass. But I'll never forget that expression; he was absolutely grim and determined—Julian, he really is behind this whole thing!" The chief pressed his head back against the outer skin of the station. *He can't be. He can't be. Maybe Julian can think of an explanation!*

"You're bounding from one ice-floe of conclusion to another," grumbled the doctor. "But what next?"

"I already told you, Julian. This is war. Worf's asked for it, he deserves it." *You don't truly believe that, Miles!*

"My God, Chief. You've known him since your *Enterprise* days. What are you saying? You think *he* has anything to do with this? You know he's no traitor!"

O'Brien looked down at the thin, wiry doctor, once again feeling the pang of jealousy at everything Bashir had that the chief didn't: good looks, thin waist, a license to cut and paste, women dripping off of him. *But he doesn't have Keiko,* thought O'Brien, *or Molly either. And they're worth fighting for.* "Comrade once, maybe, but he showed his true colors pretty damned quick! There are some things, Julian, you simply don't forgive." The chief shook his head. "I don't know . . . maybe he's been drugged or hypnotized. It seems pretty damned incredible, if you ask me." O'Brien shook his head. "What next indeed? If *Worf* can be seduced by his dark side, any one of us could be next."

Bashir rolled his eyes. "I *meant,* Chief, what do we do next *right now?* Worf has no dark side. Put aside your emotions and think more logically. He must be—I don't know, setting a trap for the Klingons? Maybe?"

O'Brien shook his head. "God, I hope you're right. I just can't picture Worf as a traitor to Starfleet, but if he is, we're in a quadrant of hurt. Come, we'd better rush, pop back in behind them, and make a run for the habitat ring. You really think anyone's going to be waiting for us in Cargo Bay Four?"

"You can rely on it," said Bashir, sounding an awful lot more certain of himself than he looked.

O'Brien gently opened the door, careful not to slip and "fall outward"; that would get him to the habitat ring an awful lot faster than he wanted, and it would be a chilly cold trip. He struggled himself up to a half-pull-up. "This used to be so much easier a few years ago!"

"You mean a few kilograms ago," retorted Bashir. The chief pretended he hadn't heard.

Struggling into the crossover corridor on his belly, he

turned to help the doctor, but Bashir whipped himself up and vaulted inside, landing on his feet. O'Brien glared, but said nothing. He led the way along the catwalk, sneaking as much as possible with hard-soled boots on a metal grill.

"Well, maybe that explains one thing," said Chief O'Brien, as they peeked cautiously around the lip of the turbolift shaft, looking for patrols.

"What explains what?"

"Why the Klingons haven't been killing us, Julian. It's Worf. Even if he's playing the traitor to fool the invaders, he wouldn't actually *murder* his crewmates."

Bashir raised his eyebrows. "That makes sense. Surely something is staying their hand. I've never seen a kinder, gentler Klingon assault."

"Well, here's at least where we get to even the odds a bit." He sidled to a weapons-storage locker, leaned close, and whispered "Emergency lock-override, O'Brien ro-delta-omega." Silence; the locker did not respond. "Pickup must be off," he muttered, tapping at the circuit with his finger.

"All right," said Dr. Bashir, "any more brilliant ideas?"

O'Brien stared, then pounded the locker with his fist. "They must've scrambled the damned codes! What vicious bastard thought of *that?*"

"Oh come on, Chief, it's not hard! If you're invading a station, you don't want the inhabitants shooting at your back."

"Of course. That makes perfect sense." The chief paused for a beat, then lunged at the door, yanking on it and hissing obscenities that made the gentlemanly Bashir blanch and put his fingers in his ears. It was, of course, a *weapons locker:* built to take a knocking and keep on locking.

"Perfect!" snarled O'Brien, punching it one last time. "What *else* is going to go wrong?"

The locker between chief and doctor abruptly lit up

like a Yule tree, and sparks showered off the shell into O'Brien's face. He whirled to face the Klingon, twenty meters distant along the habitat ring main corridor and sighting his second shot.

Instinctively, O'Brien threw up his hands to cover his face, and the disruptor struck his right palm. He yelped once, then clenched his teeth—his hand was on fire! In fact, his hand itself was numbed and the nerve endings spasming in agony, it was his sleeve that was actually aflame. He smothered it against his stomach as Bashir shoved him away from the Klingon, who, having failed with aimed shots, was now attempting spray-fire.

Fortunately, he was no better at that mode—*an uncoordinated Klingon! what're the odds?*—and neither escapee was struck. They quickly lost the soldier in the maze of twisting hallways and corridors, led by O'Brien, surefooted even while gasping in agony. Cargo Bay Four was another hundred degrees along the circle of the habitat ring, only a few minutes away—unless the next Klingon sharpshooter they ran into had actually *passed* the marksmanship test.

CHAPTER
14

JAKE TOOK HIS turn at guarding the cargo bay from a position some distance from the bickering Ferengi. He didn't want to hear them, and he felt like a voyeur at a family spat.

Quark and Rom never seemed to tire of sniping at each other and each had his own technique. Quark would overtly insult his brother: "You're *such* a profitable ambassador for the Ferengi, Rom; you go to work for a hu-man, your son joins Starfleet, you join a *strike* in my bar, and you get our entire family declared outlaws! What's next? Will you visit Ferenginar and make the sun go nova?"

Rom, in response, would play the "dumb Ferengi" while more-or-less subtly hinting that Quark was a half-witted failure, all accomplished while cringing in the proper Ferengi style of junior to senior brother: "Uh, sorry, brother. I don't mean to be such a disappointment to you. I shouldn't have kept you here, where it's so hard to make a profit. Uh, is the bar doing any better, now that you don't have to pay me?"

Jake rolled his eyes. He was so distracted by the bickering that he almost missed the faint creak of metal on metal. He leapt up from his seat, a box labeled "Danger! Highly Explosive!" and fumbled with the huge phase-wrench he had rustled up. It was as close to a weapon as he could find.

Turning wildly in every direction and hissing for silence, Jake finally located the noise. It came from a vent high over his head, at least four meters off the deck. The vent bent outward, then, with a loud click, it detached from its mounts and dropped noisily to the metal floor, followed by the soft cursing of Chief O'Brien.

The chief dropped reasonably lightly into the room, but one arm dangled limply. He was followed immediately by Dr. Bashir.

Garak stepped from the shadows in which he had secreted himself. "Welcome, Doctor! I see you got my message."

O'Brien stared at Garak, then Bashir, then back at the Cardassian. "You're not serious, are you? That really *was* a message from you?"

Garak bowed stiffly at the waist. "It brought you here, didn't it?"

Jake stepped forward. "We haven't seen any other survivors. I think—I think they're all . . ." He couldn't say it, the lump in his throat prevented further speech.

"No, they're not," said Bashir, smiling and putting his hand on Jake's shoulder. "The Klingons have been quite assiduous about *not* killing any of the residents of the station, so far as I can tell. At least, they threw me into a pile of stunned bodies—stunned, not dead—and when a Klingon patrol shot at us, they were using their disruptors on the lowest setting. Otherwise, the chief would be looking at limb-regen now."

The youngest Sisko stared at Bashir. His heart felt as if it froze in his chest then began to pound at twice the normal rate. *Alive!* "They're—all alive? All of them?" He suddenly remembered to breathe and gasped for air.

"I think so," confirmed O'Brien. "We haven't found any corpses. I think they put everybody in porta-cells inside the Promenade shops."

Jake bit his lip, wondering if he should say something about Worf, but Bashir and O'Brien had a right to know—and in any event, neither Quark nor Garak had any love for the Klingon security officer. "Chief," he began, but O'Brien was engaged in a cheery reunion with Rom and wasn't paying attention. "Dr. Bashir? I have some bad . . . I mean, I saw something that I think you should know. It's about a certain Klingon we all know—"

"The one leading the assault? Yes, we saw Commander Worf somewhat earlier."

After a moment, Jake remembered to shut his mouth. "Well, what are we going to do about it?"

Bashir looked confused. "Why are you asking me?"

Garak smirked. "Because, my dear Julian, *you* are the highest ranking officer—in fact, the only commissioned officer—in our little resistance group."

"But . . . but you, Garak! You're in the—I mean, you *were* in the Obsidian Order! They practically invented covert warfare. Can't you—?"

"Doctor, I am but a humble tailor! You are the man with pips on your collar."

Dr. Bashir hesitated only a moment. "Well, I suppose I am. All right, let's gather our resources together and see what we have. Does anybody have a weapon? Quark?"

The Ferengi scowled and kicked another explosives box. "I *had* a weapon, a phaser rifle."

"Excellent!"

"Except that *somebody* seems to have drained it completely and left a nasty note in the battery receiver."

Bashir's mouth pursed, and he grunted in annoyance. Jake held up his wrench. "I have a club."

"Club!" exploded the chief. "That's a fine, precision piece of equipment, Jake!"

"Well," said the doctor, "unless we find a bit of wiring that needs to be adjusted, it's a club."

Hesitantly, Rom stepped forward, showing O'Brien the encrypted Klingon handset he had unsuccessfully tried to rewire. "Uh, Chief, can you decrypt this comm link? I think that static is, um, the Klingons talking to each other. Maybe we can get a fix and avoid them."

"Or track 'em down and shoot 'em," muttered O'Brien, taking the handset from Rom with his good hand. "Oh. Yeah, I can pick this thing with Julian's tricorder. Or rather, I could, if I hadn't been shot. Rom, you're going to have to be my hands."

The chief turned to Jake, who was trying to follow that conversation and the one between Bashir and Garak about resistance strategy simultaneously. "Jake, I have a bit of wiring that needs adjusting, and I think I'll be needing that phase-wrench now. That is, if you don't need it to hammer nails or crack walnuts for the next few minutes."

Wordlessly, Sisko the Younger handed it to the chief and pointedly went to sit next to Quark; the Ferengi appeared not to appreciate the company. Jake allowed his mind to wander, and he found himself back on Earth, in his grandfather's restaurant. He sat in a booth at the back eating jambalaya and writing about his adventure on a deep-space station under attack by Klingons. *It always seems so much more* survivable *in novels and holo-plays.*

No, not Klingons. Klingons were so . . . outre. *Or is that* passe? *Always get those two mixed up. Nobody's going to believe Klingons, not in this day and age.* Jake squirmed deeper into his fantasy, relieved at not having to be scared, for just a few moments, at least. *Aliens,* *unknown, faceless aliens. Power suits. Oh, wait a minute—this is good! They use some really horrible weapon, not a nice, clean death ray like a disruptor, but a—*He grinned. No, it was too perfect. The aliens would use some super form of *firearm!* An actual gunpowder weapon that fired bullet after bullet, tearing up the station: faceless monsters in power suits with—what was the word?—with *machine guns.* "It could work," he mumbled aloud. Except that in real life, of course, everyone would have to die. In fiction, the author could brazenly bring them all back to life again. *Ah, that's why I don't write science fiction,* he sighed.

He was jolted from his reverie by O'Brien's triumphant crow of "That's it, you've gotten it, Rom. Here, gather around. Let's listen in on the Klingons."

Dr. Bashir took back his tricorder and leaned over the handset. The Klingon messages were as far from fascinating as they could be. The officers spoke tersely, moving squads and four-man teams around the station to hunt those few defenders remaining free. "Maybe if we listen long enough," said Jake, "we can start mapping where they are?"

"Excellent idea, Jake," said Lieutenant Bashir. "You're in charge of tracking the Klingon troop-movements."

Jake almost objected, but he caught himself. He'd opened up his big mouth and "volunteered" himself for the duty. Besides, it was certainly more interesting than standing between Quark and Rom during one of their familial spats. Jake Sisko fished in his sealed pocket for his KlipRite and stylus and activated the station route-mapper. Every few minutes, whenever a Klingon officer sent some warriors on a mission, Jake would attempt to figure out where they were going: the invaders didn't use the standard, Starfleet designation for the rooms and areas of the station, of course. He marked the troop concentrations on the map as best he could.

It was difficult writing or even viewing the screen in the gloom of Cargo Bay 4. It was especially tough to continuously strain his ears to listen to the chatter on the Klingon comm link, rather than listen to the boistrous discussion that had sprung up between Garak and Chief O'Brien. "Damn his Klingon hide!" snapped the chief. "What the hell is he up to? Why doesn't he tell us what he's doing?"

"That is simply the way they are," said Garak, shaking his head.

"They? Which *they* do you mean?" O'Brien's voice held an undercurrent of irritation.

"Klingons, of course," said Garak, failing to notice the looming shift in Chief O'Brien's body position. Jake smiled to himself; despite his smug certainties, Garak really knew very little about humans. *When a man calls his comrade a bastard, the worst thing you can do is agree with him!*

Having stepped into the quicksand, the tailor continued to stand pat, oblivious to the fact that he was sinking fast. "Well, I'm sure we've all learned a lesson about the so-called honor of Klingons. Perhaps in the future, you will listen to this older, wiser head when he tells you that the two things you can rely upon in this quadrant are that quality will rise to the top and that Klingons will betray you the first chance they get."

Jake tried to return to the map. The Klingons were following a strange, almost random search pattern. Something seemed out of kilter about it, but Jake wasn't sure exactly what was wrong.

He was just about to ask the chief what he thought when O'Brien turned on the Cardassian in sudden vehemence, slipping in an instant into the role of court-appointed counsel for the defendant. "And just what is that supposed to mean? Let me tell you something, Mr. Obsidian Order. I would trust Worf with my life—with my family's lives! And I wouldn't trust *you* as far as I could kick you!"

"Well, that is certainly the attitude I would expect from a Federation subject." Garak folded his arms and chuckled. "You have eyes, but you do not see. Chief, Worf is *leading the invasion*. You saw him yourself in the crossover tunnel. When will the Federation grow up and accept reality for what it is? It's a Cardassian trait you would do well to emulate."

Now O'Brien began to get angry. He stepped well inside Garak's "zone" and confronted the Cardassian. "Well how do *you* know what hold this Klingon general, whatever his name is, has over Worf? Did you ever think that maybe he's holding Alexander hostage, or he's threatening to blow up the station if Worf doesn't cooperate?"

"That may explain, but it doesn't excuse," lectured Garak.

"And how do you know Worf isn't really on *our* side, going along with the invasion until he's in a position to do something about it?"

Garak snorted, shaking his head. "The human capacity for wishful thinking never ceases to amaze. I certainly know enough about betrayal by friends to—"

"Oh, I'm sure you do!"

Frustrated, Garak was just about to respond when Jake thought he heard something important over the handset. "Quiet!" he shouted. "Dr. Bashir, can you make everyone shut up for a moment?" Jake listened in silence, hoping that some Klingon on the other end would request clarification or repeat of the orders.

At last, the disembodied voice over the handset continued to detail the patrols: "Search the cargo bays on the outer ring," she said, "starting with the one opposite the prison cells."

Desperately, Jake scrolled the map up and down, trying to find Odo's office and the attached brig. At last, he located it and tacked directly outward to the corresponding spot on the habitat ring: the Klingons were searching Cargo Bay 3, and depending on whether they decided to go clockwise or not, their own hiding place might be the very next one searched.

Julian Bashir began issuing orders in a crisp command tone, hoping he sounded an awful lot more confident and full of "military bearing" than he felt. "Chief, find us a way out of here other than the main doors. Everybody else, pick up any evidence of our presence here and hold it or stow it on your person. We can't let them know how few we are, or even that we were hiding here!"

O'Brien ran first to one side of the bay, then the other, hunting for an access vent low enough that they could reach. The one he had Bashir entered by was obviously far out of reach. At last, he whirled in frustration. "Julian, the only thing we can climb up into without an antigrav unit is a dead-end storage locker."

"It's better than here, Chief."

"But if they have a tricorder—"

"I can hear them right outside the door!" stage-whispered Jake, who had stationed himself near the entrance.

"No choice, Chief," Bashir ordered. He had a sinking feeling that his command was to be short-lived. O'Brien was right: all the Klingons would need to do was sweep the room with a tricorder, and they would find the escapees in a moment.

The chief made a step with his hands, hoisting the Ferengi up first because they were the lightest, then Jake. Then O'Brien and the Cardassian began doing the "after you, no after *you*" routine. After two rounds of this, an exasperated Garak picked up the chief bodily and hoisted him into the hole, leaping up to scramble inside himself. *Ah, the advantages of Cardassian musculature,* sighed Bashir to himself. He barely made it up after his troops, pulled by Garak and O'Brien together, when the doors slid open and a platoon of efficient-looking Klingon warriors entered the room.

They fell into a defensive phalanx, searching the room

visually before moving from their spot near the open doors, ready for a quick retreat if there had happened to be an army of occupation-resisters lurking inside. Bashir stayed in the shadows, watching them. Not even Klingon eyes were able to see in total darkness, he knew, but then the non-com in charge snarled, "Tricorder, scan the room."

Bashir snorted. He had a fleeting impulse to leap from his hiding place and charge across the room, hoping to draw the platoon's attention. But he knew it wouldn't work. Klingons didn't fall for the old misdirection trick. One or two of them would cut him down, and the rest would search the hole he had just left.

"We're dead meat," muttered O'Brien, who had also heard the order, evidently.

"Not if I can help it," said Garak mysteriously.

A warrior stepped from behind the other six and unlimbered a clumsy, wicked-looking Klingon toy. He started at one corner and began a slow, careful scan, arcing counterclockwise. Bashir gritted his teeth and tried to smile reassuringly, not that anyone could see him.

There was a movement behind the doctor. He heard a faint whirring noise begin. Dimly, from the corner of his eye, Bashir thought he saw a flicker of amber before the light was quickly hidden by a hand. The noise was very high frequency and quite faint, but it seemed to pulse.

When the Klingon's tricorder was pointed directly at them, the faint whirring behind the doctor rose in pitch and intensity markedly, and the Klingon continued right past! The warrior saw absolutely nothing on his tricorder, despite it being pointed directly at three humans, two Ferengi, and a Cardassian tailor holding a hissing light source cupped in his leathery hands.

The Klingon finished his sweep. "No humanoid life-forms except for ourselves," he reported in the guttural language of the invaders, instantly decoded by the universal-translator implant in Bashir's ear.

The troops milled about a little, turning over a few boxes and shining hand torches on the ground to look for telltales of recent habitation. Evidently finding nothing to interest them, they moseyed off, disruptors held at port arms as they marched. The door shut, and silence reigned once more in Cargo Bay 4.

Bashir stared after them for a moment, then back to Garak. The Cardassian crouched directly behind the doctor, watching with wide-eyed intensity; he held nothing in his hands. "Garak, what *was* that thing you used?"

"Thing? Dr. Bashir, could you perhaps be a bit more specific?"

Bashir grew annoyed. "That device you just used to nullify the tricorder field! I've never even heard of such a thing. Where did you get it?"

"Doctor, I really have no idea what you're talking about. I'm a simple tailor. I have no access to super-secret tricorder suppressors. I'm not an intergalactic spy!" He leaned close, whispering conspiratorially in Bashir's ear, "or *am* I?"

"Garak, I don't know whether anybody else saw you, but I saw, and I know what you just did."

"When a man has kicked around as long as I have, he picks up certain, shall we say, toys, tricks of tradecraft, so to speak. Is that entirely unreasonable?"

"So you admit you're a member of the Obsidian Order. You still even have spy paraphernaila—a tricorder field-suppressor, for goodness's sake!"

The Cardassian winked. "Well, let's just keep it our little secret, shall we?"

"Keep what a secret?" asked Jake, crawling from the back of the L-shaped storage locker.

"Never mind," said O'Brien. "*Sir,* hadn't we better get out of here, before that patrol comes back?" Bashir didn't quite like the way O'Brien had been saying "sir" since the doctor took charge, but he let it slide.

"On the contrary," said Bashir, "this is probably the

safest place on the whole station right now. Why search a space that you've just cleared?"

Quark, who seemed already to have grown tired of the novelty of creeping around the station like a cat burglar interrupted. "So we're staying here for a while? Does anybody have anything to eat? I guess we can't use the replicators." Rom opened his mouth, but Quark glared his brother into silence.

"We're staying put for now," agreed Bashir. "But it's time we stopped running and started coming up with a plan to beat that—that traitor Worf." *There, I said it.* Bashir waited for a retort from O'Brien, but the chief just stared downward, sullenly fascinated by the deck-plate design. O'Brien couldn't deny his own eyes.

"Chief, you know *Deep Space Nine* better than any man here," continued the doctor. "Where can we go to override the forceshield that's stopping communications, so we can somehow send a message to Bajor?"

"Well, ultimately we might have to don pressure suits and go outside. The whole subspace emitter superstructure is obliterated. The Klingons drove their bird-of-prey right through it."

"So how can we send a message?"

"We can't. Not without the subspace emitter. It's the only structure large enough to stick outside the field. That's why they sheared it off, I suppose."

"Then what's your idea?"

The chief hesitated. "Well, maybe if we could get some transmitter outside the range of the communications shield, something that could broadcast automatically—"

"You mean like a probe?" asked Bashir, seeing some solid hope.

"Exactly. Except a probe wouldn't work. The electronics would light up all the sensors on the bird-of-prey like Bajoran festival bushes."

"So," summarized Garak, "the Klingons would detect

it and blow it to constitutent atoms before it even cleared the blanking field. Nor, of course, have we any access to such a probe. And the Klingons control all the launch facilities anyway. A brilliant plan, Chief O'Brien!"

"Well, I admit it has a few rough spots," mumbled the chief.

"Please, gentlemen, we're still in the brainstorming phase," said Bashir, trying to take charge of the situation, as the manual instructed. *What a truly awful feeling . . . being in command when there's nothing one can do!* "First, let's see if we can't figure out the pattern of the Klingon searches, so we know where they're going to be looking."

"But that's just it," said Jake. "I was tracking them before, on my padd, and I noticed that the search parties keep crossing and recrossing the same areas, and missing other areas completely. It's really a stupid, mixed-up search pattern. I can't figure it out."

O'Brien suddenly grinned so wide, the corners of his mouth nearly met behind his head. "I was right. I was right!"

"Right about what, Chief?" asked the doctor.

"It's Worf! He hasn't betrayed us . . . *he's leading them in circles!*"

At once, reality began to fall in place. Julian Bashir hadn't realized just how painful was the feeling of betrayal until it began to dissipate. He had never quite accepted the image of Worf as traitor, despite his words (and despite what the conflicted Chief O'Brien had seen). Now, Bashir clutched at the offered straw, praying he wasn't simply yielding to sentiment. *We've got a man inside!* For the first time, he had a realistic hope that resistance might not be so futile after all.

CHAPTER
15

JAKE SISKO LOOKED at Dr. Bashir. The doctor's eyes were unfocused, as if he were staring at a point several kilometers away from the station. Jake turned to Chief O'Brien, who bored a hole in the deckplates with his scowl, a study in red intensity and gray strategy. Garak stroked his angular chin, shifting his eyes left and right. The Ferengi looked at each other, puzzled—Rom scratched his lobes absently, while Quark fingered the buttons on his glittery teal jacket.

There was no longer any question of Worf's loyalties. The question was, what should they do about it? *What would Dad do?* that was how Jake phrased it to himself.

"We've got to send him a message," said Jake, looking down at the beckoning handset. *Yeah, that's what Dad would do!*

"Saying what?" asked Garak in more or less of a sneer. "Good luck betraying your Klingon pals."

Jake's face grew hot, and he closed his mouth firmly,

not wanting to say the first thing that popped into his mind. Besides, the Cardassian's point stung, since Jake had no more idea than Garak of what they could say to Worf.

Rom was not quite so tongue-tied. "Uh, maybe we can tell him to shut down the environmental controls," the Ferengi gingerly suggested. "That ought to slow down the Klingons."

"Oh, *brilliant* idea!" retorted Quark. "Then we can all suffocate and float around the cargo bay like balloons! But we'll have the satisfaction of knowing the Klingons are just as dead as we."

"It was just a thought, brother."

"And so typical of your real-world understanding, Rom!"

"We could get into pressure-suits."

"Rom, shut-up. Let the rest of us common-sense adults work on it. You go sit with Jake."

Jake bristled, almost jumping up to confront the Ferengi barkeep, but then Rom, too, looked toward Jake with irritation, as if the son of the captain were still the thirteen-year-old chum of his own son, Nog. Angry but helpless, Jake settled down to listen with an ill humor.

"The handset idea is good," said the doctor, breaking silence at last. "But what in heaven can we say that will help him in any way?"

O'Brien shrugged. "Another of your secret messages, I suppose."

"Oh, *there's* a good suggestion!" It was Garak again, and Jake smiled in spite of himself.

The chief got a little heated. "Oh come on! Let's not shoot the messenger before the message is even delivered. How about a code of some sort—tell him we're here and where we can rendezvous."

Bashir snorted. "Not a *Klingon* military cipher, I hope! He's *surrounded* by Klingon military personnel, for heaven's sake."

"And," added the Cardassian, "no Federation code is safe either. I'm certain the Klingons have long since cracked them all."

"And what makes you say that?" O'Brien still hadn't forgotten Garak's *last* comment, Jake surmised.

But the chief walked right into Garak's verbal snare. "Because *we* did, Chief O'Brien. And the Klingons may be a bit slower than the Obsidian Order, but they do eventually get where they're going."

Quark spoke up, surprising everyone—especially Jake—with a suggestion that actually made some sense. "How about a pun?"

"Another one?" muttered O'Brien. Jake puzzled over the chief's remark but couldn't make sense of it.

Doctor Bashir smiled. "Yes . . . I like that. That will work, Quark—good suggestion!"

"Julian, Klingons don't have a sense of humor," said the chief.

"But Worf has been living among humans and Bajorans and Trills, and all the rest of us, for years now! Ever since the Khitomer destruction. He's Klingon, and he tries to act like a typical Klingon, but for heaven's sake, he *must* have more of a sense of humor than the rest of them."

"All right, all right! I give up."

Jake tired of sitting silently in the spectator's gallery. "You've got the form," he said, "but where's the content?"

"I beg pardon?" asked Doctor Bashir.

"We're going to send the message *as* a pun, but we still have to figure out *what* message to send."

"Oh. Yes, of course."

Everyone fell to musing. But Jake already had the answer, and a chance to pay Rom back for the little betrayal earlier, when he had looked at Jake as if Quark were banishing Rom to sit at the little kids' table at a party. "I know what message we can send," said Jake.

Dead silence. All eyes turned to the young man, who reveled in his moment, drawing it out to the breaking point.

"Well?" demanded Garak, impatient despite his years as a Cardassian spy, "are you going to tell us telepathically? Or perhaps spit out a word or two, to help us simple souls along?"

"We should tell him to turn off the environmental controls. That ought to slow down the Klingons."

Bashir and O'Brien looked at each other, nodding appreciatively, and Jake felt a sudden pinprick of guilt. Rom said nothing. His idea had been expropriated, but somehow, Jake realized, no one had taken it seriously when the far more qualified Ferengi had made it. Jake caught Rom's eye and tried to apologize with a look, but it only made things worse.

"I like it, Julian. I like it a lot!"

"This could be the key we're looking for."

"But I don't think Worf would have any opportunity to shut down the controls. They must know he's the weakest link in their chain, even if they haven't figured out he's actively fighting against them. This General Malach won't let Worf get anywhere near the environmental controls."

Garak spoke up. "Ah, but *we* have a certain freedom of movement, assuming we don't get caught."

Bashir nodded appreciatively. "Garak knows what he's talking about. This is right up his alley. We'll shut off the artificial gravity ourselves." Then Bashir smiled and got cryptic again. "Aren't you glad now, Falcon, that we spent so much time training for this mission?"

O'Brien rolled his eyes, evidently understanding the message that eluded Jake. "All right, then *we'll* shut down the gravity and evacuate the station. But we have to warn Worf to—"

"Whoa, hold that thought, Chief! Evacuate the station? You mean, dump the air into deep space?" Bashir sounded taken aback, which made sense: Jake was horrified.

"Julian, if we just cut off the station gravity, what good will that do? I'm sure the Klingons train as much in zero-G, or more, maybe, as we do."

Quark was glaring daggers at his brother. *At least one person remembers whose suggestion this was originally,* thought Jake with another slice of guilt. "If I may interject," said the Ferengi, "I repeat my question: if you cut off the gravity and pump out all the air, won't that leave *us* just as dead as the Klingons? Not to mention the Federation prisoners."

"Chief, that's just my point," exclaimed the doctor. "What about the prisoners? We must think of the prisoners! Even if we get into pressure-suits, what about them?"

O'Brien looked stumped. "Well, if we warned him what we were going to do, wouldn't he get them into some kind of protection?"

"Don't you think it would be a tad suspicious," said Garak, "if Worf were to issue pressure-suits to all the prisoners, but not to his own troops?"

"I didn't mean suits! I meant a forceshield of some sort . . . level four, it would have to be, to protect them against vacuum."

"But why would they use level four, Julian? If they're just keeping prisoners from escaping, they would set up a level two or maybe three, wouldn't they?" Again, the chief was stymied.

Jake cleared his throat. "May I make a suggestion?" He waited until he had everyone's attention. "Why don't we send the message. We still have time to decide whether we'll dump the air or not, right Chief?"

O'Brien shrugged. "I guess so. Don't have to decide until we're down in the environmental-control level."

"Then, why don't we work on the message? Doctor Bashir?"

Bashir looked at O'Brien, who looked at Rom, and the glances went all the way around until they came back to Jake. The doctor nodded. "All right, then. Let's work on that message."

You know, Jake realized to his surprise, *I'm suddenly the most qualified man here!* Words were Jake's business, not anyone else's. *Environment,* he thought to himself. *Gravity . . . a grave situation—the gravity of the situation. Yeah, that's it, something about the gravity of the situation!* "Doctor, I think I've got it! Or almost, anyway."

Lieutenant Commander, now *Colonel,* Worf called yet another arbitrary twist in the search pattern, sending the entire platoon of thirty-two Klingon warriors back into the very same rooms they just searched. When Gunnery Sergeant Komanek and Lieutenant "Rodek," Worf's erstwhile (brainwiped) brother Kurn, protested that they were searching very inefficiently, Worf roared and bellowed, *"Are you challenging my authority?"* He accompanied the threat with a vicious blow that sent Gunnery Sergeant Komanek reeling backward and caused him to twist his ankle. Worf couldn't bring himself to strike Kurn—Rodek. Fortunately, the warrior backed down.

The rest of the platoon wisely kept their mouths shut, while Komanek hopped away to beam back to the bird-of-prey for medical care. As Worf led the search team over what he already knew was old, empty territory, his comm link buzzed in his ear.

It was General Malach, Worf's blood-brother and the leader of the assault on *Deep Space Nine.* He spoke over the universal comm link to every Klingon on the station. "Heroes, I have just discovered that one of our guards was incapacitated and his handset was taken from him. He has been appropriately punished and shall remain forever nameless now."

"There is no compromise in our plans. The handset was properly encrypted, and there is no way that the rebellious subjects can listen in on our transmissions or confuse us with their own propaganda and disinformation. All the same, I am ordering my heroes to *stay off the comm link* unless it is a matter of victory or defeat. That is all."

A bright flame of hope glimmered in Worf's brain. O'Brien . . . it *had* to be O'Brien! Who else would have thought of that? More to the point, if it were someone else, then Malach was right: it would do the defenders no good at all.

But Malach did not know Miles Edward O'Brien the way Worf did. The Klingon knew with utter certainty, as only a Klingon can know, that if O'Brien indeed had gotten hold of the handset, he *could* decrypt it and probably already had. Worf decided he must operate under the premise that Chief O'Brien had done so. It was the only hope "Colonel" Worf had to repel the invasion before Gowron decided Malach was victorious and deserved reinforcements.

Almost immediately, a voice spoke over the forbidden comm link. Worf did not recognize the voice, though it spoke in Klingonese. "General Malach, I do not understand the *gravity* of the situation regarding this handset." The speaker clearly overemphasized the word "gravity," raising Worf's suspicions.

For several hours, Worf had contemplated the best way for the remaining Federation defenders to turn the tables on the Klingons, at least long enough to broadcast an emergency message to the Bajorans, but he had arrived at no satisfactory battle plan. Now, something about the message tickled the back of Worf's brain.

"Who said that?" demanded Malach angrily over the same comm link. "You buffoon, switch off your guard frequency if you want to communicate with me or any other officer—that goes for all of you! Switch off the guard channel *immediately!*"

Worf smiled: the guard frequency was a separate channel used only for emergency broadcasts. It was always monitored, but no one would broadcast on it unless he were extraordinarily stupid and incompetent—or he did it intentionally. If the broadcast were intentional, Worf had a very good idea who must have been behind it.

And that meant there *was* a hidden message behind the words, and it was meant for Worf's ears alone.

Another message sputtered in Worf's ears. "My apologies, General. In this *harsh environment,* I neglected to check my handset frequencies . . . a *grave* error, sir."

This time, there was dead silence. It seemed Malach, too, was mulling over the possibilities of who sent the message. Worf continued sending his men searching in a ludicrous and inefficient pattern while his brain churned. If the message was meant only for Worf—it was not O'Brien's voice, but surely the chief was behind it somehow—then it must have been said in a way that no other Klingon would understand. This thought led immediately to the realization that they had gone to some pains to find someone who could speak unaccented Klingon—obviously to disguise the origin, but also, perhaps, to direct Worf's attention to the *language* of the message?

Worf, of course, after so many long years among humans, spoke the standard language of the Federation as well as he spoke his native tongue. He tried translating the message into the language of his adopted parents, and, abruptly, much fell into place. In that language, the word for seriousness, "gravity," was also the word for the accelerative force created by matter and artificially generated by the station. It was what the humans called a "play on words"—the charms of which had always eluded Worf, but he had, at least, studied such subjects while living in the Federation if for no other reason, then for self-protection against secret ridicule at school.

Gravity . . . the station's gravity? Worf quickly remembered his own painful, nauseating experiences with zero-G training at the Academy—and he remembered that such instruction was not taught in any Klingon military academy he had researched. Worf could barely keep a grin of triumph off his face as the full meaning of the message popped into his head entire: the defenders were going to kill the station's gravity generators!

Perhaps not the full meaning, he amended. There was still that equally mysterious broadcast about a "harsh environment." The speaker had seemed as anxious to broadcast that clue as the other.

But now, the painful part: Worf would have to inform O'Brien, or whoever had the stolen handset, that the message was received and understood, and that meant he would incur the wrath of Malach, and perhaps even reveal his own intransigence.

Switching his own command-set to include the guard channel, Worf broadcast his own supposedly "private" message to the general. "Perhaps it was simply an untimely *levity* on someone's part," he said.

"Worf, you *idiot!*" snarled Malach on the private command-circuit. "You are broadcasting to the entire station! You, too, are echoing on guard frequency!"

"My deepest apologies," rumbled Worf, cutting off the guard echo. Once more would push credulity to the breaking point.

The Klingon strike force had quickly rounded up a small number of Federation prisoners of war—and some merchants unlucky enough to have been caught napping—and placed them, at Worf's suggestion, in a makeshift brig made from forcefields in shops along the outer ring of the Promenade, where they would be out of harm's way. By sheer good fortune, not because Worf had anticipated the Federation plan, the brevet colonel had gone beyond the call, demanding not just that the warriors of the Empire place a forcefield across a corner, trapping the prisoners against the walls of the stores, as they normally would have. Instead, Worf had insisted that gas-tight forcefield walls be placed around each entire room, all six sides (four walls, floor, and ceiling).

"To prevent any harm coming to them in the event of a counterstrike by the Federation," Worf had growled in response to Malach's raised eyebrow, and in that he had told the direct, honest truth: whatever Starfleet chose to do, Worf hoped to safeguard the hostages as well as he could.

It turned out to be the most fortunate serendipity that the forcefields would also prevent the prisoners from suffocating if something catastrophic were to happen to the environmental controls, for Worf began to speculate that that might be the second half of the Federation message—presumably from O'Brien, regardless of who spoke. Alas, the hint was too vague: "harsh environment," indeed! It could mean anything.

Worf listened through a long silence following his own broadcast over the guard channel. Even as a young boy of eight, Malach was mentally quicker than virtually anyone else, adults included, in Emperor Kahless Military City. "Worf, Worf, my little brother," he said at last. "So there is still a little bit of rebellion left in you!

"I do not know what secret code you are trying to convey—I will have the computers aboard the *Hiding Fish* work on your message—but it is of no consequence. The few remaining defenders are scattered and helpless before my heroes. You may as well stay off the guard channel and not make an even bigger fool of yourself." Worf did as instructed. He could not possibly get away with another message.

He said nothing more; there was nothing more to say. Either O'Brien knew that Worf understood, or else, by the time Starfleet found out about the loss of *Deep Space Nine,* it would already have been reinforced by Gowron himself: for the raid was a test. At that point, Starfleet Command, faced with the prospect of a major assault on their own station (with its own contingent of a *thousand* photon torpedoes), would probably back down and negotiate for some face-saving exchange. Gowron and Malach would have won.

The resulting animosity between the Federation and the Empire might well be enough to allow the Dominion to play one side against the other, despite Malach's best intentions for a strong defense. *For all of our sakes,* thought Worf, *I hope the chief is at least half as smart as he thinks he is!*

Worf gathered his bored, straggling platoon. They had figured out that the new colonel had made a stupid mistake, but were reluctant to offer the improving criticism for fear of joining the gunny back on the bird-of-prey's infirmary. "It is time to search in a brand, new location," commanded Colonel Worf. "First *stance!* Right *turn!* Forward, *step!*" Worf started the platoon marching toward the exact, opposite side of the habitat ring. *I have a feeling,* he thought, *it is going to be a good, long, slow march.*

Worf smiled. It was now time to eliminate one thorn in his side, and at the same time send one more assurance to Chief O'Brien. Colonel Worf summoned Major Krugus, the eyes and mouth of Malach, and pulled him back from the rest. "Do you see that turbolift, Major?" As if to emphasize the point, "Colonel" Worf harshly grabbed the back of Krugus's head and wrenched it around to look in the correct direction.

"Yes, I do have eyes, Colonel!" The warrior was the eleventh child of an old and honorable house. He was a fearsome warrior, and were it not for the accident of birth order, Rimakag Aganandaf would surely have been elevated to general officer by now. But in Gowron's rigid caste system, an eleventh child struck his glass ceiling at major.

Annoyed as Krugus was at Worf's assumption of superiority, he did not even notice that the hand lingered just a bit too long on Krugus's battle-helmet. "I want you to find General Malach and repeat the following message *word for word,* exactly as I give it to you."

"I will obey, O grotesquely mighty one."

Worf snarled and clenched his teeth at the back-handed slur, but he held his temper. The man was a master at saying just enough without saying too much, at baiting young superior officers into striking him—which, under Klingon law, was the only action that ever allowed a major to strike back at a colonel.

"This is the message: The *weight* of our assault should focus on the habitat ring, where we have left too much of a force *vacuum.*"

The major nodded curtly and left. Worf returned to his platoon and led them in another clumsy, ill-thought, meandering search of the decks for escapees, who surely would have heard the newly minted colonel barking orders loudly enough to be heard in the next quadrant.

Some minutes later, Worf was gratified to hear his comm link sputter to life. The major loudly repeated the confusing message Worf had given him, because he was speaking, he never noticed that every word was being broadcast over the same guard frequency that Worf and the first, unknown, voice had accidentally used . . . the same frequency he had accidentally activated on Krugus's helmet comm link while "accidentally" switching the broadcast mode to "hot mike," which broadcast everything spoken to the entire station.

A moment later, Worf's personal headset whispered in his ear, a sibilant hiss that he knew was *not* being echoed anywhere. "So, what treasonous ice are you skating across, my brother? Can this be some prearranged signal?" Malach paused for a moment, thinking deeply. "No. I cannot imagine you would have guessed such a plan as mine was possible. But you *are* conveying our every move to that Starfleet pig who stole the handset . . . a swine I am now convinced you somehow gave the decryption code. I have, of course, taken care of your treasonous ally, Major Krugus, though how you turned him, I confess I cannot imagine."

"Are you calling me a *traitor?*" Worf demanded of Malach in an outraged tone of voice. He broadcast only along the command circuit.

"But it makes no difference. It does not matter. Hear this, my brother!" Worf heard a click, then a slight buzz. He realized that Malach had just widened the broadcast to include every Klingon on *Deep Space Nine.* "Attention, heroes of the Empire! Our comm link has been compromised. Upon pain of immediate discommodation, there will be no more broadcasts. All further communication will be conducted by hand-signals and runners. Any voice you hear besides mine will be an enemy attempting to befuddle. That is all."

The buzz stopped, and Malach returned to the private command channel. "As a boy, you were no match for my intellect, Worf. And even as a man, you fall short. I have given you a chance at redemption from your own people, do not cast it away to honor those who are without honor!"

"I will not tolerate being called dishonorable!" bellowed Worf.

Malach did not rise to the bait. "You are a noble hero of a noble house. Come back to us; come back to your people. Gowron is like an angry father who must discipline his son but still *loves* his son."

"I am not a child!"

"He opens his arms to you, Worf! The Empire welcomes you back. Do not push us away. Do not push away the plate of honor untasted."

But despite his defiant words, Worf felt himself weaken, perhaps he was wrong after all. Maybe his duty to the Empire *was* greater than his duty to the oath he swore as a Starfleet officer. After all, it was not like the bad old days of expansionism, when the Klingon Empire wanted nothing less than despotic rule over the entire Alpha Quadrant.

What was Malach asking, was it really too much? He wanted—*Gowron* wanted—a strong defense against the most dangerous enemies they had ever met, Federation and Empire alike. The Founders were shapeshifters, and without a rigid screening process that would make a mockery of the Federation's soft-hearted (*soft-headed*, Worf corrected) ideas about "freedom" and "individual rights," the Founders would gradually replace more and more of the Federation's leaders, until one black day, the entire Alpha Quadrant woke up to realize it had "softly and suddenly vanished away," to be replaced by a new province of the Dominion.

Worf had already seen what decades, *centuries* of peace and indolence had done to—what was the phrase he had read in the letter?—to the grasping tentacles of the Federation, stretched infinitely far, infinitesmally thin. Today, the same people who had many times beaten back the massed warships of the Empire could no longer handle even a few raindrops on their precious pleasure-planet!

Take away their phasers and replicators and holo-suites, their transporters and medical miracles, and deposit them naked on the surface of a world no more dangerous than their own had been a few centuries ago, and how many of the highest-ranking officers in Starfleet would even survive, let alone be able to rebuild a civilization? Try as he might, Worf could not imagine *anyone* referring to the "heroes of the United Federation of Planets," unless in cold sarcasm.

So was Malach, his blood-brother, really so wrong after all?

Worf shook his head and ordered his platoon to double back upon itself to search the other end of the habitat ring. The resulting traffic jam among the ranks and file occupied his men for several minutes. *The problem with an Empire of heroes and warriors*, he realized, *is that none of us wants to be servants or soldiers*. Right or wrong, Worf could never imagine himself living his life to bring glory to another . . . Malach or Gowron. And that, after all was said, was what heroing was all about: who eats and who is eaten. The ultimate futility of that philosophy, more than his oath, was what had made Worf a Starfleet lieutenant-commander rather than a Klingon hero.

And that was why Malach was truly wrong after all. After two centuries, the Empire had become the *antithesis* to the Federation's thesis, with the Alpha Quadrant as the synthesis of the two—if the Federation became the Empire to save the quadrant, or if Empire turned into Federation, it would destroy the synthesis, and neither confederation of worlds could stand.

Sighing, Worf overtook his platoon and led them from the front, as befitted a hero of the Empire. He began a slow circuit of the habitat ring, desperately hoping that Chief O'Brien would turn out to have somewhat more of a sense of humor than he ever had demonstrated in the past.

CHAPTER
16

GARAK MADE A sour face. *He* hates *speaking in Klingonese,* realized Jake, *more even than the rest of us.* The Cardassians had had their own troubles with the Klingon Empire, long before the Cardassians ever met the Federation.

"Well," said Chief O'Brien, his brogue thicker than usual. "Well, that's two responses, as I make it. One from Worf himself, one from someone saying he was speaking for Worf. Is that good enough for you, Julian?"

The doctor shook his head. He was still reticent about evacuating the station, and Jake couldn't blame him. If Worf had somehow missed that part of the message, and if the prisoners were in unprotected, low-force pens, they would all die! It was a terrible gamble, but Jake Sisko was convinced where Dr. Bashir was not yet.

"I said you could *say* we were going to pump out all the air, Chief. I haven't yet decided whether we really can do it."

Quark had looked more and more incredulous as the

discussion continued. "Surely you're not—not *serious!*" he sputtered at last. "Even in pressure-suits, what are we going to do? We'll be balloons, I tell you . . . air-filled balloons bouncing helplessly around the station!"

Rom said nothing, and his back was turned to his brother, but that gave Jake a perfect view of a huge, wicked grin of sharpened snaggle-teeth. Rom was enjoying his brother's discomfiture!

O'Brien tried one more argument. "Julian, it's the only thing we can do . . . and if we don't do *something,* we're going to lose this station and probably everybody on board anyway."

The doctor shook his head, eyes closed. "We don't know that, Chief. But, we have sat here long enough contemplating our navels. I suggest we . . ." Bashir shrugged and gestured toward the door.

Jake moved toward the front of the column without thinking, but Bashir gently pulled him back behind Chief O'Brien, who was a few centimeters shorter, but made a wider target than the younger man. O'Brien approached the door, which snapped open without a care in the world. 'Twas Cardassian, then Federation, and now Klingon, and had been slave to thousands. The tiny brigade filed out. O'Brien looked carefully both directions, and Jake couldn't resist a quick left-right himself.

Jake still held on to the now-useless handset. He looked at his school padd, unfocusing his eyes to mentally superimpose the station diagram on their present position. "Sir," he said to Dr. Bashir, "last word we got, there was a heavy Klingon troop concentration two levels below us, working up. They could be here by now."

Garak looked at the padd as Jake held it up. "Chief, is there any way we can get down to the level of the crossover tunnel without crossing any major ladderwells or turbolift shafts? We really don't want to run into

Worf's patrol. He might not be able to stop them from stunning us."

O'Brien looked pensive. "Well, ordinarily I would say sure, if it were just me and Rom. My arm has finally stopped tingling, no thanks to our good witch-doctor." Bashir snorted, sounding almost as officious as Odo; the chief took no notice. "But I'm not so sure the rest of you can climb an unprotected ladder down four levels."

"Unprotected?"

"I mean no fall-guards, like staggered platforms. Our Cardassian friends didn't see much need for safety features."

"That is because we Cardassians assume our crewmen and servants to be competent and free from disabling phobias," sniffed Garak. "I would have no trouble climbing the antenna-well ladder, if that is what you mean; I've climbed it several times before."

"You have?" asked the doctor. "Now why would a Cardassian *tailor* find occasion to use the antenna well to sneak through a Cardassian station without detection by Gul Dukat?"

Jake smiled. The chief always enjoyed baiting Garak. *By now,* he thought, *everyone on DS9 must know Garak was a Cardassian spy.*

Garak smiled lazily, evidently enjoying the game as well. "Private fitting," he said. "And who said it was during the *Cardassian* tenure of Terek Nor?"

"Yeah," said O'Brien. "I mean the antenna well. You think you're all up to it? Jake, Quark?"

The elder Ferengi rolled his eyes. "If my brother can climb the ladder, then certainly I can! Rom isn't exactly Mr. Dexterity."

Jake just nodded. In fact, he did not at all savor the thought of climbing four levels—Cardassian-sized levels at that—down a naked ladder spaced for Cardassian limbs. But his only options were to stay behind alone or compromise the entire team's effectiveness, and these were no choices at all.

The mob headed for the door, trotting as quietly as they could, even Quark ceased grumbling and walked in subdued silence as they entered the dead, silent corridors of *Deep Space Nine*. After a few moments, Jake heard the sounds of guttural speech, the words indistinguishable but the tone of voice unmistakable. He pushed the mental picture of a mob of angry Klingons from his mind and followed behind the doctor, the tailor, the maintenance chief.

Down the black-dark corridor and through an unobtrusive doorway, hopping over a series of holes in the deckplates (where Rom had been working a day earlier), squeezing between a bank of cyan-glowing tubes that lit the company with an eerie phosphorescence, O'Brien led the sapper squad to a scaffold that only Jake and Garak could reach unaided. The pair clambored up and pulled the rest after. It took the two of them, plus Bashir on the bottom, to pull up the chief. Jake began to sweat. The air vents this deep in the bowels of *Deep Space Nine* never did work well—they were Federation add-ons—and there was no workable way to drain off the excess heat generated by humanoid bodies and radiate it to space, as there was in the rest of the station. But Jake was also shaking, and he had to force his teeth together to prevent them from chattering, and neither of those latter two reactions could be explained by too *much* heat, he noted wryly to himself.

But at last, a gasping O'Brien dragged his forearm across his dripping hair, plastering it back against his head, and pointed wordlessly to a black shaft, black as pitch, empty as the space between galaxies. Jake swallowed; moving closer, he saw a narrow ladder, the rungs spaced too far apart, leading into Stygia, or perhaps Tartarus.

Garak smiled grimly. "I see that the Federation does not believe in performing maintenance on the lighting systems," he gloated. "I would have thought better of you."

"It's hardly a high priority to light a ladderway that nobody uses!" objected the chief.

"Besides," added O'Brien's assistant engineer, Rom, "we haven't had time to do *any* maintenance, and, uh, it was next on my list after I corrected a slight problem with the comm system. I can show you the work orders if you don't—"

"Don't show this *tailor* our work schedules, Rom! It's no business of the Obsidian Order how we maintain this *military* outpost."

"Oh. Right. Sorry, Chief." Rom cringed politely, but O'Brien ignored the Ferengi ritual. Quark reached across and pinched Rom's right lobe hard enough to elicit a yelp, and the assistant engineer looked grateful. Evidently, that was the Ferengi response he sought. Garak rolled his eyes, looking very Odo-like, and then *he* snorted. *The constable is contagious!* concluded Jake.

The young man edged to the shaft and peered downward. "Careful," cautioned Bashir.

Straddling the dangerous pit, Jake fumbled in the back of his padd and extracted the emergency hand-torch. He shone it down the shaft, but the illumination petered out long before lighting the bottom. "Jeez, that's a long way down."

"Four decks," said O'Brien from right behind Jake, "and not just short decks. I mean it goes from the top of the habitat ring to the bottom—forty-two meters—and halfway in between is the deck that connects to the crossover tunnels."

Only forty meters? thought the younger Sisko. *It looks deeper, but that's probably the darkness.* He smiled; it was plenty deep enough to smash him into a pile of pumpkin remains at the bottom of a hole.

No, it's not just the fear of falling. There's something else, something I don't want to think about. Try as he might, Jake was unable to dredge up his real fear, but he knew it had something to do with his shameful behavior on Ajilon Prime. Something was pinching his cowardice nerve. There was something he was afraid of, but he couldn't put it into words yet.

"I'll take point," said O'Brien, and he plunged into the darkness without hesitation. Jake was impressed with the chief's aplomb. Rom affixed a lamp from a nearby storage locker to his waist and went next. The Ferengi was short enough that he practically had to hop from rung to rung, dangling at the end of his hands and stretching to touch one toe to the next rung down. Jake was amazed he could reach it at all.

Dr. Bashir gently pushed Jake forward, and he took the third position behind Rom after tucking his padd on his belt. For a brief moment, he felt the familiar weight of honest acrophobia; at least this fear he could understand! But there still was something else behind the simple adrenaline surge of being in a very high place with nothing to stop him from slipping and falling to his messy death: there was still a fear of *not doing something* he should be able to do. But what?

Garak, Quark, and finally the doctor fell in behind Jake, and the entire procession proceeded very slowly hand-over-hand down the ladder. Even moving cautiously, O'Brien quickly got his bulky body ahead of everyone else. His lamp shrank to a brilliant star, then a pinprick, while his figure faded altogether into the blackness. Jake kept his eyes riveted on Rom, keeping pace with the surprisingly wiry Ferengi. Young Sisko didn't look up, so he had no idea how the company above his head was doing.

At last, after an eternity, during which Jake's arms began to ache until he was honestly frightened that fatigue alone would throw him off the ladder, he noticed that the O'Brien star was moving inexorably closer: the chief must have stopped at the hatch through which they would exit the ladderway. At once, Jake felt his stomach tighten with a sickening fear—and *finally*, he understood what it was he was so afraid of: it wasn't dying, it was *failing*. Jake was afraid that once O'Brien and Rom killed the station gravity, he would panic in zero-G and humiliate himself!

He had never felt it in his life, and he knew from his father's stories that many people, upon their first exposure, became disoriented, nauseated, and completely unable to function. Jake Sisko was terrified that he would turn out to be one of those people who experience a full-blown panic attack, that he would disgrace the Sisko name.

The fear of panic itself almost made him lose control. He wrapped both arms around the ladder, hugging the metal and swearing softly, every obscene word that Captain Sisko never would allow him to utter.

Naturally, Bashir, directly above him, made things worse by completely misinterpreting the problem. "Jake, there's no need to be frightened. You're almost there. You're not going to lose your footing now."

Jake said nothing, not trusting his voice not to quiver. Garak tried again. "Do you want me to climb down and help you?"

"No," croaked the youth. It was all he could manage. Garak hesitated, presumably wondering whether to ignore the answer and climb down anyway. But Jake, desperate to avoid letting anyone get too close to him at that moment, forced himself to continue. He pressed his lips tight together and envied the Starfleet training that supposedly made the officers fearless. *What I wouldn't give for that! Anything but my writing talent, that's what I would give.* Nobody made him an offer, unfortunately.

He made himself look down. O'Brien had already gotten the hatch open and disappeared inside. Rom's torso was already within and, as Jake watched, the Ferengi's legs slithered through the hatch.

Then Jake got close enough to see the hole in the wall they vanished through: again for no reason, mindless terror threatened to rise and engulf him. Jake was not afraid that the zero-G would hurt him; he was afraid that it would make him *lose control* and panic, forcing his squadmates to waste precious time and energy quieting him . . . maybe even causing them all to get caught by the Klingons!

He waited a few moments for the overwhelming performance anxiety to subside, then, taking advantage of the brief lull, Jake practically slid the last few meters and slithered around to the inside of the ladder. He bent forward into the opening in the side of the shaft. For a brief moment he dangled, perfectly balanced between the access hatch and a fall to his death. Then he squirmed forward a fraction, and the balance shifted decisively toward the hatch. Within ten seconds, he was inside, rising shakily to his hands and feet in the narrow hatchway.

With the immediate danger past, Jake started to calm down somewhat, but his apprehension at how he would react to zero-G and being trapped in a spacesuit grew with every stoop-shouldered step forward, slouching toward the crossover tunnel, the engineering levels, and ultimately the environmental controls.

They came at last to a grating that effectively screened them from passersby in a busy corridor. The pedestrians were all Klingons, of course, and Jake quickly realized that it was Worf's lost patrol, trooping up and down the same corridor, by sheerest accident, that Bashir and his roughnecks had to cross! It was a rotten example of rotten luck, and Jake decided he never would have put it into a novel: *too stupid for words,* he raged, *to come all this way, climb down that damned ladder, and get accidentally boxed-in by our own secret ally!*

Meanwhile, O'Brien worked steadily and silently on the mag-clamps holding the grating against the power-coupling tube they crouched inside. He depolarized each magnet in turn with a slim tool extracted from the emergency kit Rom carried, and soon the grill was held against the lip of the tunnel by nothing more than the chief's knee-pressure. O'Brien gestured at the grating and raised his eyebrows in the doctor's direction, as if to ask, *Now what?*

Bashir gestured to Rom and Quark, then pointed at his own ears. The order was clear enough to Jake: the doctor was telling the Ferengi, with their notoriously sensitive hearing and monstrous earlobes, to listen for footsteps or other signs of approaching guards.

Quark pursed his lips and scrunched smaller than his already diminutive frame, then he closed his eyes and slowly swung his massive head back and forth like a deep-penetration sensor array. He held up his hand, gesturing for the crew to stay where it was. Rom, meanwhile, simply scowled, making himself look less intelligent than Jake knew him to be, and appeared to be listening intently to something he almost heard.

"Nothing, and . . . nothing," said Quark. "I think it's safe."

Garak chuckled from behind Jake, as if he knew something no one else knew. Sisko *fils* attributed it to typical Cardassian smugness.

Bashir smacked O'Brien on the shoulder, and the chief extracted the grill without making too much noise. He unfolded himself and staggered into the corridor, hopping and shaking his leg in sudden pain. "Damn thing's fallen asleep!" he whispered, as Jake and then the Ferengi hopped down beside him. O'Brien's arm still wasn't up to full range of motion, notwithstanding his earlier claim. The lingering effects of the Klingon disruptor seemed to still plague him.

Disaster struck just as Bashir was unlimbering himself from the shaft. A door slid open with a hiss, and four Klingon warriors stomped out, looking cross—even for Klingons. They halted and stared at the three humans, two Ferengi, and one Cardassian. For a second, they merely blinked, nonplussed. Then they reacted, grabbing for their weapons.

Garak reacted quicker than a pan of hot grease could

spit. He lunged toward the Klingons and shoved the first one backward hard with a well-aimed, open-handed hit to his center of gravity. The Klingon stumbed back into his comrade, who fell back onto the third. The fourth Klingon decided to charge at the same moment, and he tripped over the other three, sprawling across them.

But Garak was already pounding down the corridor in the opposite direction before the first hit the ground. By the time the Klingons untangled and leaped to their feet, Bashir's mob had already put fifteen meters between them and the Klingons, Garak leading the rout.

When the action started, Jake had stood, frozen, watching everything as if it were a holoplay staged for his amusement. The result was that he found himself tail-end of the snake as it slithered down the corridor. When the Klingons opened fire with their disruptors, Jake ducked involuntarily, feeling an itch in the middle of his back where he expected to feel a disruptor beam any moment.

He saw the crossover tunnel ahead—O'Brien was angling toward it! They might just make it . . . except for the disruptors. The Klingons were finally getting smart. Rather than try to *aim* each shot, they thought of holding down the fire-button and sweeping the beam across the floor, where it couldn't help but brush across them.

Then they heard a very familiar voice booming behind them: *"All warriors,"* bellowed Worf, *"draw and fire upon the escapees!"*

For a moment, all Jake could think was, *Betrayed!* Then he spared a glance back and realized the genius of Worf's order: the Klingons now filled the corridor several ranks deep! As expected, when the rear echelon opened fire, the *front* echelon, including Worf himself, instantly became irrelevant to the fight.

"You shot the colonel, traitorous dog!" shouted an angry voice from up front. In the ensuing donnybrook, the Federation "escapees" made it to the crossover

tunnel and dove inside, and Jake never did get to see the outcome of the friendly fire fiasco. O'Brien said something about "missing the train this time," but Jake again couldn't make heads or tails out of it.

The core of *Deep Space Nine* loomed a few dozen meters ahead. Within a few minutes, they would kill the station gravity and environmental control. Jake was about to find out whether or not he was truly worthy of the family name.

CHAPTER
17

CHIEF MILES O'BRIEN slipped down the last, slanty Jeffries tube, skinnying into the bottom well of the engineering level—below the level, actually, in the area beneath the metal-catwalk flooring that few persons apart from the engineering crew of the station even knew existed. He looked up and saw the steel-shod boots of a dozen Klingon warriors directly overhead, in the "lowest" official level of engineering above the reactors, and felt a terrible temptation to cringe back against the wall out of sight. But he knew well that the level above was much better lit, and from up there, the environmental-controls well looked like a Stygian cave.

Dr. Bashir leaned close to the chief and whispered something in his ear. *"What?"* bellowed O'Brien, enjoying the shocked look on the doctor's face. Bashir made an urgent shushing noise, which was lost in the rumbling cacophony of the atmospheric pumps and recirculators and gravitic generator itself—a low throbbing that sucked sound from the air as easily as the tide sucked away the wash from the waves. O'Brien shouted directly into the doctor's ear: *"They can't hear us down here! They can barely hear themselves talk! Trust me!"*

"What's the plan?!"

"There's the master control! The banks of blue buttons control the station gravity! There's a failsafe! You have to push this bank and that bank simultaneously!"

"What?!"

O'Brien cleared his throat, then repeated the instructions at top volume. He glanced up involuntarily, but the Klingons were not looking down at them, just shouting at each other, even their heroic howls drowned out by the machinery.

"We need another pair of hands!"

It turned out they needed *two* other pairs. O'Brien grabbed Rom and pulled him close, pointing wordlessly at the banks of turquoise-lit lamps labeled "Gravitic Generator Circuit"; the chief held up his hand showing three fingers, then two, then one in rapid succession. Rom squinted a moment, then nodded happily.

Looking over the rest of the mob, choosing between Garak, Jake, and Quark, O'Brien reluctantly gestured to the boy to come close. *"I'm going to give a visual countdown!"* yelled the chief. *"At zero, touch the bottom of all six of these slidebars! All at the same time! Got it?!"*

Jake stared at the board full of buttons and slidebars, shaking his head slowly from side to side. Feeling an increasing unease, O'Brien elbowed his way next to the lad, grabbed Jake's hands, and physically dragged them right above the proper slidebars. Jake was trembling. He kept licking his lips and dry-swallowing. *Please don't bollox it up, lad!* thought O'Brien to himself.

"Everybody else!" screamed the chief, *"find something solid to hang on! Here we go!"* He wasn't sure they understood his warning; neither Quark nor Garak acted as if they even heard him. On the other hand, O'Brien didn't particularly care whether they went for a sail or

not . . . in fact, with *those* two, it might be quite the bonny sight.

O'Brien opened a console and typed for a long interval, giving coded responses to a series of security queries. He had to type, since not even the computer could pick out his words in the din, even if it hadn't been compromised. At last, he successfully circumvented the maintenance-security subroutines and was ready to introduce a note of levity to *Deep Space Nine*.

Chief O'Brien held up his hand and waved it to grab the attention of his surrogate fingers. Three! He held it a long moment, making eye contact so he could assure himself that each person was watching.

Three!

Two!

One!

Where zero should have been, O'Brien brought seven well-spaced fingers down sharply on the bottom of the slidebars. Evidently, the others did their jobs as well, for he began to feel light-headed immediately.

It was a horrible feeling, as if he were falling, falling! O'Brien flashed back to the eerie, shattered hulk that had started the horrible adventure, the hollowed-out shell collapsing in on itself. His own pulse skyrocketed, and a burst of adrenaline pushed through his circulatory system. Panic! It was purely physical, the body screaming out in fear that it was falling. But even knowing it was just the transition to zero-G, Miles O'Brien could not calm himself down. The unreasoning fear welled up and seized hold, and he almost let go the slidebars, which would have been a disaster: without constant pressure, the safeties would kick in automatically, restoring full gravity.

His entire body began to lift against the slight pressure of his feet against the deck, his hands against the controls. Just at the point where he could no longer hold his fingers down without simply pushing himself away, the gravitic generator control passed the "point of no return," whence it would continue by itself down to zero-G.

It was a horrible sensation, worse—far worse!—than floating in the derelect ship, for this was his home, his own. This world was never supposed to be so torn apart. *Topsy-turvy, topsy-turvy* . . . the inadequate words ran through O'Brien's head like the tolling of some great bell signaling disaster, the Dire Tocsin of the Irish village, crying *fire, flood, a terrible squall off the coast among the fishers!*

Then the nausea crawled "down" his throat—no "up" or "down" left—into his stomach. He tasted the bile first, felt it ooze along his esophagus to slowly overwhelm his guts. A raging, terrible sickness far worse than he had felt in the dead hulk, because this was *Deep Space Nine,* and it was never meant to be this way.

Chief O'Brien's ears burned, and he knew if he could see them, they would first be pink as boiled corned beef, then red as a bowl of strawberries. He felt a terrific itching in his throat and ears, and dizziness shook him like a fever-chill. He noticed he was floating "upside-down" with respect to the console he had just been pressing, and he flapped his arms, trying to right himself. He had been so intent upon killing the gravitic generator that he had forgotten to secure himself to something solid.

Garak grimly clutched a chair hooked into a track, and, curiously enough, Jake Sisko had wrapped his gangly legs around the railing surrounding the well—true son of a captain that he was. Bashir was as loose as O'Brien, but the young know-it-all seemed as unperturbed by the turn of events as he had been earlier in the ship.

Thank God at least Quark looks as sick as me, and Rom too, thought the chief in unbecoming bitterness that startled even himself. *It's the spacer's revenge,* he told himself. *It's making my head funny.*

The doctor was talking, but O'Brien needed every bit

of attention to keep from dry-heaving uncontrollably and truly disgracing himself. His skin felt clammy, and he knew his flesh was as gray as the fat-scum floating in the boiling water atop the corned beef . . . soon to be white as the cream poured over the strawberries.

Suck it up, he commanded himself, *and stop thinking about food!* He forced himself to pay attention to the young pup with the pips on his collar.

"Listening to me? Chief?"

"I'm—sorry, Julian. I was—thinking." O'Brien swallowed several times. He suddenly realized that he could hear Bashir; most of the engine noise had stopped, leaving only the whine of the air pumps. *All it would take is one, little twist of the pressure-regulator . . .*

"Glad to see you're still among the living. I said," repeated Bashir, "what are you going to do next?"

"What we . . . already . . . decided. Vacuum . . . environmental controls."

"I was afraid as much," said the doctor, wincing at the thought. "I'm afraid I cannot allow you to do that."

"But why—"

"Chief, think of the prisoners! What if Worf didn't figure it out? What are they supposed to do then, suck vacuum?"

Chief O'Brien rolled his eyes, a signal of disgust that cost him dearly in the fragile sense of balance he had constructed from visual input alone. "Julian, Worf said . . . force vacuum. Must've figured it out . . . must be safe."

"Safe *how?* Did the Klingons issue them all pressure-suits, just in case some damn fool discharged the atmosphere out a porthole?" Bashir had drifted close enough to a railing to grab hold, where he fluttered gracefully, a flag on a blustery day. O'Brien found the movement disturbing enough that he began to hyperventilate. He stared away, focusing on the Ferengi. They were still bouncing slowly around the room like slow-motion balloons, waving their arms and legs and bleating.

"I don't know!" shouted the chief, too late remembering that the Klingons probably *could* hear him now that the generator was offline. "On the Klingon ship or forceshields—something! Worf wouldn't have said vacuum part if they would die."

"Maybe he didn't think of it!"

Chief O'Brien remembered in time not to roll his eyes again. "Known him longer than known you . . . *sir*. Not make . . . mistake like that!"

At last, by sheerest mischance, O'Brien drifted face-first into Bashir's boots. He grabbed hold with both hands, climbing along the lieutenant in a successful, if disturbingly familiar, drive for the railing. He latched onto the bar in a death-grip and faced the doctor from half a meter away.

This close, O'Brien saw that Bashir's own skin had grown pale. He realized that the doctor was anguishing, trying to decide whether to flush the atmosphere and risk killing every man, woman, and child held hostage aboard the station, which would be the result if Worf had somehow missed that part of the message after all, or else do nothing and, in essence, surrender the station to the Klingons. The zero-G was a nuisance, but not disruptive enough by itself to prevent them from holding their conquest until reinforcements arrived from the Empire. Without the evacuation of the station atmosphere, the six of them could not hope to overwhelm the Klingons.

Bashir hesitated on the precipice of decision, too perfectly balanced to go either way. But the chief knew what to do, perhaps because, of all things in the world, he trusted Worf *not* to be as thick-skulled and humorless as his Klingon brethren. The problem was, how to persuade the doctor? For obvious reasons, the potential death of the prisoners was far more *real* to Julian Bashir than was the joke-getting ability of a Klingon he had met for the first time just a couple of years earlier.

For a moment, O'Brien was at a loss, then abruptly,

the words jumped into his mouth almost before they appeared clearly in his brain. "Julian, you said it yourself!"

"Said what? *What?*" shouted the doctor, staring back and forth between the chief and the environmental control panel.

"You said yourself that the Klingons were moving heaven and earth *not* to kill anyone . . . you said it!"

"So-o-o?"

"So they know there's going to be a counterattack by the Federation. There has to be! And the only place the prisoners would possibly be safe on a station under bombardment is behind a level-four forcefield!" When he finished the thought, the chief noted with surprise that his nausea was almost entirely gone, even though he was still dizzy and disoriented; the pressure of logical thought calmed him down.

"Maybe they just plan to release them when——"

"No, I mean that's what Worf must've argued with them, that's how he got them to store the prisoners behind the forcefields, even *before* we broadcast the warning. That's why he told us so quickly to go ahead and do it!"

It wasn't much. There were logical arguments that might be advanced against the point, if Bashir were looking for them. But it was just enough to tip the balance in the doctor's mind, the one, final stick that broke the logjam. "Yes," said Dr. Bashir quietly.

"Julian?"

"Yes, Chief, I believe we can. Chief O'Brien, get everyone in pressure suits. What Worf said about the station atmosphere . . . *make it so.*"

"Aye, sir!" Now that he wasn't thinking so hard about the lack of gravity, his Starfleet training reasserted itself. He spun around, using his hand on the railing as a pivot point, and kicked across the room toward the bank of storage lockers. One contained ESO pressure suits for Extra-Station Operations in the unlikely event that such a thing was required; it hadn't been in all the years O'Brien had been aboard *Deep Space Nine*.

Fortunately, the lockers were too old to have been connected into the station computers, therefore, the combinations were not scrambled as were the rest of the locks. O'Brien punched his own code, and the locker snicked open with the cold efficiency of Cardassian machinery.

Garak materialized by O'Brien's side. "Do I take it we are about to embark upon an invigorating swim to Bajor?" he smirked.

"Take it any way you want. Just stay *out* of my way." In the closet were eight Starfleet pressure suits and, miraculously enough, two Cardassian suits left over from the old days. "Here," mumbled the chief, extracting one of the latter and launching it toward Garak. "I wouldn't want you to be underdressed."

"It would spoil my image," agreed Garak, efficiently shedding shoes and outer garments to slither into the suit.

O'Brien turned around and gave one suit a gentle push in Bashir's direction. *If he can kick my butt at darts, he can bloody well catch this damned thing!* Then he slipped into a suit himself.

"Chief!" hissed Jake Sisko from a few meters away. The lad dangled at an impossible angle from the cage separating their deck from the one that used to be "above," a concept now meaningless. "Chief, what are we supposed to do with those?"

"Watch!" commanded O'Brien. He kicked off his boots—they were included in the suit, of course—and gently pulled apart the front seam of the suit. Maneuvering it so that the chest opening just touched his feet, O'Brien slithered his way into the tight-fitting, accordion-jointed, head-to-toe jumper. Pulling his arms inside and ducking his head into the helmet, O'Brien pressed the chest seam together again and dialed the mode-select to seal. He heard the soft thunk as the suit pressurized itself to three-quarters station normal, and his ear cracked at the sudden change.

Holding three suits, he reset his feet and launched toward the Ferengis, who were still bumping around in the corner. He stretched and handed-off one ESO to Jake *en passant.* When O'Brien reached Quark and Rom, the bartender turned reluctant revolutionary was already eyeing the suits with horror. "Chief O'Brien, you had better not be telling me that *I* have to wear one of those!"

"Here you go, Rom. No, Quark, I wouldn't be telling you anything. Leave it off if you think it might clash with your teal jacket, I don't care."

"Oh, right," sneered Quark. "So I can die and allow *Rom* to take over my bar? Not for a Ferengi's grace period!" Quark snatched the remaining suit, which was marked for a supervisor. "But don't you imagine for *one microsecond* that I'm going to forget about this cross-species humiliation!"

Humiliation? What the hell is he on about? Then the chief saw Rom squirming into his own suit, and he understood immediately. When the young Ferengi finally managed to get himself inside and work the air seal, it was all O'Brien could do to avoid actually laughing out loud at the absurd picture of a tiny Ferengi inside an ESO built to accommodate a burly human: the arms and legs flopped uselessly, and Rom could barely see over the lip of the helmet. The assistant engineer looked like an egg stuffed into a sock.

Quark, when he struggled into his suit (with help from Rom), looked even more ridiculous. Unlike his brother, Quark tried to look dapper and dignified and succeeded only in making himself look like Molly playing dress-up in Keiko's clothes.

But it was good enough; everyone was secured inside the pressure-suits. The moment of truth had arrived.

O'Brien kicked gently back toward the environmental-control panel. He plucked a delicate probe from his pocket and carefully bypassed the final security subsystems, literally rewiring the environmental interface to delete the interminable requests for passwords and superuser status. The environmental-control password system had been designed by the Cardassians to prevent some idiot from accidentally purging all air from the station—or a Bajoran terrorist from doing it on purpose—but they had no time for it now!

But now it was O'Brien who hesitated, nervously stopping his hand just a centimeter away from the purge. *Do I really have the guts? Was I right about Worf? Was Worf right about the Klingons not wanting to hurt the prisoners or use them as human shields?*

He hesitated for three seconds, then looked up to see Bashir staring at him with such intensity, O'Brien jerked backward, almost pushing himself away from the console. "Have to move," he muttered to himself, too quietly to be overheard through the helmet. "Somebody's got to make the decision, and that somebody's me."

He sighed a long, resigned breath, then flexed his digits the final two centimeters and poked the "Emergency purge" touchplate. At first, O'Brien heard nothing inside his suit except for his own breathing, loud in his ears, then he started to hear the roar of escaping gas as the mighty circulation system began the eight-minute process of evacuating all the air from the station in an emergency, crash-priority purge. Accompanying this was the red-alert warning shriek and an insistent voice warning of imminent doom from hard vacuum. O'Brien quickly reached into the open control panel and slew the sound effects. When the wind-roar reached its peak, the chief had to grip the console tightly to avoid being sucked toward the nearest air vent.

Gradually, the external sounds became faint and tinny. He heard horrified shouts from the level "above." Glancing up, he saw four Klingons caroming off the walls of the engineering level in panic, searching for pressure suits, oxygen masks, *something* to save themselves! They finally located a locker and blasted it open with disruptors, but it was too late for all but one Klingon, who flung himself into a suit in a desperate frenzy.

He made it . . . barely. But his comrades were dead, by the most horrible means O'Brien could imagine: slow suffocation as the atmospheric pressure plummeted.

The remaining Klingon was alive, but incapacitated by the trauma to his lungs and tissues. The Federation counteroffensive had finally begun.

CHAPTER
18

JULIAN BASHIR BEGAN to get cold feet as the air pumped from the rest of the station. The dimly remembered manual insisted they had another ten minutes before the larger spaces in *Deep Space Nine* were evacuated, and he determined to make use of those precious moments. "Jake, give me the handset," he said. The boy looked blank until Bashir remembered to say "Open comm link to, ah, pressure suit 224A, codename Jake Sisko." He repeated his request for the handset, and Jake fumbled the recovered Cardassian communicator to the doctor.

Licking his lips, Bashir activated the device. "Open comm link to handset. Scan for frequency squawk, link to broadcast." The commands were unfamiliar, but then, he had never tried to link from a pressure-suit to a Klingon communicator before. After a moment, he heard a fast click-click in his ears that he presumed was maintenance shorthand for "link established," and he breathed a sigh of relief.

"Attention General Malach. This is Lieutenant Julian

Bashir, commanding officer of the *Deep Space Nine* defense forces." Bashir paused. He had deliberately not mentioned that he was a doctor—*let him sweat at the thought that we're trained counterterrorists!* "We are evacuating all air from this facility. The process cannot now be reversed. You must *immediately* move all Federation prisoners to airtight confinement or they will die, and Starfleet will hold you personally, and the entire Klingon Empire, responsible for the deaths of all men, women, and children under your control!"

Nothing but static. Bashir waited thirty seconds and was just about the try again when the voice he recognized as "Malach" came over his suit comm link. The general sounded as though he were whispering directly into Bashir's ears. "If you value the lives of your fellow Federations, you will instantly restore the atmosphere of this station!"

"Negative, the process cannot be reversed. It is beyond our control now. Only you can save their lives . . . and I *demand* that you do so or suffer the wrath of the Federation for all time to come—against you and your *house* for all eternity!"

The ruse having failed, Malach responded immediately this time. "The prisoners are safe. We wish to discuss terms of your surrender. You will not be harmed."

"Oh, we have no intention of surrendering, *Malach.*" Bashir deliberately did not use the term 'general.' "We shall fight to the last man. I suggest you pray that your Klingon warriors have trained as assiduously in zero-G vacuum warfare as we have. *We are coming for you,* Malach. Today will be a good day to die . . . for you." He thumbed off the handset broadcast switch and listened, but Malach did not respond.

Bashir looked up to find the entire company staring at him, each from his own peculiar attitude in the weightless environment. "Maintain open comm link with pressure suits 224A, 228A, 172A, 173A, and 175A."

Click-click. "Men, I have just informed Malach that we are evacuating the station, and ordered him to get the Federation prisoners to airtight spaces."

"Yeah?" demanded Quark aggressively, "and what about the *non-Federation* prisoners, like Morn and Captain Kobei?"

"Malach has no reason to suddenly start killing them now, Quark. But we need a plan of action—he knows we're coming for him, but he has no idea how many we are or how heavily armed. He only knows we're here and we can monitor their communications."

"And he knows that Worf is on our side," added O'Brien, who floated directly "above" Bashir and upside-down from the doctor's point of view. "I hope to hell Worf knows the game is up!"

Bashir said nothing. His own breath was loud in his ears. Quark and Rom were still flailing, and Rom's helmeted head struck a bulkhead. Bashir jerked when he heard the thump loud and clear over the comm link.

Malach's voice returned in the doctor's ears . . . everyone's ears, presumably, with the open circuit: "We had no choice. The Federation does not understand that this is the greatest crisis ever to face the Empire—the entire Alpha Quadrant. More even than the Borg! *Somebody had to act.*"

"We have the advantage," Bashir nearly shouted, ignoring the Klingon. "Let us strike quickly, while they're still getting their sea-legs, so to speak. We must retake Ops and get a message through to Bajor!" The handset did not broadcast, so Malach heard only silence in response to his evident urge to rationalize. *Good, let him sweat for a change.*

"We want no war with the Federation. We are not asserting control over your territory, do you not understand? We saw a leak, and we moved to plug it. You would have done the same, if you would have allowed your warriors to act. Lieutenant Bashir, *listen to me.* We are not your enemies. Our *mutual* enemy lies beyond this gateway in the Gamma Quadrant. *Listen to me!"*

Bashir found a solid railing with his feet. Grace under any condition, including zero-G, came easily to the doctor; always had. He launched himself toward the hatch that mediated between the "upper" and "lower" levels of the engineering department, though the terms were meaningless now. Garak followed close at his heels, and Jake and the chief took a moment to retrieve the squawking, flapping Ferengi and tow them along behind.

Arriving at the hatch, Bashir gripped the ladder with his legs while he worked the manual override—not an easy task in zero-G, since it had never occurred to the Cardassians who built the station that anyone would try such a damn-fool stunt. But by bracing himself and applying dynamic tension in opposite directions simultaneously, he managed to twist the screw and dial back the bolts. The door opened, and Bashir wriggled through.

He spared barely a glance at the four Klingon soldiers who had guarded engineering: three clearly were dead, but he couldn't tell about the fourth. *You're a doctor, damn it,* insisted one part of his brain, but another part screamed, *No time, no time!* Feeling a wave of guilt, he bypassed the possible patient and pushed toward the next level up.

"Lieutenant Bashir, I do not want to fight you. Join me—join us in glorious defense of the Alpha Quadrant against these invaders from the Dominion. Join the Empire, and arm-in-arm, we shall repell the Founders and secure our borders. Lieutenant, answer me! You dishonor me by this stony silence. I require an answer. *I* demand *an answer!"*

Major Kira Nerys tensed when Dax said it, tensed though she was expecting it, ready for it: "Wormhole ahead," said Dax, dry-mouthed enough to have to clear her throat. The normally irrepressible Trill seemed to be entering in the general spirit of doom and anxiety that gripped the rest of the bridge crew of the *Defiant*.

Kira tensed and licked her own lips. Her fingers sought out the torpedo controls, and though they trembled with anticipation, she knew, if the order came, she could fire cleanly and without hesitation. Passing through the wormhole, she scanned constantly for a hidden invader. The realm of the Prophets seemed an especially blasphemous place to plant an ambush, hence quite attractive to a would-be Klingon enemy. But nothing happened in the wormhole itself.

As usual, she felt a twist wrench her guts outward, like tidal forces, as they passed through. The wormhole was neither *here* nor precisely *there,* nowhere in particular, in fact. It was everywhere along its route at once, and nowhere with any great specificity. In fact, she felt no passage of time, per se, just the vague, disquieting sense of being where she came from and where she was going all at the same, drawn-out instant. She felt foreboding, too, and that emotion at least was new for her.

"Exiting the wormhole, Benjamin," announced Dax, as though she were saying *Leaping out of the frying pan, Captain.*

Kira held her breath. *This is it,* she thought; if there were to be an ambush, this was where it would have to be, so close to home. But no ball of energy met them, no cascade of disruptor blasts to pulverize the cloaked but unshielded skin of the ship. There were no torpedoes, disruptors, large rocks, or buckets of sand flung into their path.

But—but we're not alone, she realized. She felt the squeezing fist in her belly that always told her whenever there were a Cardassian patrol lurking nearby, back in the bad old days. The fist clenched tighter as the *Defiant* exited the wormhole, accompanied by the usual, spectacular starburst pattern that she had seen so many times from aboard the station. "Great," she muttered, "may as well fire off a flare gun to announce our arrival."

"I am sorry, Major," said Captain Sisko, "but I didn't quite catch that."

"I mean, sir, that it's frustrating to be running silent in a cloak and pass through the wormhole with an announcement loud enough to be seen three sectors away!" Suddenly, something didn't look quite right. "Stand by, Captain. Dax! Check for . . . check for warp signatures. There was nothing recent when we left, remember?"

"Checking. Uh-oh . . . Kira, there *has* been somebody here, snooping around."

And there definitely was something different about *Deep Space Nine.* "Hail them, sir?"

"Negative," said Sisko immediately. "Did you notice the curious incident of the dog in the nighttime, Major Kira?"

"Huh? What dog?"

"The dog did nothing in the nighttime, Benjamin," said Dax with a mysterious sing-song quality, as if quoting.

"That was the curious incident," remarked Benjamin Sisko.

Riddles, always riddles with those two! "Oh, I get it: we just came through the wormhole. Why didn't *they* hail *us?*"

"Exactly, Kira. Let's poke around here for a while until we understand what's going on."

Kira brought the station up on the viewer and began systematically examining the image from top-left to bottom-right. Definitely, something was wrong. Now she had to find it.

A presence loomed over Kira's shoulder. "Now this is funny," said Constable Odo, her closest friend among all the inhabitants of *Deep Space Nine,* "there's no chatter."

"No what?" she asked.

"Humans—and Bajorans—are the noisiest mob of people I have ever encountered, Major. It's a constant source of irritation to me, having to filter out the incessant *chattering* you people do all the time: Bajor to the station, the station to Starfleet, the station to ships in the area, wanted smugglers to Quark and vice versa."

"All right, so we talk a lot. We like to keep in touch!"

"But Kira, there is no chatter."

"No chatter? You mean, no communications? At all?"

"Ordinarily, at any one moment, there are three comm links between the station and Bajor. Even recently, with the station blessedly quiet and even Quark starved for want of criminal enterprise, we should have seen *some* idle chatting in the ten minutes since we entered the station's space. But there hasn't been a word, not a single communication from the station. The Bajoran high council just sent a new batch of wanted holos, and nobody in my office even acknowledged receipt!"

"Captain!" cried Kira, "I've got it! Look at the main emitter . . . there's just a great big hole where the antenna used to sit." She tapped rapidly at her keyboard console. On the main viewer at the front of the *Defiant,* a red circle appeared circling the jagged scar where the emitter array used to squat.

"Can we beam onto the station, Old Man?"

"No chance, Benjamin. The station shields are up."

"I do not like the looks of this at all," said Sisko quietly. Abruptly, he sat bolt upright in his command chair and said, "Dax, take us around the station, but keep the impulse engines below a quarter." The captain rose, absently stroking his beard as he stared at the forward viewer. "We're not alone," he said at last.

The words sent a shiver through Major Kira, and she almost began sneezing again, though it was months beyond when the pregnancy should have stopped causing that reaction. "A cloaked ship," she said, not particularly surprised. "Klingon?"

"Who else?" asked the constable, who had not moved

from his spot behind Sisko's chair. "The station is compromised," added Odo. "The Klingons have captured it in our absence and thrown a communications shield around it so the survivors cannot call for help."

"That does seem the most logical solution," said the captain.

Kira felt her stomach clench even tighter into a ball at the icy, emotionless tone of the statement. *Jake's on board!* she thought. She did not dare say the words aloud. "Do they know we're here? Oh. Stupid question."

Dax snorted. "Even if they weren't looking for a warp signature, they sure couldn't miss our spectacular floral arrangement a few minutes ago." She was referring to the opening of the wormhole, which Dax claimed resembled the flowering of some monstrous, cosmic tulip bulb.

"Should we send a message to Bajor?" Kira's hands hovered over the console.

"No!" said Sisko sharply.

The major jumped. "Why not? We need reinforcements to—"

"Because opening a channel is like clicking on a handtorch in a dark room. They'll decloak and fry us before we get two syllables out."

"How about making a speed-run toward Bajor?" suggested Constable Odo. "Once inside Bajoran space, surely the Klingons wouldn't shoot."

"They're cloaked, Odo," reminded Dax, a mere second before Kira would have.

"They can burn us and cruise quietly away," added the major from Bajor, "with no one the wiser. We're like two black cats," she continued, "maneuvering around a pitch-black room, stalking each other. Playing cat-and-cat."

"Play ball," muttered Sisko.

Kira wasted no time staring out the viewer as they rounded the station, hunting for the Klingons. The ship was cloaked, as were they, and would be invisible to the naked eye. Instead, she watched for the tiniest fluctuations of energy readings on her threat-board: faint changes in temperature, a flicker of the cosmic background radiation as the enemy ship passed between them and the rest of the universe. A star that suddenly *moved* the slightest amount, detectable only by astrogational instruments, would indicate a slight *refocusing* of the image of the star due to the fact that the cloaking shield was not equally thick all along its length—the effect was like holding an ancient contact lens at arm's length and finding it by the visual distortions it caused. Any of these would give the *Defiant* a bearing but no range on the Klingon ship—or ships!

"Run us closer," said Sisko, sounding and looking completely calm, but Kira had enough experience with professional killers during the Occupation to recognize the mark of the beast beneath his skin and behind the corneas of his eyes. "Run us right in and among the pylons, Old Man. Let's see how badly that . . . gentleman wants to play hide-and-seek."

"Heat surge bearing one seven zero mark plus fifteen!" called out Major Kira, almost before she realized herself what she had just seen.

"Come about, all engines stop!" snapped Sisko. The viewer spun sharply as Dax turned the *Defiant* 170 degrees, so that she pointed directly at the heat source Kira had spotted. The major performed an extremely sensitive, passive scan of the immediate area, but she found nothing. The surge was gone.

"They must've banked their own engines," she muttered. "If they tamped them down to a quarter impulse—well, make that a fifth impulse, with that noisy Klingon ship—they'd be a silent as we are."

"They spotted us the same time you spotted them," said Odo. The captain grunted in disappointed agreement.

"All right, keep moving, Old Man; in and around the pylons. Perhaps we'll get lucky again. Major Kira, consider this a wartime situation. Don't try to hail them, don't give them a chance to surrender. We've been fired upon already, and we're within our rights to blow them out of the sky without warning."

"Yes *sir,*" she grinned.

Kira forced her eyes off the viewer, enticing though it was to watch Dax's skill as she threaded the needles of *Deep Space Nine.* The major stared intently at her targeting computers, her fingers hovering lightly over the fire key . . . though that was quite an arm-stretch, considering how far the baby-on-board made her sit from the console. But she couldn't help catching the looming obstacles in her peripheral vision, just enough to gasp every now and then as the captain's "old man" cut a turn a little too close.

"Heat flume!" called out Kira. "Wait, neg that. "It's from the station." A moment later, she added, "For Prophet's sake, there goes another. They're getting pretty careless with the outgasing back there."

With the sixth venting, she began to get suspicious. "Hands of the Prophets," she whispered. "Captain, the whole station is lit up like a Bajoran festival bush in the infrared . . . they're leaking atmosphere from every joint and seam!"

"Leaking atmosphere?" said Sisko, sounding, if anything, even colder and more controlled. *He's living through hell right now,* she realized; even she couldn't help but picture the slowly suffocating residents, dropping to the ground and grabbing their ears as the atmospheric pressure plummeted. "Dax, where's it coming from?"

The Trill shook her head. "From everywhere, Benjamin! It's—they're *purging the entire atmosphere!* Benjamin, this is crazy . . . it's going to take them hours to be able to restore it again, and there're not enough pressure suits for even a third of the station population, even considering how few people are left!"

For the first time on the mission, Captain Sisko almost lost control. He jumped to his feet and shouted, *"Son of a*—" He swallowed the rest of the statement, choking on a long string of ear-burning obscenities that Major Kira dutifully supplied in her own mind. The captain clenched his hands so tightly, she could hear the knuckles crack from where she sat. After a moment, he sat again with exaggerated calm, false control. "The situation has become urgent, Kira," he said, not even bothering with the formalities of rank. "Secure the station. *Now.*"

She could not stop her eyes from staring up at the viewer, despite the fact that her sensors were far more sensitive. Her gaze bored into the screen as if to rip right through it and penetrate the Klingon ship by force of will. As though some force held her vision and wouldn't let her look away, she stared, unblinking, riveted, *and she saw the ship.* She sucked in a breath. The Prophets had answered her prayer, for the Klingon ship had become visible! Then it flickered from view again, and Kira's brain finally caught up with her eyes: she knew what she had seen.

"Captain! It's the air—the steam—I mean, frozen water droplets in the venting atmosphere, and they look like steam, like fog, and the *damned Klingon ship is swirling through the fog!* I can see it! I can *target* it!"

Lieutenant Commander Dax's cold voice suddenly cut through Kira's mounting excitement. "Computer, overlay forward viewer with thermal imaging." The viewer color-palate suddenly shifted to shades of red from the ruddy black of cosmic background temperature of three Kelvin to the pinpoint white of the station nuclear reactors; the visible-light outline of the station, still visible behind the thermal image, showed as a stark, metallic base surrounded by a deep amber, almost burnt umber, that represented the normal heat-radiation of the station skin.

But dancing all along that skin at regular intervals were fountains of prismatic beauty, rare rubies spouting plumes of fiery spirals, like fire-flowers or the swirl of a dancing Firebird's tail. The hot atmosphere escaping from a dozen joints and nozzles turned the entirety of *Deep Space Nine* into a miniature galaxy in yellowing red: the streams began in electric yellow at their core, where they sprouted from the station arteries; they spiraled around the rotating station, darkening through orange, umber, and finally turning the color of bright, oxygenated blood as the venting atmospheric gases cooled, darkening along the yellow-red color axis on the viewer.

There were several breaks and eddys in the scintillant image, too many! Kira almost fired a torpedo at the station's own ventral sensor array before she realized what was causing that particular disturbance in the pattern. She looked from ripple to cut, identifying each one as a normal piece of the station disrupting the fluid flow, like rocks forming cascades in a rushing river. She was looking for the singular, inexplicable splash that would signify the presence, not of just another rock, but of a hidden fish lurking beneath the surface.

CHAPTER
19

MAJOR KIRA NERYS stared at the slowly rotating swirls, thinking of the sunberry ices they sold on the streets back home. *They're here, they're here somewhere, the bastards, can't sit still forever, have to move sometime. Come on you cowards move somewhere! Don't be frightened of the gases that are going to kill you in the end. Just cut through them, just get up and move from one side to the other and I've—*

Except, for all her staring, it was Constable Odo who spotted the moving disturbance with the telltale bow wake. "There!" he shouted, running forward to the viewer to point directly at the track. For a moment, he seemed to forget himself, and he kept stretching his arm as if still a changeling, able to turn the limb into a telescoping pointer.

"I see it!" snapped Kira, desperately bringing her fire-control sensors to bear on her best guess, based on Klingon bird-of-prey profiles, of where the bridge would be. *But—no, that's impossible! Don't do that!*

"It's moving behind a pylon! Our own *pylon* is in the way!"

"Fire, Major," said Sisko calmly, having regained his sense of self.

"But we'll shoot—"

"To hell with the pylon—take the shot, soldier!"

Kira obeyed without another moment's hesitation, but she shifted to phasers, since a photon torpedo would merely hit the pylon and *stop*. The phaser struck the metal protuberance six meters from its end. After a moment, the heavy blast sheared through the pylon and continued to the next target in its line of sight.

For an instant, the thermal image on the viewer burned as white as the snows on Mount Turyeil Bajori. Then the filters adjusted, shifting the color-palette toward a lower frequency, and Kira could see the ghostly image of a *burning hole,* streaming hot gas and black specks that must be metal debris. The Klingon ship was silhouetted black against the eye-straining yellow-white of hellish heat. The bird-of-prey's power plant had ruptured, spraying a stream of antimatter into the swirling oxygen and nitrogen, where it reacted, producing enough heat to swamp the infrared sensors.

"Computer," said Captain Sisko, his command-tone cutting through the ice of fascinated reverie that gripped the bridge crew, "remove thermal imaging, restore forward viewer to normal visual light reception."

At once, the viewer went nearly black, so quickly that Kira still saw the afterimage of the burning hole in the antimatter-containment shell. Yet the hole was still visible, the antimatter stream still reacting brightly enough to produce a monstrous arrow pointing directly at the bird-of-prey. The *Defiant* began to roll and vibrate as it was buffeted by the shock waves from the initial explosion and the subsequent matter-antimatter reactions. The inertial dampers mostly compensated, but the ship still pitched and yawed like an old-fashioned sailing vessel of centuries past.

Kira grabbed her console and held tight. Dax and Sisko likewise rode it out, and Odo reacted more quickly than a human would have and braced himself. But the two ensigns were neither so quick-thinking nor so lucky. Tarvak Amar was thrown out of his chair by the first jolt. When he struggled up against the shaking a minute later, Kira noticed he was cradling his left arm, which did not move, and his face was bone white. Ensign Janine Wheeler had been standing at her post near the astrogation console, but now she lay on her side, unmoving, her head against the bare-metal railing separating the upper from the lower bridge.

Kira tapped her comm badge. "Medical emergency on the bridge, send a head-trauma team, blue alert."

If the captain noticed the casualties, he didn't have time to fret about them; he was still in the middle of a battle. "Drop cloak and raise shields, Old Man. Keep the pylon between us. Is he shooting or running?"

"Both," answered Dax. A pair of photon torpedoes launched directly at the *Defiant,* followed by a narrow-beam disruptor blast. It was a standard Klingon tactical trick: fire the torpedoes, then shoot the shields to punch a hole for them to push through. It never worked perfectly—but then, it didn't need to. The disruptor burned a hole partway through the shields, and before they could compensate, the photon torpedoes overloaded the system and crippled the ship.

Kira ducked involuntarily as the disruptor beam washed across the forward sensor array, then she returned fire with an identical spread of two torpedoes and a phaser blast to light their way. "Damn," she muttered, "they got their shields up."

"But they're badly hurt!" shouted Dax.

"So are we! Shields damaged, I mean, not the ship, not yet—"

"Containment breach on the bird-of-prey has turned into a hull breach, and they're turning tail."

"They're shooting as they go," added Kira, "and our

forward shields are still trying to recover. Captain, they'd better not shoot us or we could be cooked *rajelah.*"

Demanding control from herself, she maintained an even strain by meditating upon the Fifth Fire-Verse of the Prophets:

> *The gentle breeze dies,*
> *But the gale builds in passionate intensity;*
> *The fire is ever in the breaching,*
> *Not the building.*

"Never mind, Benjamin," said Dax. "They're not even targeting, just popping shots over their shoulder. Hundred to one against them hitting—"

Kira continued to monitor her sensors. *"Incoming!"* she shouted, before even realizing what she saw: torpedo, constant bearing, decreasing distance . . . it was coming right down their throats!

"Shields!" barked Captain Sisko, but Kira could only look back at him and sadly shake her head. "Brace for impact," said the captain. "Lie down if you're standing."

Dax evaded, but the Klingon torpedo tracked. If the initial shot hadn't been so perfect, so lucky, the torpedo's eye could not have found the *Defiant* in time. Unfortunately for the Starfleet crew, the Klingons had thrown the dice and rolled a double. Dax swerved and bucked, but the torpedo exploded three thousand meters off their port bow, where the shields were still weak from the two-pronged assault of a few seconds earlier.

The *Defiant* shuddered with the initial shock. *The white whale breached by a harpoon,* thought Kira, who was working her way through the great human literature of centuries past. The ship took the blow badly, bucking and yawing so that it was all the major could do to wrap her arms around the mast and not be cast into the sea with Ahab. The jerky visuals were making her sick, so she shut her eyes, unable to block the inner vision of another ship, the *Pequod*, tossed in the water by a living leviathan, rather than the shock waves from matter and antimatter crashing together in the froth of energy that drove Kira's own vessel.

Sisko stood, glaring at Dax. "Good call on the odds of a hit, *Old Man*."

"Oh come on, Benjamin! That's not fair."

"How fast?"

"The leak? Oh, we're not going to be sucking vacuum in the next hour. But we're not going anywhere, either. We could wait and hope we drift out of the communications containment shield, then call Bajor for help."

"No time, we have more important fish to fry," said the captain. "Prepare to beam the entire crew aboard *Deep Space Nine*."

"Benjamin, the shields are up, we can't transport. And the station is in hard vacuum and zero-G," said the science officer, staring at her sensors. "And there are forty-three live Klingons aboard!"

Sisko thought for a long moment, eyes closed. "There is one place on the station you *can* beam to," he said, lips curling into a marrow-freezing smile. "Target the pylon that Major Kira so kindly tore up with her phasers. I'll bet good latinum the pylon shield is compromised."

"Oh! Um, yeah. I suppose it is. What do you know?" Dax's face turned a pinkish shade, and Kira couldn't stop a quick smile.

"Kira," barked Captain Sisko, "break out pressure suits and issue phaser-rifles. We're going in. Instruct the ship to break outside the comm-blanking field and send a priority-one distress call to Bajor after we—"

"Can't," said Dax unhappily.

"Are you saying, Old Man, that you can't program the *Defiant* to leave the station and send a subspace message?"

Dax sat heavily. "Yes, sir."

"Aye, Captain," said Kira, finally able to respond to the order for suits and phaser-rifles. She rose and began cranking open emergency lockers.

Sisko seemed to notice the fallen ensign for the first time. The medical team had arrived up the turbolift, and the ship's medic crouched over Janine Wheeler, doing something to her skull. "Senior Chief," said Captain Sisko, his voice softening now that the crisis had passed, "is she going to be all right?"

The MedTech looked up blankly, unsure who had spoken. "That depends," she said, "can we get the ensign to the station infirmary?"

"This is not possible to determine just yet," said the captain, elaborately casual, but again, Kira could tell that inside, Sisko was ready to explode.

"Then I can't say whether she'll be all right, because that's what she needs, sir. I can't do anything else. I immobilized her head, but there's brain trauma from the cranial impact: pupils not equally reactive, with the left barely responding at all; no coring response, no response to verbal stimuli."

The other MedTech, a petty officer second class, indicated Ensign Amar, who had taken the captain's advice to hit the ground before the torpedo impact. "This one has a busted wing, but that's it."

"Suits and phaser-rifles, Captain," said Kira, laying them across the railing. She stared at the suit, then felt her bulging abdomen, wondering whether she would fit into it.

Sisko grunted and nodded, evidently not trusting himself to speak. "All right, everybody except the medical personnel and the injured—oh, and except for you, Major; sorry about that—suit up and grab a rifle. You've all been drafted onto the away team." Kira started to protest, then realized that Miles O'Brien might very possibly be dead, and if that were so, what Kira carried would be all that Keiko had left of her husband.

The away team—Sisko, Dax, Odo, and nine other crew members—slid into their ziplock suits and headed down for the transporter room.

At first, Worf thought his weight-loss was only his imagination. He had desperately been hoping that O'Brien would catch the rather broad hints the Klingon had thrown out, at great danger to himself. For a few moments, Worf was certain it was merely wishful thinking.

He was double-timing his squadron around the perimeter of the habitat ring, dragging them behind in an ever-more raggedy formation as they struggled to keep up, when he realized that every long stride in his march-step was bouncing him higher into the air than the last. The sign was unmistakable—the sometimes stubbornly thick-headed chief had finally gotten it! And if O'Brien had figured out the *rest* of the message, then Worf had better start looking for an emergency pressure-suit locker immediately.

Without saying a word to his alleged command, Worf shifted his gaze left and right as he walked. There were not that many lockers, it had never occurred either to the Cardassian construction crew or the new Federation landlords that *depressurization* was a likely emergency. Not surprising, since that particular emergency had never happened in thirty years, except as a result of ship-to-ship or ship-to-station combat.

Within a few more strides, Worf was feeling decidedly light-headed, but he wasn't sure whether that was because of the low-gravity or a drop in the atmosphere. Then he began to pant from the faint exertion of fast walking, and all doubt disappeared. *"We are under attack!"* he bellowed, paying for his air expenditure with a dizzy spell that almost dumped him onto the deck. "The enemy is on the other side . . . *break ranks and charge!"*

Worf himself led the charge, pounding along the corridor, bounding higher and higher until his head began to graze the overhead with every leap. He gasped for air, seeing sparkles before his eyes. Colonel Worf—*No, Lieutenant Commander!*—began to laugh at the absurdity of everything. He slipped and fell, sliding across the deckplates like an ancient *Farak* disk across the ice, with gravity a tiny fraction of normal, friction was proportionally diminished.

Worf laughed until the tears rolled, then he felt a wave of unreasoning terror, and *finally,* the rational thought rolled lazily into his brain that he was experiencing the narcotic effects of oxygen-deprivation: his brain simply wasn't getting enough oxygen because of the plummeting atmospheric pressure, and the rational faculties were shutting down.

The terror transformed suddenly to rage and hatred, emotions never too far from the surface anyway in a good Klingon warrior. He spun as quickly as he could in the low-G, ready to confront the devil-Klingons behind him with bloody-minded ferocity.

But the troops, his erstwhile command, had their own problems: they were tearing into each other like a pack of starving *gravka* beasts. Some had drawn their short-bladed *d'k tahg* knives, but others were using hands and feet. Their flesh varied in color from ashen gray to white with blue highlights around the lips. Several had collapsed and lay still. Worf had run them into unconsciousness, perhaps death.

Worf turned away, another thought drifting into his feeble excuse for a cerebral cortex: *I must find a pressure-suit or I shall die.* The thought aroused no particular emotion, neither fear nor glory in a heroic death—and *that* lack of emotion frightened him a little, galvanizing the Klingon to action.

He pushed himself to his feet and staggered onward, struggling against unconsciousness, which lapped at his mind—waves along the seashore, gently tugging him toward the vast deep. Ahead, he spied the symbol he had been looking for: the stylized pointy cylinder with a hose snaking from the top and around the body, which meant "pressure-suits inside"—something the other Klingons would probably never figure out until it was too late. Humans, who dominated the Federation, prided themselves on their "universal" emergency symbols, which of course no one but a human could decipher.

Worf tried to leap the remaining distance, but he fell over instead and bounced face-first into the bulkhead. His head jerked, as if a giant held it in cupped hands and yanked to the right and up, over and over. Nausea overwhelmed the warrior, and, for a moment, he was so sick and dizzy, he forgot that he was also quickly suffocating to death.

Time . . . I have time! I have five minutes before permanent brain damage. The words echoed inside Worf's skull. He squirmed along the ground, a sick and dying rodent headed for the comfort of a hole in which to die.

For a moment, blackness claimed him. The room spun, but Worf no longer cared. It was over. Death wasn't so bad after all. *Sto-vo-kor.* More words, but this time from another time, another voice: *But that will not help the Empire much. Or the Federation.*

Who said that? He could not remember, but it had something to do with a war, or a raid, and blood entered into the transaction, as it always did. What happened to the lights? *Oh. Eyes closed. Open them.*

Still not much, but it was enough to see by. Worf saw a pointy cylinder with what looked like a rope coming out of one end. It was painted onto a door his hand was almost touching.

With effort bordering on that of the heroes of old, Worf struggled back to a shadow of consciousness and was rewarded by another wave of nausea. He was floating now, all the station gravity gone: he was held against the locker door only by the station's spin, which imparted a slight acceleration outward—one thirtieth of a G on the habitat ring. Less than fifty Newtons held him against the pressure-suit locker; he could push himself away by flexing his hand.

Problem: the doorplate required far more than fifty Newtons pressure to open the door. Worf stretched his feet back as far as they would go, and his groping toe faintly brushed the opposite bulkhead. A smaller man would never have been able to reach. He shifted his fingers, centering them on the touchplate, and pressed outward simultaneously with fingers and toes.

The plate depressed silently, and the door slowly rolled back, its grating noise lost in the filmy wisps of atmosphere. When it was halfway open, Worf pulled his hand back and pushed once again, hard, with his foot. He drifted into the opening, shoulders barely clearing the doorframe.

He wasted no time on a full pressure-suit. He had one overriding, desperate need. He grabbed the back of a helmet and twisted the air-flow valve full forward, then he opened the helmet and stuck his face into the neckhole. His lungs were heaving, gasping at the nothingness that surrounded him. He felt himself blacking out again, and this time, there was no stopping the sensation.

He blinked, wondering where he was, what he was supposed to be doing. *Who* he was. In panic, he realized he did not even know his name.

He blinked. *Any minute now, I will remember who I am.* He heard a rushing in his ears that meant . . . that meant something. *Any minute, I will remember my name. I know this—I should know what this is!*

Wo-ooo-oooooooo-orf! The name whooshed back on the North Wind, but a second later, it was followed by the most violent headache ever to batter his skull—a

223

bat'telh caving into his cranium from behind wouldn't have brought so much agony! Worf gritted his teeth, refusing to scream and disgrace himself, a Klingon warrior.

Klingon . . . warrior. He shook his head—big mistake. A wave of nausea hit him full force, as all his memories rushed back at hurricane force. Lieutenant Commander Worf was floating in the pressure-suit locker, his arms wrapped in a death-grip around a helmet, his face pushed against the neckhole, whence he sucked the life-giving oxygen into his lungs, clearing his head.

Dressing in a pressure suit in zero-G was hard enough without also having to stop every few seconds to suck another lungful of air from a detached helmet. His head still pounded from the oxygen-pummeling his brain had received, but at least the nausea retreated under the onslaught of urgent action. It took the Klingon a full *fifteen minutes* to struggle his way into the suit, but when he did, he was fully in command of himself again.

Malach was screaming in Worf's ears, the voice coming over the command headset: ". . . the prisoners behind force shields, *now,* you lazy—!" The rest of Malach's order could be represented in Worf's mind only by a long string of vile dashes, language appropriate to a gunnery sergeant, perhaps, but not a commissioned officer from a fine, old house. In the flush of the crisis, Malach's lack of true breeding was leaking through, confirming what Worf had always dimly suspected about the "noble" lineage of the house of Razg.

Worf did not know exactly where Malach was. The "general" could be anywhere. Worf smiled, *but I know where you are, O'Brien my comrade.* The environmental controls could only have been monkey-wrenched from one of two places, and there was no way that the chief could have fought his way through to Ops. Therefore, he was in the lowest level of all, the bottom of the engineering section—or had been, at least.

Worf grabbed a phaser rifle from the "upper" section of the pressure-suit locker and set out for the nearest crossover tunnel. It was time for hammer to meet anvil—with several dozen Klingon warriors in between.

CHAPTER
20

LIEUTENANT COMMANDER WORF, shucking off the ersatz rank of colonel, bounded clumsily through the crossover tunnel, cursing himself for not taking extra time practicing zero-G combat in the holodeck on the *Enterprise,* or even in Quark's holosuites on the station! *I shall rectify that immediately, should we retake the station,* he told himself. Thinking, forming words and sentences, helped stave off the persistent effects that zero-G had on his middle-ear: vertigo, dizziness, nausea, and a pervasive and clearly clinical sense of impending doom.

His only consolation was that everyone else must be feeling the same set of symptoms, and Worf at least had recent experience with it in the derelict hulk. *Except the doctor,* he corrected darkly. Dr. Bashir never seemed bothered by anything.

At first, the Klingon warrior struck his helmet with virtually every "step," until he forced himself to stop jumping *up* and instead to point himself the way he wanted to go and jump *straight.* By the time he figured out the technique for double-timing in the weightless station, Worf had managed to give himself a concussion right through his helmet, or at least a headache angry enough to fell anyone but a Klingon.

Worf saw the airlock at the inner end of the tunnel looming. He flapped his arms and legs and slammed into the titanium door with a loud clank, head-first. Fortunately for the mighty warrior, the pressure-suit helmet was built to withstand asteroid-mining accidents and cargo-bay misadventures. Seeing stars, Worf braced his legs and twisted the manual release on the airlock door, which had sealed automatically when it detected depressurization.

The door retracted; it was silly, actually, there was as much hard vacuum on the inside as the outside, so what good was an airtight seal? But Cardassians were known for following rules and maintaining good discipline, not for subtle logic. Worf dialed the door until it was open enough to admit his bulky frame, made even bulkier by the pressure suit. Then, dragging his phaser-rifle behind him, he twisted his body into line with the door's "pupil" and propelled himself into the Promenade level.

A spate of pressure-suited Klingon warriors, none lower in rank than staff sergeant, waited to greet him. They had set their ambuscade halfway between crossover tunnels two and three, since there was no way of knowing which he would take. But there was no question they were floating in ambush for Worf, because they opened fire on him as soon as he shot into the Promenade.

But these Klingons were not as well trained as most in the art of zero-G combat, and they didn't expect Worf to rocket into the huge cylinder and continue all the way to the inner bulkhead. Their disruptor shots passed the pressure-suited projectile.

"Fools," muttered Worf, before realizing his mike was probably hot. It was clear what had happened: Malach had figured out that Worf really *was* a traitor, and he had cut Worf's headset out of the communications loop. Thus, Worf had never heard the orders sending a hit-squad to the Promenade to intercept him.

He struck the inner bulkhead, ironically crashing into the door to Constable Odo's office. The squad was already coming after him, clumsy in their movements. At first, he thought it was because they were trying to move and fight in unfamiliar, Federation pressure-suits they had managed to don, but then he realized there was an even more ridiculous explanation.

Are they trying to walk? he wondered in amazement. Indeed, the battle-hardened warriors were trying to keep their feet in contact with the deck! They windmilled their arms (against what?), trying to find a balance that of course no longer existed. Their middle ears screamed, *Falling! Falling!* And they desperately needed an "up" and a "down" to avoid the terrible feeling of vertigo that still lurked at the back of Worf's brain, as well.

But the lieutenant commander had a huge advantage: he had already had a dry run in zero-G ops just four days earlier. And Worf remembered his lesson well.

While the hit-squad advanced slowly, struggling to maintain familiar contact with the deck, Worf took the opposite tack: he aimed himself at what would have been the ceiling of the Promenade, nearly ten meters "over-head," and pushed off with his friction boots against the constable's door. He soared in the airless, weightless environment angling slightly toward the crew. He calculated well, ending up directly "above" the squad. Only a few of the warriors had even seen where he went. The rest stared and pointed, presumably shouting that Worf was *over there* or *hiding behind that kiosk.*

As Worf headed toward the overhead, he fumbled at his phaser-rifle. His normally nimble fingers were hampered by the thick, insulated gloves. Even so, he managed to click the phaser beam–dispersal to the widest pattern, the power setting to the highest level.

He twisted his body and opened fire on his erstwhile

comrades even before he struck the ceiling. The combination of high power and wide beam dispersal created a cone of stun-force phaser shot. The Klingons fell like *pu'tahk* lizards on too hot a rock. Nine jerked and spasmed, sending themselves careening through the Promenade on random courses, unconscious and likely to stay that way for several minutes. Only three reacted quickly enough to grab hold of a bench and slide themselves under it for cover.

The Klingon shooters returned fire with their disruptors. Just then, Worf passed the upper-level catwalks, the same perch from which Jake Sisko and his Ferengi cohort, Nog, used to spy on the people below. Worf made a grab and managed to hook one hand on the railing, yanking himself to a halt. He rotated through 270 degrees around the railing, striking the catwalk on the opposite side from the Klingons, far "below." The metal mesh of the walk partially shielded him from the disruptor blasts, and what little destructive energy got through dissipated around his pressure-suit, which was shielded against cosmic particles and gamma radiation.

Alas, the same could be said of the three warriors still left unstunned below. Above—where Worf hung on to the top of the catwalk to avoid drifting away with the slight movements of respiration and twitching—the weapons officer fumed at his lack of weapons. His opponents were behind a wall too thick for his depleted phaser to cut through. *What I really need,* he grumbled to himself, *is a photon torpedo instead of a phaser running low on power.*

He stared at the station core in frustration. He had to link up with O'Brien and whichever station personnel the chief had managed to rescue. But if he made a dash for the inner bulkhead of the Promenade, he wouldn't get even halfway before the massed disruptor fire of the Klingons tore him to shreds—or stunned him into submission, if Malach's no-killing order still stood.

He stared through the grillwork, knowing that his

counterparts were staring up at him. Their eyes might even be meeting, though none of the parties could possibly tell. And a thought occurred: what he really needed was a photon torpedo, and what was he holding in his hands but a potential bomb? Like any other phaser, with a little electronic surgery, the rifle could be cross-wired and made to overload and explode.

There was one small drawback, of course: it was a one-shot weapon, after which Worf would be disarmed, save for his *d'k tahg* knife, which of course, was *inside* his suit! On the other hand, if he *didn't* take the chance, he could stay on the catwalk all day and all night, or until enough reinforcements arrived to take him out by a swarm attack.

Worf was a Klingon warrior, and that meant that a decision was quick in coming and was always followed immediately by action. He turned the rifle over, popped the case, and pried open the power-pack. He held on to the catwalk with his feet, hoping they were too small a target for the sharpshooters to notice.

"Worf, Worf," sounded a mellifluous voice over his headset. He jumped, startled by the unexpected resumption of communications from his blood-brother. "I know you believe your treachery is irretrievable, and perhaps you believe it is now an affair of honor. But it is not too late. You can still come back to me, back to your people."

Worf sighed. "You are not my people . . . my brother."

"The final triumph of the Empire is inevitable, Worf. Do not find yourself on the losing side of an impossible war."

For a moment, Worf said nothing. He struggled to remember his engineering year back at the Starfleet Academy, where a classmate had showed him one night how to overload a phaser. Needless to say, it was not a skill taught officially in the curriculum, nor could it be found in the standard Federation engineering manuals on the weapons. *If the chief were here,* he could not help thinking, *he would have finished this task in thirty seconds.*

He realized he was sweating and biting his lip, not an auspicious reaction for a mighty warrior of the mighty Empire. "I cannot predict about the war, but you are not going to win this battle, Malach. You must withdraw with what honor and dignity you can. Starfleet must have already sent a ship to discover why the station stopped communicating."

"They will wait, Worf. They have already been informed about the communications failure and instructed that all is well. When the Starfleet ship finally arrives, it will find a surprise. Worf, once we have the station and can decrypt the weapons-lock, we can use the station defenses themselves to defend *our* station from Starfleet. Starfleet will relent and negotiate, as they always do."

"Your plan is flawed and will never work. The captain will return and will not negotiate with terrorists and madmen."

"Mad? You call me *mad?* The general who pulls off the greatest feat in recent military history must surely be the *sanest* man in the Empire!" Malach's voice rose to a crescendo, and Worf paused in his labors. *I struck a nerve,* he realized with a chill. *Malach is terrified that he is losing his mind!* That, Worf realized, might have been a major motivation for the stunning attack on *Deep Space Nine.*

"They all said you were mad, did they not, my brother? You told them your plan, and they laughed at you, told you it was insane. But you showed them, bloodbrother. You showed them all."

"You see how alike we are?" whispered Malach in Worf's ear, a disturbing intimacy that angered the lieutenant commander. "You are the only one who ever understood me. They thought I was mad even when we were children—Commandant Gacht'g told me so himself, right to my face! Where was honor then, eh Worf? You have been my rock, my support all these years that I had to hide myself in simple service to the Empire as a mere major. The one friend I could depend upon. Now, I am the general, and I shall remember your support. Come back to me!"

Worf frowned. He found the wires he thought he wanted, but hesitated before crossing them: if he had guessed wrong, rather than overload for eight seconds then blow, the phaser would melt in Worf's hand, probably taking half his arm with it. *So either way, I shall be disarmed,* he thought grimly.

Malach's delusional state was more advanced than Worf ever imagined. He had had no contact whatsoever with his "blood-brother" since they both left Emperor Kahless Military City. Yet, evidently, Malach had fantasized a whole relationship that never existed, visualizing his boyhood friend into his adult ally. Then another thought struck Worf: as a mere *major?* Like Major Krugus?

"I am sorry to disappoint you," said Worf, then realized with a start that it was quite true. "I am no man's rock. I walk my own path, and that path does not include your . . . invasion of this station." At the last moment, Worf changed his mind; he had been about to say *"your mad scheme."*

Taking a deep breath, Worf crossed the wires. The rifle did not melt. Instead, it began to emit a high-pitched noise over the comm link; its frequency at the extreme edge of Worf's auditory range. He was committed. The wires, once crossed, could not be uncrossed. As he leaned over and gently pushed the phaser rifle toward the floor of the Promenade, he thought about blood-brotherhood, wondering whether it, too could never be uncrossed.

Abruptly, another revelation crossed Worf's mind, this one purely tactical: it was clear from his conversation with Malach that Worf's own comm link had not been disabled. He was still able to hear *and broadcast*. He had been cut out of the communications loop between Malach and the other Klingon warriors, and probably they could not hear him, having been instructed to accept only communications preceded by a digital code.

But the handset that O'Brien had—was proven to have by his response to Worf's hints—had no such filter. *The chief can still hear me,* Worf realized, and filed away the datum for an unexpected tactical advantage . . . later.

The rifle drifted lazily "downward," tumbling end-over-end, but neither gaining nor losing velocity. He had not timed the push perfectly; the phaser exploded before it struck the ground. But it turned out to be close enough. Two Klingons were flung to the sides by the force of the explosion. They jerked in agony at their violent injuries, then they began convulsing in earnest, clawing at their Federation helmets, as if tugging them off their heads would allow them to breathe the vacuum more easily. The suits had been breached.

Worf waited until they stopped moving. *Odd,* he thought, *I thought there was a third* . . . But no one else reacted to the blast. Tentatively at first, Worf pulled himself over the catwalk rail and pushed off toward the floor. No one moved to impede him, either by disruptor fire or by grappling with him as he bounced past. Worf decided to enter the core through the doctor's office, so he headed in that direction as quickly as he could in the zero-G. Malach evidently had nothing more to say—for the moment.

Once again, Miles Edward O'Brien, in a long life of such violent encounters, found himself fighting Klingons hand-to-hand, a torn iron stanchion against a *bat'telh*— *they weren't supposed to use them!* screamed his brain— kicking stomachs and trying to tear holes in Federation pressure-suits that now protected the enemies of the Federation. *My God, doesn't it ever end?* They fought in zero-G, worse yet! And with every blow, the Klingon foe would shoot one direction while O'Brien tumbled the other in a perfect demonstration of Sir Isaac Bloody Newton's Second Law of Mechanical Physics.

Garak seemed to be swarmed, the brave little tailor. *He ought to be able to kill seven at one blow,* thought the chief, his mind wandering at the hopelessness of their plight. There were too damned many Klingons! They were everywhere! They came out of the woodwork, though admittedly, the Resistance (as O'Brien termed the six of them) encountered more dead Klingons than live, pressure-suited warriors.

The Resistance had barely made it up three levels— though "up" was a relative term—and were still mired in the higher levels of engineering. Whatever monkey business General Malach had worked on the computers still eluded the chief's ability to undo, so there was no multilevel communication except through the handset, which had ceased receiving useful information. Malach himself had gotten online more than once, however, and patiently explained to the "rebels" why they couldn't possibly win. So the device still worked, it was simply locked out of the comm loop. The suit communicators worked, so long as everyone was in one room together. If there was no line-of-sight, the Klingon jammers prevented a relay.

"Chief!" bellowed Bashir, making O'Brien wince. The doctor couldn't get it through his head that when speaking over a comm link, even inside a pressure-suit, a whisper was as good as a shout, and it didn't matter how far apart they were, so long as Bashir was in direct line-of-sight with the chief.

"I'm here, for God's sake, Julian! Stop screaming."

"Chief, I'm trapped! They're pressing me back through the number two access port!"

The Resistance had been driven sideways, into the outer edge of the large engineering deck, in a section connected to the main engineering deck by only two doors and whose outer skin was the outer hull of the station itself. O'Brien and Garak perched at one door, beating back the Klingons whenever they tried to force their way inside. Bashir and the Ferengi were at the other door, with Jake Sisko shuttling between the two camps as the "reserves," lending what assistance he could to whoever was being driven back most quickly.

This is futile! Another never-ending war, another . . . O'Brien blinked. The germ of an idea sprouted in his backbrain. Across the room, Jake Sisko plowed into the marauding Klingons with a torpedolike swoop. Directly in front of Chief O'Brien, the Klingon with the *bat'telh* abruptly stiffened, then drifted slowly to the side— stunned by his own non-com, who still remembered the "no kill" order of General Malach.

O'Brien barely slammed the door in time to avoid the sergeant's second shot, which would have stunned him. The chief's thought grew, and in a moment, he had the answer . . . "The Resistance can win!" he muttered.

"What's—what's that?" gasped the doctor, leaning against the door. The Klingons on his side had withdrawn to regroup, as they had on O'Brien's. Garak grasped the remaining piece of stanchion from which the chief had torn his weapon. The Cardassian gasped huge lungfuls of air and looked distinctly blue.

"Julian, I've got it!"

"Got what? A plan?"

"Yes, we just keep fighting!"

"Oh. Well, that's simply wizard, Chief."

An angry Quark piped up from the corner into which he had drifted. "Oh *thank you,* Chief, for that insightful analysis!" Because of the size of their suits, the Ferengi could control either hands or feet, but not both at once. Quark had a mini-phaser found in a locker, while the more technically sophisticated Rom was using a disruptor taken from the body of an atmospherically challenged Klingon warrior. But neither Ferengi could control where he drifted or which way he pointed, not while operating a weapon. So they ended up spinning lazily, taking pot shots whenever they happened to rotate to a good field of view.

"No, you don't understand, either of you. We just *keep fighting*, keep them fighting every minute—we should open these doors and start shooting."

Jake gasped in understanding. "Chief, I get it! You're thinking about the *oxygen*, aren't you?"

O'Brien grinned. It was good that at least one other person had seen it before he explained; it was a good test of the idea. "The kid's got it right, fellas. We *keep the Klingons moving*, keep them active and fighting. Julian, you should know this. They've got a larger lung capacity, right?"

"Yes . . ." admitted the doctor, evidently still puzzled.

"So if we keep their lungs pumping, shouldn't they run through their air tanks much faster than we will?"

Silence. Then after a long several seconds, Bashir's voice over the comm link. "Good Lord, Miles—that's brilliant!"

"Well, Quark? Does this plan meet with your approval?" O'Brien threw every gram of sarcasm into the question he could muster. Of course, the Ferengi took it seriously, instead.

"Yes, Chief, that's inspired! It's almost . . . Ferengi. Have you been reading the Rules of Acquisition recently?"

"No, Quark, and I wouldn't touch 'em with a three-meter positronic discharge tube. Now let's open the door and not give them time to rest or, God forbid, change air tanks!"

CHAPTER
21

THE FIGHT WAS furious, but didn't last long. Quark was torn by his natural tendency to stay out of barroom brawls, a technique mastered after years of running a haven for the scum of the quadrant, and a very un-Ferengi-like urge to leap to the defense of his comrades in the Resistance. Weighing against the latter option was the fact that his hands and feet, even at maximum stretch, came far short of the gloves and booties of the gargantuan suit into which Quark had crammed himself in panic as the air vanished: at first, he literally could do *nothing* but flap his arms and legs and squawk in humiliated rage over the comm link. His only consolation was that Rom was in the same boat. Then, he had figured out (though Rom tried to grab credit) that he could clumsily operate a phaser two-handed with his hands at the elbow joints of the pressure-suit, but it was undignified and not terribly useful.

The Klingons swarmed all over Bashir, O'Brien, and the Cardassian tailor. Even the boy was swinging a steel pipe, despite his earlier peculiar insistance to Nog (who told Rom, who told his brother) that he was a total coward. *Why not phasers?* wondered Quark, then realized that the suits were probably tough enough to deflect the low-powered hand phasers and hand disruptors, which were all either party had. Nobody had rifles.

There were four Klingons to four Resistance fighters, but because of O'Brien's tactic of using the hu-man boy as *reserves,* shuttling back and forth between Garak and the O'Brien-Bashir tag team, the Klingons ended up being outnumbered in both fights.

The invaders fought lustily and recklessly, however, and might still have won, had the chief's plan not finally worked. Even from his upside-down vantage point, as he fired the occasional, relatively useless phaser shot, Quark was able to see Klingon heads gulping for air and turning a bluish-purple as they found themselves inhaling nothing but their own exhalation. O'Brien was right: Klingons, with their bigger, more powerful lungs, used much more oxygen than did their hu-man (and Cardassian) counterparts. The warriors had sucked their tanks dry when Quark's pressure-gauge showed a full hour and thirty-four minutes of air left!

And then the battle was over before Quark could work up a sufficiently greedy argument to compel him to find a wall and launch into the thick of the fray, to strike at least one blow for his economic right to cheat customers in his *own* bar, his *own* way. The Klingons went down fighting, every one. They died rather than surrender. The only injury was to O'Brien, who got his arm wrenched and the sleeve of his suit torn. The last was by far the more serious "injury," and everything stopped while Bashir frantically tore open every drawer and locker in the engineering deck before finally finding a pressure-patch, a thick piece of plasticized cloth with *very* sticky glue on one side, to seal up the chief's torn sleeve.

While patching the chief, Bashir conducted a hurried conference, with O'Brien, the hu-man boy, and the

Cardassian (each at his own angle, which made Quark's head spin more even than the zero-G). Nobody thought to fetch the Ferengi and include them, though of course Quark could hear and participate via the radio. It was disconcerting to collude while rotating slowly on his axis, however.

"This isn't going to do it," said O'Brien. "We can't go from deck to deck, fighting Klingons with no plan. It stands to reason we'll be clipped, taken out finally, and Malach will win after all."

"You're so cheery," griped the doctor, his pride wounded at O'Brien's grim assessment. "Isn't it a bit early for a dirge?"

"Julian, it's a mathematical certainty that long before we overcome them, we'll be captured—or killed, even accidentally. There might be as many as *forty* Klingons still left aboard!"

"I'm afraid I must agree with our esteemed chief," chimed in Garak. "I'm not averse to risking death or imprisonment in order to defend the station, but isn't it a terrible waste of spirit and manpower?"

"Thanks, Garak, for that vote of confidence in my leadership."

"I have nothing but the greatest respect for your leadership, Dr. Bashir! I'm simply pointing out a few realities, unpleasant though they may be: we're not *getting anywhere*, to put it bluntly. What's our purpose?"

"Jake," asked Bashir, "what's your take? You're as much a part of this as the rest of us."

"Hey, remember me?" demanded Quark, at that moment facing directly away from the huddle in the center of the room. "Isn't anyone interested in *my* take on strategy?"

"Quark, I'm terribly sorry . . . you don't feel left out, do you?"

"No, Doctor, I'm simply filled with gratitude when we move from room to room, and Chief O'Brien says 'don't forget to bring the beachballs!' How come everyone but us gets to hatch plans? Ferengi are very good at scheming, you know! It's one of our best traits. Isn't that right, brother?"

"Uh, yeah. Quark's right. We really are good at it," confirmed Rom. He didn't sound particularly convincing, though, not even to Quark's lobes.

"All right, Quark," said the chief. "Do you want to scheme? Fine, then come up with something, some plan. Oh, and I'm sorry about the beachball crack, but you really do look funny, you know."

"Well it so happens," said Quark, with all the frozen dignity he could muster, "that I *have* thought of a plan. Actually, you said it yourself a day or so ago, but I think you thought you were joking."

"If you would care to enlighten us," purred the Cardassian tailor, "I'm certain we would all be eternally grateful."

"It's very simple. Obviously, the Federation has no idea what's happened to the station, right? They must have bought Malach's crude lie about the comm grid being offline for repairs."

"Unfortunately," said Bashir, sounding petulant, "Starfleet appears to be so uninterested that they haven't even bothered to come over and scan us."

"And if Malach can secure this station and send for reinforcements from the Klingon Empire—Gowron, is it?—then by the time the Federation gets off its butt and comes out here, they'll have to fight a Klingon fleet *and* their own station. Am I right?"

"That's Malach's theory. It appears to be logical . . . again, unfortunately."

"So our best chance of stopping him is to get a message to the Federation, or to Bajor."

"But we can't," explained O'Brien with ill-disguised impatience. "We can't get a message through the comm shield the Klingons put around us. We could have used the subspace emitter, since it sticks out quite a ways from the station, but that was the first thing the bastards took out. I think they sheared it off with their ship."

"But chief," asked Quark, "why does the emitter need to be attached to the station?"

"Don't be an ass, Quark! How's it going to broadcast if it's not—"

"Chief, what if the transmitter were intelligent enough to broadcast all on its own? And suppose you could get it far enough away from the station that it was outside the communications damping field. Wouldn't that work?"

Quark had finally rotated around on his axis to look at the assembled "Resistance." It was a scuffy-looking bunch, even by hu-man standards. O'Brien was staring at him. Even though the helmet faceplate, Quark could see the chief's typical look of annoyed puzzlement. "I don't have the resources to build an intelligent transmitter, Quark. And the Klingons would detect the electronics and blow it apart. We've been through all that!"

"You idiot, I'm talking about launching *one of us!*"

Dead silence. For a moment, Quark became terrified that his comm link had suddenly died. Then Bashir spoke. "One of *us?* One of us here?"

"Of course! What else? You don't need a computer, Chief—you just need to open an airlock and throw one of us, probably Jake Sisko, in the general direction of Bajor. As soon as he clears the damping field, he starts transmitting. Chief, can you boost the gain on these cheap, little comm sets in the suits?"

"Quark!" exclaimed Garak. "That's . . . that's brilliant! I never knew a Ferengi had such potential." Quark was losing sight of the conference out his peripheral vision as he continued to rotate. He harbored a desperate hope that he would drift close enough to a wall that he could grab it and stop his slow spin.

"Oh, my brother is too smart for the Ferengi Alliance," bragged Quark's brother. "That's, uh, why they wouldn't let him back on Ferenginar."

"Shut-*up*, Rom!"

"Quark," said Bashir patiently, "I cannot allow one of my—"

"No, Julian, it's a *great* idea! You wanted a plan? Well, here's one dropped right in your lap. We get to the Promenade, where the emergency airlocks are; I short-circuit the computer locks; we stick Quark inside, and when the doors open, he kicks out away from the station!"

"Perfection itself," said the Ferengi.

"But, how long can he survive just in his suit?"

"A Ferengi?" asked the chief. "Oh, six hours, easily, if he takes it slow and doesn't make any unnecessary movements. The suit has a transponder. The Bajorans or a Starfleet vessel can pick Quark up anytime after the Klingons have been subdued."

Something odd had happened. Quark couldn't quite put his finger on it, but the hu-mans had gotten some aspect of his plan terribly wrong. He scowled, replaying the conversation in his lobes, listening for the mixup.

"Wouldn't the Klingons just shoot him before he broadcasts?" asked the good doctor, fretting about the humanity of it all.

"How would they even know to look for him? They've got all the runabouts, they've got the bird-of-prey. They know we don't have a subspace emitter antenna because they sliced it off; they know we can't even communicate with each other out of line-of-sight, because of the damping field. And we can't use the station comm links or computers even if we got to them, because it would take a couple of days to break the encryption scheme . . . without access to a starship computer, I mean.

"Julian, *they think they've already won!* There's nothing we can do anyway. How vigilant do you think they'll really be? Are they likely to spot one tiny Ferengi in a spacesuit, zooming through space under a communications blackout? It's not like he has enough electrical activity to ring alarm bells on their sensor arrays!"

Like a puzzle, the fine strands came together in the center of Quark's mind. Abruptly, he realized the terrible flaw in the implementation of his plan. "A tiny *Ferengi?* Wait! Wait! How did *I* get to be the one who—"

Jake Sisko chimed in. "Quark has a point, sir. Maybe I should be the one to—"

"Oh Jake, really! Do you think your father would allow me to keep my *head,* let alone my collar-pips, if I allowed you to take such a terrible risk with your life?"

"Such a terrible risk?" screamed the impressed volunteer. "Let the boy do it! He's much more the heroic type . . . I'm an idea man, a thinker, not a doer!" Quark struggled wildly, flailing his arms and legs like an agitated rodent. He twisted and tried to swim in the air, but he couldn't manage to give himself any faster of a spin or turn himself around. Something to do with conservation of angular momentum, he glumly decided.

While three hu-mans and a Cardassian tailor, all quite unsympathetic to Ferengi in general, debated the life and all-too-likely death of Quark, the subject of their discussion could only stare helplessly at a very uninteresting bulkhead, his back to the roundtable. Beads of perspiration popped out on his face, where they stuck. In zero-G, there was no "down" for them to run. It was the most uncomfortable feeling in the world, piled on top of the general zero-G–induced sickness: warm, salty drops of sweat glued to his flesh. He couldn't wipe them away because he couldn't get at them! The helmet shielded Quark's face from all possible relief.

Not that Quark's discomfort mattered to anyone, *oh no.* Though he often thought himself the only sane person left on the station, since the departure of the Cardassians—who were admittedly cruel and coldhearted, but so what? was that a *crime?*—he was generally treated worse by the inmates than the Cardassians used to treat Bajorans. Harassed at every step by Constable Odo, prevented from making a decent living, not allowed a moment's respite, subject to being hauled into

Odo's security office at any moment when the call went out to "round up the usual suspects."

Quark sighed, but no one caught the subtle hint. By the time he rotated around to face the mob again, they had reached a consensus. Whether by voting or by Bashir's exercising dictatorial fiat, Quark couldn't care less. The unchangeable upshot was that they would happily accept Quark's idea, but Quark would be the expendable one!

"Do your worst," he snarled, and they did. For the next hour, the self-styled Resistance battled its way up, so to speak, level after level, until they were only two down from the Promenade. The Promenade was the nearest level that had an airlock. Not that an airlock was strictly necessary. With the station in vacuum, Quark was grateful they didn't simply break a window and defenestrate him.

But there, two levels below the Promenade, they stuck fast: they ran into a pocket of resistance that quite outnumbered them, twelve Klingons to their four (plus two involuntary noncombatants), and they had to retreat behind a door the opening circuitry of which Chief O'Brien shot out with a phaser blast, jamming it.

"For God's sake, Chief!" shouted the doctor, straining to hold the door shut by bracing his feet against one side of the jamb and pulling back on the door's emergency manual bolt. "Isn't there *any* other way up to the Promenade?"

O'Brien was exhausted. He drifted loose, gasping for each breath, probably grateful for the zero-G. Unlike Quark, who still cursed the stupid chief for his brilliant idea. Garak looked grim and alert, but the Ferengi's years tending bar made him extraordinarily sensitive to falsity, and the Cardassian tailor's heart pounded so hard that Quark's sensitive lobes could actually pick it up through the line-of-sight comm link.

Jake Sisko made no pretense of spirit. He had pulled

himself into a upside-down fetal position and held the top of the same manual bolt that Bashir braced without trying to help the doctor. The boy was exhausted. *Great, another useless appendage better left behind,* groused the Ferengi, floating helplessly—as usual.

For half an hour, they had done nothing more than parry the Klingons' attempts to force the door, the only door, thank the Divine Auditor. But all the while, the sibilant voice of the Klingon commander whispered to them through the captured handset. The voice was soft in Quark's lobes through the jury-rigged relay O'Brien had set up between handset and the suit com-links.

"You cannot win; the game is over. You have already lost. Now is the time to surrender yourselves. You will be spared, I give you my word of honor as Malach of House Razg! Federation, there simply is no further escape. You can go no farther, though the distance you have covered and the warriors you have slain attest to your remarkable courage and warrior spirit. But every battle must end, and I have maneuvered sufficient force to prevent your further advance. Surrender now, and I *personally* guarantee not only your own lives, but the lives and *freedom* of all the prisoners I hold!

"The prisoners are safe. They are within forceshields. Not one Federation or luckless neutral has been harmed, I swear it! But you *must surrender now,* or I simply will not be able to restrain my troops any longer."

"Maybe he's right," conceded Chief O'Brien, finally being sensible, though his voice sounded beaten and discouraged rather than calculating. "He's not killed anyone yet, at least not that I've seen. And he did shoot one of his own men when the man almost knocked Jake off the railing."

"It's what *we* would do, surrender, I mean," said Rom, surprising Quark with such a proper Ferengi attitude. "Rule of Acquisition number—"

"Oh, shut-up, Rom!" snapped Bashir, proving himself

as cranky as the rest of them. "Look, I will *not* surrender my command, just because a bunch of punk Klingons gain a little, temporary advantage over—"

"Julian, face the facts! He's got twelve out there already, he says there are more on the way, and I'm inclined to believe him! We're only four—"

"Six!"

"Four who can fight, Julian, and one of us is a teenaged boy! What more can you expect us to do?"

"Much as I loathe admitting it," said Garak, keeping his voice remarkably steady, "the chief is being quite practical. Now, had Malach been fighting the *Cardassian* station of *Terek Nor,* instead of the Federation *Deep Space Nine,* it might have been a different story."

"Oh, yes," sneered the chief, "the Cardassians gave them real hell when they overran your entire so-called empire in a few hours!"

But Garak's inevitable retort was cut short by another crackle from the handset. When the voice sounded, Quark was startled first to realize that it was not the voice of General Malach, the only Klingon voice they had heard since the Klingons realized they could be heard. But the Ferengi bartender was utterly nonplussed when he realized whose voice it was. It was the prune juice, extra large!

"You must do as General Malach suggests," said Worf, his voice fizzing and popping like the hu-man drink called root beer. "You cannot win this battle, and no one will come to your aid if you burst through those doors. *This is not like Captain Sisko's famous victory on the glorious Kobyashi-Maru campaign.* Surrender immediately, and do not even think about further resistance."

The coin flips once again, thought Quark in surprise.

Three voices spoke simultaneously, the first in triumph, the latter two in complete bafflement: "You see?" crowed the general who had masterminded the strike against the station, "even your own spy and saboteur

246

agrees that you have no choice but to surrender this station and accept my generous offer!"

"Glorious victory?" exclaimed Doctor Bashir, "glorious—*victory?*"

And Chief O'Brien had his own contribution: "Kobyashi? Who the *hell* is Captain Kobyashi?"

CHAPTER
22

DR. JULIAN BASHIR looked from one blank face to another. Only Jake looked pensive, the others clearly had no clue to the significance of what Worf had just said. *No clue?* Bashir stared at O'Brien. "Chief, the *glorious victory* of the Kobyashi-Maru! Don't you get it?"

"Get what? Julian, it's just more gibberish. What the hell is Worf on about? What's this Kobyashi Maroon thing?"

"The Kobyashi-Maru! Chief, the Koby—" Bashir froze in mid-shout, feeling his face turn hot. Master Chief Petty Officer Miles Edward O'Brien was so damned useful around the station, included in so many high-level meetings, treated like any other department head, that sometimes, that *nearly always,* Bashir forgot that O'Brien wasn't a commissioned officer. The chief had never been to Starfleet Academy in his entire life!

Of course he had no idea about the Kobyashi-Maru, the secret exercise given to all cadets not once but many times. The exercise that *could not be won* . . . that was designed for failure. The purpose was so simple, it took most Academy cadets their entire school career to figure it out. Starfleet wanted to see how they reacted to failure. What would the cadet and future officer do when everything he tried, no matter how brilliant or unexpected, still led to his ship exploding in a fiery death, taking the cadet and all the crew with it?

Glorious victory? The Kobyashi-Maru was so much the opposite that there was no way Worf could be mistaken or misremembering. It was a code, a deliberate message.

Unexpectedly, the boy spoke up from his disconcerting vantage point at the other end of the tog-wheel that Bashir was wedging shut, upside-down with respect to the other three combatants. "Chief, the Kobyashi-Maru is . . . well, let's just say it was an important battle, and the Federation lost. Big time."

"I never heard of it," retorted the chief. "I've studied every military engagement listed in every casebook, and I never—"

"It's something they only study at the Academy. It's not in the books. The—Starfleet is sort of embarrassed, they don't want to let anybody know about it."

"Which raises the rather interesting question," said the doctor quietly. "Of how you, Jake, seem to have found out."

"Oh. Uh, I was . . . told."

"By your friend Nog, I take it."

"No! Um, no. Nog wouldn't do that, not while he's still at . . . I mean, my source was kind of higher rank than Nog. A Starfleet officer."

Bashir smiled sardonically. "Wouldn't happen to hold the rank of captain, would he?"

"Anything's possible," said Jake noncommitally. "Anyway, my source waited until it was certain that I would never attend Starfleet Academy. He wouldn't have wanted to, ah, ruin the effect, if you know what I mean."

"This is all charming," interrupted O'Brien. "But

what's the point? So Worf thinks a defeat is a victory. It's probably one of those Klingon honor things. Big deal!"

"No, Chief. It's decidedly more than that. It's a clue, maybe the last clue he can give us—he called the engagement a glorious victory, but it was a terrible defeat. What does that mean?"

Long, pregnant silence, during which Bashir strained every neural fiber in his head to concoct increasingly complex meanings for the bizarre faux-pas. The silence was broken at last by the small, tentative voice of Quark's brother Rom. *Probably the most commonsensical voice among us,* Bashir told himself. "Uh, that he means the exact opposite of whatever he says?"

Thud. The Latinum dropped. Of course, when all else fails, try the most obvious answer!

"So, what else did he say? Anybody remember? O'Brien, Rom, Jake?"

"I notice you chose not to ask me," muttered Garak, perhaps forgetting that they were all "hot-miked," and everyone could hear every smallest utterance.

"I can remember exactly," said Rom. "A Ferengi businessman is expected to memorize his business accounts going back five years—"

"Yes, yes," said Bashir hastily. "We've been through all that! What *exactly* did Worf say, besides the bit about the . . . the famous battle?"

"He said, 'You must do as General Malach suggests. You cannot win this battle, and no one will come to your aid if you burst through those doors. This is not like Captain Sisko's famous victory on the glorious Kobyashi-Maru campaign. Surrender immediately, and do not even think about further resistance.'"

"But that's it!" shouted O'Brien. "He said *no one would come to our aid* if we crashed through the door—he's saying he *will* come to our aid!"

"'You can't win the battle,'" quoted Jake; "Worf's saying we *can* win the battle *if* we make an all-out attack right now, coming through the doors, and he'll join us, and—and maybe Malach doesn't have the manpower to reinforce those guards out there."

Sensitive to the Cardassian's previous remark, Bashir rotated to face him. "Garak? I know you have a lot more experience in these matters than you like to let on. Any thoughts?"

"My only thought, my friend, is that we are doing precious little good cowering here wishing everything would get all better. At this point, I'm quite ready to die of sheer boredom. Death by disruptor fire would be a welcome relief!" Garak smiled, barely visible through the faceplate of his pressure-suit, which was styled to look much more *imperial* than the Federation suits, but which was otherwise reasonably well-tailored. "Thank you for asking, Dr. Bashir."

Encouraged by the unanimity, Bashir twisted until he located the two Ferengi, clutching an odd-looking wall that he realized, on second glance, was a catwalk when the station was under gravity. "Quark, Rom? Do we have a consensus?"

"Oh, you're bothering to ask the *torpedo's* opinion?" sneered the former. "How civilized of you, Doctor. Better watch yourself; you might start to recognize that I have certain rights that are being—"

"We think the plan is fine," said Rom, cutting off his bitterly cynical brother.

"Then," said Bashir, "on the count of three, here we go. It's Armageddon time, troops."

The sudden opening of the door caught the Klingons flat-footed, or perhaps "randomly floating" was a better term: they were huddled in a conference of their own, helmets pressed together to speak too quietly for Malach to hear on his channel. Presumably, they were discussing their inability to break through the defenses of the Resistance and deciding what they were going to tell the general. One by one, they stared in surprise as the door rolled quickly open (with both Bashir and Jake spinning the tog, their feet braced as best they could manage). One

Klingon pointed and shouted something, then the mighty Klingon warriors fumbled for their disruptors.

Simultaneously with that motion, a red disruptor beam lanced from a dark, shadow-painted tube—one of the auxiliary power-conduits, Bashir reckoned. Two Klingon invaders were tagged from behind before the rest even knew they were fighting on more than one front.

Cleverly, the entire platoon of Klingons tried to rotate to deal with the new threat—not an easy task in zero-G! They grabbed each other, of course, and Conservation of Angular Momentum insured that for every Klingon who rotated to face Worf, the one he grabbed was spun in the opposite direction!

Bashir kicked away from the door and into the room, taking hip-shots with his own phaser as he drifted. He careened off one bulkhead, kicking again to make up for the momentum absorbed by his body. Another shot, and another, and finally a hit! Three of twelve Klingons down, and so far, no casualties for the Resistance.

It became instantly obvious that these warriors were not as experienced as he in zero-G combat—and Julian Bashir regretted every second he had spent badmouthing Captain Sisko for requiring extra training! Klingon warriors used their comrades as launching platforms, kicking off from one another, sending the launching pad tumbling off in the opposite direction.

Worse still: as they kicked off their compadres, the launchees tried simultaneously to spin around to return fire. But of course, they didn't stop spinning just because they were pointing, for a moment, in the right direction! Like any other object in a zero-G vacuum, once they started rotating, they continued rotating, spinning like gyroscopes and firing desperate salvos during the brief intervals they could see their targets.

Worf—it *must* be Worf!—crouched absolutely still in a dark corner, and he had the eye of a demon: every shot was unerring. Of course, against enemies as disoriented as these, even Julian Bashir could play Wyatt Earp, picking off the Klingons as if shooting desperadoes in a Wild West holonovel. Even so, even with O'Brien, and with Garak—who, unsurprisingly, was quite a good shot—and Jake, who couldn't hit the port bulkhead with the starboard bulkhead, even so, without Worf, the tide of battle would eventually have turned against them. Worf alone accounted for half the casualties among the Klingons. Caught in the crossfire, gyrating uncontrollably, and rebounding from walls and pieces of equipment in unexpected directions, the Klingons had no chance at all.

The war was over virtually before it began. Twelve Klingons floated about the cabin in various states of incapacitation—sadly, up to and including death, several by suffocation when their suits were ripped open by sharp projections they ran into. For a terrible moment, Bashir was driven by his Hippocratic oath to want to try to save those who were still alive, but dying. It tore his guts out to float motionless, hand gripping a seat-back, doing nothing—*withholding medical care!*—while men died around him, even Klingon warriors.

But there were many others still on the station, prisoners folded into forceshields somewhere, whose air might be running out, or who might be at risk of being slaughtered if the Klingons became desperate enough to forget their orders. Doctor Bashir had to make way for Lieutenant Bashir, who had an entire station to tend.

Or did he? Worf kicked from the opposite wall, aiming at the tangle of seats and railings that decorated one wall. *Must be the floor when the gravity's on,* thought Bashir lamely. The Starfleet Klingon rotated to crash into a chair shoulder first, bringing himself to a halt. "Is there any senior officer in your group, Doctor Bashir?"

"No, Worf. I'm in charge."

"You are in charge no longer, Doctor. I will take command."

"I beg your pardon, Worf!"

"I am assuming command, *lieutenant*. We have no time for this sparring! We must find a way to alert Starfleet to the danger."

"Well, begging the lieutant-commander's pardon," said O'Brien, with a decidedly sneering air, which he relished good-humoredly, "but if he'll stop taking command for a couple of seconds and listen, we've got the plan all worked out."

Worf's face through his faceplate contorted in a brief flicker of fury. *I wonder whether the chief realizes how on-the-edge his old friend is?* Bashir thought of stories he had read about people who had tried to domesticate wild animals, only to be torn limb from limb when the beast reverted, even for a moment, to its natural state. Then the doctor flushed hotly, realizing how xenophobic such an analogy would sound! *But I didn't mean it that way!*

Worf was not an animal, and within a second, his fury turned to mild annoyance. "Please tell me what your plan is—Julian."

Speaking in turns, Bashir and O'Brien explained Quark's plan, careful to give credit, though Worf looked incredulous at the thought of the Ferengi coming up with something useful. O'Brien, meanwhile, was modifying Quark's comm link, presumably boosting the broadcast power.

Feeling a terrible sense of urgency, Dr. Bashir urged Worf to let him stay behind to offer medical care, but the Klingon refused to waste time on the defeated enemy and led them quickly "upward," toward the Promenade. Under the circumstances, Bashir didn't push the point.

"Malach still has quite a few soldiers roaming about, at least twenty," Worf warned. "Keep your phasers out and get ready for an excellent firefight, with plenty of glory for us all. Today may turn out to be a good day to die." Worf smiled like the hero of a Klingon opera in the final act, before the entire stage was washed with the red *kazl* syrup they traditionally used for blood.

"God, I hate it when he talks like that," muttered

O'Brien. Bashir didn't answer. He was too busy *not* looking at the bodies of the patients he would not treat.

Against all his expectations and every Ferengi rule of survival, Quark discovered to his horror that he actually *liked* being in the thick of things, even if his own military contribution was minimal. He couldn't shoot well because his hands, when he stretched, reached only to the wrists of the suit, which was too bulky to bunch up further. He could grip a phaser halfheartedly by clamping it between his flippers, but he couldn't aim well enough to guarantee not frying his own comrades. *At least Rom is in the same stupid fix,* he thought uncharitably, pleased to feel a bit more Ferengi-like. It was intolerable on those few occasions when, due to sheer, dumb luck, his little brother ended up saving the day, while Quark uselessly flapped his arms like a bankrupt madman.

They were still two levels away from the Promenade airlock and had to fight their way through Klingon forces. But soon, the battles blended into one another; they were all so much alike. The so-called Resistance would stumble across a lone Klingon, or maybe three, and there would be a brief exchange of phasers and disruptors, because the Resistance nearly always took the Klingons by surprise, and had the advantage of cover and concealment (tactics that were distinctly Ferengi, not at all like the "scream and leap" tactics Quark usually associated with hu-mans), they won with no casualties each time. They walked through six invaders that way, and only one time was there any real excitement for the pair of Ferengi.

They surprised a pair of invaders. One performed the normal, expected, Klingon course of action when ambushed by a numerically superior band of enemy soldiers: he spun, grabbed some feeble cover, and began spraying disruptor blasts as if he were at the Final Audit. Worf and O'Brien took care of him quickly.

But the other, a dangerously clever chap, did the

utterly unexpected: he got his feet behind him and *launched himself directly at the party*. The shots from his partner drew the fire of everybody else, and amazingly, they didn't even see the Klingon swoop past their heads, close enough to reach out and touch them.

He made no contact with Bashir, O'Brien, Worf, Jake, or Garak, but his trajectory put him on a direct collision course with Quark and Rom! The Klingon fired a shot. But he was agitated and tumbling slightly, and his shot split the pair of Ferengi. Before he could fire another, he collided first with Quark, then, on the rebound, with Rom.

Quark was terrified, but he never had the chance to freeze. He reacted as his savage, precapitalist ancestors must have: he wrapped his arms and legs around his attacker, managing to catch the Klingon's throat in the crook of one arm, and squeezed and jerked for all he was worth in bars of latinum. Rom grappled the Klingon's feet, taking a couple of brutal kicks to the chest. If there were atmosphere, reflected Quark dully, he probably would have heard the crack as one or more of his brother's ribs broke.

Then Quark's groping hand found the emergency-release on the neck valve of the Federation pressure-suit the Klingon wore. He tore it open and snapped the lever, detaching the helmet, and that spelled the end of Mr. Clever. It was Quark's only kill . . . and he had to split it with his idiot brother!

Two decks later, with Quark and Rom being towed behind the rest like balloons behind a thoughtless child, they finally reached their goal, the Promenade, and there they found their reward: the main body of Malach's remaining army, sixteen warriors, and the general himself. Evidently, one or more of the ambushed Klingon lookouts had managed a comm link call to Malach, and the general knew just where they were coming. He had set up an ambush, but then he allowed them to enter the

Promenade unmolested! Quark shook his head in amazement—the arrogance of the Klingons!

The bedraggled members of the rag-tag Resistance fluttered like flags, rippling with every slight movement of their anchor hands. Quark and Rom gripped an ornate sign with both arms . . . ironically, the sign for Quark's Place. *If only this were one of those hu-man holonovels!* lamented the Ferengi, but Quark knew that no cavalry would come to the rescue, and there was no way out of the trap: Malach had them where he wanted them.

"You have done astonishingly well to get to this point," allowed Malach, speaking through his own comm link. His words were received by the handset, forwarded to the receivers on each helmet. Quark cringed at the cold cruelty behind the compliment. Malach thought he had been made a fool of, and that was not a healthy way to start a relationship with a Klingon.

"But the game is played out, and, in the end, you see, I wear the Empire crown." The general touched his helmeted head. Quark had the vague idea that Malach was making a reference to some impossibly bloody Klingon opera. General Malach, bulky even for a Klingon, nearly as big as the frightening Worf, was stuffed tight in the Federation suit he had "liberated."

"We won't surrender," said O'Brien, who had patched his own suit's transmitter into the handset as well. "You're going to have to take us by force, and we'll die, and you'll have a full-blown war with the Federation. Is that what you want?"

"No," admitted Malach. "I want only the station." He smiled, visible through his faceplate, as his troops scattered to all directions, as if by prearranged signal. "But I will take what I can get and hold it against the enemies of the Empire."

"You said we weren't enemies!"

Malach's face contorted in anger. *"All who oppose the*

right of self-defense for the Empire are enemies of the Empire!" He seemed to catch himself, turning left and right off his pivot-point. His right hand gripped the sculpture near the turbolift and the airlock . . . *the airlock,* whispered a very un-Ferengi-like voice in Quark's inner lobe. "Surrender, and we shall be enemies no more," continued the Klingon general. "Restore air and gravity to this station. When we have sent you under truce-flag to your Federation, along with the other involuntary guests, they shall not want war between us."

"Stuff it up your . . . Jeffries tube."

Quark cringed, waiting for the explosion; it never came. Malach merely smiled again, unperturbed by the rude suggestion. He raised his hand to give the order to attack.

Worf beat him to it. The lieutenant commander fired a full-power phaser shot directly at Malach, but bad luck dogged the Resistance still. By raising his hand, the general had twisted his body inadvertently, and the beam barely brushed his side. The pressure suit deflected what little wash it took (at a bad angle), and Malach was unhurt.

The Klingons returned fire, of course, and the battle raged. There was so much debris, so many metal bits and protruding spars, that *everyone* had cover. The fight was a standoff, beams lancing back and forth in eerie silence in the vacuum, nobody hitting anyone. But Malach dispatched five of his warriors to circle the Promenade and flank the Resistance from behind. When that happened, there would be nowhere to hide—the Resistance would fall!

Minutes passed, and everyone stopped the useless shooting. Garak and Bashir turned to face back the other way, leaving Worf, Jake, and O'Brien to hold the main force of Klingons tight behind their cover. But it was a losing game of Moogie's Auction, where the asking price started high and worked slowly downward until the first person accepted the bid from the seller. You waited and waited, and some altruistic clod always got the first bid in before you could! Everyone was just waiting for the flanking team to show up and catch the Resistance in a crossfire. The game would be lost at that moment.

Quark had just resigned himself to possible death and was rehearsing his final tally for the Divine Treasury when he saw the most amazing thing he had ever seen in his life: the turbolift doors abruptly slid open, and half a dozen beams of phaser fire flickered toward the Klingons from behind—it was Malach caught in the same hammer-and-anvil attack he had set up for the Resistance!

Quark stared wildly at the suited figures bursting from the now-empty turbolift shaft. One looked familiar. The figure twisted in mid-trajectory, shooting in every direction at once. Lieutenant Commander Jadzia Dax grinned with a bit of battlelust as she decimated the last remnants of Malach's victorious invasion force.

Quark made a mental note to stock up on old hu-man holoprograms . . . the cavalry to the rescue!

CHAPTER
23

FUR AND PHASERS continued to fly in the airless, weight-less, curiously peaceful war zone: without the noises usually associated with battle—the shriek of phasers, the snarl of disruptors, the screams of victims, the screech of torn metal, the hiss of escaping air from ruptured hulls, the bellow of commands, the the froth of curses, threats, imprecations, and insults, the ululation of a Klingon battle cry, even the hysterical sobbing of terrified by-standers. War just wasn't the same. Quark shook his head, sighing to himself. The party was over. Sisko was back with Odo (of course) in tow.

Ordinarily, the Ferengi would have cringed and cow-ered in classic Ferengi fashion behind something thick, solid, and opaque, but he simply had seen too much in the past few days. The old fear-glands were bled dry. The Ferengi adrenalyte had flowed so freely, it no longer affected Quark's physiology. It was like the ancient Ferengi story of the boy who cried "Audit!" once too often, and nobody came when a *real* auditor showed up.

He yawned inside his helmet, watching the battle rage silently around him, above and below, left and right, all directions being arbitrary, of course. The pincer maneuver drove Malach and his warriors back about thirty degrees around the Promenade concourse, but Quark was too filled with ennui to follow.

Abruptly, he was shaken from his reverie by a rude hand grabbing him by the shoulder of his suit. "—Wake up!" blistered Chief O'Brien, who evidently had been calling him for some time. Quark continued to tumble in the direction he had been jerked, spinning majestically end around end toward the open turbolift doors. "God Almighty, Quark, get your head out of the stars! How much pull have you got on the tanks?"

Disoriented by the spin, Quark didn't understand the question at first. He crashed into the bulkhead next to the doors and clutched a mapboard, stopping his tumble. "Wh-what?"

"Your air tanks! Your air tanks, you giant earlobe! You just donned new tanks. How much air have they got left in there?"

"Uh—oh! Uh, it says seventeen point three."

"Hm . . . that's enough for—"

"Seventeen point three *what?*"

"For about five hours, if you don't kick around much out there. Yeah, that's plenty. All right, Quark, into the lock!"

"The lock? The lock! Chief, surely you weren't serious about that idea! I mean, I could never—I would panic, I'm sure—*I can't hurl myself into empty space!*"

"I figured that," said O'Brien, nodding inside his own suit. He had kicked across to join the Ferengi. "So I'll do the hurling."

"You!"

"Sure, it'll be just like throwing darts. Except with a big, clumsy, pointless missile." O'Brien grabbed Quark's loose suit and kicked, launching the two of them across the Promenade toward the outer wall, directly opposite the turbolift. They gently bumped into a small, innocuous, recessed door labeled "Emergency Exit Airlock" in Cardassian. Quark had never noticed it before, but then, why would he have? He had never before contemplated leaping into the endless void riding only a spacesuit!

"You can't do this! I have rights!"

Silently, O'Brien began to untog the door, one bolt after another. After the eighth, the ninth, and the tenth bolt, Quark felt a sudden chill of terror thrill through his body and up his spine, driving away any lingering apathy he felt.

"Ha! ha! ha! He! he! A very good joke indeed. We'll have a good laugh about it at the bar—he! he! he!—over our synthale—he! he! he!" Quark was aware he was losing it.

"The synthale," said the chief.

"He! he! he! He! he! he! Yes, the synthale. But isn't it getting late? Won't they be waiting for us at Quark's Place, Jadzia Dax and the rest? Let us be gone."

"Yes," said O'Brien, "let us be gone."

"For the love of latinum, Miles O'Brien!"

"Yes," he said, "for the love of latinum."

Quark stammered wordlessly in reply, staring at the door. Eleven togs; twelve; thirteen togs, and the door rotated slowly to the side, rolling like the docking airlocks in the station arms. After a few moments, O'Brien looked impatient. "Quark!" he barked.

No answer. He shouted again: "Quark!" No answer still.

Chief O'Brien shoved Quark inside the Cardassian tomb and began to crank. Slowly, the door rolled back into place, the airlock darkening to black, as there was no working illumination. When only a crack remained, and Quark stared at the world he had known for ten years or more, probably his last glimpse of the station, O'Brien spoke a final time. once the door was shut, there could be no further communication. "You know what to do? Don't waste your breath until you've got a good way away from the station. Then start broadcasting. I've set you to full gain on your comm link. And don't panic! You've got five hours of oxygen if you don't panic . . . maybe two and a half if you waste it screaming or thrashing about. Got it?"

Quark stared dumbly, then, against his will, he found himself nodding slowly. Chief O'Brien grinned a sadistic, little smile (in Quark's opinion), and ground the door the rest of the way shut.

Don't panic! That was a laugh. The Ferengi could already feel his heart pounding so hard that his chest already ached. The adrenalyte he thought was drained rushed back like the returning tide, and his entire body shook like a misaligned impulse engine. His extremities were cold, heading quickly toward *numb,* and he was dimly aware, in some corner of his mind, that he was probably going into shock.

He wasn't going to make it. *You're going to die out there,* whispered a matter-of-fact voice in his inner lobe. *In the coldest, loneliest place in all of* Deep Space Nine: *the great outdoors!* He began to hear a hiss. O'Brien was flooding the airlock with air . . . Quark was to be fired from the chamber like a dart from a blowgun!

Quark reached back to touch the bulkhead behind him, the last, seemingly flimsy barrier remaining between himself and the starry abyss of emptiness. Defying O'Brien's last orders, Quark made quite a production out of wasting precious oxygen by screwing his eyes shut and screaming for all his lungs were worth.

When he finished, he opened his eyes. He was still in the airlock, of course. Numbly, he grabbed hold of the handle above his head, rotated his body until his feet were planted against the place where O'Brien had walled him in—out. With no more warning, the outer door exploded away from Quark with a loud bang. After hours of silence in the vacuum of *Deep Space Nine,* the noise of the explosive bolts made his whole body convulse. Then he was pushed from the lock by one, single atmosphere of force that felt like a thousand, enough anyway to hurl him outward, spinning slowly on two axes.

After the brief surge of acceleration from the mini-hurricane, Quark was surprised to discover that there was not the slightest sensation of moving. Rather, it looked like the station was receding from *him*, growing more distant every time his spin brought it back into view. It pulled away slowly, majestically: the stately core fell away from his feet. After many minutes, the monstrous habitat ring passed before his face—it took a hundred heartbeats to pass. Pressing far away were the twin "coat hooks" of the pylons, sticking out either direction from the ring. Another fifty meters to the right, and he would have collided with the "lower" pylon (the other looked severely damaged, as if someone or something had used it for target practice).

Dimly, Quark tried to remember why he was where he was, why he had been cast out to die among the stars and the interstellar dust clouds. Something came back, a dim memory hiding behind the evil, malicious grin of O'Brien the Executioner. Something about a comm link.

"Awk!" he said. "Ack—back—gack!" No, that wasn't quite it . . . Quark snapped from his state of shock, staring wildly around the inside of his helmet as if he had never seen it before. It didn't *look* like the Divine Treasury . . . could he have gone—to the *other* place?

Wait, wait, there's something I must—I'm supposed to do . . . Quark convulsed. All the memory flooded back at once, and he remembered who he was and why he was drifting among the stars. The comm link! Sweat beaded on Quark's forehead, turning icy in the recirculated air of his pressure-suit. He felt a distinct nausea that he thought he had banished hours before: the stars spinning past his visor raised again the old specter of space sickness. Quark closed his eyes for a moment, but it only helped a little.

A small fact had just occurred to him: if he *couldn't* raise anyone on the comm link, then he *would*, without fail, die the loneliest and coldest death in the universe: to freeze or suffocate or die of fear a hundred kilometers from the nearest air, light, and life.

He tried to talk, to shout over the open comm link, but his throat was frozen shut! He couldn't utter a sound . . . he couldn't even breathe. Panic gripped him like a living thing. He opened his eyes wide and thrashed and bucked, trying to throw it off. His vision dimmed; the bright pinpoint jewels surrounding him flickered and began to fade. *I'm dying of hypoxia!* he raged to himself.

Then the scream he had been suppressing since kicking off from the station finally forced its way up his throat, breaking the data-jam. *"Help me! Help me, for the love of latinum! Please, somebody—Bajor, Starfleet, anybody!"*

No answer. Quark breathed deeply, then his heart almost stopped when he caught sight of his air gauge: *8.8!* He had already burned up half his oxygen, and he had only been cruising for a few minutes, a couple of seconds, a—he stared at the chronometer reading inside the helmet—for *two hours?*

Stunned, Quark watched the chronometer and continued to broadcast his distress call every ten minutes. In between broadcasts, he tried to calm himself, breathing slowly, shallowly, husbanding his air supply. He lowered his air intake so dramatically—meditating upon an enormous room, a whole station full of bars and strips and shavings of latinum—that he actually began to see stars and sparkles at the edge of his vision. His color perception grayed-out, and it was difficult to see the numbers on his chronometer. His mind wandered through a fanciful corridor in the Divine Treasury, a long, curving hallway that looped back into itself (swapping inside and outside, like what the hu-mans called a Klein bottle). Something tickled his lobes. He ignored it, mechanically repeating his distress call over and over, mumbling like an employee. The tickling grew louder, more insistent.

Words . . . a voice, a shape of sound. His lobes burned cold, but they could hear perfectly well.

He heard a sound, a voice, a *response.* "This is Commander Tureilav of Bajor Naval Rescue. Vessel calling distress signal, *please identify!* We cannot locate you on our sensors."

Quark blinked in surprise. Stunned, he realized his mind was a total blank. For the first time in his long, painful, profitless life, Quark had absolutely nothing to say.

Then he shook all over, as if he had just been granted stock options in the Grand Nagus's personal corporation. Words popped into his head: "Quark! I'm Quark! I'm Quark!"

"Tureilav to Quark, what is the nature of your emergency? We are en route from Bajor. What are your coordinates?"

"Commander Tur—Tureilav," said Quark with a sigh, "you are not going to *believe* what I'm about to tell you!" As the stupid cliché left his lips, Quark had the terrible premonition that it might turn out to be prophetic— what if the Bajorans *didn't* believe him?

But they simply had to believe . . . *The most idiotic altruist in the quadrant wouldn't make up a story this crazy!*

"What have you done? Colonel Worf, *what have you done?"* Malach screamed through his comm link, bringing a grim smile to "Colonel" Worf's lips.

"I cannot say for certain what Mr. O'Brien has done," answered the lieutenant commander, "but I can guess." In fact, Worf did not have to guess; the stroke was obvious (and brilliant) the moment Quark dove into the airlock: *Quark the ballistic hero!* thought Worf, unusually poetic for a tactical officer, but the grand scheme reminded Worf of one of his favorite Klingon operas, and the poetry came naturally to his brain.

O'Brien, his back still to the hidden airlock that even Worf had never noticed before, broke into the conversation through his own link in the Klingon communications chain. "I'll tell you what I've done, Malach, whoever the hell you are. I've put a stop to your daf' scheme!"

Malach ignored the chief and spoke directly to Worf. "And what, exactly, have you had your man do to 'put a stop' to my strike?" He smiled, exposing his teeth in a gesture more fierce than friendly.

"Worf had nothing to do with it, you—dishonorable pig! I just sent out my own comm link, and by now, there's nothing you or anyone else can do!"

The general seemed to notice O'Brien for the first time, holding the lip of the door to Quark's Place and rotating to face the chief. "You! You are a rankless man. Who granted you this authority?"

"Admiral Benevidez."

Worf scowled, staring back at O'Brien. *Has the combat driven him mad?* he wondered.

Malach stared too, his eyes widening just for a moment. "He is the senior admiral of Starfleet, is he not?"

"Yeah, he's a good friend," explained O'Brien. "In fact, he's been hiding in my closet ever since the attack began. We keep in contact by subspace carrier pigeons."

Worf, in a long and infamous career in and out of the Klingon Empire, through more adventures than he could count on fingers and toes, had seen more than his share of angry, irritated, and downright furious Klingon faces. General Malach's, however, was one of the angriest Worf had ever seen. Malach's flesh turned white as the pressure-suit he was wearing, and his eyes widened into twin reflector dishes.

Worf had seen Malach lose his composure now and again during the long campaign, but it was nothing compared to this time as Malach finally realized that a tiny handful of Federation defenders had finally broken the final campaign of "General" Malach, and almost assured discommodation of whatever shreds remained of the "noble" House of Razg. Malach screamed a long string of threats and obscenities. However, the specifics were left to Worf's imagination, for Malach wisely severed his comm link before cutting loose.

"Malach!" shouted Worf. When the general—Worf's blood-brother—failed to respond, Worf kicked the gain to maximum and shouted again.

Instead of answering, however, Malach abruptly pulled his feet to rest against the doorframe of the bar and kicked off, away from Worf and O'Brien. The maneuver caught Worf by surprise. *He is abandoning his men!* realized Worf, shocked. He never thought his blood-brother could do such an un-Klingon-like thing. *It is only in the final extremity that honor and dishonor show themselves unmasked,* remembered Worf, quoting an old children's proverb he had learned . . . at the academy at Emperor Kahless Military City.

But as Malach faded from sight, his voice came clear and peremptory over the scrambled comm link: "The fight was glorious, my brothers. The gods have turned the dice, and the the victory goes to the enemy. But you fought well and bravely, and with honor.

"Those of you who joined my cause because your houses were discommodated, you have the word of Gowron that they are restored. Those who joined for the sheer Klingon joy of battle are satisfied.

"Honor is satisfied! There is no need *for the rest of you* to commit Mauk to'Vor. Lay down your weapons, you who are left alive. Yield as men do when they know the fight is lost. We gambled; we lost. But we have shown these spineless worms what it is to be *Klingons!* We have shown them what face they must keep if they are to serve effectively as the front line against the Dominion . . . and that means we won, in the long view: we have helped the cause of Empire, of Gowron, of Kahless.

"To honor! To Empire! Stand tall until we meet again in *Sto-vo-kor*. Farewell, of all my military commands, this last was my greatest." Then Malach fell silent.

Inside his helmet, rapidly running out of air, Worf's mind worked furiously: following Malach would be nearly impossible—one warrior with a disruptor could certainly seal off tunnels behind him! No, not to follow . . . Worf would have to *reason* where Malach was headed.

He has gone to die, Worf knew, but where? How?

The lieutenant commander, in desperation, turned to his closest friend on *Deep Space Nine.* Covering the distance between himself and Miles O'Brien with a blurry leap, impacting with a bone-jarring crunch, Worf quickly killed the comm link—he couldn't have the other Klingons overhear him—and instead pressed his helmet directly against the chief's. "He has gone to kill himself," he explained tersely to O'Brien. "We must deduce where!"

"Worf, he just saw Quark go through the airlock. It's got to be heavy on his brain! He'll throw himself out an airlock, and we'd have the devil of a time finding him, especially with so much of the station damaged, and not knowing exactly where to look."

Worf closed his eyes, putting himself into the heart and spirit of his blood-brother. *Yes . . . yes! That would be his path.* "But where, Chief? Where will he do it? Is there another secret airlock?"

"Well if there were, how the hell would Malach know about it?"

Worf and O'Brien looked at each other and said the obvious at the same moment—"The cargo bays." Of course! With the station forceshields down and all the air evacuated, Malach could crank open the main door of any one of the cargo bays with his hands, and there would be nothing stopping him from pushing off into bright space beyond those doors. It involved time and work, but Malach had no other appointments to keep.

"There are many cargo bays," said Worf. "I may find Malach before he can get the door open, but this duty is mine alone. You cannot say to my blood-brother what must be said. Find the prisoners and *make sure they have air!* That is my last order before turning command over to Captain Sisko."

Malach, when last seen, had been heading vaguely toward Cargo Bay 2. Worf shot for the turbolift shaft to intercept.

CHAPTER
24

MALACH WAS NOT in Cargo Bay 2, not in Cargo Bay 3. One advantage of zero-G was the speed with which Worf could bounce, literally, from point to point around the Habitat Ring. Worf continued on his trek, and in Cargo Bay 4, he found Malach. The general had already opened the cargo-bay doors, but he was waiting for Worf.

"I see your deductive skills have not diminished with age," said Malach. At the academy in Emperor Kahless Military City, Worf had taken top honors in Logic and Opera Appreciation; Malach had beaten him in Mathematics, Military History, Military Bearing.

"You knew I would come," said Worf.

And Individual Psychology.

Malach smiled behind the crystaline faceplate. "I have six minutes of air left," he noted, glancing at the gauge at chin-level inside the helmet.

"There is plenty of spare air."

"We have five minutes, Worf. I require one minute to see the universe before I die." General Malach let go of

271

the pile of lock-stacked cargo he was gripping—dolimite for some colony in the Gamma Quadrant—and stared hard into Worf's face. The general smiled. *Contemptuous,* thought Worf, *almost a sneer.* Worf fought down the instant Klingon-rage at the implied dishonor in the look . . . this was, after everything, his brother—blood-brother. "So this is what a traitor looks like," said Malach.

"I am *not* a traitor," answered the security officer of *Deep Space Nine.* "I have a duty to Starfleet!"

"Does it supersede your duty to your own people? To the Empire?" Malach shook his head. He really wasn't interested in the answer, Worf knew. *He probably will not believe me anyway.*

But Worf had to try. For the sake of what they both had learned at Emperor Kahless Military City, where Worf's father had sent the boy when he began to have disciplinary problems at age five, Worf was desperate to explain the "betrayal" to his blood-brother. "My father died in the attack on Khitomer," Worf began. "It was the year after he placed me in the academy. We had just moved to Khitomer, and I resented being taken from the academy after such a short time, when I had just found my feet. I was still a problem—you remember how I was when we first met—but I had learned much. For the first time, brother, my father spoke to me with respect! You do not know what that is like, since you never knew your father."

Malach merely smiled wistfully. He looked over his shoulder out the open door at the beckoning stars. "And the Romulan attack left no time for the happy reconciliation, father and son. How mawkish, Worf. You *have* changed, and grown stupid, if you think that will make a difference to me. The pleading of traitors does not interest me."

"Silence, Defeated One!" thundered Worf over the special command comm link. *That did it,* he thought,

that snapped his eyes back. Worf curled his lip. Worf had invoked the sacred Klingon relationship of victor to vanquished, and Malach was now honor-bound to treat Worf with respect. "You owe me these minutes by our witnessed blood oath, but if I cannot compel you to obey a debt of memory, you will at least pay me the courtesy of recognizing my victory!"

Malach bowed, as much as one could in zero-G. He inclined his head slightly, but still smiled with bitterness and ill-humor. "Speak, now that you have recognized me as your enemy, you cannot deny me a death with honor, not by our past or your recent service. You have invoked the Speech of Victory. You cannot retract it."

"Underneath this uniform—well, the uniform I usually wear—I am still a Klingon! I obey the old ways. And the core duty of old was the Sword Oath, is it not so?"

Malach said nothing, nor did he acknowledge the question. He was skating on brittle ice.

"Do you not understand, Malach? I did not desert the Empire—*the Empire deserted me!* I had sworn an oath, a Sword Oath, to Starfleet and to Captain Sisko, and Gowron knew that! He could have given me dispensation under the Code of Houses—he did not have to discommodate my House!" Worf realized he was shouting with anger. Years of pent-up frustration and fury spilled out of his heart into the cargo bay, globules of cruel, cold disillusionment that floated, spinning, toward his blood-brother. "Can you not see yet? I swore to Captain Sisko *as if he were my father!*"

Worf fell to silence, shocked by what he had said. He never would have dreamed of saying such a thing to anyone on the station, not even Miles O'Brien. Malach was the only person he could talk to about this dark, forbidden subject . . . Malach, the last remaining link between Worf and a time when his father, his real father, was still alive and the focus of his aspirations.

In so many ways, Captain Benjamin Sisko reminded

Worf of the father he had known for such a short while, at once deep and lighthearted, poured from equal parts grim determination and practical jokery. Worf often heard his father's voice, whispering amusing stories, but he kept them to himself, not out of fear for his dignity, but out of simple selfishness: Worf wanted to keep all of his father for himself, sharing none with his colleagues—especially not with Jadzia Dax, who shared too much of Worf's life as it was! He wanted just one thing that was his and his alone, and that one thing was his father, still imprinted on the lieutenant commander's memory.

But now, he had shared . . . with a man he had just formally declared his enemy. *I am a fool,* thought Worf bitterly, *he will now use this weakness against me.*

"You fool," began Malach, echoing Worf's own thoughts, but then, the broken general surprised Worf. "I am not dying because a single raid failed! I have suffered defeat before. I am not so fragile."

"Then why? Why, my brother? *Why* have you chosen Mauk to'Vor?"

Malach sighed, looking deckward toward his feet. "It is you who does not understand, *brother.* I lost a minor raid. My men will be returned to the Empire eventually, and so would I have been. Gowron will shout at his wife and kick his personal aide, but I am not afraid of Gowron's temper."

The general paused, but Worf did not interrupt. He had begun to realize what Malach was saying.

"I lost a minor raid, Worf, but I have also lost my most important campaign." Worf said nothing; there was nothing to say. He knew what campaign Malach meant, and it was not the raid, or even the chance to gain true glory for House of Razg (*probably for the first time,* thought Worf) that motivated Malach. *It was me; I was Malach's final campaign. He sought to bring me back . . . and he has lost.* Worf looked away, so as not to allow his emotions to seize hold of his face.

"Fare well under your Sword Oath, brother," concluded Malach, "as the Defeated One, I claim my rights."

Without speaking another word or waiting for Worf's answer, General Malach pressed his feet against the lock-stacked boxes and pushed himself backward. He passed through the door a few seconds beyond the five minutes he had planned. *If he breathes slowly,* thought the blood-brother Malach left behind, *he can still have his full minute to appreciate the cold, unwinking brilliance of the stars.*

Worf watched the body as it receded, until it was no longer visible to the naked eye. Malach did not speak for the last minute of life, but he did spread his arms in the sign meaning, *I journey to Sto-vo-kor with no weapon but my warrior's heart.*

Gowron would deny any involvement in Malach's "scheme," Worf knew. He sighed. Young as he was, he remembered a time when the High Council had enough honor at least to admit their own misdeeds when caught red-handed. But Gowron would insist he had no knowledge of what Malach intended, the Council would back him up, and the Federation, recognizing a feint but having no evidence of anything beyond one renegade Klingon warrior, would diplomatically conclude that they had no quarrel with the Empire. In other words, Worf's blood-brother Malach would have no more effect in death than he ever did in life: it would be as if General Malach of the presumed-to-be-noble and honorable House of Razg had *never even existed.* As Malach faded from view, he likewise faded from history. He became an un-Klingon, falling down the infinite memory hole.

Is that the end my destiny holds for me, too? What place in history was there for a "traitor" to the Empire?

Is it truly better, he wondered not for the first time, *to know one is an outcast?* Or would it have been better to live like his brother, his real brother—once Kurn, now

Rodek—who had survived this battle uninjured, but also undistinguished. And still unconscious of his true heritage. Still bereft of his true self.

When Worf could no longer see Malach, he turned and headed back toward the Promenade, thinking more than was good for him, for any Klingon.

"There," said Master Chief Miles Edward O'Brien, making the final adjustment to his portable field-generator, "that should just about—" With a loud *pop,* the small machine died and went dark. O'Brien stared for a moment, then gave it a solid kick. The porta-gen burped and flickered back to life. "Just about do it," he concluded.

"Com restored!" shouted Dax, and the ragged crew in Ops cheered, except for Captain Sisko, who only smiled as if he had known all along that the chief would come through.

Instantly, the message programmed by Major Kira on the *Defiant* began to repeat, apprising Bajor that the station had been seized by Klingons and requesting urgent help. Until O'Brien activated his field-generator, Kira's emergency beacon was swallowed by the Klingon comm-damping field before it could reach even as far as the station, let along Bajor. The Bajorans responded immediately: *"Evening Sky to Defiant,* we're already on our way; ETA twenty minutes. We detect no Klingon ships near your station."

Already on their way? thought Chief O'Brien, puzzled for a moment, then he broke out into a broad grin. It had worked! Quark must have gotten clear of the damping field and caught the attention of the Bajoran planetary defense perimeter! "So that's why our young general finally gave it up," he muttered.

"How's that?" asked Constable Odo, standing beside the chief.

"Nothing. I'll tell you later. I have to keep this thing constantly adjusted, matting out the comm-blanking field, or we'll lose communications again." O'Brien had generated a field the same frequency and amplitude as the one used by the Klingons, but phase-shifted exactly 180 degrees. The net effect was to create pinpoint "holes" in the field where waves perfectly canceled out troughs, holes through which they could receive and transmit comm signals—riddled with static, but intelligible.

The repeating message abruptly ceased, and Kira's own voice cut into the comm link. "They're cloaked! There might still be a ship . . . advise caution."

"Major Kira? This is Jad Davas."

"Captain Jad?"

"Lieutenant colonel."

"Davvi! When did all this happen?"

"Kill the audio and monitor, Old Man," said the captain. Dax cut the feed and allowed Kira privacy to chat up her old chum. As soon as the loud ship communications ceased, they heard what at first sounded like an annoying buzz. They could barely make out words.

"Dax? What is that?" asked Sisko, leaning forward and cocking one ear. He turned to O'Brien. "Chief, is that insect-buzzing a voice communication?"

You bet your sweet pips it is, thought O'Brien. "Yes sir, and you can thank the insect himself for saving your station."

"You will explain that, won't you, Chief?"

"Let me just isolate it and crank up the gain, sir. You'll see what I mean." With gravity and atmosphere restored and O'Brien safely ensconced in his engineering pit once more, he set the computer to cheerfully contact each comm circuit using the encryption key-code on the handset, thus restoring normal functionality, then he turned to the specific task of isolating Quark's weak comm signal and boosting it to pull it through the dueling comm blanking fields.

Worf was up in Ops, and Dr. Bashir as well. In fact, everyone who was anyone found a duty station (or at least a seat) in Ops, wanting to savor every moment of their sweet victory. The doctor had just joined them a few minutes earlier, after stabilizing Ensign Janine Wheeler's concussion and healing Ensign Tarvak Amar's broken humerus.

"Worf," asked the doctor, standing just behind O'Brien, "how did you know I was with the chief?"

"I did not know you were present, Doctor. I knew only that O'Brien had taken a handset and decrypted the signal."

"But, why did you send the Kobyashi-Maru message, then? What made you think Chief O'Brien would understand the reference? He never went to Starfleet Academy."

There was a long, long pause, during which O'Brien stopped working and tilted his head to hear better. *Yeah, what about that? I didn't have a clue what that was all about!*

When Worf spoke at last, the voice was reluctant and irritated, in that singular, "embarrassed-Klingon" way: "Because, Dr. Bashir, I . . . forgot." The last word was said so softly, O'Brien could barely overhear it.

"What?"

"Because I forgot that O'Brien never went to the Academy! Is that what you wanted to hear?"

"Good heavens," muttered Julian. "Well, thank goodness for a faulty Klingon memory!"

The chief's body shook with the struggle to hold back three days of pent-up laughter. He finished extracting Quark's message.

"Help," said the listless, Ferengi voice. "Oh, don't bother. I know no one can hear me anyway."

Everyone stared at Dax for some reason. Dax stared back at O'Brien, who shrugged and said, "It's Quark. He's still out there, you know."

"How much air does he have?" snapped Sisko, all business again.

"Oh, couple of hours, I figure," said the chief, "unless he's been thrashing about."

"Advise the *Evening Sky,* Old Man. I think it's safe to pick up Quark before they come here."

"Aye-aye, Benjamin," said the lovely Trill lieutenant commander.

"Chief, open a channel to our ballistic hero. I want to reassure him that he's going to be fine."

"Wait, sir!" cried Odo, grinning like a . . . *like a solid,* thought O'Brien. "I request permission to make the Quark contact."

Captain Sisko raised his eyebrows. "If you wish. Be my guest, Constable." The captain sat back in his command chair and crossed his legs, smiling in anticipation.

O'Brien opened the channel, then gestured to Odo. Before he could speak, however, the Ferengi's voice came over the comm link again: "This is Quark, and I know now I'm going to die. Out here! It's an outrage! But there you have it; that's what comes from dealing with hu-mans. All right then, I approach the Divine Treasury with head high and pockets stuffed with latinum. Consider this my *final* last will and testament, which supersedes the will of Stardate . . . well, whatever four days ago would be.

"I, Quark, being of fiscal solvency, a business owner, and of sound mind—"

"That is debatable," sneered Odo over the comm link.

There was a long pause, then, astonishingly, Quark *began again!* "I, Quark, being of fiscal solvency, a business-owner, and of *reasonably* sound mind, except for an occasional auditory hallucination, do solemnly—"

"Quark, you idiot! This is no hallucination, this is Odo, and we've restored full functionality of the station. The Klingons are gone. You saved the day, much as it pains me to say."

"Odo . . . *Odo!* Is that you? No, scratch that, you're the only person who could insult me and praise me all in the same breath. Odo, you've got to get me out of here! I mean, into there! For greed's sake, *beam me back aboard the station!"*

"Why Quark, you want to come back?"

"Yes of course I do, you stupid cop! No, wait! I didn't mean that! I just want—"

"You just want me to beam you back aboard."

"Yes."

"Now."

"Yes!"

"Rather as a favor, would you say?"

"Yes!"

"Certainly, Quark . . . so, how much is it worth to you?"

"What?"

"Everyone has his price, Quark. You could go insane out there, all alone, just you and stars. . . . Just how much is your sanity worth to you, Quark?"

"Just rescue me out of simple gratitude!"

"Well, that's not the *Ferengi way,* is it? How do you expect me to get to, oh, the *Divine Treasury* if I got caught doing free favors for every Tom, Dick, and *Quark?"*

"All right," gasped the Ferengi, defeat evident in his voice even to O'Brien. "What do you want? Latinum? I have sev—I have three bars to my name. You can have . . . one."

"Why, Quark! Are you trying to *bribe* a peace officer?"

"Of course I'm trying to—I mean, no! It's the furthest thing from my mind! Uh, if you don't want latinum, then, um, what do you want?"

Odo smiled, clasping his hands behind his back. "I think I would like . . . a name. No, make that *three* names, one for every bar of latinum you intend to fondle."

"Names?"

"Of three of your smuggler friends intending to pass through this station in the next, oh, forty-five days."

"But I don't know any smugglers!"

"Have a nice trip, Quark. We're having a wonderful time. I'd say, 'Wish you were here,' but you know I never lie."

"Wait! Wait! I think I might remember one or two, ah, *rumors* I've picked up about . . . that sort of thing. Is anyone else listening, Odo?"

"No, Quark," reassured the constable. "We're entirely alone." The rest of the Ops personnel snickered. Chief O'Brien quickly filtered out the sound, lest Quark hear it and clam up.

"All right, then, and remember: you never heard it from me. Here are the names . . ."

While Odo took them down, O'Brien noticed the warp signature of a Bajoran ship approaching fast. The *Evening Sky* swooped upon the station, closing on the comm-source dot that the chief had already identified as Quark. The dots merged, but still Quark hadn't said a word. O'Brien scratched his head in puzzlement until he realized that the ship must be nearly on top of the Ferengi, but behind him, where he couldn't see.

Not wanting to interrupt the entertainment, O'Brien caught the captain's eye and mouthed the words, *Bajorans here now*. Sisko nodded, as did Constable Odo.

"Thank you ever so much, Quark," said Odo. "Perhaps your 'friends' will understand the pressures you were under. But just in case they don't . . ." Odo smiled, closing his eyes. "You're about to be swallowed by a sea monster, Quark. Perhaps you'd do well to stay inside and let it digest you all the way back to Bajor."

"What the—? What are you . . ."

"Oh, just think of it as a leveraged buyout. Goodbye, Quark. I'll let you know when it's safe to come back."

"Signal just died, Captain," said O'Brien.

Dax spoke up a moment later. *"Evening Sky* reports one sputtering Ferengi requesting transport to Bajor."

"Oh please," whispered Odo. "Don't let the alarm clock ring."

Chief O'Brien scratched his head about the bizarre remark for a moment, then returned to the task of rebuilding *Deep Space Nine* from the engineering levels on up.

STAR TREK®
VULCAN'S FORGE
by
Josepha Sherman and Susan Shwartz

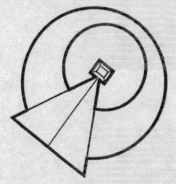

Please turn the page for an excerpt from
Vulcan's Forge . . .